"Lila?" Devon asked, going on alert.
"What's wrong?"

"Blood. Over there."

I headed in that direction. Devon stepped up beside me, with Felix behind him.

"Stay behind me," I growled at Devon. "I'm your bodyguard, remember?"

"And Sinclairs take care of each other, remember?" he shot right back.

I shook my head, but I couldn't stop Devon from drawing his own sword, ready to attack whatever danger was lurking here.

Together, the two of us crept closer and closer to the dumpster, with Felix right behind us, gripping his own sword and literally breathing down our necks. I held up three fingers and looked at Devon. He nodded back. We silently mouthed the words together:

One . . . two . . . three!

The Mythos Academy Series
by JENNIFER ESTEP

Touch of Frost

Kiss of Frost

Dark Frost

Crimson Frost

Midnight Frost

Killer Frost

In e-book only

First Frost

Spartan Frost

The Black Blade Series

Cold Burn of Magic

Dark Heart of Magic

JENNIFER ESTEP

KENSINGTON PUBLISHING CORP.
www.kensingtonbooks.com

KENSINGTON BOOKS are published by

Kensington Publishing Corp.
119 West 40th Street
New York, NY 10018

All Kensington titles, imprints, and distributed lines are available at special quantity discounts for bulk purchases for sales promotions, premiums, fund-raising, educational, or institutional use.

Special book excerpts or customized printings can also be created to fit specific needs. For details, write or phone the office of the Kensington sales manager: Kensington Publishing Corp., 119 West 40th Street, New York, NY 10018, attn: Sales Department; phone 1-800-221-2647.

ISBN-13: 978-1-61773-826-5
ISBN-10: 1-61773-826-3

First Trade Paperback Printing: November 2015

10 9 8 7 6 5 4 3 2 1

Printed in the United States of America

First electronic edition: November 2015

ISBN-13: 978-1-61773-827-2
ISBN-10: 1-61773-827-1

As always, to my mom,
my grandma,
and Andre,

for all their love, help, support, and patience
with my books
and everything else in my life.

ACKNOWLEDGMENTS

Any author will tell you that her book would not be possible without the hard work of many, many people. Here are some of the folks who helped bring Lila Merriweather and the world of Cloudburst Falls to life:

Thanks to my agent, Annelise Robey, for all her helpful advice.

Thanks to my editor, Alicia Condon, for her sharp editorial eye and thoughtful suggestions. They always make the book so much better.

Thanks to everyone at Kensington who worked on the project, and thanks to Alexandra Nicolajsen, Vida Engstrand, and Lauren Jennings for all their promotional efforts. Thanks to Justine Willis as well.

And finally, thanks to all the readers out there. Entertaining you is why I write books, and it's always an honor and privilege. I hope you have as much fun reading about Lila's adventures as I do writing them.

Happy reading!

DARK HEART
OF
MAGIC

CHAPTER ONE

Working for the mob isn't all that it's cracked up to be.

Oh, sure. It always looks all glitzy and glamorous on TV and in the movies: folks wearing snazzy suits, eating in fancy restaurants, and talking about how to best deal with their enemies over coffee and cannolis. And maybe I'd actually done some of those things, during the few weeks I'd been working for the Sinclair Family. But most of the time, taking care of Family business was a boring, tedious job, just like any other—

"Watch out, Lila!" Devon Sinclair shouted.

I ducked just in time to keep from getting pelted in the face by a blood persimmon. The ripe, apple-size fruit sailed over my head and splattered against the ground. The skin exploded on impact, painting red pulp and seeds all over the cobblestones and filling the summer air with a sweet, sticky scent.

Sadly, the cobblestones weren't the only things covered in fruit—so was I. Red pulp had soaked into my blue T-shirt and gray cargo pants, while seeds and bits of skin clung to my gray sneakers.

An angry, high-pitched *cheep-cheep-cheep* sounded, the noise somewhere between a crow's cawing and a chipmunk's chirping. I glared up at the tree where the persimmon had come from. A creature with charcoal-gray fur and emerald-green eyes jumped up and down on its hind legs on a branch about ten feet above my head. The creature's jumps were so hard and powerful that more ripe blood persimmons dropped from their branches and hit the ground, bursting open and adding to the oozing mess. Oh, yeah. The tree troll was definitely upset that it had missed me with its latest fruit bomb.

Tree trolls were among the many monsters that made their home in and around Cloudburst Falls, West Virginia, along with mortals and magicks, like me. I'd always thought of the trolls as sort of a cross between an oversize squirrel and the flying monkeys from *The Wizard of Oz*. Oh, tree trolls couldn't actually fly, but the black webbing under their arms helped them catch wind currents as they hopped from one branch to the next, while their long, bushy tails let them dangle upside down. The trolls were only about a foot tall, so they weren't nearly as dangerous as copper crushers or many of the other monsters that inhabited the town. Most of the time, they were pretty harmless, unless you got them riled up. And this one was certainly riled up.

Careful of the falling persimmons, Devon Sinclair stepped up beside me and craned his neck back. His black T-shirt and khaki cargo pants were splattered with even more persimmon pulp than mine, making it look as though he'd been caught in a red rainstorm. Just about the only part of him that wasn't covered in fruit was the silver cuff that glimmered on his right wrist, one stamped with the Sinclair Family crest—a hand holding a sword aloft.

"He's not a very happy fellow, is he?" Devon murmured in his deep, rumbling voice. "No wonder the tourists are complaining."

Cloudburst Falls was known far and wide as "the most magical place in America," a town where "fairy tales are real," so tourism was the name of the game around here. People came from all over the country and the world to see the magnificent views from Cloudburst Mountain, the rugged, fog-covered peak that loomed over the city, as well as spend their money in all the shops, casinos, restaurants, hotels, and other attractions that ringed the Midway, the main drag in the center of town.

But monsters were also drawn to the area because of all the bloodiron, a magical metal that had been mined out of Cloudburst Mountain for years. At least, that's what many of the local legends and tall tales claimed. Tourist rubes might like to *ooh* and *aah* at the monsters in the various zoos in the Midway and photograph the creatures in their natural habitats during expeditions up the mountain, but the out-of-towners didn't appreciate tree trolls chucking persimmons at them as they strolled down the sidewalk. And the tourists especially didn't like to get attacked by some of the more dangerous monsters that lurked in the dark alleys and shadowy spots in and around town. So it was the job of the Families to make sure that the monsters stayed in their designated areas—or at least didn't snack on too many tourists at one time.

This particular troll had taken up residence in a tall blood persimmon tree that sat in the center of one of the shopping squares that branched off the Midway. Since this square was part of the Sinclair territory, we were the ones who'd been called in to deal with the creature. For the last three days, the troll had been fruit bombing everyone who dared walk by its tree, causing several tourists to drop and break their expensive phones and cameras. *Nothing* pissed off a tourist more than losing their fancy new phone. I knew, since I'd spent the last few years swiping phones out of the pockets, purses, and fanny packs of every out-of-towner that looked like an easy mark.

Beside me, Devon shifted on his feet, moving out of the

bright, direct sun into a pool of dappled shadows closer to the tree. The warm rays filtered down through the branches and danced across his muscled body, showing off his rugged features, intense green eyes, and the honey highlights in his dark-chocolate-brown hair. I breathed in, catching a whiff of his crisp pine scent, mixed in with the sticky sweetness of the splattered persimmons. Just standing near Devon made my heart do a funny little pitter-patter in my chest, but I ignored the sensation, just as I'd been doing for weeks now.

"What do you want to do about the troll?" I asked. "Because I don't think he's coming down from there without a fight."

Devon was the bruiser, or second-in-command of the Sinclair Family, responsible for overseeing all the Family guards and dealing with all the monster problems that arose in Sinclair territory. Most of the bruisers for the various Families were arrogant jerks who enjoyed bossing people around and taking advantage of their powerful position. But Devon was a genuinely good guy who treated everyone in his Family equally, from the smallest pixie to the toughest guard. Plus, he would do anything to help the people he cared about, something he'd proven by putting himself in danger time and time again.

Devon's inherent goodness and devotion to others were some of the many things that made me like him way more than I should have. His soulful green eyes, teasing grin, and rocking body didn't hurt either.

Me? Good and I weren't exactly close friends, and the only devotion I had was to myself and making sure that I had plenty of cash in my pockets and food in my stomach. I was a loner thief who'd spent the last four years living in the shadows until I'd been recruited to be Devon's bodyguard a few weeks ago. Not that he really needed a guard.

Devon was a tough fighter who could take care of himself—and then some.

"Well, I say that we pick up all the fruit that's still in one piece and chuck it right back at the troll," another voice snarked. "Let *him* see how it feels to get splattered."

I looked over at Felix Morales, Devon's best friend and another member of the Sinclair Family. With his wavy black hair, bronze skin, and dark brown eyes, Felix was even more handsome than Devon, despite the fact that he was also covered in pulp—not that I would ever tell him that. Felix was already a terrible flirt. We'd been in the square for ten minutes, and he'd spent more time grinning at the tourist girls who wandered by than figuring out what to do about the troll, which was why he'd gotten hit with the ripe fruit so many more times than Devon and me.

Felix winked at two girls in tank tops and short shorts who were sitting on a nearby bench sipping lemonade, then waggled his fingers at them. The girls giggled and waved back.

I rolled my eyes and elbowed him in the side. "Try to pay attention."

Felix shot me a sour look and rubbed his side.

"What do you normally do about tree trolls who throw things at tourists?" I asked.

Devon shrugged. "Usually, we don't have to do all that much. Most of the trolls stay in the trees in their designated habitat areas. Whenever they start making pests of themselves, we send some guards over to tell them to either cut it out or move back up the mountain where they can do whatever they want."

I nodded. Like most monsters, tree trolls could understand human speech, even if mortals and magicks couldn't really understand them all that well.

"Usually, that's the end of it, but this guy doesn't seem

to want to leave," Devon said. "He's still here, despite the guards I sent over yesterday. And he's not the only one. I've heard rumors that all the other Families are having similar problems with trolls right now. Seems like something has them spooked and they're coming down off the mountain in record numbers."

As soon as Devon said the word *leave*, the tree troll started jumping up and down even faster than before, his *cheep-cheep-cheeps* growing louder and louder. The high-pitched shrieks stabbed into my brain, making me grateful that enhanced hearing wasn't one of my Talents. The creature was plenty loud enough already without the sound being magically amplified.

All around us, the tourists stopped slurping down their jumbo sodas, noshing on their giant wads of cotton candy, and snapping photos of the bubbling fountain in the middle of the square. They stared in our direction, curious about the commotion. I dropped my head and slid behind Felix, trying to blend into the background as much as possible. As a thief, I'd never liked being the center of attention. Kind of hard to pick someone's pocket or snag a watch off her wrist when she was looking straight at you. I might not be here to steal anything, but old habits die hard.

Devon looked at me. "Do you think you can use your soulsight to see what he's so upset about?"

"Yeah," Felix chimed in. "Let the great Lila Merriweather do her magic mojo. She is the monster whisperer, after all."

I reached over and punched him in the shoulder.

"Hey!" Felix said, rubbing his arm. "What was that for?"

"I am *not* a monster whisperer."

He rolled his eyes. "Did you or did you not feed three guys to a lochness a few weeks ago?"

I winced. That was *exactly* what I'd done. I didn't even feel bad about it, since the guys had been trying to kill Devon and me at the time. But I'd always been secretive about my magic, my Talents, and all the things that my mom had taught me about how to deal with monsters. I'd had to be, since I wanted to keep my magic firmly inside my own body and not have someone rip it out of me and take it for himself. So I wasn't used to Felix joking about it so openly. Every time he or Devon made a comment about my magic, I always looked around, wondering who might have overheard and what they might do to me in order to get my Talents.

Devon noticed my worried expression, and he put his hand on my shoulder. The warmth of his fingers soaked through my T-shirt and burned into my skin. That was something else I liked a lot more than I should have. I shrugged out from under his touch, trying not to notice the flash of hurt in his eyes.

"Please, Lila," Devon said. "Try to talk to the troll."

I sighed. "Sure. Why not?"

Most magic fell into three categories—strength, speed, and senses, such as sight, smell, sound, taste, and touch. So lots of magicks had a Talent for sight, whether it was the ability to see great distances, in microscopic detail, or even in the dark. But I had the more unusual Talent of also being able to see *into* people and feel their emotions as though they were my own, whether it was love, anger, jealousy, or something else. Soulsight, it was called. I'd never used it on a monster before, though, but I supposed there was a first time for everything.

So I stepped forward, tipped my head back, and peered up at the creature. Maybe it sensed what I was trying to do because it stopped jumping up and down and focused on me as intently as I was staring at it. My eyes locked with the monster's, and my soulsight kicked in.

The tree troll's red-hot anger slammed into my chest like a flaming fist, but that emotion, that feeling, was quickly smothered by another, stronger one—stomach-churning fear.

I frowned. What could the troll have to be so worried about? Sure, Devon, Felix, and I were all wearing swords belted to our waists, but so did most everyone in the Families. It wasn't like we were actually going to hurt the creature. Or maybe that's what the other mobs did. I wouldn't put it past the Draconi Family to slaughter the monsters that dared to wander into their territory, either down here in the city or up on Cloudburst Mountain, where the Draconi mansion was located.

But whatever the troll was so worried about, it wasn't going to leave or even calm down until it had been taken care of. As if the troll could sense my thoughts, it *cheeped* again, then skittered up a branch, moving higher and higher into the tree, and disappearing into the green clusters of leaves.

"What did you do to it?" Felix asked.

"I didn't do anything to it," I said. "Here. Hold this."

I unbuckled the black leather belt from around my waist and passed it over to Felix. He clutched the belt and the attached sword and scabbard in his hands.

"What are you doing, Lila?" Devon asked.

"It's worried about something. I'm going to find out what that is."

I went over and circled around the tree, my dark blue gaze going from one branch to the next as I mentally calculated how I could best get up to where the troll was.

Felix looked at me, then at the tree. "You're going to climb up there? With the troll?" He shook his head. "Sometimes, I forget how totally cray-cray you are."

I scoffed. "The only one here who is cray-cray is you, Romeo."

Felix's face scrunched up with worry at my not-so-veiled reference to his love life. On the surface, Felix might seem like a terrible flirt, but it was all an act to hide how crazy he was about Deah Draconi, daughter of Victor Draconi, the most powerful man in town. Naturally, Victor hated all the other Families, especially the Sinclairs, because that's how these kinds of doomed love stories always went. My mom and dad were proof of that.

Devon glanced back and forth between Felix and me, but he didn't say anything. If he knew what I was talking about, he didn't pipe up and say so.

I shut Devon and Felix out of my mind, stepped forward, and took hold of the tree. The blood persimmon was old and sturdy, with lots of thick branches that would hold my weight. I'd always enjoyed climbing, no matter the surface or what I was scaling, and it was practically a job requirement for a thief.

So I shimmied up the trunk, then reached up for the first branch. I quickly went up ten, fifteen, twenty feet, smiling all the while and enjoying the earthy smell of the tree and the rough scrape of the bark against my hands. I might be an official member of the Sinclair Family now, with a thin veneer of legitimacy, but I still liked practicing all my old tricks. You never knew when they might come in handy, especially with Victor Draconi plotting something against all the other Families.

Finally, when I was about thirty feet up, that distinctive *cheep-cheep-cheeping* sounded again. I looked up to find the troll perched on a branch up and off to my left. The creature regarded me with open suspicion, its emerald-green eyes narrowed to slits, another blood persimmon clutched in its long, curved black claws. Three fresh, jagged scars raked down the right side of the troll's face, as if it had tangled with a much bigger monster recently—and won. This one was a fighter. Good thing I was too.

I wrapped my legs around the branch, making sure that I wouldn't fall, then held my hands out to my sides, trying to let the troll know that I wasn't here to hurt it. The creature kept staring at me, but it didn't make a move to bean me in the face with the fruit. Finally, some progress.

I dropped my right hand down to my side and unzipped one of the pockets on my cargo pants. The troll cocked its head to the side, its small, gray, triangle-shaped ears twitching at the sound of several quarters *jingle-jangling* together in my pocket.

But instead of coins, I drew out a dark chocolate bar, held it up above my head, and waved it back and forth. The troll's black nose twitched, and its green eyes brightened in appreciation and anticipation.

Monsters might have more teeth and talons than the rest of us, but it was easy enough to deal with most of them. You just had to know what to bribe them with, something I totally appreciated as a thief. Most of the time, a drop of blood or a lock of hair was enough to get you safe passage through a monster's territory. Some monsters, like the lochness that Felix had mentioned, required quarters and other shiny coins, but tree trolls went in for more immediate gratification.

Dark chocolate, and lots of it.

"C'mon," I crooned. "You know you want it. I'm just paying the toll for climbing your tree and invading your personal space—"

The troll scrambled down, snatched the chocolate bar out of my hand, and returned to its previous branch, its lightning-quick movements almost too fast for me to follow.

Zip-zip-zip.

Its black claws made quick work of the wrapper, and the troll sank its needle-sharp teeth into the chocolate. More little *cheep-cheeps* sounded, but this time they were squeaks of pleasure.

I waited until the troll had downed another bite before starting my spiel, such as it was. "Listen, little furry dude. I'm not here to make trouble. But you know how it is. If you start acting out and throwing stuff at tourists, then the Sinclairs are going to make you move on. You know that. So what's got you so upset?"

The troll chomped down on another piece of chocolate, staring at me all the while, his green eyes locked with mine. Once again, his anger and worry rippled through my body, mixed in with a bit of warm happiness brought on by eating the chocolate. Nothing strange there. Chocolate made me happy too.

But the longer I stared at the troll, the brighter and greener its eyes became, until they were practically glowing like stars in its furry face. It almost seemed as if the creature had the same soulsight that I did and was peering into me the same way I was into him—judging whether or not I was trustworthy. So I focused on remaining calm and trying to look as nonthreatening as possible.

Maybe it was a trick of the sunlight streaming down through the leaves, but I swear that I felt something . . . shift inside me. It was as if I was somehow calming down the troll just by staring at it and thinking good thoughts. Despite the hot summer day, a chill swept over me, cold enough to raise goose bumps on my arms.

I shivered and blinked, breaking the strange spell. The troll was just a troll again, and everything was normal. No glowing eyes, no odd emotions in my chest, no more cold chills. Weird—even for me.

The troll *cheeped* again, then reached up and pushed back a branch beside its head, revealing a large nest.

Twigs, leaves, and grasses had been braided together in

a crook of the tree, along with several candy bar wrappers. Looked like this troll really loved his chocolate. I scooted up higher on my branch so that my head was level with the nest. A moment later, another tree troll—a female given her dark gray fur—popped her head up out of the nest, along with a much smaller, fuzzier head. A pair of tiny, innocent green eyes stared back at me. The male tree troll handed the rest of the candy bar to the female, and she and the baby vanished back down into the bottom of the nest, out of my line of sight.

So the monster was watching out for his family, which was the reason for all the fruit bombs. No doubt the creature saw everyone who approached the tree as a potential threat. Well, I couldn't blame him for that. I might be a thief, but I knew what it was like to try to protect your Family—mob and otherwise.

And to fail miserably.

The old, familiar, soul-crushing grief stabbed my chest, but I shoved the emotion deep down into the bottom of my heart where it belonged.

"All right," I said. "You can stay here until your baby is big enough to travel. If you're looking for someplace a little quieter, there are some nice, tall trees over by the lochness bridge. You should scout them out."

The tree troll *cheeped* at me again. I hoped that meant he understood me.

I pointed at him. "But no more throwing fruit at people, okay? You leave them alone, and they'll leave you alone. *Capisce?*"

The troll *cheeped* at me a final time, which I was going to take for a *yes*.

I unhooked my legs from around the branch and started climbing down. The troll watched me all the while, jumping from one branch to the next and following me all the way down the tree, but he didn't throw any more blood persimmons. More progress. Maybe I really was a monster whisperer after all. I wasn't sure how I felt about that.

When I was about ten feet off the ground, I sat down on a branch, flipped over, and let go. I plummeted through the air, letting out a happy laugh at the rush of the wind through my hair, before landing in a low crouch. I made a gallant flourish with my hand to add to my dramatic dismount, then got to my feet.

Felix grinned. "Show-off."

I grinned back. "Absolutely."

Devon craned his neck back, trying to see the troll. "So what did he do?"

"He's got his family up there, so he's not going anywhere," I said. "I told him to stop throwing fruit at people, and it seemed like he agreed to it. I guess we'll just have to wait and see."

Devon nodded. "Thanks, Lila. Good job."

His face crinkled into a smile. I looked away from him before my soulsight kicked in, but the dizzying rush in my heart had nothing to do with my magic. It was just Devon being Devon, and how hopelessly into him I was, despite my need to keep my distance.

Devon sensed my mood swing, and his grin dropped from his face. I felt like I'd reached up and snuffed out the sun with my bare fingers, and more than a little guilt curled up in my stomach. He really was a good guy, and I kept pushing him away, hurting him without even meaning to.

But I'd been hurt too—horribly so—and I didn't want my heart to be broken again. Not even for someone as all-around hot, charming, and wonderful as Devon Sinclair.

Devon waited until Felix had handed over my black leather belt and I'd buckled my sword around my waist again before jerking his thumb over his shoulder.

"Come on," Devon said. "Let's go home and get cleaned up."

He and Felix turned and headed out of the square, but something made me stop and look back over my shoulder. Thanks to my sight, I easily spotted the troll staring at me through the leafy branches, his green eyes brighter and more wary than ever before, as if he knew about some lurking danger that I didn't. Our eyes locked, and once again, the creature's worry, fear, and dread made my heart sink, my stomach churn, and a chill slither down my spine.

I shivered, dropped my gaze from the monster, and hurried after my friends.

CHAPTER TWO

Devon, Felix, and I left the square, strode down a walkway, and stepped out into the Midway, the commercial heart of Cloudburst Falls.

The square and its shops had been busy enough, but the Midway was jam-packed, as throngs of tourists moved from one side of the enormous circular area to the other, flowing into the shops and restaurants, and back out again. Every single business tied in to the town's overall fairy-tale theme, from the smallest Olde Tyme Fudge Shacke to Camelot Court, one of the largest hotels. Oh, there were plenty of real magical attractions, like the zoos where you could pet rockmunks and other small monsters. But really, the Midway was nothing more than the world's largest—and cheesiest—renaissance faire.

Adding to the atmosphere were men and women wearing knee-high black boots and black pants, along with poofy silk shirts, colorful cloaks, and cavalier hats topped with feathers. Gold, silver, and bronze cuffs stamped with various crests glimmered on their wrists, while swords were belted to their waists. The guards moved from one food cart and clothing shop to the next, like sharks circling around and around, making sure that everything was running smoothly. They were constantly on the lookout for everything from obnoxious tourists who'd had a few too many drinks to employees taking more out of the till than they put in.

The tourists thought that the dressed-up guards were just part of the fun, and several folks stopped to snap photos of them. What the rubes didn't realize was that the color of their cloaks and the symbols stamped into their cuffs designated which Family the guards belonged to—and that they all took their jobs very, very seriously.

Each Family owned a different piece of the Midway, and we were in the Sinclair section, which consisted of banks, several petting zoos, and a museum displaying artifacts made of the bloodiron that had been mined out of Cloudburst Mountain.

The guards here all wore black cloaks and silver cuffs stamped with the Sinclair crest—a hand holding a sword. Devon stopped and spoke to one of the guards, telling her that the tree troll had been dealt with, while Felix waved and called out to the folks he knew, which was practically everyone. Felix had never met a stranger.

The guards all nodded at me, their gazes lingering on the hand-and-sword cuff that adorned my right wrist. I shifted on my feet, my fingers tracing over the small, star-shaped sapphire embedded in the silver cuff. It matched the sapphire ring on my finger. I forced myself to nod back to the guards, wishing all the while that I could melt into the crowd and disappear. As far as I was concerned, the fewer people who knew me the better, even if I was an official member of the Sinclair Family now.

Devon finished with the guard, then cut through the park in the center of the Midway, choosing a cobblestone path that curved past several bubbling fountains. He turned his face toward the cool, refreshing mist, letting it soak into his black T-shirt. The water made the cotton cling to his broad shoulders in all the right places, not to mention his muscled chest. I couldn't take my eyes off him, and I didn't really want to.

Felix jabbed his elbow into my side, breaking the spell. "Looks like I'm not the only one with romantic problems, eh, Juliet?"

I crossed my arms over my chest. "Devon and I are just friends."

"*Right*," Felix drawled. "Because the two of you haven't spent the last few weeks making googly eyes at each other when you think the other person isn't looking. I might be a flirt, but at least I'm honest about it. You two just need to make out already and be done with it."

Luckily, the steady *rush-rush-rush* of the fountains and the chatter of the crowd drowned out his words so that Devon didn't hear them. I glared at Felix, but he smirked and elbowed me in the side again.

Devon faced us, using the bottom of his T-shirt to wipe off his face and revealing his stomach muscles. Yeah, I totally stared at him again.

Devon dropped his shirt and looked at me. "Something wrong?"

I shook my head hard enough to make my ponytail flap against my shoulders. "Nope. Nothing's wrong. Nothing at all. Not one little thing."

"Okay," he said, although I could tell he didn't really believe me.

I moved past Devon, heading deeper into the park. Carts lined the winding path, with vendors selling everything from frozen lemonade and caramel popcorn to sunglasses and T-shirts. The scents of bacon-wrapped hot dogs and fried funnel cakes topped with snowy mounds of powdered sugar filled the air, making me sigh with longing.

Felix eyed me. "Don't tell me you're hungry again

already—especially after all those BLTs you inhaled for lunch."

"Climbing trees and bargaining with monsters is hard work." My stomach rumbled in time to my words. "I need to keep my strength up."

Felix groaned, but Devon laughed.

"I think we have time to get Lila a snack before we go back to the mansion," Devon said.

We veered into a section of the park that was all food. Several wrought iron benches were spaced in between the carts, and folks chowed down on everything from ice cream to nachos to deep-fried pickles. And just like the rest of the Midway, guards patrolled this area, all of them sporting swords and bronze cuffs stamped with a hacienda—the Salazar Family crest.

As the Sinclair bruiser, Devon was well-known by all the Families, and the Salazar guards gave him respectful nods, which he returned. Felix was much more sociable, going over to and chatting with a cute Salazar guard who was about our age. I rolled my eyes. Sometimes, I thought that Felix knew every single girl in Cloudburst Falls, especially the pretty ones.

The Salazar guards eyed me, their stares cautious and curious, since I was a new member of the Sinclairs and a relative unknown. Their sharp gazes took in everything from my black hair and dark blue eyes to the silver cuff on my wrist to my pulp-covered clothes and sneakers.

But the thing that really caught their attention was the sword belted to my waist.

The weapon was sheathed in a plain black scabbard, but the hilt was exposed, showing off the five-pointed star carved into the metal there. Smaller stars ran down the hilt and were also etched into the blade itself.

Surprise flashed in the guards' eyes, and a few of them whispered to each other, wondering whether my sword was really made out of bloodiron. Given the metal's name, you would expect the weapon to be a rusty red, but the sword was actually a dull, ashy gray. They were called black blades by most magicks because of one simple, horrifying fact—the more blood you got on the blade, the blacker the metal became.

I didn't like the Salazar guards' scrutiny, and I had to curl my fingers into a tight fist to stop myself from wrapping my hand around the sword's hilt and hiding the beautiful scrollwork from sight.

Bloodiron was rare, and most weapons made out of it were highly prized—so highly prized that family symbols and crests were carved into the metal to make the weapons easy to identify and harder to sell on the black market. Even I had never stolen a black blade because it just wasn't worth all the trouble it would take Mo Kaminsky, my pawnbroker friend, to fence it.

Not that I would ever even *consider* selling my black blade. The sword had been my mom's, and it was one of the few things I had left of her, along with my star-shaped sapphire ring.

"The more you try to hide your sword, the more attention you draw to it, and yourself too," Devon murmured, noticing how tense I was. "You're a Sinclair now, Lila. You don't have to hide in the shadows anymore. Not from the Salazars, not from anyone. We watch out for each other, remember?"

"Yeah. Right."

I smiled at him, but I curled my fingers even tighter together to keep from reaching for my sword again.

Devon bought us dark chocolate-covered apples dipped in crushed, toasted almonds and drizzled with raspberry syrup. Felix grabbed his apple, then went back over to the Salazar guard to continue his flirting.

"Let's go sit in the shade for a few minutes," Devon said.

"That's how long it will take before Felix runs out of steam."

I snorted. "Run out of steam? Are you kidding? He's eating that apple even faster than he talks. All that sugar will just rev up his engine that much more."

Devon laughed, and we headed toward the nearest bench, which was shaded by a tall maple. I peered up at the tree, but I didn't spot any trolls, just a couple of rockmunks running up and down the branches, chattering to their chipmunk cousins.

We'd almost reached the bench when I realized exactly where we were in the park—the spot where my mom had once saved Devon from being kidnapped.

White stars flashed on and off in front of my eyes, threatening to crash together, form a solid wall, blot out the here and now, and throw me back into the past.

And make me relive all the horrible memories I wanted to forget.

Devon noticed the stricken look on my face. He stared at me, then at the bench. He winced, realizing exactly what I was thinking about.

"I'm sorry," he said. "I didn't realize. . . . We can go somewhere else—"

I forced myself to blink away the white stars and shake my head. "No, it's fine. Really. Let's sit."

I went over and plopped down on the bench, trying not to think about the last time I'd sat here, eating ice cream with my mom. Those white stars rose up in my mind again, but I ruthlessly forced them away. I'd relived that awful day a thousand times in my head, and I didn't want to do it anymore. Not when I had other things to think about.

Like getting revenge on Victor Draconi for murdering my mom.

Devon sat down beside me, his shoulder brushing mine

in a silent show of support. I didn't look at him because I didn't want to see or especially feel the soft sympathy that was surely shining in his eyes right now. It would just make me like him more than I already did. I might be a sucker for a cute guy, but I was no fool. And since I planned on leaving the Sinclairs and Cloudburst Falls as soon as I could, there was no point in starting something up with Devon when it would just end all too soon.

Especially when I already cared way too much about him.

Devon pressed his shoulder against mine again, then slid a couple of inches away, giving me the space he realized I needed.

We sat there, munched on our apples, and watched the flow of tourists. The tense, awkward silence between us slowly eased and mellowed, and the white stars and bad memories faded away. Yeah, I wished that my mom was still alive, but she would have been happy that I was here with Devon. My mom had worked for the Sinclairs before me, and she would have been proud to see what a great guy Devon had become—and that her saving him, sacrificing herself for him, hadn't all been for nothing.

Ten minutes later, Devon and I finished our apples and tossed the sticks into a nearby trash can.

Devon looked over at Felix, who was still chatting up that Salazar guard. "If he keeps that up, he's going to get in trouble with his girlfriend."

"What girlfriend?" I tried to make my voice light, but it didn't quite work.

Devon snorted. "The one he's always sneaking off to see. Don't tell me you haven't noticed. Felix is always slipping out of the mansion with a rose or some chocolate or something else he thinks she'll like. The boy's got it bad."

I shrugged. "I'm sure he'll move on to someone else soon enough. Look how he's flirting with that guard. Do you really think any girl—much less a bona fide girlfriend—would put up with that?"

Devon shrugged back. "Depends on the girl and how she feels about Felix. I don't know why he bothers flirting with other girls when it's obvious how crazy he is about her." He drew in a deep breath and slowly let it out. "I know exactly how he feels."

He didn't look at me, which was a good thing, considering the tomato-red blush staining my cheeks. A couple of weeks ago, Devon had told me how he felt about me, but I'd shot him down, saying we should stick to being friends. This was the first time he'd directly mentioned his feelings since then. I wondered why he was bringing them up now and how much longer I could keep turning him down, instead of giving in and seeing if he kissed as good as he looked—

"Oh, look," a snide voice called out. "It's Tweedledum and Tweedledee."

A shadow fell over me, blocking out the sun, and I looked up to find a tall, blond guy with cold brown eyes standing in front of me. He wore a red T-shirt with a snarling gold dragon stretched across his wide chest, and a gold cuff with the same dragon crest flashed on his right wrist.

Blake Draconi, the Draconi Family bruiser, Victor's son.

And the guy who'd helped murder my mom.

CHAPTER THREE

White-hot rage surged through me, burning away everything else.

Blake was Victor's second-in-command, and he was just as dangerous and depraved as his father was. He'd been in our apartment the day Victor had tortured my mom, leaving nothing behind but her bloody, broken body.

This time, I couldn't stop my hand from curling around the hilt of my sword. Devon put his arm across the back of the bench, cupping his hand around my shoulder, his fingers pressing into my arm in a faint, but clear warning.

"Blake," Devon said in a cool voice. "Where are your friends? It's odd to see you without your entourage. Or did you give them the day off?"

Blake smiled, but it was an ugly expression. "I don't need my friends the way you do, Sinclair. I see you're out with your *bodyguard* again." He turned his gaze to me. "If you ever want to see how a real man would treat you, honey, just give me a call."

Blake puckered his lips and blew me a kiss. I focused on his smug smile instead of his eyes. I had no desire for my soulsight to kick in and let me feel all of Blake's perverted imaginings.

"Sure," I replied. "And the next time you want someone to make you whimper and bring you to your knees, just give me a call, honey. I've got lots of practice doing that. Or don't you remember that wrist lock I put you in a few weeks ago?"

Blake's cheeks flushed with anger. His hand dropped to his own sword, and he stepped forward—

"Blake! There you are."

A beautiful girl with golden hair and dark blue eyes rushed up to Blake. Deah Draconi, his younger sister, who just happened to be the Juliet to Felix's Romeo.

Deah realized that her brother had stopped to talk to someone, and she turned and smiled, ready to greet whoever it was. Then she realized that it was Devon and me, and the smile slipped off her face.

"Devon. Lila," she said.

"Deah," Devon and I replied in unison.

Deah looked at Devon and me; then her gaze flicked left and right, searching for Felix. She spotted him, still talking to that pretty Salazar guard. Anger sparked in her eyes, and her mouth pinched in a frown.

Felix must have felt Deah's hot stare because he glanced over at her. He froze, then shot the Salazar guard a quick smile and scurried over to us. Devon and I both got to our feet so that we were standing in front of Blake and Deah. Felix took up a position by my side. He shrugged his shoulders to Deah in a silent apology, but he didn't dare say anything to her. Not with Blake around.

"Oh, look," Blake sneered again. "There's another Tweedle to add to this collection of stupid."

Felix's hands clenched into fists, and a muscle ticked in his jaw. I sidled forward so that I was closer to Blake than he was. Felix could throw a few punches, but Blake had a strength Talent and would hurt Felix just because it amused him. Devon stepped up beside me.

Blake looked back and forth between the three of us. He scoffed and opened his mouth—

"Hey! Felix! Devon! Blake! Deah!" a cheerful voice called out.

Startled, all five of us turned to look at the girl who came bouncing up to our hostile group, wondering who would dare to include Devon and Blake in the same sentence.

The girl was gorgeous. Seriously, model gorgeous, with dark red hair and the biggest, brightest hazel eyes I'd ever seen. She was one of those petite people you'd describe as a whirlwind of energy—a real dynamo, despite her small size. She smiled at Devon, revealing a perfect set of dimples that made her even prettier.

I didn't know who she was, but the others did because they all nodded at her, even Blake and Deah.

The girl wore a green peasant blouse and black shorts with cute, strappy black sandals. An emerald solitaire pendant glinted in the hollow of her throat, the stone sparkling in a way that told me how real and expensive it was. Oversize sunglasses perched on top of her head, while a green handbag dangled off her right arm.

I focused on the sword belted to her waist, admiring the wolf scrollwork that covered the hilt. A black blade like that was worth even more than her necklace. And the girl carried herself in a confident manner that said she knew exactly how to use the weapon.

Devon smiled back at the girl, and the two of them exchanged a quick hug. "Katia. It's nice to see you again."

Deah noticed me frowning at them. She raised her eyebrow and smirked, clearly realizing that I was jealous. I ignored her.

Katia turned to Felix and gave him a slow, lingering smile that deepened her dimples. "Hey, Felix."

"I . . . uh. . . ." Felix's mouth kept opening and closing, and opening and closing, as though the sight of her stunned him so much that he couldn't form a single coherent thought.

Something that made Deah frown and me smirk at her.

"Hey, Katia," Felix finally mumbled.

Despite the fact that his clothes were still slathered with persimmon pulp from our encounter with the tree troll, Katia went over, opened her arms, and enfolded Felix in a tight hug that went on . . . and on . . . and on . . . before she pulled back and kissed his cheek.

Deah's expression cranked up from frown to all-out glower. I smirked at her again, and she focused her glare on me for a moment before turning it back to Katia.

But Katia didn't seem to notice the other girl's hostile expression, and she nodded at Deah and Blake. A wink of light caught my eye, and I realized that Katia was wearing a silver cuff stamped with a wolf's head. So she belonged to the Volkov Family. Weird. I'd never seen her around before, and I'd made it a point to know all the guards and important members of the Families, so I wouldn't be tempted to steal from the wrong person when I was picking pockets on the Midway.

Devon realized that I didn't know who the girl was, and he held out his hand, pointing to her, then me. "Katia Volkov, this is Lila Merriweather. Lila, Katia."

"Nice to meet you," Katia said, smiling.

I nodded. "You too."

"Katia lives up north in New York, near Bigtime," Devon explained. "Carl, her dad, is Nikolai Volkov's brother. Carl and Katia head up the Family branch where they live."

"A much smaller branch, from the rumors I've heard," Blake piped up. "It's just you and your dad now, right?"

Katia's smile slipped a bit. "Yeah. Just us now."

"Come to town for the tournament?" Devon asked.

Katia's unease melted away, and her face warmed again. "Yep, representing the Volkovs. Are you competing again this year?"

Devon nodded. "I am."

Blake snorted. "Not that he has any chance of winning." He slung his arm around his sister's shoulder. "In case you all have forgotten, Deah is the defending champion, and she's the favorite to win the tournament again this year."

Deah shrugged off his arm, then looked at Katia. "But you gave me a really good fight last year."

Her voice wasn't unkind, but Katia's smile vanished, and she didn't respond. Nobody liked to be reminded that she'd lost.

I hated to be a totally clueless tourist rube, but I had no idea what they were talking about. "Um, what tournament?"

All five of them looked at me like they couldn't believe I'd asked that question.

"The Tournament of Blades," Devon said. "The Families sponsor it every summer."

"Yeah," Felix added. "Several people are picked from each Family, and they all compete out at the fairgrounds until there's just one person left."

"Oh. That."

I did know what they were talking about—I'd just never actually gone to the tournament. I'd asked my mom once if we could go, the last summer she'd been alive, but she'd told me no, that there was too great a risk of someone from one of the Families recognizing her. She'd left the Sinclairs and Cloudburst Falls before I'd been born, and she had never let anyone except for Mo know that we came back to town every summer.

After she'd been murdered, I'd been so busy getting shipped from one foster home to another, then striking out on my own and trying to steal enough to make ends meet, that I hadn't paid much attention to the tournament, except for all the extra tourists it brought to town, giving me more phones and cameras to swipe and take to Mo to fence.

"You seem to know an awful lot about the tournament, Morales," Blake sneered, "for someone who's never actually entered."

Felix's hands clenched into fists again, and an embarrassed blush spread across his cheeks.

"And you talk a lot for someone whose kid sister beat him out at the tournament last year," I shot right back.

Blake opened his mouth to make some snide remark, but Deah put her hand on his arm.

"Let's go," she said. "We've wasted enough time with these losers. We need to practice for the tournament, remember?"

"Yeah. Right."

But Blake wasn't nearly as enthusiastic about the contest as he'd been before. He glowered at me again; then he and Deah headed down the path away from us.

Devon, Felix, and Katia all relaxed as soon as the Draconis vanished from view, but I kept glaring at the spot where Blake had disappeared.

Katia wrinkled her nose. "Um, what's that smell?"

Felix winced. "Oh, that's us. We were dealing with a tree troll earlier."

"We were just on our way back to the mansion to get cleaned up," Devon said.

Katia nodded. "Maybe we can catch up tomorrow then."

She might have been talking to Devon, but she looked at Felix as she said the words.

"Sure," Felix said. "That would be great. Just text me."

"I'll do that."

Katia leaned over and kissed him on the cheek again. She

gave him another bright smile, waved goodbye to Devon and me, and moved off into the crowd.

Devon and I waited until she was gone before we both looked at Felix.

"What's your girlfriend going to think about Katia?" Devon asked in an amused voice.

"Shut up," Felix growled and stomped away.

"What was that all about?" I asked.

Devon grinned. "Felix and Katia spent a *lot* of time together during the tournament last year."

"Ah. Summer love?"

His grin widened. "More like summer lust. Felix said that it was fun while it lasted. But now with his new mystery girl, I don't know what he'll do."

"Probably just talk faster so he can juggle both of them at once," I said, knowing full well that Deah Draconi would never, ever let herself be juggled any more than I would.

Devon laughed, and we went after Felix.

We left the Midway behind, cut through an alley, and entered a parking lot reserved for Family vehicles. Each one of the expensive SUVs and sports cars boasted some sort of crest on its doors, and for the Sinclairs, it was that hand holding a sword, done in white against the SUV's black paint.

Felix was leaning against the side of the vehicle, his arms crossed over his chest. "Took you long enough," he muttered.

I made a big show of scanning the parking lot. "Why? Because there weren't any pretty girls around to keep you company? However did you make it five whole minutes standing here by yourself?"

"Shut up," Felix growled again.

"So," I drawled. "Let's talk about you and Katia. She seems . . . nice."

Devon snickered. "Felix certainly thought so last summer. Or at least he thought her lips were nice, since he spent a fair amount of time studying them up close and personal."

I waggled my eyebrows. "And it looks like Katia wants to pick up right where they left off."

Devon laughed. Felix gave us both a sour look, but his lips slowly twitched up in a sheepish smile.

"I doubt Katia will have time for me," Felix said. "She was really upset she lost the tournament to Deah last year. She's probably going to spend all her time training."

"And being with you would, what, sap her strength?" I snarked.

Felix glared at me again, so I decided to be merciful and quit teasing him—for now.

"Tell me about her. What's her Talent?"

"Katia is fast," Felix said. "Like, superfast. She has a major Talent for speed. That's one of the reasons she got to the final round of the tournament last year."

Speed was a hard magic to defend against because by the time you realized what was happening, your opponent had already gutted you. In my experience, the best way to deal with someone with a speed Talent was to knock them on their ass. Hard to be superquick when you were scrambling around, trying to get back up onto your feet.

"Just speed?" I asked. "Nothing else? No other magic?"

Felix shook his head. "Nothing like Devon's compulsion or your transference power, if that's what you're asking. But she's a good fighter, one of the best in all the Families. She always wins the tournament up in New York every year, but she's come up short against Deah twice now."

"Well, maybe this will be her year."

"I doubt that," Devon chimed in. "Not with Deah's mimic magic. It makes her almost impossible to beat. She's won the tournament two years in a row, and she beat Katia in the finals both times."

I frowned. "Deah's a mimic? What does that mean?"

"Deah has the ability to mimic anybody she meets," Devon said. "The way they walk, talk, move. So when she's battling someone, she can mimic their fighting style, whatever it is, and use it against the other person. And that's not all. It's almost like her mimic Talent actually lets her tap into and use the other person's magic too."

"She's amazing to watch," Felix said in a dreamy voice. "She can throw around the biggest guard like it's nothing."

My frown deepened. That almost sounded like a version of my soulsight—like Deah could see the way people moved so well that she could copy their style. And if she could use their own magic against them as well. . . . That sounded suspiciously like my own transference power—the Talent that let me absorb other people's magic and then use it for myself. Weird. I wouldn't have thought that Deah and I had anything in common.

"What about the Sinclairs?" I asked. "How did you guys do in the tournament last year?"

Devon shrugged. "Katia beat me to advance to the final round. I thought I had her at one point, but she got the better of me."

I eyed the muscles in Devon's arms and shoulders. He spent his free time working out on one of the roofs at the Family mansion, so I knew how tough he was. Beating him in a fight was no small task.

"Katia and Deah must be really good."

Devon shrugged again. "They are. Maybe you'll get to find out for yourself."

"What do you mean?"

He glanced at Felix, and they both grinned.

"Oh, you know, when we go watch the tournament." Devon's voice was just a little too casual to be believable.

I waited for him to look at me, so I could use my soul-sight and feel what he really meant, but Devon pulled out his keys and stepped toward the SUV. I glanced at Felix, but he pulled a pair of sunglasses out of his pocket and slid them onto his face, hiding his eyes. Oh, yeah. They both knew something that I didn't, and they didn't want me to guess what it was.

Devon unlocked the SUV. He started to get into the driver's seat, then stopped and glanced down at his persimmon-spattered clothes. "Reginald is going to kill us for dirtying up the leather."

"Oh, Reginald's bark is worse than his bite." Felix arched an eyebrow at him. "Besides, you're the Family bruiser. You're not supposed to be afraid of anyone."

Devon snorted. "Everyone's afraid of Reginald. Especially you."

"You'd better believe it." Felix grinned. "But it's your car, so *you* can be the one to tell him why it smells like a juice box."

"Thanks."

"That's what friends are for."

Devon laughed, and the two of them kept talking, debating whether they should ask the pixies to try to wash their clothes or just go ahead and throw them away when we got back to the mansion.

Instead of listening to them, I found myself focusing on the sudden, odd lack of noise. Sure, murmurs, music, and more floated down the alley from the Midway, but the parking lot itself was quiet.

Too quiet.

Devon and I had been attacked and kidnapped in this very spot a few weeks ago, and he, Felix, and I were the only folks here now. There was no love lost between Blake and us, so I wouldn't put it past Blake to try to sneak back here with some Draconi guards in hopes of beating us senseless—if not worse.

My gaze scanned over the cars, and I used my sight to peer in through the tinted windows, just to make sure that no one was lurking inside, watching us. All the vehicles were empty, but it didn't lessen my worry.

Something was wrong here.

My hand dropped to my sword, my fingers tracing over the star carved into the hilt. Whether it was a parking lot, a pit, or a palace, there were three rules when it came to a place being too quiet.

Too quiet meant you weren't as alone as you thought you were.

Too quiet meant someone was up to something.

Too quiet all too often meant death.

So I scanned the parking lot again, looking—*really* looking—at everything with my sight. The cars, the pavement, even the access doors on the backs of the buildings to see if someone was peering out one of them at us. And I finally spotted something out of place—a small, dark, glistening pool oozing out from behind one of the dumpsters.

Blood.

I drew my sword. The rasp of the black blade sliding free of its scabbard caught Devon's and Felix's attention.

"Lila?" Devon asked, going on alert. "What's wrong?"

"Blood. Over there."

I headed in that direction. Devon stepped up beside me, with Felix behind him.

"Stay behind me," I growled at Devon. "I'm your bodyguard, remember?"

"And Sinclairs take care of each other, remember?" he shot right back.

I shook my head, but I couldn't stop Devon from drawing his own sword, ready to attack whatever danger was lurking here.

Together, the two of us crept closer and closer to the dumpster, with Felix right behind us, gripping his own sword and literally breathing down our necks. I held up three fingers and looked at Devon. He nodded back. We silently mouthed the words together:

One . . . two . . . three!

Together, we rushed around the side of the dumpster, our swords held high.

But nobody was hiding behind the container.

Instead, a tree troll lay in the dumpster's shadow, its gray, furry body propped up against the brick wall like it was a drunk tourist sleeping off a bender. But the monster wasn't drunk.

It was dead—its throat cut open.

Devon and I lowered our swords. Behind us, Felix let out a tense breath and did the same.

"What do you think did this?" Felix asked. "Another troll? Some other monster?"

I moved forward and crouched down, scanning the troll's body. It looked small in death, sad, deflated, and crumpled, like a piece of garbage that someone had tossed aside with no care or concern about where the creature had landed.

But there wasn't nearly as much blood as there should have been. With a wound that deep and vicious, the monster's blood should have been splattered all over the dumpster, the wall, and the asphalt. But only a small pool gleamed by the creature's leg, the one I'd spotted from across the parking lot. So where had the rest of the blood gone? Had some other monster come along and lapped it up? My stomach twisted with disgust.

"I don't think so," I said. "If the troll had been attacked

by another monster, it would have been clawed, more torn up. That looks like a clean slice to me. I think . . . maybe a person did this."

I crept even closer, leaning down and tilting my head to the side so that I could stare into the troll's emerald-green eyes, which were dull and glassy with death—

White stars exploded in front of my face the second my gaze locked with the monster's.

It wasn't like looking back into my own past with my soulsight and watching everything unspool like a movie. These images were all quick, hazy, disoriented, like I was glimpsing random photos I'd never seen before. And I felt all the pain that went along with them as if it were my own; a shadow sneaking up on me; something grabbing hold of my arm and throwing me forward; my face slamming into the wall, stunning me; and finally, a hand rolling me over and a dagger lashing out toward my throat—

I choked down a scream and staggered back, my sword slipping from my suddenly nerveless fingers. My feet slid out from under me, and my ass hit the asphalt. I blinked at the hard jolt, and the images vanished, although the feelings—especially the fear—lingered.

"Lila!" Devon crouched down by my side. "Are you okay? What happened?"

My hand latched onto my neck, but the skin there was smooth and unbroken, despite the blood roaring in my ears, the terrified *thump-thump-thump* of my heart, and the hot, phantom sting throbbing from one side of my throat to the other.

I shook my head. The last of the white stars vanished, and my vision returned to normal. The sting in my throat lingered, though. So did the fear squeezing my chest.

I'd seen dead monsters before, but I'd never looked one directly in the eyes. Apparently, my soulsight worked just as well on dead creatures as it did on living ones, and I realized that I'd just seen the last few moments of the troll's life. I shuddered, wishing I hadn't.

"Lila?" Devon asked again.

"I'm fine. Just lost my balance. Clumsy me." I let out a weak laugh.

Devon frowned. He knew I was lying, but instead of calling me on it, he held out his hand and helped me back to my feet.

"Are you sure you're okay?"

I forced myself to let go of his hand before he noticed how much mine was trembling. "Yeah. I'm fine."

He kept staring at me, so I fixed a smile on my face and made a big show out of dusting off my pants, picking up my sword, and sliding it back into the scabbard on my belt.

"Why would anyone want to kill a tree troll?" Devon asked.

"Well, they can be annoying pests, but this. . . ." Felix trailed off. "This is kind of extreme."

"No," I cut in, my voice cold and harsh. "This is just *cruel*."

The two of them didn't have my soulsight, so they hadn't seen or felt the troll's terror, shock, and suffering like I had. And they hadn't heard the worst thing of all, the one thing that was still ringing in my ears and making me sick to my stomach, even now.

The mocking, heartless laughter that had sounded as the killer had sliced open the troll's neck with that dagger.

CHAPTER FOUR

Devon called some guards over to the parking lot to properly bury the tree troll's body and clean up what little blood there was. He also asked the guards to e-mail the day's security footage to him so he could try to figure out who might have done this, but I knew it would be a dead end. Hundreds of people walked through the Midway, the alley, and this parking lot every day, and there were no cameras back here in the parking lot. He wouldn't be able to pinpoint who had murdered the troll, although I admired him for trying.

Once the guards arrived, there was nothing more for us to do, and Devon and Felix headed back to the SUV. But I lingered by the troll's body, staring at that one, small pool of blood on the asphalt, still wondering why there wasn't more of it.

"Lila!" Devon called out. "Let's go!"

I turned to walk over to the SUV when a small shadow fell over me. My head snapped up, and my hand dropped to my sword, wondering if the murderer might have come back to admire his sick handiwork.

But it wasn't the killer—it was the tree troll that I'd given the chocolate bar to earlier, the one with three jagged scars on its face.

The troll was perched on the roof above my head. It

stared down at me, its green eyes bright and accusing, as if to say, "I tried to tell you something was wrong, but you didn't believe me."

I shivered, dropped my gaze from the creature, and hurried over to the SUV.

Devon drove, with me in the front passenger's seat and Felix lounging across the back, smearing persimmon pulp and seeds everywhere. Devon maneuvered through town, passing the trolleys that hauled tourists around Cloudburst Falls. We stopped at a red light and watched several bicycles cruise by, the magicks that were steering them using their speed and strength Talents to churn their legs and pull cutesy carriages full of tourist rubes along behind them.

The light turned green, and Devon left the main drag and headed through the side streets. My stomach clenched with nervous anticipation. He always went this way now, whenever we came into town. And so did I.

A few minutes later, we reached a gray cobblestone bridge that arched over the Bloodiron River. With its dilapidated buildings, abandoned warehouses, and shadow-filled alleys, this definitely wasn't the nice part of town, and no other vehicles were on the bridge or the surrounding streets. Mortals and magicks alike avoided this area and the others like it in town. Not because there were any obvious dangers, but because the lizard parts of their brains whispered a warning to them.

Here be monsters.

Devon eased the SUV onto the cobblestones and stopped in the middle of the span. I fished three quarters out of my pants pocket to pay the toll, just like I had when I gave that chocolate bar to the tree troll earlier. Except the consequences of not giving the lochness that lived under the bridge the tribute it required would be much, much worse than getting pelted with fruit.

So I rolled down my window, stretched my hand out, and laid the coins on a worn, smooth stone marked with three Xs in the center of the bridge.

Clink-clink-clink.

The quarters clattered onto the Xs, the sounds soft, no more than rasps of metal scraping against the stone, but I felt like I was banging a drum, drawing the attention of everyone—and everything—around us. I stared at the three coins, wondering if the lochness would scoop up the quarters with one of its long, black tentacles.

Nothing happened.

I waited ten seconds, twenty, thirty, before sitting back in the SUV and rolling up the window. I looked at Devon and shrugged. He hissed out a breath between his teeth, took his foot off the brake, and drove on, but I stared in the rearview mirror, watching the coins glimmer in the afternoon sun.

The second the vehicle's tires rolled off the bridge, a black tentacle shot up out of the water and swiped the quarters from the center stone.

I blinked, and the tentacle was gone, although the surface of the river rippled from far more than just the current.

"Did you see it?" I asked.

Devon's gaze was focused on the rearview mirror. "Yeah. Just for a second."

Felix had been staring out the back of the SUV, and he shivered and faced the front again. "Have I told you guys how creepy it is that we *always* drive over the lochness bridge now? And that you *always* stop and pay the toll?"

"Well, when a monster saves your life, it's only fair to give it what it wants," I murmured. "Unless you want to end up like Grant."

Grant Sanderson had been the Sinclair broker, but what he'd really coveted had been Devon's compulsion magic—

the power to make people do whatever Devon said, even if they didn't want to. Grant had kidnapped Devon and me and tried to take our magic for his own. But we'd escaped, and I'd tricked Grant and two other men into crossing the bridge on foot without paying the toll.

The lochness had dragged all three of them into the river—and eaten them.

I didn't have any regrets about what I'd done to Grant, since he'd been trying to kill us, but Devon winced, his face creasing with guilt. He still thought he should have seen Grant for the cruel, jealous person that Grant really was and tried to help him somehow. It was just another way in which Devon was a good guy, and I wasn't.

I wasn't going to lose a wink of sleep over Grant, but the same couldn't be said for the murdered tree troll we'd found. Even now, I kept picturing its lifeless body, dull, empty gaze, and the vicious slash through its throat. Even worse, that soft, heartless laughter echoed in my head all the while, sending a chill down my spine. It all just reinforced a cold, hard truth that I'd learned the day Victor Draconi murdered my mom.

Sometimes, humans were more monstrous than anything else.

CHAPTER FIVE

Devon left town behind and headed for the mountain, steering the SUV up the curvy, narrow roads.

We passed house after house, each one bigger and more impressive than the last. Lots of mortals and magicks had built vacation and other homes up here to take advantage of the sweeping views. Your mansion's size and location on the mountain was a status symbol that let all your neighbors know how much money, magic, and power you had. Bigger and higher were better. Naturally.

But the mansions quickly thinned out and disappeared, replaced by thick stone walls set with closed iron gates that led into the compounds of the various Families. Guards wearing boots, cloaks, hats, and swords patrolled behind the walls and gates, and thick screens of pine trees hid most of the compounds from view. Towers soared up out of the greenery, all of them topped with colorful flags bearing the crests of the different Families, including a wolf's head for the Volkovs and a cluster of purple wisteria flowers for the Itos.

Finally, we reached the Sinclair Family compound. The gates opened at our approach, and Devon steered through them, over a bridge, and along a circular driveway. An enormous mansion made out of black stone rose up in front of us—a rough, blocky structure that looked as if it had been carved out of the side of the mountain itself. Balconies, patios, and walkways fronted much of the sprawling, seven-story structure, swooping from one floor to the next, while several sections rose up and formed actual towers, just like at the other Family compounds.

The Sinclair mansion was the highest structure on Cloudburst Mountain, so close to the top that the thick clouds that rimmed the peak year-round would often sink down into the trees and cloak the grounds at night. The white fog was actually mist that continually drifted up from the dozens of waterfalls tumbling down the mountain's rocky ridges. Given that it was late afternoon, the sun was keeping the worst of the fog away; although the clouds were close enough to kiss the black flags on the tops of the towers.

Devon parked the SUV next to the mansion's main entrance. We'd barely gotten out of the vehicle when an older man with snow-white hair strode out the front door and stopped in the driveway, his stance as stiff and crisp as his three-piece black tweed suit.

William Reginald eyed the three of us and our persimmon-spattered clothes, his nose twitching with obvious distaste. "I take it that things didn't go so well with the tree troll?" an English accent colored his voice, making him sound exactly like the butler he was.

Being a Family butler involved a lot more than supervising the cooking and cleaning. Reginald basically ran the mansion, overseeing the day-to-day operations of everything from the kitchen and cleaning staff to the groundskeepers to who got admitted inside the compound to talk business with the Sinclair higher-ups. Butler was one of the three most important positions in the Family—along with the bruiser and broker—making Reginald equal to Devon in terms of power.

Felix threw his arm around Devon's shoulder, making bits of persimmon slide off both their T-shirts. "Oh, it went just fine and dandy. Can't you tell?"

Reginald sniffed, clearly not amused. "Very well. Off with the lot of you. I will see about cleaning up this . . . mess." He pointed his finger at us in a warning. "And don't you dare touch or sit on anything in those clothes."

He waited until we'd all nodded our agreement before turning back to the vehicle. Reginald peered through the window into the backseat and grimaced, as though it physically pained him to see all the red stains on the leather.

We left Reginald standing by the vehicle, muttering about cleaning solutions. Devon opened the front door, and he, Felix, and I headed inside.

The outside of the mansion might be black, blocky stone, but the inside was white, airy elegance. Everything glimmered, from the white marble floors to the flecks of gold, silver, and bronze that swirled through the painted walls to the crystal chandeliers that dripped down like clusters of icicles hanging from the ceilings. Faceted gemstones decorated much of the dark, heavy furniture, adding even more sparkle and color, along with the rich, vibrant stained glass that was set into many of the windows.

As a thief, I had let myself into my share of fine homes and had swiped more than a few valuable objects, but the luxe mansion still took my breath away, despite all the weeks I'd been living here. It was a good thing I wasn't casing the place. I wouldn't have known what to steal first.

"See you guys at dinner," Devon said.

Felix and I nodded, and the three of us went our separate ways.

I headed up the stairs to my bedroom, which was just as

finely furnished as the rest of the mansion. The front of the room was an entertainment area, with a black leather couch and matching recliners arranged around a glass coffee table, all of which faced a flat-screen TV mounted to the wall. A four-poster bed covered with a black-and-white-striped comforter and mounds of pillows took up part of the back wall, along with a white vanity table. Another table that featured a miniature ebony trailer, a grassy corral, and a small barn sat next to some French doors that led out to a balcony.

I sighed, went over, and started to plop down on the couch, when a sharp, twangy voice called out.

"Don't you dare sit down on that!"

The front door on the ebony trailer slammed open, and something *zip-zip-zipped* through the air, rushing straight at me. A second later, a six-inch-tall man with shimmering, translucent wings attached to his back hovered right in front of me, his arms crossed over his tiny chest. Oscar, the pixie who took care of my room and, by extension, me. He must have been getting dressed for dinner because he only wore a white tank top, along with blue boxers and black cowboy boots. He never went anywhere without his boots on. He was a little redneck that way.

I groaned. "Not you too. Can't I sit down on something? Just for a minute. It's been a long day."

"Not if I have to clean it up afterward." Oscar regarded me with critical violet eyes, his nose twitching. "You smell like a fruit cobbler—and not in a good way."

I pulled my sticky T-shirt away from my chest, wincing as another wave of too-sweet persimmon pulp filled my nose. "Really? I hadn't noticed."

"Sarcasm's not going to help you with me, cupcake," Oscar said, making shooing motions with his hands. "So instead of sitting down and getting something else dirty, you might as well strip off those nasty clothes and get in the shower. I'll put you some fresh clothes on the hanger on the back of the bathroom door. Go on, now. Git."

He zoomed back and forth in front of my face, like I was a cow he was trying to herd.

"Yes, master," I grumbled.

Technically, pixies were monsters, since they weren't human-size, but I'd always thought of them as miniature people. They were also the housekeepers of the world, hiring themselves out to mortals, magicks, and even other monsters in exchange for a place to live, protection, money, and more. Oscar and I had gotten off to a rocky start when I'd first moved in, but I now considered him a friend. He was also one of the few people who had known my mom, because she'd worked for the Family for years, until she'd had a falling out with Claudia Sinclair.

Oscar might not be much bigger than my hand, but he made up for his small size with plenty of attitude. He was the bossiest pixie I'd ever met, barking out order after order in his twangy, hillbilly voice to anyone who dared get within earshot. Over the past few weeks, I'd learned that it was better just to humor him in most things, like wearing the clothes he laid out for me and eating the food he brought up to my room when I was out on Family business and couldn't get down to the dining hall for the regular meal.

So I obediently headed into the bathroom, shut the door behind me, stripped off my clothes, and took a long, hot shower to wash off all the blood persimmon juice that had soaked into my hair and skin. When I was done, I reached an arm out of the bathroom and grabbed the fresh clothes off the hook on the door.

I expected to find my usual T-shirt and cargo pants, but Oscar had put out a tight, sleeveless, sapphire-blue top, along with a pair of fitted black pants and matching heels. Apparently, he wanted me to dress up for dinner. I grumbled again, but I didn't feel like arguing with him, so I put on the clothes with one substitution. I ditched the heels in favor of black sneakers.

I'd already dried my hair, so I plopped down in front of the vanity mirror and pulled my black locks back into a sleek ponytail before sticking two black lacquered chopsticks through it. The thin sticks might look like innocent hair accessories, but they were far more useful, since the hollow wooden tubes featured a set of lock picks. My star-sapphire ring completed the ensemble, along with my silver Sinclair cuff.

When I finished, I headed over to the table next to the patio doors where Oscar's pixie house sat. Most folks would have thought that the ebony trailer was some sort of dollhouse, despite the fact that the roof was missing several shingles, the porch sagged like a wet newspaper, and several tiny honeybeer cans littered the front steps. A grassy yard led over to a corral and a barn, also made out of ebony, making the entire table look like a diorama of some western dude ranch. Rustic, people would say, if they were being kind.

Behind the fence, Tiny, Oscar's pet tortoise, was lying on his back, his green legs sticking up in the air as he snoozed the day away in a sunspot. Tiny cracked open a black eye at the sound of my footsteps, but when he realized that I didn't have any lettuce or strawberries, he went back to his nap. I tickled one of his feet, making him snort and rock back and forth on his shell before he settled down again.

The trailer's front door slammed open again, and Oscar hopped down the creaky porch steps and strutted out onto the lawn. He held his arms out to his sides and turned around.

"Well?" he drawled. "How do I look?"

While I'd been getting dressed, Oscar had been doing

the same. His sandy mop of hair was slicked back under a black cowboy hat, and he wore a pair of new, creased black jeans and a white button-up shirt with black trim, along with his usual cowboy boots. I squinted. Were those black pearl buttons on his shirt? Probably, knowing Oscar.

"Nice," I said. "What's the occasion? And why did you make me dress up too?"

He grinned. "You'll see. Bet you can't beat me to the dining hall!"

Oscar zipped over to the bedroom door, opened it, and flew away before I could answer him.

I looked at Tiny. "Have you been feeding him sugar again?"

The tortoise just snorted again.

I went down to the dining hall, which was one of the biggest rooms in the mansion. Tall, skinny windows lined the back wall from floor to ceiling, showing off the deep, dark evergreen woods that surrounded the mansion. Sunlight streaming in through the glass made the chandeliers overhead sparkle even more than usual, the crystals painting rainbow patterns on the black-and-white Persian rugs that covered the floor. Long tables that could seat more than thirty people each clustered together in the middle of the room, while still more tables were set up along one of the walls, each one covered with food.

I headed straight for the buffet tables to see what the pixies had whipped up tonight. Their excellent home-cooking was one of the best perks of living at the Sinclair mansion. Tonight's menu was one of my favorites—grilled steak with horseradish mashed potatoes and a summer salad of ripe tomatoes, crunchy cucumbers, and tangy red onions that the pixies grew up in the greenlab. I heaped a plate full of steak, potatoes, and salad, along with dates that had been stuffed with gorgonzola cheese and wrapped in bacon, which was my absolute favorite food. Bacon made *everything* better.

A guy swaggered up next to me. "You gonna leave some of those for the rest of us?"

My fingers curled a little tighter around the tongs I was using to pick up the dates. "Vance."

"Lila."

Vance Groves was one of the top Sinclair guards with Talents for both speed and strength. At twenty, he'd already been serving the Family for a couple of years. Vance patrolled down on the Midway, and he was one of the few guards who actually enjoyed strutting around in the cheesy black cloak and feathered cavalier hat, both of which he was wearing right now. He thought that the ren-faire gear made him look oh so dashing, and he was absolutely right about that. With his golden hair and blue eyes, Vance was seriously handsome, something he took great pride in. He was always posing for photos with the giggly tourist girls—and then slipping them his phone number afterward.

Vance also thought that he was the best fighter in the Family, something I'd disproven over and over by disarming him every time we sparred together. Vance didn't like anyone beating him at anything, especially not a newbie recruit like me, and he went out of his way to annoy me every chance he got.

Vance sneered at me, snatched the tongs out of my hand, and started piling the bacon-wrapped dates onto his plate.

"You don't want to do that."

His blue eyes narrowed. "Why not?"

"You're watching your weight, remember?" My voice was oh so kind but loud enough for everyone around us to hear. "Good for you, trying to get rid of your potbelly.

Not to mention that male pattern baldness that's starting to set in. But hey, the hat covers that up, right?"

Vance's eyes bulged with anger, and his mouth dropped open, but only strangled syllables escaped.

I gave him a sweet smile, slipped the tongs out of his hand, and piled the rest of the dates onto my plate so that he would have to wait for the pixies to bring out another tray.

I slapped the tongs into his chest. "Later, Vance."

His fingers fisted around the utensil like he wanted to brain me with it, but I was already grabbing a glass of sweet iced tea and striding away.

I put Vance out of my mind and carried my food over to the table where Devon and Felix were sitting, along with a tall, muscular man with onyx skin and black hair peppered with silver threads. Oscar was hanging out with some of the other pixies at a table next to the windows.

Devon and Felix were dressed in nice shirts and black pants, just like me, but the man was a completely different story. He sported white linen pants and a lime-green Hawaiian shirt patterned with exploding volcanoes spewing scarlet lava. The garish combination of green and red made him the most colorful thing in the room. White flip-flops covered his feet, while a white straw hat was hooked on the back of his chair.

Mo Kaminsky, my friend and fence, looked at me as I pulled out a chair and sat down next to him. "So, kid, whatcha got for me today?"

I reached into my pocket, drew out the small stone statue of a Fenrir wolf that I'd swiped on my way to the dining hall, and set it down on the table. "And you?"

Mo grinned, reached into one of his own pockets, and drew out a crystal paperweight shaped like a tree troll.

I grinned back. "Nice."

Felix eyed the statue and the paperweight. "Um, aren't those supposed to be in one of the downstairs living rooms? Don't you guys ever get tired of stealing stuff?"

Mo and I looked at each other, our grins widening. "Never," we said in unison.

Every day, Mo and I each swiped some trinket from somewhere in the mansion, then brought it to dinner to see what our spoils were, so to speak. Last week, we'd both gone for a pair of silver bookends in the library. He'd gotten one and I'd snagged the other. Of course, since we both officially worked for the Family now, we weren't actually *stealing* the items. If we had been, Mo would have been taking the pilfered goods down to the Razzle Dazzle, his pawnshop, and either fencing them to one of his shady contacts or foisting them off on some unsuspecting tourist—for twice the items' value.

Every day after Mo and I showed off our spoils, we switched items and tried to figure out where the other person had gotten their trinket from so we could return it to its proper place. I didn't mind putting everything back . . . too much. It was a fun game and it kept my skills sharp. But I'd been so busy helping Devon with the tree troll and other Family problems the past few days that I'd fallen behind and had a backlog of shiny knickknacks sitting on the vanity table in my bedroom.

So Mo slid the Fenrir wolf statue into his pants pocket, while I slipped the troll paperweight into mine. Then, we both resumed eating as though we hadn't stolen anything at all. Mo and I weren't exactly troubled by things like sticky fingers and guilty consciences.

Felix eyed my plate. "You and the bacon again—it's like a disease or something."

I picked up one of the bacon-wrapped dates. "How can something that tastes this good possibly be wrong?"

Felix groaned, but I grinned and popped the date into my mouth. The bacon and fruit combined for a rich, smoky-sweet flavor, while the gorgonzola cheese added a bit of creaminess. A perfect little bite and so good that I polished off the others on my plate, went back to the buffet, and got several more.

Vance Groves glared at me as I walked by, since he was sitting close to the buffet, but I ignored him and returned to my table.

Dinner was fun and boisterous, with Felix and Mo competing to see who could outtalk the other. Felix told Mo all about our tree troll problem, while Mo chattered on about all the odd items that people had pawned at his shop today. The two of them barely shut up, except to take a bite of food every now and then. As much and as fast as they talked, it was a wonder there was enough oxygen in the room for both of them at the same time.

Since I couldn't get a word in edgewise, I concentrated on my food, which was just as delicious as it looked. The steak was perfectly cooked with a black-pepper crust, while the crispy, cool crunch of the salad offset the slow burn of the horseradish in the buttery mashed potatoes. I washed everything down with the sweet iced tea.

Every so often, I'd look up to find Devon staring at me, a thoughtful expression on his face. He'd been a little cool and distant the past few weeks, ever since I'd told him that I didn't want to take our friendship—or whatever this thing between us was—to the next level. We'd been so busy with the troll in the square and then finding that poor, murdered monster behind the dumpster that today had been the first day things had felt somewhat normal between us. At least, until he looked at me the way he was right now.

I felt the same way about Devon that he did about me,

but I didn't plan on sticking around here forever. As soon as I figured out what Victor Draconi was plotting against the other Families and found a way to finally make him pay for my mom's murder, I was on the next bus out of Cloudburst Falls. I didn't know where I would go or what I would do, but I'd figure it out . . . eventually.

Besides, I already cared about Devon way too much. I didn't want to get my heart broken when whatever was between us finally ended.

And it *would* end.

Every good thing in my life had so far, and there was no reason to think that Devon would be any different. Yeah, yeah. I know that folks always say that it's better to have loved and lost, than never to have loved at all. Bullshit. Those people hadn't loved and lost all the things that I had—my mom, my innocence, my childhood. At seventeen, I'd already had enough hurt to last a lifetime.

So I ignored Devon and focused on my food. I'd just popped the last of the bacon-wrapped dates into my mouth when Claudia Sinclair strode into the dining hall.

Claudia was Devon's mom and the leader of the Family—the big cheese, the top dog, the head honcho. And she looked the part, with her fitted black pantsuit, stiletto heels, and expensive but understated jewelry. A silver cuff flashed on her right wrist, a bit wider, thicker, and brighter than everyone else's, further marking her as the boss.

Claudia was quite beautiful, with auburn hair and expressive features. It was only when you looked into her green eyes that you saw the strength, determination, and coldness lurking beneath her smooth, polished surface.

Claudia ate most of her meals in the library, which doubled as her office, since she always had some sort of work to do. But even more surprising than her presence in the dining room was the wide smile stretching across her face.

It made me more nervous than if she'd stormed in here snarling at everyone.

Reginald followed Claudia into the dining hall, along with Angelo Morales, Felix's dad. Claudia took up a position at the front of the room, with Reginald and Angelo flanking her.

A pixie zipped over and handed Claudia a glass of sparkling apple cider, along with a fork. More pixies fluttered through the room, depositing a glass next to everyone's elbow. Oscar flew over with my apple cider, grinning and leaning up against the glass, which was taller than he was.

When everyone had been served, Claudia *tink-tink-tinked* the fork against her glass, and the room hushed.

"What's going on? What are we celebrating?" I asked Mo.

He winked. "Just wait and see, kid. It's a Sinclair tradition."

Everyone faced Claudia, and she looked out over her Family members, the pixies who kept the mansion spotless, the guards who patrolled down in the Midway, the folks who worked at the banks, museums, and other businesses. Her eyes met mine and my soulsight kicked in, letting me feel her rock-hard strength and determination—and sly satisfaction.

Oh, yeah. Claudia was *definitely* up to something.

She stared at me another moment, then looked out over the dining hall again. "As you all know," she began, "the Tournament of Blades, the annual contest that all the Families sponsor and participate in, will begin in the morning. It's one of the summer's most popular events with the tourists, and this year's crowd looks to be larger than ever before."

Several *woot-woots* of excitement rang out, including some from Mo. I rolled my eyes. He didn't care about the tournament so much as he did about all the people it would bring into the Razzle Dazzle to buy the junk he had for sale.

"Every year, Reginald, Angelo, and I select those who will represent the Sinclair Family in the tournament and announce them here, at dinner, the night before the competition starts," Claudia continued. "The tournament requires a unique combination of speed, strength, smarts, and fighting skills, all of which we take into account when making our selections. Tonight, I am happy to share those names with the entire Family."

More *woot-woots* rang out, along with a round of applause. But eventually the cheers and claps died down, and a charged silence filled the room. Everyone leaned forward, perched on the edge of their seats in anticipation, especially the guards, waiting to hear the names Claudia would call.

She smiled. "I think the first name will please you all: your bruiser, Devon Sinclair."

Another, louder round of applause rang out, while Felix let loose with some ear-splitting whistles. A faint blush colored Devon's cheeks, but his green eyes were warm and happy as he got up, walked across the room, and stood beside his mom. He looked at me, and I grinned and flashed him a thumbs-up, which made him blush even more.

His selection was hardly surprising, though. Bruiser was one of the most important positions in the Family, so Devon's not being in the tournament would have been the real shock. But everyone knew how hard he worked, how tough and strong he was, and how he genuinely cared about and looked out for everyone in the Family. That's why the guards, workers, and even the pixies were cheering so long and loud for him. Devon deserved to be in the tournament, and he'd do his best to make everyone proud.

Claudia called out several more names, all guards whom I'd sparred against a time or two. I clapped and cheered with everyone else, approving of the selections. Claudia, Reginald, and Angelo had picked a good mix of people with a variety of Talents, including speed, strength, and enhanced senses, all of which would come in handy during the tournament.

"Vance Groves," Claudia announced.

I rolled my eyes, but I clapped politely for him. Vance might be cocky and arrogant, but he was a good fighter. Vance pushed back from his table, high-fived his friends, then strutted up to the front of the room, preening and taking his place with the other participants.

"And now, for the last person who will be representing the Sinclairs in this year's Tournament of Blades."

Claudia paused and looked around the room, her gaze going from one face to the next. Silence fell over the dining hall again, even more intense than before, since this was the last chance to be chosen. People froze, eyes wide, hands clenched tight, breath caught in their throats. I just wanted her to go ahead and say the lucky name already. It seemed kind of cruel to keep everyone in suspense for so long.

Claudia turned her head, her green gaze meeting mine. Her sly satisfaction filled my body, and I finally realized what she was up to. I cringed, even as she called out the last two words I wanted to hear.

"Lila Merriweather."

CHAPTER SIX

Shock surged through me, as though some magick had just blasted me with a lightning bolt.

I'd never, ever thought that Claudia would call *my* name. I'd only been here a few weeks, and some of the guards had served the Family for years. Sure, I'd saved Devon's life a couple times, but that had been more sneakiness and luck on my part than anything else, along with a fair amount of help from the lochness. So why pick me to compete in the tournament?

My shock and surprise quickly melted into absolute horror as every eye in the room fixed on me. I was a thief who did her best work in the shadows when no one was looking. I *hated* being the center of attention, but that's exactly what I was right now.

Mo beamed at me, his black eyes shining with warm pride, and Felix and Oscar were grinning like fools, all three of them clapping as hard and loud as they could. Oscar's transparent wings were twitching so hard with excitement that I thought they might fly right off his back.

Mo nudged me with his elbow. "Go on up there, kid. Take a bow with the rest of the competitors. You've earned it."

Everyone was still staring at me, so I had no choice but to get up and take my place with the others. Vance snorted, but the other guards gave me friendly smiles. Devon scooted over so that I could stand next to him, but I still shifted uncomfortably on my feet, trying to sidle behind him as much as I could so that I wouldn't be quite so front and center.

By this point, everyone in the dining hall was standing, clapping, cheering, and whistling for all the folks who'd been chosen. I fixed a smile on my face and clapped along, even though all I really wanted to do was slink out of the room as quickly and quietly as possible.

Devon leaned over. "I know you didn't expect this, but I'm glad you'll be part of the tournament. Out of all of us, I think you have the best chance to win."

"But what about the competitors from the other Families? What about Deah and Katia?"

He leaned even closer, his crisp pine scent washing over me. "You're the best fighter I've ever seen. And more important, you're smart, especially with your magic. You'll win. Trust me, Lila. A couple of days from now, we'll be standing here again, celebrating your victory." He hesitated, his voice dropping to a low, husky whisper. "And I'll be cheering louder than anyone else."

His green gaze locked with my blue one. My soulsight kicked in, letting me see and feel all his emotions—warm pride, rock-hard certainty, and that hot, hot spark that made an answering heat sizzle through my entire body. He really believed what he said. Devon really thought that I could win the Tournament of Blades.

And in that moment, I desperately wanted to do it, if only so he would keep on looking at me the way he was right now.

Everyone left their tables and streamed forward, wanting to congratulate all the folks who'd been chosen to compete. I shook hand after hand and endured back slaps from Mo, Felix, and countless others. Oscar buzzed around my head, whooping, hollering, and throwing his tiny cowboy hat up into the air, then darting forward to catch it.

"I still don't understand why Claudia picked me," I muttered.

"Relax, Lila," Felix said. "It's not like no one's never heard of you before. All the other Families have seen you with Devon and me in the Midway. And all the Sinclairs know what you did for Devon at the lochness bridge. They know you've earned this."

Maybe that's what was making me so uncomfortable. I didn't *earn* things. I was a bloody thief. I took what I wanted whenever I wanted it. So this was a whole new experience for me.

"You should be happy that Claudia picked you," Oscar piped up.

"Why is that?"

"Because the tournament winner gets a gold cup and a check for twenty-five thousand dollars."

"Oh." My eyes widened. "*Oh.*"

The pixie laughed. "I thought that might interest you."

"Lila is sure to win." Mo clapped me on the back again. "You know what, kid? I should be your trainer. Keep you focused on the tournament."

I gave him a suspicious look. "Why do I think you're mentally playing the *Rocky* theme music in your head right now?"

Mo grinned. "I'm sure I can find you some steps to run up somewhere around here."

I groaned, wondering how much more this was going to complicate my life.

Felix and Mo went over to talk to Devon, with Oscar flitting along behind them. I headed in the other direction, hoping that I could escape from the dining hall, but Vance blocked my retreat.

"Well, I see it pays to date the boss's son," he sneered. "That's the only reason you're in the tournament."

"And I see that they must need a rodeo clown for the tournament," I shot right back. "Guess the organizers are lucky you volunteered, huh?"

"I'll see you on the field tomorrow, Merriweather," Vance snarled.

"Looking forward to it, Groves."

He stormed off, his black cloak flapping around his shoulders.

I glanced around, but no one had noticed our confrontation, and I was finally able to slip out of the dining hall.

Instead of going back to my bedroom, I headed to the mansion's library, which took up three levels, all of which featured balconies bristling with bookshelves. The square area sloped up to form a tower, with the ceiling made out of alternating panes of black-and-white stained glass. With the sun setting, the glass cast more shadows than light.

Claudia had left the celebration as well and was sitting behind an ebony desk on the first floor of the library. Behind her, a series of glass doors led out to a balcony that offered more sweeping views of the grounds. A pair of silver reading glasses perched on her nose, but she didn't glance up from the papers she was poring over as I stalked toward her.

"I was wondering how long it would take you to charge in here," Claudia murmured. "You're late. I expected you five minutes ago."

"Sorry," I sniped. "I got waylaid by well-wishers."

Claudia arched an eyebrow, but she kept right on reading.

"What's so fascinating?" I sniped again. "Are you jotting down all your secret desires there in your diary?"

That finally got her to snort, pull off her glasses, and raise her gaze to mine. "Hardly. I was reviewing Devon's report about the tree troll incident in the square. What did you bribe the troll with to get it to stop throwing fruit at people?"

"How do you know that I bribed it with anything?"

"Because that's what your mother would have done." Claudia leaned back in her chair. "Serena always preferred trying to reason with the monsters to killing them. It was one of the things I admired most about her."

I stared at her, wondering at her soft, sad tone, but Claudia knew better than to look into my eyes and let me see what she was really feeling. Annoyance spurted through me. That was the problem with letting people in on your secrets, especially your magic and what you could do with it. They started figuring out ways to get around your Talents. I liked knowing what other people were feeling—it had helped me stay alive this long.

Talking about my mom was another one of those things that made me uncomfortable, so I wandered over to a bookcase that took up one wall of the library. All sorts of pretty knickknacks gleamed on the shelves—porcelain keepsake boxes, sterling silver letter openers, crystal picture frames. I scanned the items, wondering if I might pocket one or two while Claudia wasn't watching and use them for my game with Mo. I might ostensibly be going straight these days, but it was good to keep in practice. You never knew when a pair of light fingers might help you out of a sticky situation.

So I bent down, pretending to admire a photo of my mom with a blond woman I didn't recognize. There were lots of shots of my mom in here, since she'd been a member of the Family for years before she'd left Cloudburst

Falls. But she seemed especially happy in this photo, grinning at the blond woman as if the two of them were good friends.

"See anything you like?" Claudia called out.

As I turned to face her, I dropped my hand down by my side and palmed a small jet statue shaped like a lochness, complete with sapphire eyes and several small tentacles, off one of the shelves.

I shrugged and slid the statue into my pants pocket. "Nothing that would interest Mo."

Claudia scowled. As part of my agreeing to work for the Sinclairs, I'd forced Claudia to appoint Mo as the Family broker, the person responsible for, well, brokering all the Family's business deals. Claudia and Mo had some history I didn't know about, but she seemed to almost openly loathe him at times, while he enjoyed needling her like it was his new favorite sport.

I leaned my elbow on one of the bookcase shelves, knocking a few pictures out of alignment. Claudia's nose wrinkled. She was almost as fussy about things being in place in her library as Reginald was about the rest of the mansion looking up to snuff. I grinned. I liked annoying her. It wasn't smart, but it was the only bit of rebellion I could get away with, since I was stuck here for the next year.

Providing I lived that long, of course.

"Where are we with the Draconis?" Claudia said. "Have you heard anything new?"

Everyone was always interested in gossip about the other Families, especially the Draconis, since they were our main rivals. But Claudia had even more reason than others to be concerned about them. A few weeks ago, I'd used my soulsight on Victor Draconi, and I'd realized that he was plotting against Claudia and all the other Families.

Something big.

Something dangerous.

Something deadly.

"Nothing out of the ordinary," I said. "We ran into Blake and Deah today, but all they were interested in was crowing about how Deah's going to win the tournament again this year; especially since there was another girl there, Katia Volkov."

Claudia nodded. "That's to be expected this time of year. I doubt that even Victor would try something before the tournament, since it's such a big draw and money-maker for everyone in town, mortals and magicks alike. He'll wait until afterward to put his plan into motion, whatever it is."

She rubbed her forehead as though it was aching. I didn't have to use my soulsight to see the tension pinching her face. Whatever Victor was up to, it worried Claudia more than anything else. And she had good reason. I'd seen into the black, rotten depths of Victor Draconi, and the only thing that beat in his dark heart was cold, cruel calculation—and his icy desire to destroy Claudia and all the other Families.

"Maybe we'll get lucky and Victor will let something slip during the tournament," she said. "At the very least, I can see who he meets with and talks to. That might tell us something about what he's planning."

"Yeah. About the tournament."

She arched her eyebrows.

"Why did you pick *me* to compete? I thought we had an agreement. I would be your eyes and ears and find out everything I could about the Draconis. Kind of hard to be a spy when you're the center of attention."

"Because I think you can win it."

I snorted. "Bullshit. Devon has just as good a chance to win as I do. So does Vance, for that matter. So what's the *real* reason?"

Claudia paused a moment, considering her answer. "Because your mother was the only person that Victor was ever truly afraid of."

Her soft words punched me in the gut, but I didn't let any of my hurt and heartache show. "He certainly didn't seem to be afraid when he cut her to pieces."

Claudia stared at me, her green eyes blazing with conviction. "Victor was *always* afraid of Serena—of her sight magic, of her fighting skills, and especially of her ways of communicating with the monsters."

"And what does all that have to do with picking me for the tournament?"

"I want him to know there's someone else he should be afraid of."

My mouth dropped open in surprise, but Claudia kept staring at me, the conviction in her gaze burning even brighter and hotter than before.

I didn't know how to respond, so I turned toward the doors, desperate to leave and trying to hide my shock, sorrow, and all the other emotions surging through me.

"Good luck," Claudia called out in a soft voice.

I didn't know if she was talking about the tournament or my turbulent feelings. Probably both. But I didn't trust myself to speak, so I nodded, strode over, pulled open one of the doors, and left the library as fast as I could.

CHAPTER SEVEN

"It's too early for this," I grumbled. "*Way* too early."

It was seven o'clock the next morning, and I was lying in bed, the covers pulled up to my chin, watching Oscar zip around the room putting clothes into a black duffel bag sitting on the couch. The pixie had been up for an hour already, rustling around in my closet, flying from here, into the bathroom, and back out again, and muttering to himself all the while.

"Why can't they start the tournament at a reasonable hour?" I grumbled again. "Like noon-thirty."

Oscar stopped in midair and slapped his hands on his hips. The pixie had ditched his formal cowboy getup from last night in favor of a black T-shirt boasting the Sinclairs' white hand-and-sword crest, faded jeans with holes in the knees, and black cowboy boots. A black cavalier hat with a plume of white feathers perched on his head, while a tiny black cloak fluttered around his shoulders. It was an odd mix of redneck and ren-faire. He'd even dressed up Tiny in a matching hat and cloak, although the tortoise had already knocked the hat off his head and was busy sniffing the feathers to see if they were edible.

"The tournament starts so early because it is an entire day of *awesome*," Oscar said. "Trust me. You're going to love it. Now get your lazy *tuchas* out of bed, cupcake—unless you don't want any breakfast bacon."

"Are you crazy? I always want breakfast bacon, and noon bacon, and afternoon bacon—"

Oscar threw a black T-shirt with the white hand-and-sword crest at me, hitting me in the chest and silencing my argument. A pair of matching black athletic shorts followed a few seconds later, landing on top of my head.

"Don't make me bean you in the face with your own socks and sneakers," he warned.

Bullied by a six-inch-tall pixie at seven in the morning. Yep, my life as a mobster was certainly a glamorous one.

"Do you want any bacon or not?" Oscar snapped.

And just like that, he won. I groaned and crawled out of bed.

After a quick breakfast that was extra heavy on the bacon, I went outside and got into the back of an SUV, along with Devon and Felix. Angelo was driving, with Mo in the front passenger's seat. Another SUV rolling down the driveway in front of us held Claudia, Reginald, Oscar, and some of the guards chosen to compete in the tournament, including Vance Groves, who'd been as arrogant and insufferable as ever at breakfast, showing off some of his fighting moves for his friends. Behind us, several more cars held other members of the Family, everyone from the Midway workers to the other guards to the pixies.

"What's with the convoy?" I asked.

Mo glanced over his shoulder at me. "The tournament is a big deal to all the Families. Practically everyone attends all the rounds, except for the bare minimum of folks needed to work the booths, patrol the Midway, or watch over the compounds on the mountain."

"Even then, the guards and all the other workers take shifts so that everyone has a chance to see at least part of the tournament," Angelo chimed in. "It's almost like a minivacation for everyone in the Families, and we all try to put aside our differences. At least while the tournament is going on."

"And after that?" I asked.

Mo grinned. "Then it's back to business, blood, and battles as usual, kid."

I snorted. I would expect nothing less from the Families. It was amazing they could call a truce long enough to hold the tournament in the first place.

Angelo drove down the mountain, but instead of heading for the Midway, he took a different route, snaking around the tourist area and heading toward the outskirts of town. He drove over the lochness bridge, slowing down long enough for Devon and me to fling several handfuls of quarters out the windows to pay the toll for all the Sinclair vehicles crossing the span today. I peered out the windows, but I didn't see any long black tentacles, rippling water, or other signs of the lochness. Then again, it was early. Perhaps the monster hadn't roused itself from its watery bed on the bottom of the river yet. At least someone got to sleep in today.

Angelo drove on. A couple of miles later, the cracked sidewalks, abandoned warehouses, and dilapidated buildings gave way to rolling hills covered with grassy lawns and dense thickets of trees. In the distance, I spotted a wide swath of white sand and the dark blue waters of Bloodiron Lake.

A wooden sign planted in one of the lawns featured a carving of a red boat sitting on blue waves, announcing that we were entering the Cloudburst Falls Fairgrounds and Recreation Area. My heart twisted in my chest. My mom used to bring me out here every summer to swim in the lake, play on the beach, and hike the trails in the surrounding forests, but I hadn't been here since her death four years ago.

Angelo turned into a paved lot and parked the car. We all got out, with Devon and me grabbing our duffel bags, which held extra clothes and shoes, along with the weapons we would be using in the tournament. My mom's black-blade sword was stuffed into my bag, while Devon had his father, Lawrence's sword, the hilt engraved with the Sinclair hand-and-sword crest. Angelo, Mo, and Felix grabbed some other bags filled with supplies out of the SUV, and we all headed toward the fairgrounds.

The fairgrounds spread across several acres, with the evergreen woods rising up all around them like soldiers protecting a precious jewel. Gray cobblestone paths led from the parking lots to the fairgrounds, winding past vendors selling everything from sunscreen to replica black blades to hats covered with Family crests. Food carts also clustered along the paths, and the smells of cinnamon rolls, chocolate chip cookies, and deep-fried fudge filled the air, making my mouth water and stomach rumble, even though we'd just finished breakfast an hour ago. Wooden booths offered spectators the chance to try their hands at carnival games, like a ring toss with plastic lochness tentacles as the targets. As part of a strong man test, a kid was enthusiastically beating a plastic bat on top of a fake tree troll head. The harmless game reminded me of the murdered monster we'd found yesterday. And just like that, my appetite vanished.

We moved past the carts and game booths and fell in with the crowd streaming toward the center of the fairgrounds. Gold, silver, and bronze cuffs flashed on many wrists, but there was more mixing between the members of the Families than usual, and everyone seemed to be in a cheery mood, laughing, smiling, and teasing their friends and everyone else they knew. The tournament hadn't started yet, which meant that everyone still had a chance to win. I wondered how long the collective goodwill would last once people started being eliminated.

The main drag of the fairgrounds led into a large, circular stadium, with gray stone bleachers rising up all around it, and private, glassed-in boxes set at the very tops. Each of the private boxes boasted a flag bearing the crest and colors of the Family it belonged to. The Sinclair box was directly across the stadium from the Draconi one. Naturally.

Five tents had been set up around the stadium entrance, close to a waist-high, chain-link fence that circled the grassy field that would serve as the competition area. Each tent was patterned with a Family crest and topped by a matching flag, while a sixth, much larger tent, done in neutral white fabric, perched off to one side.

Angelo, Mo, Felix, Devon, and I headed for the Sinclair tent. Just as Angelo and Mo had said, practically everyone in the Families had turned out for the tournament, and many folks wearing Family T-shirts and hats were already perched on the bleachers, noshing on nachos and buffalo wings, and waiting for the action to start. Workers moved back and forth across the stadium floor, carrying hurdles, balance beams, and more, setting up what looked like an obstacle course.

Flocks of tourists had also come out for the tournament. I could tell they were tourist rubes by the cameras hanging around their necks and the way many used their cameras and phones to snap photos of everything around them, including the pixies zipping through the air like swarms of bees, their translucent wings shimmering in the morning sunlight, carrying ice cream cones that were twice their size.

I snorted. From their constant photo snapping and excited chatter, you'd think that the tourists had never seen pixies before, but the creatures were everywhere, just like all the other monsters that the rubes came to Cloudburst Falls to gawk at. Our town just happened to have more magic and monsters than anywhere else. At least, that's what the tourism officials claimed.

We reached the Sinclair tent and stepped through the opening. Chairs had been set up inside, along with tables full of food and drinks and several oscillating fans to combat the day's growing heat. Reginald stood in the center of the tent, wearing another one of his black tweed suits and directing the pixies, who were passing out bottles of water. Claudia was sitting by herself along one of the walls, checking her phone.

Angelo, Mo, and Felix split off to see if Reginald needed any help, but Devon and I didn't get five steps into the tent before people started coming up to us and talking about the tournament. For once, I didn't mind the attention. The mood was light and happy, and everyone was back-slapping, high-fiving, and wishing all the competitors good luck.

"Ready to choke, Lila?" a snide voice murmured in my ear. "Because that's exactly what you're going to do today."

Well, not everyone.

Vance stepped up beside me, a smug grin stretching across his handsome face. He made a slow slashing gesture with his finger across his throat, then raised his hands to his neck and started making fake choking sounds.

I gave him a sweet smile in return. "If you don't move along, I'm going to shove my fist into your throat and make you choke for real."

Vance dropped his hands and glared at me, and I glared right back at him.

Devon stepped in between us. "Good luck, Vance," he said in a pointed tone.

Vance rolled his eyes. "I don't need luck. That's for all the other losers here."

Devon's face hardened at the insult. "Well, I guess we'll see who the real losers are at the end of the tournament."

"Whatever, dude." Vance rolled his eyes again and moved over to his friends, who were clustered around one of the drink tables.

"What a jackass," Devon muttered.

"No argument here."

We moved deeper into the tent, both of us giving and receiving more well-wishes. I might be supercynical, but even I had to admit that the camaraderie was . . . nice. It made me feel like I truly was a member of the Family and part of something bigger and more important than just myself.

It made me proud to be a Sinclair.

"Isn't this great!" Oscar said, zooming over to me, his violet eyes bright with excitement.

I eyed the caramel apple in his hand, which was about twice the size of his entire body. "I think that you've had too much sugar already. You're worse than a little kid when you get all hopped up on it."

"Too much sugar?" Oscar said, his voice high and twangy. "Too much sugar? There is no such thing!"

He took another bite of his apple, and his wings started twitching even faster than before, making the black cape flutter around his shoulders. Oscar gave me a manic grin, then zoomed off to chatter to another pixie.

Devon was talking to a couple of the other competitors, so I wandered over to where Mo was standing along one of the tent walls, scribbling on a notepad. Several pens were stuck through the brim of his white straw hat, while still more pens bristled in the pocket of his Hawaiian shirt, which was black and patterned with white orchids.

"What are you doing?"

Mo's eyes never left his notepad. "Overseeing some friendly wagers about the tournament—for the good of the Family, of course."

"You mean you've gone from pawnbroker to bookie."

The corner of his mouth lifted up in a sly smile. "Can't get anything past you, kid."

"Just be sure I get my cut."

Mo arched an eyebrow. "Would *I* try to cheat *you* out of money that I've made betting on you?"

"Absolutely."

He grinned. "You know me too well, Lila."

I laughed.

The cheery conversation went on for several more minutes, until Claudia put her phone away, rose to her feet, and strolled to the center of the tent. Devon handed his sword to her, and she twirled the Sinclair Family black blade around in her hand. Everyone stopped what they were doing, quieted down, and faced her. She straightened to her full height, her green gaze sweeping back and forth over everyone gathered here. Beyond the fabric walls, the murmur of the crowd continued, but everything was still and silent in here.

"No matter what happens in the tournament, who wins and who loses, I want you all to know how very proud I am that you are members of my Family," Claudia said, looking at each one of us in turn.

My eyes locked with hers, and her warm pride filled my chest. She really was happy to call us her Family, in more ways than one, and it wasn't just some pep talk to get us excited for the tournament.

"That being said," Claudia continued, a wry smile curving her lips, "if we manage to show the other Families how strong we are by excelling in the tournament, well, I wouldn't be opposed to that either. Would any of you?"

We all grinned back at her.

Claudia raised her black blade, her hand holding the sword high, mimicking her Family crest. "To the Sinclairs!"

"To the Sinclairs!" we all roared back to her.

There were more cheers, laughs, and well-wishes; then Devon and I filed out of the tent with the other competitors. Vance made kissy noises when I walked past, but I ignored him. Devon was right. Vance was a total jackass.

Several tables had been set up outside the white tent, which was serving as command central and the medical center, and we got in line with the other competitors. In an instant, everyone turned from cheery and loud to tense and quiet, their gazes cutting left and right, scanning the lines, and checking out the competition.

As the Sinclair bruiser, Devon got his share of speculative looks, but most folks were focused on Deah, who stood at the front of one of the lines, along with Blake and the rest of the Draconis.

Deah was dressed in a red T-shirt with a gold snarling dragon crest and matching shorts, just like the rest of the Draconis. Her blond hair was pulled back into a ponytail, and her gold cuff glimmered on her wrist. Instead of smirking at everyone like Blake was, Deah stared straight ahead, pretending she didn't notice everyone staring at her. She didn't seem to like being the center of attention any more than I did.

Each competitor was assigned a random number. Devon drew number seventeen, while I was number three. Naturally. Bad things *always* came in threes. I wondered if this was an omen that I wouldn't do well in the tournament. Probably. But I pinned the paper number to my T-shirt anyway.

Once we got our numbers, there was nothing to do until the first event, an obstacle course. So Devon, Felix, and I ended up hanging around outside the Sinclair tent, watching the ebb and flow of people and pixies.

"You guys are going to do great," Felix said. "It wouldn't surprise me if you both ended up facing off in the final round against each other."

Devon groaned. "I hope not. Lila will kick my ass for sure."

I lightly punched him in the shoulder. "You'd better believe it, Sinclair."

He laughed and looked at me, and I found myself falling into his green, green eyes—

"Felix! There you are!" a voice called out.

The three of us turned to see Katia Volkov weaving through the crowd and heading our way. She bounced up beside Felix and gave him a dazzling smile, her dark red braid swishing across her back. Like everyone else, Katia was dressed in a Family T-shirt and matching shorts, dark green with the silver wolf head that was the Volkov crest. A matching silver cuff glimmered on her wrist, while the number thirty-three was pinned to her T-shirt.

"Hey, Katia," Felix said.

He smiled, but it quickly turned into more of a grimace, and he dropped his eyes from hers and started glancing around the tents, probably looking for Deah.

But Katia had no idea that something was wrong and sidled a little closer to him.

"I haven't heard from you lately," she said. "We used to text all the time, but not so much anymore."

Felix's grimace deepened. "Oh, I've been . . . busy. You know, with school and Family stuff and everything. Haven't you?"

Katia frowned. "Yeah, I guess." Another sunny smile split her face, lighting up her hazel eyes. "But I thought that we could catch up after the tournament is over for the day. Maybe go over to the Midway, get some food, and . . . talk."

"Oh, um, I . . . well, you see—" Felix stammered, trying to find an excuse to turn her down.

Whispers surged through the crowd, saving him from having to answer her. People moved aside, and Blake strutted over to us, along with the other Draconi competitors, with Deah trailing along behind them.

"Oh, look," Blake said, stopping and sneering at us. "It's the losers' bracket."

"Always nice to see you too, Blake," Devon replied in a calm tone.

Blake's brown eyes narrowed. "I don't know why you guys even bothered to show up. Everyone knows that Deah's going to win again. Isn't that right, Sis?"

He nudged her with his elbow, but Deah wasn't paying attention to him. Instead, her gaze was locked on to exactly how close Katia was standing to Felix.

Her face turned as cold and hard as her brother's. "Yeah. That's right."

Felix winced and opened his mouth, as if he wanted to explain himself to her, but he couldn't do that with Blake and the other Draconis standing there.

Blake ignored the rest of us, his gaze moving up and down Katia's body. "You know, I meant to tell you yesterday, but you are looking good as usual, Katia: too good to hang out with these losers."

Katia looked at Blake, then Felix, then back at Blake. "Thanks," she said in a neutral voice. "Good luck out there today."

"Baby, I don't need luck." He smirked. "And neither do the rest of the Draconis. Come on, Deah. Let's go tell Dad how much we're going to enjoy beating these losers."

Blake shoved his way right in between Devon and

Felix, knocking them both aside. Devon glared at Blake's back, his hands clenching into tight fists, but Felix stared at Deah the whole time. She dropped her head, skirted past him, and hurried to catch up with her obnoxious brother. Felix held his hand out, as if he was going to grab her shoulder, but he dropped it to his side at the last second.

Deah didn't see the motion, but Katia did. The other girl looked back and forth between Felix and Deah. She frowned, realizing that something was going on between them, even if she didn't know exactly what it was.

"Forget about them," Devon said. "We should go over to the fence and scope out the obstacle course. They'll announce the competitors for the first heat soon."

"I'll go with you guys," Felix volunteered. He forced himself to smile at Katia. "We'll catch up later, okay?"

"Sure," she said, still frowning and looking at Deah's back. "That will be great."

"Great," Felix replied in a too-bright voice.

He nodded at her, then whirled around and started walking toward the chain-link fence. Not quite running, but close enough to it. Katia's frown deepened, but she nodded at Devon and me and headed back toward the Volkov tent.

"Let the games begin," I muttered.

CHAPTER EIGHT

Devon and I caught up with Felix at the fence, where he was looking out over the obstacle course, along with most of the competitors.

The workers had completely transformed the stadium floor. Gone was the flat, empty, grassy field, and in its place stood hurdles, balance beams, a zip line, and a fifty-foot-tall rope ladder.

But the centerpiece of the stadium was a large, natural cold spring filled with fresh, clear water that constantly bubbled. Legend had it that the spring had the same healing properties as the water that flowed down the falls on Cloudburst Mountain, and tourists used to come and bathe in the spring, before the Families decided to build the stadium around it.

Natural rock formations shot through with veins of bloodiron ore rose up out of the ground around the spring, making it look like a miniature Stonehenge. Oh, sure, the rocks and grass and water made the spring seem pretty and inviting, like an oasis in the middle of the stadium, but really, the rocks, grass, and water were just more obstacles to get through.

Because this event was also for the tourists, all the obstacles, from the hurdles to the balance beams to the zip line, were decorated in cheesy ren-faire style, with flags, banners, and feathers, or adorned with snarling monster faces, just like all the Midway shops and restaurants. Fake tree trolls hung from portions of the rope ladder, while black plastic lochness tentacles stuck up out of the spring. The bubbling water made it look like there was a real lochness lurking in the cold depths there.

"Tough course," I said.

"Yeah," Devon agreed. "But how fast you finish it determines where you'll be seeded in the tournament. So you want to get through as quickly as you can."

The tournament had one hundred twenty-eight competitors, all members of the Families. After we finished the obstacle course, the one-on-one matches would begin, continuing over the next couple of days until there were two folks left standing, who would duke it out to see who won.

When I finished sizing up the obstacle course, I turned my attention to the competition. I recognized almost all the guards milling around the fence, since they were the same guards that I'd spent the last four years ducking when I was picking pockets, stealing cameras, and swiping phones on the Midway. But there were a few people I didn't recognize.

Lucky for me, Felix was already chattering a hundred words a minute, telling me all about the Family members, including their strengths and weaknesses.

"See that Volkov guard? He has a major strength Talent. Don't let him hit you, or he'll knock you out with one blow. And that Salazar dude? He can form fireballs with his bare hands. Don't let him touch you, or he'll burn you so badly you won't even be able to hold your own sword. And that Ito woman over there, well, she's been known to. . . ."

After a while, all the names, faces, and Talents ran together, and I couldn't remember who did what. And still,

Felix kept right on talking. Sometimes, I thought that he must have speed magic to talk as much and as fast as he did.

"Hey, guys," a voice called out, interrupting Felix. "What's up?"

We turned to find a slim, petite girl standing behind us. She was wearing a purple T-shirt patterned with a cluster of purple wisteria flowers and matching shorts, along with a silver cuff stamped with the same design. The number twenty-one was pinned to her shirt, and her black hair was pulled back into a pretty braid.

"Poppy!" I said, reaching out and hugging the other girl. "It's so good to see you."

Poppy Ito laughed and returned my hug. "You too, Lila."

She hugged Felix and Devon as well, then drew back, grinning at us. "You guys ready to rock 'n' roll?"

Felix jerked his thumb at Devon and me. "They are. I'm just a spectator, as usual."

"Well, I'll be hanging out with you soon enough," Poppy said. "Probably by round three or four."

"I'm sure you'll do great," Devon said.

She waved her hand. "Don't sugarcoat it. I'm quick, but my fighting skills aren't the best. But it's always fun to compete."

Poppy was the daughter of Hiroshi Ito, the head of the Ito Family, and was training to take over as the Family broker. She was as powerful and well respected in her Family as Devon was with the Sinclairs.

She grinned again, her dark eyes gleaming with mischief, then balled her hands into fists and threw a couple of mock punches. "Besides, this is the only chance I get during the year to bust out all the cool moves I see in the movies. Right, Lila?"

I laughed. "Don't you know it."

Poppy loved action movies just like I did; a couple of weeks ago, we'd had a girls' night in where we'd stayed up late, eaten way too much junk food, and watched a whole bunch of superhero and other movies we both loved.

Felix slung his arm around her shoulder. "Well, no matter where you finish, you're still my girl."

Poppy huffed at his flirty tone and smacked his arm away. "I'm not your girl, remember? That would be Katia. I'm surprised you're not glued to her side, like you were last year."

Felix winced. "Is every single person going to bring up Katia and me? It was just a summer fling."

"Not from the looks she's giving you right now," Poppy said.

Katia was standing about twenty feet away, staring at Felix and frowning at how close he was standing to the other girl. But Poppy, being Poppy, waved at Katia and went over to talk to her. Soon, the two of them were smiling and laughing.

Devon drifted off to talk to some of the Sinclair guards, but I stayed with Felix.

"You need to talk to Katia," I said. "It's obvious that she still likes you. You need to tell her there's someone else. It's not fair to keep avoiding her and letting her think the two of you are going to hook up again."

Felix sighed. "I know. I'll tell her . . . after the tournament today."

I eyed him.

"What?" he said in a defensive tone. "The tournament's going to start in a few minutes. I wouldn't want to wreck her concentration."

"Someone has a rather high opinion of himself."

"I am rather handsome. And charming. And an exceptionally good kisser." Felix waggled his eyebrows. "Or so I've been told."

I snorted. "Well, you'd better tell her soon, or she's likely to punch you right in your good kisser. And don't worry about upsetting Katia's mojo for the tournament. You might even help her."

"How do you figure that?"

I shrugged. "Because there's nothing more vicious than a girl who's just had her heart broken."

The workers put a few finishing touches on the obstacle course, and the officials strolled out into the middle of the stadium and lined up in front of the cold spring. There were five of them, one from each Family, dressed in white cloaks and cavalier hats, which was supposed to be a sign of their neutrality. Heh. We'd see about that.

I looked around the stadium, scanning the crowd. Claudia, Reginald, and Mo were sitting up in the Sinclair box, with Oscar buzzing back and forth from one side of the glass windows to the other, a stick of cherry cotton candy clutched in his hand. The pixie noticed me staring and whipped his cotton candy back and forth like a flag, almost knocking Mo's hat off. Mo grabbed for the cotton candy, but Oscar was too quick and darted out of his reach. I grinned and waved back at them.

I swung my gaze to the opposite side of the stadium and the Draconi box. To my surprise, the box was empty except for a single woman. She was wearing a large white hat with a black ribbon around the floppy brim, so I couldn't see her face, just the long, blond hair trailing down her shoulders. I wondered who she was, but it didn't matter. If she was sitting in the Family box, then she was a Draconi and an enemy.

Three men carrying trumpets strode out into the middle of the stadium and blasted out several loud, cheery notes. The crowd hushed, and a low drumbeat rang out, getting louder and faster with every second. Everyone on the bleachers leaned forward, while the competitors did the same around the chain-link fence.

"And now, the event you've all been waiting for, the Tournament of Blades!" a voice called out through the sound system.

Everyone inside the stadium went wild, including me. I didn't know why, but I was yelling, cheering, and clapping as loudly as everyone else. The noise went on for more than a minute before the officials waved their hands, calling for quiet.

"And now, to get things started, let's welcome last year's returning champion, Deah Draconi!" the announcer boomed.

Hearty cheers filled the air as Deah left the fence behind and strode over to the start of the obstacle course. As the reigning champion, she had the honor of being introduced first. A smile split her face, and she bowed to one side of the stadium, then the other.

Beside me, Felix clapped and clapped his hands before letting out a loud, ear-splitting whistle. I looked at him, and he grinned and shrugged his shoulders. He couldn't help himself. Not where Deah was concerned. I didn't know if that was sweet or stupid.

Once the cheers died down, the officials welcomed everyone, then started randomly calling out numbers, since the competitors would be split into four groups for the obstacle course.

Devon's number was the first one called. He winked at me, waved to the crowd, and went over to stand beside Deah. They nodded at each other.

More numbers were called, including Blake's, Poppy's, Katia's, and Vance's, until there was only one spot left for the opening round of the obstacle course.

"Number three, Lila Merriweather!"

What was it with me always being picked last? If this

kept up, I was going to develop a complex or something. But I fist-bumped Felix, waved to the crowd, and took my place at the starting line next to Devon.

"I would wish you good luck, but you don't need it," he said.

I grinned. "You're right. I don't. Eat my dust, Sinclair."

He laughed and nudged me with his shoulder. I nudged him back, staring into his eyes—

"Well, isn't this sweet?" a snide voice said. "You going to help your girlfriend get through the course too, Devon? I mean, you already got her into the tournament."

Vance swaggered up next to me, the number nine pinned to his chest. He nudged me with his elbow too, but it wasn't a friendly gesture. I nudged him back even harder, right in his stomach, making him wince.

"The only one who needs help here is you, Vance," I snarked. "How are you going to get through the course without messing up your hair?"

Vance reached up to pat his golden locks and make sure they were slicked back into place. When he realized what he was doing, he dropped his hand and scowled at me.

Then, he noticed Katia standing on his other side, and he perked right back up again. "Hello, there," he purred. "I don't think we've met. Vance Groves, future winner of this tournament."

"Charmed," Katia replied in a dry tone, rolling her greenish eyes.

Vance would have kept trying to flirt with her, but the officials called us to the starting line, and we all took our places single file. I looked out over the course, the hurdles, the cold spring in the middle, the towering rope ladder at the far end of the stadium, visualizing how I would get from here to there.

An official stepped forward, drew the sword from the scabbard belted to his waist, and raised the weapon high.

The crowd hushed, and we all leaned forward, trying to get every inch of advantage we could.

"For honor . . . for glory . . . for Family!"

The official dropped his sword, and the tournament was on.

The first stretch of the obstacle course was a flat, straight, mad dash, and the folks with speed Talents sprinted to the front of the pack, led by Katia. Felix was right. She was *fast*—faster than anyone else—and she jumped out to a big lead. Katia had already reached the hurdles before I was even halfway there. But there were plenty of obstacles up ahead to slow her and the other speedsters down.

I hit the hurdles right in the middle of the pack, which was exactly where I wanted to be. Despite Devon, Mo, and Claudia claiming that I could win the tournament, I didn't necessarily *want* to. Oh, I enjoyed winning as much as the next person, but doing so would draw the unwanted attention of everyone in town, including Victor Draconi. So my plan was to do just enough to appear completely average.

But everyone else was giving it their all, including Devon, who was several feet ahead of me, along with Blake and Vance. Deah and Poppy were right on Katia's tail, something that the other girl didn't like, judging from the dark scowls she kept shooting over her shoulder at them, especially Deah.

All the while, the crowd cheered, yelled, and screamed, urging us to *go, go, go, go!* I blocked the noise out of my mind and concentrated on getting through the course.

I cleared the hurdles and sprinted over to the next section, where the competitors had to climb one of several knotted ropes twenty feet up to a platform. Katia slowed down considerably here, since she wasn't nearly as strong as she was fast, but climbing was one of my specialties, and I was able to make up some time on her and everyone else ahead of me.

Katia, Deah, and Poppy all reached the platform at the same time, with Devon, Blake, and Vance right behind them. The girls took hold of the multiple zip lines that had been strung up and leaped off the platform, causing the crowd to cheer even louder. I got to the top of the platform just in time to see the three of them drop into the soft sand at the bottom, scramble to their feet, and start running again.

Then it was my turn.

I grabbed hold of the metal handles attached to the zip line and pushed off from the platform, the air rushing over my body. The sensation was almost as good as free-falling down a drainpipe, and a happy laugh escaped my lips. Maybe the tournament would be more fun than I'd thought.

I let go, landed in the sandpit, and rolled up onto my feet. Vance grunted as he landed beside me. I glanced at him, and he scooped up a handful of sand and flung it at my face, trying to blind me. I jerked my head to the side, barely avoiding getting the wad of sand in my eyes, although it still hit my neck and sprayed all over my body. Vance laughed, surged to his feet, and rushed over to the cold spring.

So that's how it was going to be? Well, if Vance wanted to play dirty, I could give as good as I got.

It was so *on*.

I put on an extra burst of speed and leaped out as far as I could into the spring, tucking my knees up into my chest.

"Cannonball!" I yelled.

Vance's head snapped up, and I landed right beside him.

Splash!

I went all the way under. The water was shockingly cold, and I came up shivering. But it was worth it to see Vance soaked through and through. He growled and pretended to stumble into me. Down in the water, out of sight, Vance hooked his foot around mine, trying to use his strength magic to trip me and make me plunge under the surface again.

But the instant he touched me, my transference Talent kicked in, and my body absorbed all the energy, all the power, he was using to try to take me down.

I welcomed the cold burn of magic in my veins and used the extra burst of strength to put my shoulder down and plow right through him. Vance slipped and did a faceplant into the water. I kept going, grabbed the far edge of the spring, and pulled myself up and out of the water. Behind me, I could hear Vance sputtering and cursing.

I grinned. Oh, yeah. This was *fun*.

After the cold spring, there were more sprints and hurdles, along with several balance beams, and then the big finale of the fifty-foot rope ladder. I made it through the other obstacles and ran over to the base of the ladder, glancing up.

Katia was still in the lead, but Deah was right behind her, with Poppy a few feet farther down and about ten feet off to the side, on the far section of the ladder. Devon was directly below Poppy, with Blake beneath Katia and Deah. The ladder was as wide as it was tall, and since I didn't want to impact Poppy's and Devon's climbs, I took hold of the side where Katia, Deah, and Blake were. I'd just started to pull myself up the first rung, when I felt a shoulder slam into mine, knocking me to the ground.

"See you at the top, loser," Vance hissed, throwing himself up onto the ladder.

I cursed and got to my feet, determined to beat him to the platform.

But it wasn't going to happen.

Vance had the perfect combination of speed and strength magic to scale the rope ladder, and he was already halfway up before I even got started. But I moved as quickly as I could, stretching and reaching and climbing, trying to make up as much ground as possible.

I looked up, judging my progress. Several feet above my head, near the top of the platform, something flashed a bright silver before winking out. I blinked. What was that?

A loud cheer rang out all around the stadium, telling me that someone had already reached the top, but I couldn't tell if it was Katia or Deah. A few seconds later, Vance joined them, leaning over the edge and sneering down at me.

I ground my teeth together, angry that he'd beaten me, but I kept climbing. Poppy and Blake had both made it to the top as well, but Devon was still on the ladder, and he glanced over at me.

"Race you to the top!" he called out, a grin spreading across his face.

"You're on!" I shouted back.

I was only about ten feet from the platform now, and I reached up for the next rung.

An ominous *creak* sounded.

My head snapped up. Above me, at the very top of the ladder, long, thick fibers sprouted up like weeds where one of the ropes connected to the wooden platform. It took me a second to realize that the rope was actually unraveling.

And it wasn't the only one.

More and more of those fibers appeared, running all along the top of the ladder like kudzu unfurling everywhere. A sick feeling filled my stomach. I knew what was going to happen next.

"Watch out!" I yelled, hoping to warn everyone else on

the ladder and trying to scramble to my right, away from the unraveling ropes.

But it was already too late.

With a series of loud, *crack-crack-cracks*, this entire section of rope snapped free from the top of the wooden platform, and the ladder started to fall.

Dragging me down with it.

CHAPTER NINE

Screams and shouts sounded as the crowd realized what was happening, and horrible thoughts shot through my mind one after another as I started to fall.

I was forty feet up in the air, and there was no soft sandpit at the bottom of the ladder. This was going to hurt—*a lot.* I'd be lucky if I only broke an arm or leg, instead of my neck—

I stopped in midair, my right arm feeling like it was being torn out of my shoulder socket. A hand gripped my wrist, and I looked up.

Devon grimaced, his fingers digging into my arm. "I've got you, Lila!"

Somehow, he had realized what was happening and had crawled close enough to reach out and catch me. Gasps rang out from the crowd, but I blocked out the noise and focused on Devon.

He stared at me, his green gaze locking with mine. "*Hold on!*"

His voice cracked with his compulsion magic, and his power wrapped around my entire body as though I were nothing more than a puppet and he was the one pulling my strings. I had no choice but to do as he asked, so I locked my fingers around his wrist.

But my own transference magic kicked in as well, and

Devon's compulsion quickly melted into pure, cold power surging through me. He wasn't controlling me anymore, and his magic increased my own, giving me a welcome boost of extra strength and making my grip even tighter than his.

We held on to each other while I kicked my leg out and hooked my foot through a section of rope that was still firmly attached to the platform. Devon helped swing me over so that I could grab on to the ladder with my free hand.

"I'm good!" I called out.

He nodded, the tension draining from his face, and let go of my wrist. We were closer to the top than the bottom, so we kept climbing. Poppy leaned over and helped us both up and onto the wooden platform.

Devon and I sprawled on our backs, both of us sweating and breathing hard. My heart *thump-thump-thumped* loud enough to drown out the crowd's cheers, and the metallic taste of my own shock, dread, and fear filled my mouth.

"Are you guys okay?" Poppy asked, her dark eyes wide. "What happened?"

"No idea," Devon said, sitting up. "One second the rope was fine. The next, it wasn't. Lila, are you all right?"

I sat up as well. "Yeah, I'm okay. Thanks to you."

I nudged his shoulder. Devon smiled and nudged me back.

"Just watching out for you. That's what Sinclairs do, remember?"

I nodded, my throat tight with emotion. It had been a long time since anyone had helped me the way Devon just had. He could have easily fallen off the ladder trying to grab me, or I could have dragged him down off it, but he hadn't hesitated, and he'd saved me.

Slowly, the cheers died down, but other sounds rose to take their place—hoarse, raspy moans of pain.

Devon and I both got to our feet and peered over the side of the platform. Two guards were sprawled at the bottom of the rope ladder. I didn't know how far up they'd been, but they'd both landed awkwardly. One of them—a Draconi—was moaning, rocking back and forth, and clutching her arm to her chest as though it was broken. The other competitor was one of ours—Henry, a Sinclair guard. His left leg was twisted underneath his body, and I could see the broken bone pressing against his skin from up here. The pain was so bad that he was crying and choking down screams.

A hush fell over the crowd, and shouts rose up as the medical staff raced over to the bottom of the ladder. Angelo was with them. He took one look at Henry's wound, then gestured for a stretcher. A few seconds later, Henry was being rolled away toward the white medical tent. The crowd got to its feet, clapping, but the polite noise didn't come close to drowning out Henry's screams.

I looked down again. Henry had hit the ground so hard that his body had made an outline in the grass, like a drawing of a murder victim on a crime show. I shivered. That could have been me down there with a busted leg.

Or worse—dead.

Everyone on the top of the platform was yelling, pointing, and running back and forth, including Deah and Blake, who had their heads together, whispering to each other. Poppy was gesturing with her hands and talking to Devon, but I wasn't paying attention to her sharp, worried words.

Instead, I kept thinking about the ropes and how they had snapped away from the platform. I'd climbed up my fair share of ropes, and they didn't just unravel like that, especially not these thick, heavy ones. Even someone with a strength Talent would have had a hard time tearing through them. But the ropes had fallen away from the platform as easily as I could swipe my hand through a spider's web.

So what had really happened to them?

The officials stopped the tournament, and we all climbed down the ladders attached to the side of the platform. The other competitors who hadn't been on the course came over, along with the higher-ups in the Families, and everyone checked on their friends. Claudia, Reginald, Mo, and Felix hurried over to Devon and me, with Oscar zipping along behind them.

"You okay, kid?" Mo asked, his eyes dark with concern.

"Yeah, I'm fine, thanks to Devon."

I looked over, but Devon was reassuring his mom, Reginald, Felix, and Oscar that he was okay.

Mo took off his white hat and started whipping it back and forth in front of his face to create a breeze. He stared up at the ladder. "Scariest thing I've ever seen, the way the rope just fell like that. What happened up there?"

"I have no idea, but I'm going to find out. Give me your phone, and cover me."

I jerked my head at the ladder. Mo handed over his phone, slapped his hat back on his head, and followed me.

Several officials were already gathered around the ladder, talking, taking photos, and more. The ropes lay where they had fallen—the long, thick brown strands looking like copper crushers lazily sunning themselves in the grass.

"How do you want to play this?" Mo asked.

I grinned. "Just be your usual loud, charming, demanding self."

He grinned back, then barreled over to the officials. "What is the meaning of this? Did you guys not check the ladder before you let everyone start climbing it?"

One of the officials stepped forward and held his hands out, trying to placate Mo. "Mr. Kaminsky, I assure you that we are looking into the situation—"

Mo poked his finger into the guy's chest. "Looking into the situation? *Looking into the situation?* I'd say that we've all *looked into the situation* since everyone saw the ladder fall like it was made out of cotton candy. What I want to know is what you're going to do about the fact that my guy has a broken leg and there's a Draconi guard with a busted arm. . . ."

And Mo was off, bellowing at the officials. People stared at him, and I used the distraction to sidle forward, moving closer to the ladder. Everyone was clustered at the base where the majority of the ropes had landed, but one strand had curled around the side of the platform. I bent down, as though I was tying my sneaker, and stared at the rope.

The end was frayed, as though the rope was worn and weak and the weight of the competitors hanging on to it had just been too much. That was exactly what I would expect, given how it had snapped away from the top of the platform. So I looked at it—*really* looked at it—using my sight magic to pull the rope into supersharp detail.

The rope was frayed—but it had also been cut.

A small, clean slice went about halfway through the strand, one that I wouldn't have even noticed if I hadn't been looking for it with my magic. Cut away half the rope, and the weight of the competitors *would* have been too much for it. It was no wonder that the other half of the rope had unraveled as quickly as it had.

No way that slice was any sort of normal wear and tear. That was the kind of mark that couldn't have been made by anything other than a knife. I thought of that flash of silver I'd seen when I'd peered up the ladder, trying to catch up to Vance.

Someone had deliberately cut the rope.

I was sure of it. And I was willing to bet that the other strands had similar slices.

But who had cut the ropes? And why?

I thought back, trying to remember who had been where and when, but the course had been a mad scramble from start to finish, and the ladder had been no different. It would have been easy for someone to pause at the top before they pulled themselves onto the platform, pretend they were winded, pull a knife from their shorts pocket, and slice through some of the ropes, especially if they had a speed Talent to help them pull it off.

This was supposed to be a friendly competition. Did someone really want to win so badly that they would try to take out other people? In the very first event on the very first day? Henry and the Draconi guard could have easily broken their necks. They were lucky they hadn't been killed. I'd always known that the competition between the Families was cutthroat, but this was something else.

Something dark. Something sinister.

Something deadly.

By this point, the official had herded Mo off to the side of the ladder, and Mo was running out of things to yell at the other man. Time to go. So I angled his phone at the rope, taking several shots of the cut and frayed end. Then I got to my feet, slid the phone into my shorts pocket, and walked behind the official that Mo was still berating. I jerked my head, letting him know that he could wrap things up. Mo winked back at me.

"Well, perhaps I have been a bit hasty," he said, his voice suddenly charming instead of angry. "I should let you fellas do your job. Thanks for the info, buddy. Keep up the good work."

Mo clapped the official on the shoulder, leaving the other man with a dazed expression on his face.

Mo fell in step beside me. "What did you find out, kid?"

"Later," I whispered back. "When it's just the Family."

He nodded, and we headed over to Claudia, Reginald, Devon, Felix, and Oscar, who were checking on the other Sinclair guards.

Through the crowd, I noticed Vance watching me. He realized that I was okay, and he snorted and started talking to Katia, who was frowning, her hazel eyes dark with thought.

I remembered how Vance had thrown sand at me, tried to trip me in the spring, and shoved me out of the way when I was starting up the ladder. He had been directly above me and had just crawled onto the platform when the ropes had given way. He had Talents for speed and strength, so he could have easily cut the ropes in all the confusion. Vance was a jackass, but was he really that much of a monster? I didn't know.

And he wasn't the only suspect. Blake had been on top of the platform too, and he outright hated me. He could have cut the ropes to hurt me, or maybe even ordered another one of the Draconis to do it for him in order to take out as many of the other competitors as possible.

Anger and worry surged through my body, and my hands clenched into fists, even as another shiver slithered up my spine. I found myself looking over my shoulder and staring at the imprint of Henry's body in the grass again.

Oh, yeah. That could have easily been me.

But the far more troubling thought was that maybe someone had *wanted* it to be me.

CHAPTER TEN

The crowd on the stadium floor was breaking up and drifting away when Mo and I rejoined the others.

"Lila!" Oscar shouted. "There you are! Are you okay?"

If anything, the danger and excitement had added to his sugar high, and the pixie *buzz-buzzed-buzzed* around and around my head like a helicopter.

"I'm fine," I said, holding out my hand so he could land on it. "Really, I am."

Oscar stalked back and forth on my palm, looking me up and down, his black cape fluttering around his shoulders, and his cowboy boots tickling my skin. It was several seconds before he was satisfied enough to fly up, sit on my shoulder, and hug my neck.

"I'm glad you're okay," he said.

"Me too."

I reached out and patted his tiny back, careful not to crush his wings. Oscar hugged my neck again, then stayed perched on my shoulder.

Felix shook his head. "Well, you and Devon put on quite the show. Everyone here got their money's worth today."

"How's Henry?" I asked.

"Dad's working on him right now. He's in a lot of pain, and his leg is definitely broken," Felix replied, his face troubled. "I'm on my way to help. I just wanted to make sure that you guys were okay first."

He nodded at Devon and me, then broke into a jog, leaving us behind and heading toward the white medical tent.

Claudia stepped up beside me, looking me over just as the others had. When she realized that I was okay, some of the tension eased out of her slender shoulders and her jaw unclenched.

"You had me worried there for a second," she murmured.

"Yeah. Me too."

I opened my mouth to tell her what I'd found out about the rope, but she shook her head, stopping me. A second later, I realized why.

Victor Draconi was heading in our direction.

The folks still milling around scrambled out of his way, and whispers sprang up in his wake. Everyone stopped what they were doing to stare at us, wondering what sort of fireworks might explode between the heads of the two most powerful Families.

Victor stopped in front of Claudia, looking poised, polished, and powerful in his dark gray suit and red tie, which was patterned with tiny gold dragons. Another, larger dragon was stamped into the middle of the wide gold cuff that flashed on his right wrist. He straightened up to his full height, and the sun bounced off his thick, wavy, blond hair and highlighted the sharp angles of his handsome face.

This was the closest I'd ever been to Victor, so close that I could smell his faint, spicy cologne and see exactly how cold his eyes were, despite their rich golden color.

White-hot rage boiled through me, and I had the sudden urge to scream, raise my fists, and charge at him. So many times, I'd dreamed of getting close enough to Victor to run him through with my black blade. Of course, the one time I was actually within striking distance, I didn't have my sword, much less any other weapon that I could hurt him with.

So I forced myself to smother my rage with reason—because Victor wasn't alone. Blake and Deah stepped up beside him, with more Draconi guards behind them. Even if I could have gotten past Blake, Deah, and the guards, Victor was more than capable of defending himself.

Especially given all the Talents he had.

Magic radiated off his body, the sensation cold and strong enough to make me shiver, despite the hot, humid day. Claudia didn't know how many Talents Victor actually had or what he could do with all the magic he'd stolen from other people over the years, but I could feel *exactly* how powerful he was.

Most of the time, someone had to use their strength, speed, or other Talents against me in some physical way—punch me, shove me, restrain me, whatever—before my transference power flared to life and let me absorb their magic. In a way, anyone who attacked me with his Talents was just hurting himself, since all the magic that soaked into my body made me stronger. But Victor was so powerful that just standing next to him was enough to make my own transference magic stir to life and my body chill with magic.

Normally I welcomed the surge of strength that went along with my Talent, but right now, it made me sick to my stomach.

Victor realized that I was staring at him, and his gaze met mine.

The icy knives of his hate stabbed into my heart, and I had to bite my tongue to keep from gasping in shock or showing any sort of emotion. Victor stared at me a second longer, then swung his golden gaze back to Claudia, dismissing me as unimportant. The feeling of his hate lingered, though, even colder than the invisible waves of magic rolling off his body. I ground my teeth together to keep them from chattering.

"Claudia."

"Victor."

The two of them stared at each other, their faces hard and flat. All around us, the whispers faded, and everyone leaned forward, eager to hear every single word they said.

"The officials are telling me that it's an accident," Victor said in his deep, rumbling voice. "It's unfortunate that both of our Families had competitors who were injured."

"Indeed," Claudia said, her voice as smooth as his. "I was on my way to check on Henry. How is your guard?"

Victor shrugged. "Just a broken arm. She'll live. Although I've already given her spot in the tournament to someone else."

Claudia frowned. "Why would you do that?"

He shrugged again. "She shouldn't have fallen."

"Or once she did, she should have gotten right back up and started climbing again," Blake chimed in. "Not sat on the ground crying like a little kid who scraped her knee."

He scoffed, as though he couldn't believe one of his Family members could be so weak. I looked at Deah, who winced and stared at the ground. She might not agree with Blake and her dad, but she wasn't going to stand up and tell them how wrong and cruel they were either.

"Funny, I remember you moaning and crying," Devon drawled. "I'm sure you remember too. It was back in the arcade a few weeks ago when Lila put you in that wrist lock."

Blake glared at Devon, who smirked back. Even worse, Victor stared at me again, his eyes narrowed in thought as he studied me far more closely than he had before.

"Well, please give my regards to your guard and tell her that I hope she feels better soon," Claudia said.

"Of course," Victor murmured, still staring at me.

His gaze locked with mine. Once again, his icy hate for Claudia and all the Sinclairs surged through me, along with cold curiosity about who I was and what I'd done to his son. This time, I couldn't hold back my shiver.

Victor looked at me a moment longer, then turned his attention back to Claudia. "I'll be interested to see how your guards do in the tournament."

"And I yours," she replied. "And my congratulations to Deah for finishing second today. She really gave Katia Volkov a run for her money on the course—before the incident."

Victor's mouth flattened out. "Yes, well, second place is really only first loser, isn't it?"

Deah winced again, but she finally spoke up. "I should have beaten her. It won't happen again. And I'm still going to win the tournament. Don't worry about that."

"We'll talk about that when we get home," Victor said, his voice as cold with his daughter as it had been with everyone else.

Hurt flashed in Deah's eyes, and her shoulders drooped. She fixed her gaze on the grass again, as though that would hide the embarrassed blush in her cheeks.

"Until tomorrow then," Claudia said.

"Until tomorrow," Victor replied.

He and Claudia tipped their heads at each other; then Victor turned and headed out of the stadium. Blake glared at Devon and me one more time and followed his father. The guards fell in step behind them.

Deah nodded at Claudia, then turned to go. I don't know why, but something urged me forward, and I stepped up, reached out, and touched her shoulder.

"You really did do a great job today," I said. "You flew through all the obstacles like they weren't even there. I couldn't have done that. I *didn't* do that."

Deah gave me a cold look. "Don't be an idiot. I lost to Katia, just like my father said."

She shook off my hand, whipped around, and hurried after Victor and Blake.

Deah fell in step beside them, but Victor and Blake were talking to each other, and they didn't so much as glance at her. Her shoulders slumped again, but Deah kept walking right beside them.

I frowned, wondering at the tight, twisting sensation in my own chest. It took me a second to realize that it was pity.

For the first time, it occurred to me that maybe I wasn't the only one Victor and Blake had hurt.

The officials announced that the obstacle course was closed so they could investigate further. They canceled the other heats for the day and announced that the competitors would be randomly seeded, with the individual matches starting in the morning. The crowd groaned, but everyone packed up their belongings and headed home. We did the same.

Two hours later, I was back in the library, sitting on a white velvet settee by the fireplace, along with Mo. Claudia and Devon were sitting in chairs across from us.

Angelo, Felix, Reginald, and Oscar were watching over Henry, who was in the mansion infirmary. They'd fixed his broken leg with some stitch-sting, and he was resting now. I didn't envy him. A broken leg was bad enough, but I thought the pain of the liquid stitch-sting seeping into your wound and yanking, pulling, and sewing all your skin, muscles, and bones back together was even worse.

"So you think the ropes were deliberately cut," Claudia said, scrolling through the photos I'd taken on Mo's phone.

"I know they were—I could *see* it."

"Maybe you could, but the officials didn't," she said. "Or they chose to ignore it. Either way, they've ruled it an accident. The tournament will proceed as planned in the morning."

I frowned. "Why wouldn't they admit that someone cut the ropes?"

"Because the Tournament of Blades is one of the biggest events of the summer," Mo chimed in. "Nobody wants to cancel it. Even if one of the officials did realize that the ropes were cut, they would still declare it an accident. There's too much pressure from the Families to let the tournament continue for the officials to rock the boat. Too much money from ticket sales and concessions is at stake."

Claudia handed Mo his phone. "The bigger question is who cut the ropes and why?"

I shrugged. "I don't know. I was too far down on the ladder—all I saw was the flash of the knife. Devon?"

"Katia and Deah were both on the platform when the ropes started unraveling. So were Poppy, Blake, and a few other folks." Devon shook his head. "I didn't see anything either. Then again, I wasn't really looking."

I drew in a breath. They wouldn't like what I was about to say, but the suspicion had been running through my mind for hours now. "What about Vance? He was up there too."

The three of them stared at me in surprise.

"You think Vance cut the ropes?" Devon asked. "Why?"

"Well, he was right above me when it happened. And he wasn't exactly thrilled that I was in the tournament."

I told them how Vance had tried to sabotage me before we'd reached the rope ladder.

"Throwing sand in your eyes, tripping you, shoving you out of the way. Yeah, Vance can be a jerk like that.

But actually cutting the ropes?" Devon shook his head again. "That's pretty hardcore. Besides, Vance and Henry are friends. Vance wouldn't have wanted to hurt him."

"Maybe Vance didn't realize that Henry was on the ladder too," I said. "Or maybe he just didn't care."

Nobody had any answers, and we all fell silent, lost in our own thoughts. Finally, Claudia got to her feet.

"Well, no matter who cut the ropes, I want you two to be careful," she said, looking at Devon and me. "The tournament is always a bit volatile, with all the Families in one place."

"What if it happens again?" I asked. "What if someone tries to hurt the other competitors again?"

"I don't see how they can," Devon replied. "The individual rounds start tomorrow; so it will be all one-on-one matches, just two people fighting in the ring. Hard to sabotage that."

Claudia and Mo murmured their agreement. Even if the saboteur was already thinking about striking again, there was nothing we could do about it tonight. So Mo left to check in with his sources and see if they had heard anything else, while Devon went to clean up for dinner.

Claudia moved over to her desk, sat down behind it, slid on her glasses, and started shuffling through her papers. I ambled in her direction. I waited until Devon had closed the library doors behind him before I spoke.

"Interesting run-in you had with Victor."

"Yes, he was as charming as always," she replied in a dry tone.

"Does he always treat Deah like that?"

"Unfortunately, yes."

"Why?"

Claudia looked up from her papers. "Why does Victor do anything? The short answer is simply because he can, or he thinks that it will benefit him in some way, or both. But he's always been hard on Deah, much harder than he's ever been on Blake."

And Victor had hurt Deah much more than he ever had Blake. Victor should have been proud that she'd finished second in the obstacle course, but he'd been cold and dismissive instead, calling her a loser in front of his sworn enemies. I wondered if anything Deah ever did was good enough for him.

"How does making his own daughter feel terrible benefit him?"

Claudia pulled off her glasses and set them aside. "I have never claimed to understand the inner workings of Victor Draconi's twisted mind. The only answer I can give you is that he has a dark heart, which you've seen for yourself."

I still remembered the icy knives of his hate ripping into my chest. Even now, the phantom sensation made me shiver—and made me more determined than ever to figure out what he was up to.

"You know, I haven't been getting anywhere doing things your way."

"What do you mean?"

I shrugged. "Talking to people and using my soulsight on them is all well and good, but I can't actually read minds, you know—just emotions. And emotions can mean a lot of different things. So I was thinking that I might try a more direct approach to get the lowdown on what Victor and Blake are up to."

Claudia arched an eyebrow. "Meaning what, exactly?"

"Meaning that I was planning to mosey on over to the Draconi compound and do a little spying," I said. "If that meets with her majesty's approval."

At my snarky tone, Claudia arched her other eyebrow so that she had a matching set. She didn't like me calling her *her majesty*, but that's what she was—the Sinclair Family queen.

She picked up her glasses and *tap-tap-tapped* them on top of the papers on her desk. Emotions flared in her eyes one after another: curiosity, concern, hope, guilt. Despite her cool exterior, Claudia really did care about me in her own way. She didn't like the thought of my spying on Victor, especially since she knew what the consequences would be if I got caught—and that my death wouldn't be the worst of it.

But it was a risk I was willing to take. I'd do anything to make Victor pay for murdering my mom, and so would Claudia.

Her face hardened, and she laid her glasses down on the desk. "Do you really think that you can slip into the Draconi compound? Without getting caught?"

She might not like putting me in danger, but she was willing to do it if it meant finding information that could derail Victor's scheme or at least help protect the Sinclairs. I admired her for that—for her ability to make those kinds of hard choices—although I would never tell her so.

"You're talking to Lila Merriweather, remember? Thief extraordinaire." I gave an elegant, elaborate flourish of my hand and bowed low.

Claudia huffed. "Perhaps instead of asking whether you'll get caught, I should be asking whether you can keep your ego in check long enough to get over there and back again. Or will you be too busy patting yourself on the back the whole time?"

I tapped my finger against my lips, pretending to consider her question. "I don't know. My ego really likes being a badass thief—gives me the warm and fuzzies inside."

Claudia raised her eyes skyward, as if asking what she'd ever done to get stuck with me. "If Serena hadn't been my best friend and I hadn't sworn to watch out for you. . ."

"I know, I know, you'd tan my hide and send me to bed with no supper."

She sniffed. "For starters."

I grinned. "Then aren't you glad that you made that promise to my mom all those years ago? You don't have to worry about any hide tanning or worse, depriving me of food. Face it. You're stuck with me, toots. Like a bad rash you can't get rid of."

"Lucky me." Her voice was as cool as mine was cheery.

I winked at her. For a moment, Claudia's lips quirked up in what almost looked like a smile; then her face turned serious again.

"When were you thinking about doing this?"

"Tonight. The Draconi guards will be distracted, thinking about the tournament instead of keeping as good a watch as they should. And maybe I can find out something about who cut the rope ladder, if Blake or one of the other Draconis was behind it."

"All right—do it. We're running out of time. Victor might not do anything during the tournament, but I wouldn't put it past him to strike the second it's over." Claudia hesitated. "But be careful. Because if the Draconis catch you. . . ."

Her voice trailed off, and her jaw clenched. It was best for both of us not to think about how Victor would torture me before he ripped out my magic, killing me in the process.

"I'll be careful." I crossed my finger over my heart in a large X. "Promise."

Claudia nodded, then slid her glasses back on and started reading through her papers again. I headed out of the library, making a mental list of the things I would need to infiltrate the Draconi compound. Just before I reached the double doors, she spoke again.

"Good luck," she called out.

"That's the second time in two days you've said that to me," I said, looking over my shoulder.

"I think you're going to need it."

"Yeah. Me too."

I nodded at her, then pulled open one of the doors and left the library.

CHAPTER ELEVEN

I went to my room, took a shower, and hung out with Oscar and Tiny for a while before going down to dinner in the dining hall. Of course, all anyone wanted to talk about was what had happened at the tournament, and I once again found myself the center of attention, as a steady stream of folks dropped by the table where I was sitting with Devon and Felix.

"Are you guys okay?"

"How's Henry?"

"It was so amazing the way Devon caught you before you fell!"

The questions and comments went on and on. I stayed quiet and let Devon and Felix do most of the talking. After all, they were the ones who deserved the glory, Devon for grabbing me and Felix for helping to heal Henry.

But the curious looks and constant talking, smiling, and nodding politely got to be too much, so I downed the rest of my lemonade, grabbed my glass and plate, and headed over to the buffet for some refills.

The pixies had set out another delectable spread of sandwiches and summer salads, along with fresh fruit and several different kinds of cookies. I poured myself some more lemonade, then grabbed three chocolate chip cookies, along with some strawberries to take back up to my room to Tiny.

"I see you're looking no worse for wear," a voice called out. "Especially not when it comes to your appetite."

Vance swaggered up to the table, elbowed me out of the way, and started heaping triangles of toasted club sandwiches onto his plate. "Got to get some of these beauties before you steal them all."

My hand tightened around my plate, but I didn't respond, and Vance glanced over at me.

"What's the matter? Monster got your tongue?" He clucked his own tongue, mocking me. "Then again, I suppose you did have a scare today. Maybe next time you won't be so lucky, Lila."

My eyes narrowed. "Is that a threat?"

He dropped his gaze and grabbed another sandwich off the tray, so I couldn't use my soulsight to see what he was really feeling.

"Nah," Vance finally said. "I'm going to win the tournament, and that's all there is to it. In a couple of days, everybody will be gathered around *my* table. Not yours. So enjoy the attention while it lasts."

He smirked again, shouldered past me, and went back over to where his friends were sitting. Vance took a seat, smiling, joking, and laughing with the other guards.

But my feet felt glued to the floor, and all I could do was stand there, frozen in place, wondering if there had been a far more sinister meaning to Vance's words than what he'd actually said.

I wasn't hungry anymore, and Devon and Felix were still busy talking, so I slipped out of the dining hall and went up to my room.

Oscar was still eating and gossiping with everyone else, so he wasn't around to see me get ready for my night of skulking, much less ask awkward questions about where I was going and what I was doing. Tiny was in his corral, but the tortoise wasn't going to tell anyone anything, especially since I dropped several strawberries onto the grass in front of him. Tiny nodded his green head in approval at my buying his silence, lumbered over to the berries, and started eating them.

Oscar had insisted that I wear nice clothes to dinner again, but I stripped them off in favor of a pale blue T-shirt, gray cargo pants, and gray sneakers. The soft, muted colors would be perfect for blending in with the shadows. My hair was already in its usual ponytail, with my chopstick lock picks stuck through it, so I moved on to the next things I needed.

Weapons.

I buckled my sword and scabbard to my black leather belt, which was studded with three stars. At first glance, the metal pieces looked like pretty decorations, but they were actually throwing stars made out of the same bloodiron as my sword. If things went according to plan, no one would see me enter or leave the Draconi compound, but I wanted to be prepared in case I had to fight my way out.

I also grabbed a long, sapphire-blue trench coat from where it was hanging on one of the knobs on the four-poster bed. The spidersilk coat had belonged to my mom, along with the ironmesh gloves sticking out of one of the pockets. Despite its rich, vibrant color, the coat would also help me blend into the shadows, since spidersilk had the unusual property of melting into the landscape around it—sort of like the way people walked straight into spider webs without even realizing they were there.

I stuck my hands into the coat pockets, making sure I had the rest of my usual supplies, which included dark chocolate bars, several quarters, and a couple of locks of my own black hair tied up with different colored ribbons.

Just in case I ran into some monsters and had to pay a toll or two. It would be rather humiliating to make it in and out of the Draconi compound undetected, only to get eaten by a copper crusher or some other creature on the way home.

When I was fully attired for the night, I opened one of the doors, stepped out onto the balcony, and looked out over the stone wall. It was after eight now, and the long summer day was finally dimming to a twilight dusk that would soon give way to full night. Down in the valley far, far below, the neon lights of the Midway formed a solid circle, with the shopping squares branching off in all directions, like the carts on a Ferris wheel. The lights flared, flickered, and flashed in every color of the rainbow, gleaming like a carpet of electrified jewels that had been scattered in the middle of the dark, rugged mountains.

I pulled on my ironmesh gloves, then took hold of the drainpipe attached to one side of the balcony. The drainpipe was part of the stone of the mansion, so I didn't have to worry about it coming loose from the wall, unlike the tournament rope ladder. So I stepped out into the open air and let myself free-fall, enjoying the rush of the wind against my body. Sure, I could have used the stairs that snaked from one level of the mansion to the other, but this was faster—and *way* more fun. It was so much fun that I laughed, although the wind tore the soft, happy sound away from my lips and sent it spinning up into the humid night air.

Just before I hit the ground, I tightened my grip on the drainpipe, causing a bit of smoke to waft up from my gloves. Ironmesh was another special metal, one that was thin, flexible, and protective all at the same time. If I'd tried to free-fall down the drainpipe with my bare hands, I would have burned and bloodied my palms, at the very least, or laid them open to the bone, at the very worst. But the inherent grip in the ironmesh would help me climb up or slide down practically any surface, including this glass-smooth stone.

Once my sneakers touched the ground, I slid into the nearest shadow and dropped into a crouch, studying the landscape. Most everyone was still in the dining hall, but a few guards patrolled the grounds, like always. But I'd spent the last four years being as invisible as possible, so it was easy for me to wait until the guards' backs were turned, sprint across the lawn, and disappear into the surrounding trees.

I moved deeper and deeper into the woods, following a faint trail that led to a clearing ringed by a wrought iron fence. Blocks of black marble had been set into the grass, marking the spot as the Sinclair Family cemetery—the place where the Sinclairs themselves were buried, along with all the people who'd loyally served the Family.

Including my mom.

I crouched down and plucked a small blue forget-me-not from a patch of them growing wild in the clearing. Then I got to my feet and opened the gate, wincing at the faint *creak*, before walking to her tombstone at the back of the cemetery. *Serena Sterling* flowed across the marker, while her symbol, the Sterling Family symbol—that five-pointed star—was carved into the top of the black stone.

I stared at her tombstone, all the usual emotions squeezing my heart: guilt, grief, loss, longing, anger. But no matter what I felt, no matter how much I still missed my mom, the world kept right on turning, the way it always did, the way it always would. Birds chirped, bees buzzed, rockmunks scuttled through the underbrush. So I drew in a breath, then let it out, pushing away my turbulent feelings even as the air seeped out of my lungs.

I stayed by her grave for several minutes, soaking up the peace and quiet, especially after all the conversations and questions in the dining hall. I'd been on my own for so long that I was still adjusting to living in the mansion and being around so many people all the time. Whenever I needed a breather from the Family, I'd slip out of the mansion and come here, since no one seemed to visit the cemetery but Claudia and me.

I twirled the forget-me-not back and forth in my fingers, watching the fading sunlight play over the blue petals. Then I placed the flower on my mom's tombstone, mumbled how much I still missed her to whatever ghosts and monsters might be watching, and left the cemetery.

I hiked through the woods, passing through growing clouds of cool, damp mist. The summer sun was hot enough to burn off most of the waterfall spray during the day, but as the sun set, the fog increased, sliding lower and lower on the mountain, like vanilla ice cream melting in a sundae and oozing everywhere. Most of the mist was still stuck in the trees above my head, but when night fell, it would filter down through the branches and completely saturate the forest. I wasn't worried, though. No matter how low and thick the fog got, I would still be able to see everything as clearly as if it were noon, thanks to my sight.

No, what bothered me was the noise—or lack of it.

I don't know how far I'd gone into the woods before I noticed that it was quiet—too quiet.

The chirp of birds and lazy drone of bugs that had surrounded the Sinclair cemetery had vanished, replaced by dead, still silence. I dropped my hand to my sword, stopped, and turned in a slow circle, peering at everything, but I didn't spot anything out of the ordinary. Just towering trees and tangled branches and white mist as far as even I could see.

Normally, this deep in the woods, I would have expected to spot at least a couple of sets of bright, glowing, jewel-toned eyes watching me from the shadows—

sapphire-blue, emerald-green, and ruby-red orbs that belonged to various monsters. But even the shadows were quiet, still, and empty. Weird. And a little creepy. So I hurried on, keeping my hand on my sword, just in case.

The Draconi compound was on the eastern slope of the mountain, directly opposite the Sinclair mansion on the west side, but it wasn't all that far between them distance-wise, only about three miles cutting straight through the forest. So it took me less than an hour to reach the edge of the woods that flanked the Draconi stronghold.

In addition to being on the other side of the mountain, the Draconi compound was also the exact opposite of the Sinclair mansion in every possible way. It wasn't even a mansion so much as it was a castle, made out of gleaming white stone that rose up into a series of towers, each one topped with a red flag bearing a snarling gold dragon. Everything about the structure was slick and elegant, from the tall, diamond-paned windows to the red roses twining through the white wooden trellises to the cobblestone bridge that arched over the moat in front. Seriously, it was an actual moat with water running through it and everything. That was a bit much, if you asked me.

The Draconi compound was certainly beautiful, but I preferred the Sinclair mansion. The rough, black, blocky stone there seemed much more natural and honest than this too-perfect castle with its ivory towers.

But there was one thing I did like about the Draconi castle—all the trees and bushes that dotted the sloping lawns. Thick clusters of greenery ran all the way from the woods right up to a patio on the west side of the structure. I hadn't mentioned it to Claudia, but this wasn't the first night I'd come here. I'd been hiking over to the Draconi compound every few days and familiarizing myself with the guard routes, doors, windows, and more, in anticipation of this night, when I would actually break into the castle itself. A good thief did her homework, and this was the same routine I'd used countless times before, whenever Mo had sent me out to retrieve an expensive item from someone's house on the sly.

I waited until the guards turned away from my location, then sprinted forward, keeping low and moving from one cluster of bushes to the next. It took me less than a minute to creep from the woods up to the side patio. I reached for the door to see if it was locked, but the *crunch-crunch-crunch* of tires made me stop. I hunkered down and peered around a white marble planter shaped like a snarling dragon blowing red roses out of its mouth, instead of flames.

A dark green SUV pulled up to the front of the mansion and stopped. A silver wolf's head gleamed on each one of the vehicle's doors. My eyes narrowed. What were the Volkovs doing here?

The driver got out of the SUV and hurried to open the back door. A second later, a short, muscular man with a bushy brown beard emerged from the vehicle. Nikolai Volkov, the head of his Family. And he wasn't the only person I recognized. Katia got out of the vehicle as well, along with a middle-aged man who had to be Carl Volkov, her father, since he had the same dark red hair she did.

Nikolai, Katia, and Carl stood by the car, their faces neutral, waiting for the king himself to emerge.

The front doors of the mansion swung open, and Victor Draconi stepped outside, with Blake right beside him, just like always. I looked for Deah, but she didn't appear.

"Nikolai, Katia, Carl," Victor called out. "Thank you for coming."

The Volkovs murmured their greetings, and Victor held out his hand, gesturing for them to follow him inside. "This way. My chef has prepared a fine meal for us tonight . . ."

They all disappeared inside the mansion, along with Blake. The Volkov driver stayed with his SUV, eyeing the Draconi guards as though he was worried that they might attack him, now that their respective bosses were gone. The Draconis returned his hostile glares, their hands on their swords, but they went back to their rotations, and no one spotted me lurking on the patio.

I waited five minutes, hoping that was enough time for Victor and the others to reach whatever dining room they would be eating in, then reached up and tried the patio door.

Locked.

But I could fix that.

I plucked the chopsticks out of my hair and twisted the black lacquered wood, revealing the picks inside, then went to work on the lock. Several seconds later, the tumblers *click-click-clicked* into place, and the door *snicked* open. I stuck the chopsticks back into my ponytail, slipped inside, and shut and locked the door behind me.

I'd told Mo that I was planning to break into the Draconi compound at some point during the summer. He hadn't liked the idea any more than Claudia had, but he'd realized that he couldn't talk me out of it, and he'd come through for me the way he always did. Thanks to his shady connections, Mo had gotten his hands on the castle's blueprints, so I knew which hallway to head down and which stairs to climb to get to where I wanted—Victor's office.

According to the gossip I'd heard, only a few folks had access to Victor's office, and it was the most logical place for him to keep any incriminating files on whatever he was plotting against the other Families. Maybe I'd find out something about the rope ladder too, if Blake or one of the other Draconis had sabotaged it, although my money was still on Vance for that crime.

The Sinclair mansion was richly furnished, but it looked as rundown and rickety as Oscar's pixie trailer compared to the sheer, overwhelming opulence of the Draconi compound. Everything inside the castle gleamed with some sort of gold, whether it was the threads in the couch cushions, the gilt-edged mirrors on the walls, or even the solid gold chandeliers dangling from the ceilings.

I'll admit it. I stopped and stared at one of the chandeliers, greedily dreaming about how I could put that in my pocket and sneak away with it. But that would be impossible, even for me, at least without a ladder, a cart, and some power tools, so I hurried on.

Besides the gold, the other most notable ornament was the snarling dragon crest. It was embroidered, carved, and chiseled into practically everything, from the scarlet curtains to the dark mahogany furniture to the white flagstones embedded in the floors. Victor had his symbol displayed on everything inside his castle, and I had no doubt that he wanted to stamp it on the rest of Cloudburst Falls too.

Only the Draconis themselves—Victor, Blake, and Deah—actually lived in the castle, with the rest of the Family housed in various outbuildings. So the guards only patrolled the perimeter of the structure, and I didn't see anyone, not even pixie housekeepers, as I slipped from one hallway to the next. The inside of the castle was as eerily too-quiet as the woods had been, and unease curled up in my stomach. Something was wrong here. Other than, you know, me breaking into a place where I would be tortured and killed if I were caught sneaking around.

I'd just started down another hallway that would get me closer to Victor's office when the murmur of voices sounded, along with the *clink-clank* of silverware. So I followed the noise until I spotted a set of closed double doors at the end. From the blueprints Mo had given me, I knew that the doors led into one of the mansion's dining rooms, but of course I couldn't go in there.

That didn't mean that I couldn't spy on what was going on inside, though.

I climbed a set of stairs to the second floor and another door directly above the ones on the ground level. It wasn't locked, so I turned the knob and cracked it open. Since no lights blazed on this level, I felt safe enough to ease the door open and tiptoe through to the other side.

The door led out onto a balcony that overlooked the first-floor dining room. The area was deserted, so I dropped down onto my stomach, pulled up my spidersilk coat until it covered most of my head, and slithered up to the edge of the balcony, staring down through the slats in the white marble railing.

In the dining room below, Victor sat at the head of a rectangular table, with Blake to his right and Deah to his left. Katia was next to Blake, with Carl across from her. Nikolai Volkov sat at the other end of the table. The pixies had already served the food, and everyone was digging into cheesy lasagna, buttery garlic bread, and a green salad full of colorful veggies.

"So, Katia," Victor said, picking up his glass and swirling around the red wine inside. "Congratulations. Your performance in the obstacle course today was quite impressive. Your speed Talent served you well. I've never seen anyone move quite so fast before."

His words were innocent enough, but he stared at her, his golden gaze sly, as if he knew some secret about her victory. But there was nothing to know. Katia had used her speed magic to win fair and square . . . right? That's how it had looked to me. Then again, I hadn't been up front with her and Deah.

For a moment, Katia chewed on her lower lip, worry filling her face, but then she smiled and nodded. "Thank you, sir."

"Never thank someone for something you've earned by being smarter than everyone else," Victor corrected.

Smarter than everyone else? What did *that* mean? The way Victor talked, it was almost as if he knew that Katia had somehow cheated. Even more puzzling, it seemed to make him *happy*, as if she'd done something that he heartily approved of, although I had no idea what it could be. Maybe she'd pulled the same sort of dirty tricks on Deah that Vance had on me. If so, you would think that Victor would be upset about that, instead of pleased.

"Your victory is one of the reasons I asked you and Nikolai here tonight," Victor continued. "I always enjoy dining with winners."

He arched his eyebrow and gave his daughter a pointed look, telling everyone that he didn't consider her to be a winner tonight.

Deah's lips twisted with misery, but she sat up straight and tried to rally. "Well, it's always nice to have some competition. But it's only the first day of the tournament. What matters is who is left standing at the end, right?"

Katia scowled at her, and Deah shot her a dirty look in return. Victor glanced back and forth between the two girls, nodding his approval. A smile curved his lips, and I realized that he was enjoying pitting them against each other. It was just another sign of his cruelty.

Deah's phone buzzed, and she picked it up off the table and read the message on the screen. But when she realized that her father was still staring at her, she set her phone aside, dropped her head, and concentrated on her lasagna.

"I'm glad that Deah enjoys the *competition*," Nikolai drawled. "Perhaps this will be the year when that competition finally beats her."

His voice was pleasant enough, but his brown gaze was hard and expectant when he looked at Katia. She gave him a curt nod, as if promising that she wouldn't let Deah defeat her again.

Victor's smile widened. "Care to make a friendly wager on that?"

Nikolai reached up and stroked his brown beard, giving himself time to think. "What sort of wager?"

"Oh, I'm sure I can think of something that will be to our mutual benefit," Victor said, his voice smooth and seductive. "We are allies now, remember?"

"Mmm." Nikolai's tone was far more noncommittal.

The two men stared each other down, the silent tension between them growing and growing.

I looked back and forth between them, but the angle was too high for me to use my soulsight to see what they were really feeling. Still, Victor's words troubled me.

Allies? Since when were the Draconis and Volkovs *allies*? The Volkovs were the third most powerful Family in town, behind the Draconis and the Sinclairs. Everyone knew that the Volkovs wanted the top two Families to destroy each other so they could step up and seize power. So what had changed to make Nikolai join Victor?

More worry rippled through me. Maybe Claudia was wrong. Maybe Victor wasn't going to wait until after the tournament to strike out against the Sinclairs.

Maybe he'd already set his plan in motion—whatever it was.

Carl broke the silence by reaching out, grabbing a bottle of wine from the middle of the table, and filling his glass all the way to the brim with the blood-red liquid. Then he raised the glass to his lips and guzzled down all the wine like it was water and he was dying of thirst. *Glug-glug-glug.* He let out a happy sigh, smacked his lips together, and refilled his glass as quickly as he had drained it.

He held up the full glass and used it to gesture at the others.

"You should take Victor up on his bet, brother," Carl proclaimed in a loud voice, slurring his words. A few drops of wine sloshed out of his glass and stained the white tablecloth. "And you should bet a lot. Because my girl will win this year. She's got a secret weapon. Don't you, Katia?"

Katia's cheeks flamed in embarrassment, and she gave her father a sharp, disapproving look, but he was too busy gulping down his wine to notice, much less care. A spurt of sympathy filled my chest. It was obvious that Katia's father drank—a lot.

Victor's eyes narrowed with interest. "Really?" he asked, his voice taking on a sly, knowing tone. "And what would this secret weapon be?"

Katia's cheeks were still red, but she shrugged, trying to deflect the question. "I've just been training extra hard. That's all. But my father's right. It's going to pay off. I *know* it will."

She stared at Deah, waiting for the other girl to react to her challenging words, but Deah was busy checking her phone again, and she didn't even glance at Katia. Apparently, talking about the tournament wasn't nearly as important as whatever texts were on her phone.

Blake had been shoveling food into his mouth during the whole conversation, but he stopped long enough to snicker. "Looks like some folks don't care about your training."

Katia's cheeks burned again, with anger this time, and her lips flattened out in a harsh line. She didn't like Deah ignoring her. I wondered what Katia would think when she found out that Deah was dating Felix, or whatever the two of them were doing besides stupidly sneaking around.

It had been obvious at the tournament that Katia wanted to hook up with Felix again. I wondered if Felix had talked to Katia yet and told her that he was seeing someone else. Probably not, given everything that had happened with the rope ladder.

"Well," Victor murmured. "I suppose we'll see when the tournament resumes tomorrow."

"Yeah," Katia muttered, stabbing her fork into the salad on her plate.

"I'll be interested in watching you compete, Katia," Victor continued. "I always admire strong fighters who are determined to win. Perhaps if things go well, Nikolai might let me borrow you for some . . . special projects that the two of us are going to be working on together."

Katia blushed again, and her hazel eyes lit up with pleasure, as if she would actually enjoy working for Victor.

My stomach twisted with a combination of worry, disgust, and dread. *Special projects?* That certainly had an ominous tone to it. I waited, hoping that Victor would elaborate, but of course he didn't.

Victor and Nikolai kept talking about the tournament, mainly who the other Families had entered. Blake and Katia both chimed in with their opinions. So did Carl, although his words slurred so badly that the others just ignored him. Deah kept sneaking glances at her phone.

They also chatted about the rope ladder, but everyone agreed that it was an unfortunate accident. If Victor or Blake had been behind someone cutting the ropes, they weren't going to come right out and say so. Or maybe they hadn't had anything to do with it and Vance was the guilty one, as I suspected.

I waited a few minutes, but Victor and Nikolai didn't talk about anything else interesting or sinister, so I slithered away from the edge of the balcony and left my view of the dining hall. I probably had at least forty-five minutes before dinner would end, and I needed to get to Victor's office, search it, and get out of here before then.

Still keeping to the shadows, I skulked through the mansion, moving from one hallway and staircase to the next, climbing higher and higher all the while. According to the blueprints Mo had given me, Victor's office was located close to the greenlab, the space where both common and magical plants were grown, including stitch-sting bushes, which were harvested for their healing properties. I headed in that direction, and soon, the delicious smells of dinner were replaced by the softer, floral scents of flowers.

I sidled up to and peered in through the glass doors that fronted the Draconi greenlab. Just as in the Sinclair greenlab, tables covered with beakers, burners, and other scientific equipment took up the front part of the lab, surrounded by all sorts of plants, bushes, and even a few small, potted trees. The lights were turned down low, and I didn't see any guards patrolling inside or pixies flying over the tables. Good. Cutting through here would get me to Victor's office more quickly and would be marginally safer than continuing to skulk down the hallways. The castle might be mostly deserted, but sooner or later, I was bound to round a corner and run face-first into a pixie, who would be sure to yell and sound the alarm that I was here.

I tried one of the doors, surprised that it was already open. I would have thought that Victor would have the greenlab locked up tight, given all the stitch-sting and other important, expensive supplies inside, but I wasn't about to overlook this bit of good luck. So I slipped inside and shut the door behind me.

I looked over the front part of the greenlab, but science had never been my thing, so nothing stood out to me.

Still, I pulled my phone out of my coat pocket and snapped photos of the equipment and the lab setup to show Felix and Angelo later. I also took several shots of an area off to the left side of the lab—one that was filled with shelves full of bottled liquid stitch-sting.

Just like at the Sinclair mansion, heavy metal grates covered the shelves, locking away the healing liquid, but there was more of it here than I'd ever seen in one place before. Hundreds upon hundreds of bottles lined the shelves from top to bottom. It made sense, though. If Victor was thinking about attacking the other Families, he'd need a lot of stitch-sting to patch up the Draconi guards.

I put my phone away, moved through the lab area, and stepped into the greenhouse section. Herbs and vegetables stretched out in all directions, along with row after row of stitch-sting bushes. The dark, evergreen bushes weren't quite monsters, not like tree trolls and copper crushers, but they would still poke out their sharp needles and try to scratch you if you got too close to them without paying their toll. But I hadn't felt like carrying around a jar of honey tonight to drizzle on their roots, so I made sure to stay clear of the bushes.

And just like in the rest of the castle, everywhere I looked, I spotted something else emblazoned with that snarling dragon crest, including each and every one of the white flagstones that curled across the floor. The crest looked so fierce, so lifelike, that I thought the dragons might rise up and bite me on the ankles for stepping on their snouts.

Finally, I reached the center of the greenlab, a round, open space with paths snaking off in all directions. One enormous dragon made out of red and gold stained glass was set into the middle of the floor here, with matching flames streaming out of its mouth and wrapping around the dragon's body, as though the creature were continuously breathing fire and about to incinerate everything around it, including itself.

Just like Victor killed anyone who displeased him in the slightest way.

Maybe it was stupid, but I skirted around the stained glass crest, not wanting to step on any part of it, especially since the dragon's red eyes seemed to follow every move I made. I crossed to the far side of the open space and ducked behind another stitch-sting bush, ready to cut through the rest of the greenlab and find Victor's office—

"What do you think you're doing?" a voice hissed.

CHAPTER TWELVE

I froze, my breath caught in my throat, my heart hammering in my chest, my fingers curling around the hilt of my sword. I thought I'd been so careful, so quiet, sneaking around and keeping to the shadows like the perfect thief, but someone had spotted me. Now, all I could do was hope that I could fight my way out of the greenlab, make a mad dash for the woods, and disappear into the trees and the mist—

"I wanted to see you," another, deeper voice murmured.

Wait a second.

I knew that voice and the first one too. I sighed. Seriously? They were meeting *here*? Did they not know how stupid and dangerous this was?

I hunkered down, crept forward, and peered around a white marble dragon planter full of sprigs of stitch-sting. Sure enough, Deah and Felix were standing in the middle of the open space, right in the center of the stained glass dragon. The glimmering bits of red and gold glass made it look like fire was licking at their feet and that the snarling creature was about to erupt out of the ground and gobble them up. Well, that's certainly what Victor and Blake would do if they ever found out what was going on. Felix and Deah were taking their whole Romeo-and-Juliet romance to new extremes.

Felix grinned and held out a single red rose. Deah slid her phone into her pocket, then crossed her arms over her chest and glared at him. So Felix was the one who'd been blowing up her phone at dinner. I should have known. I wondered how she'd managed to get herself excused from the meal to come here.

"And why would you want to see me now that Katia's back in town?" she snarked.

He winced. "Um, I don't know what you mean?"

"I just bet you don't," she snapped back. "Funny thing, though. I remember you and Katia being *all over* each other during the tournament last summer, especially at the after-party at the lake. Don't you remember? Oh, wait. You probably don't, since the two of you were sucking face the *whole time*."

Felix opened his mouth, but Deah cut him off and kept right on going.

"And from the looks of things today, Katia is ready for round two." A note of bitterness crept into Deah's voice. "She kissed you. Yesterday, when we all met on the Midway—she kissed you right in front of Blake, Devon, and Lila, and I had to keep my mouth shut, stand there like an idiot, and watch her flirt with you. Just like I had to do at the tournament again today."

Felix winced again, but his face turned serious. "Listen, Katia is cool, but you're the one I want to be with, Deah. Not her. You know how I feel about you. How I've felt about you for *months* now."

He held out the rose to her again. Deah stared at the flower, and I shifted to one side so that I could look into her dark blue eyes. Her emotions slammed into me a second later.

Lingering, numbing boredom from dinner. Pinching hurt from her father's harsh words and high expectations. Rock-hard confidence that she was going to beat Katia and win the Tournament of Blades again. Sharp worry that someone was going to catch Felix in the greenlab. But most of all, I felt how much she cared about Felix. The hot spark of her feelings for him was like a firecracker exploding in my heart over and over again.

Despite her longing, Deah didn't take the rose. Instead, she shook her head and stepped back. Her eyes dulled and dimmed, and that hot spark was snuffed out.

"You should leave," she said in a sad, tired voice. "This is never going to work. Not with you being a Sinclair and me a Draconi. You should go before one of the pixies sees you—or worse, Blake or my dad. Maybe it's a good thing that Katia's back in town. So we can make a clean break now, before things get any worse than they already are."

Felix's smile wilted, and he dropped the rose to his side. "You don't mean that. Not really."

Deah shrugged, her face blank. "It doesn't matter. Nothing does except the fact that my father and brother hate your Family. There's no getting past that, Felix. No matter what you think."

"But—"

"No," she said in a firm voice, shaking her head and making her blond hair fly around her shoulders. "Don't tell me again that nothing matters but us. That's not true and you know it. Too many other things matter. And how we feel about each other isn't one of them."

Felix kept staring at her, his eyes dark with hurt, pain, love, and longing.

Deah sighed again. "Just leave, okay? And don't come back. That's what's best—for both of us."

She turned to go, which spurred Felix into action. He dropped the rose, stepped forward, pulled her into his arms, and planted his lips on hers.

Deah stiffened, her hands coming up to his chest as

though she was going to push him away. But then, her fingers curled into his shirt, and she swayed forward and melted into the kiss. Her arms snaked up and around Felix's neck so that she could pull him closer. They broke apart and stared into each other's eyes, both of them breathing heavily.

Then they kissed again, as close together as two people could possibly be, their lips crashing together again and again as though their lives depended on it.

Guilt flickered in my chest at spying on such a private moment—along with more than a little jealousy. I wished I could kiss Devon like that. Hold him like that. Or that I just had the courage to tell him how I really felt about him, to take a chance and see what might happen between us.

But I pushed aside my feelings and turned away from Felix and Deah. I still had a job to do, one that was far more important than hiding in the shadows mooning about Devon.

Because if I didn't figure out what Victor was planning, he would destroy us all.

I slipped deeper into the greenlab, careful not to make any noises that would alert Felix and Deah to my presence. But they were too wrapped up in each other to notice the whisper of my sneakers on the flagstones, and I left them behind and reached the far side of the greenlab.

I peered through this set of glass doors, but the hallway beyond was deserted, so I stepped outside and hurried on my way. I rounded the corner and finally reached my destination—the double doors that led into Victor's office.

The gold knobs were shaped like snarling dragons, and I gingerly tried one, half expecting it to come to life and bite off my fingers. Of course, that didn't happen, but the door was locked, so I pulled out my chopstick lock picks and went to work. Less than a minute later, the door *snicked* open. I waited, listening for noise and movement on the other side of the wood, but I didn't hear anything, so I felt safe enough to slip inside, shut, and relock the door behind me.

Lights burned in the office, which was easily twice the size of the Sinclair library. And just like with the rest of the castle, gold glimmered everywhere I looked, from the pillows on the couches to the trim on the furniture to the chandeliers hanging from the ceiling. Shelves took up two of the walls, filled with books, photos, and trophies. I spotted two gold cups with Deah's name engraved on them, proclaiming her as the winner of the Tournament of Blades. I wondered why they were in here, instead of her bedroom, since she was the one who'd earned them, not Victor. I snorted. Then again, he probably considered them *his* trophies, since she was *his* daughter and a member of *his* Family. Sometimes, I didn't know which I hated more—Victor's cruelty or his ego.

I scanned the rest of the shelves, my greedy little heart wondering how many precious things I could stuff into my pockets and how much cold, hard cash Mo would give me for them. I particularly admired a set of diamond-crusted dragon bookends. But I forced myself to keep my sticky fingers in my coat pockets where they belonged. I didn't dare steal so much as the smallest knickknack. Not from Victor and especially not from his office. Swiping those bookends would tip him off that someone had been in here, and that was the last thing I wanted.

So I hurried over to Victor's desk, which was close to another wall. It was three separate sections joined together in a U shape and featured your usual office setup—laptop, mouse, keyboard, phone, a couple of reading lamps. I'd just reached for the laptop to wake it up when a spark of red caught my eye.

I looked up into the face of a dragon.

I staggered back against a corner of the desk, making a cup full of pens *rattle-rattle*, and I had to clamp my lips together to keep from shrieking. After a few sweaty, heart-pounding seconds, I realized that it wasn't an actual dragon staring at me, just one that had been carved into the white stone wall behind Victor's desk.

It was the same snarling dragon crest that was on everything else, the biggest I'd seen in the entire castle, but this dragon's head was turned to the side, with a fist-size ruby for an eye embedded in the stone. Flames curled all around the dragon, and its head and the ruby eye were particularly prominent, as if the creature continuously peered over the shoulder of whoever sat at the desk. I shivered and dropped my gaze from it.

I focused on the desk again, starting with the left section since that's where Victor's laptop was. I jiggled the mouse and made the screen flare to life, but the laptop was password protected. I tried a few combinations, like Blake's and Deah's names, but nothing worked, so I moved on, scanning through all the papers on top of the middle section of the desk: invoices, contracts, shipping orders. The same sort of stuff that Claudia had on her desk—all the things that dealt with the Families' business interests. Stuff that would tell me nothing about what Victor was planning.

Still concentrating on the left and middle sections, I opened and closed all the drawers, scanning through the items inside. There were more papers, along with pens, staplers, and rolls of tape. Nothing interesting, but I still made sure to put everything back *exactly* where I had found it. I didn't want Victor to even *think* that someone had been in his office, much less rifled through his desk.

When I finished with the drawers, I turned to the right and final section of the desk, the one that was the closest to the dragon carving's eerie ruby eye. And I finally found something interesting.

Files—on everyone in the Tournament of Blades.

There were five stacks of files, one for each major Family—the Draconis, Sinclairs, Volkovs, Itos, and Salazars. I flipped through the top file in each stack. Name, age, height, weight, hair and eye color. It was all detailed, from first-time competitors to folks who had been in the tournament for years. A photo of the person was also clipped to every file. But what was really interesting—and totally creepy—was that the information was so specific and so detailed, especially when it came to a person's magic.

Victor had chronicled every person's Talents, cataloging them as minor, moderate, and major, and listing all the things that person could do with his or her magic. The more powerful a person was, the thicker the file and the more notes crowded into the margins, ones that I was betting Victor himself had written in blood-red ink.

Devon's file was on top of the Sinclair stack, and I held my breath as I opened it and read through the notes.

No strength or speed Talents, and no obvious magic at all. Although I still believe that he has to have some sort of power. More careful study is needed.

I exhaled. Victor didn't know about Devon's compulsion magic. Good. That was good. Compulsion was the sort of rare, special Talent Victor would do anything to have for himself, including kidnapping and killing Devon—just as he'd tried to do when Devon was younger. Victor would have succeeded back then, too, if my mom hadn't intervened.

I put Devon's file back and scanned through some others. The longer I looked, the more I realized that Victor's notes were different when it came to the various competitors. For the folks in other Families, he'd just jotted down observations about their magic. But for the Draconis, he had gone a step further, almost as if he were planning how to best use their magic for something.

Moderate Talent for speed. Would benefit from TT29.
Major Talent for strength. Augment even more with CC2.
Minor Talent for sight. Possibly use RM55?

The notes on the Draconi competitors went on and on, and I had no idea what any of them meant. I didn't dare steal any of the files, so I pulled out my phone and snapped several photos to show Claudia and Mo. Maybe they'd be able to decipher Victor's code.

I spotted a file with Deah's name on it. Curious about what Victor had written on his own daughter, I pulled it out of the stack and opened it up.

Major mimic Talent. Will have to find right combination to make her truly exceptional. Possible experiments needed to maximize her potential.

The notes chilled me more than any others I'd seen so far. Victor wanted to experiment on his own daughter? With what, exactly? And why?

I snapped photos of her entire file, concentrating on

Victor's notes, then put it back in the stack where I'd found it. Below Deah's file was one with Blake's name. I took pictures of it as well, although Victor had only written a few notes in it. Apparently, he wasn't nearly as interested in Blake's magic as he was Deah's. Then again, her mimic power was a much rarer Talent than his strength magic.

I worked as fast as I could. Dinner had to be winding down by now, and Victor could come back here any second. I put Blake's file back where I'd found it and was about to move away from the desk when I spotted a final folder sitting off to the side all by itself. The name on the tab caught my eye.

Lila Merriweather.

A chill slithered down my spine. Victor had a file on me too? I snorted. Of course he did—because I was in the tournament and finally worthy of a bit of his attention. I opened the file.

Name, age, height. All of it was listed there, and there was even a photo of me that had been taken at the tournament sometime today, since I was wearing the black T-shirt and shorts I'd had on during the obstacle course. I hadn't noticed anyone taking my photo, but there had been tons of people with phones and cameras. I shivered at the thought that someone had been watching me.

Hard to tell what, if any, magic she has. Rumored to have a sight Talent. Perhaps a bit of strength as well? Something familiar about her, though. Must keep an eye on her and see how she progresses through the tournament.

I exhaled again, longer and louder than before. Victor didn't know about my soulsight and transference magic, and he hadn't realized who I really was—the daughter of his old enemy, Serena Sterling. I didn't know what he would do if he ever found out the truth, but it wouldn't be anything good.

I took photos of my file as well, thin though it was, and put it back where it belonged. My time was up, and I was about to head over to the doors and slip out of the office, when I realized that I was shivering in a way that only meant one thing.

There was magic in here—and a lot of it.

I stopped and looked around the office, scanning the fine furnishings and wondering what might be emanating enough magic for me to feel it so strongly and at such a great distance in this huge room. I moved out from behind the desk and headed toward one of the bookcases, thinking that maybe Victor had a black blade stuffed back on one of the shelves.

But the farther I moved away from the desk, the more that chill of magic lessened. So I turned around and found myself staring at the dragon carving in the wall, the ruby eye still fixed on me.

Hmm.

I had been a thief long enough and had watched enough of those old *Scooby-Doo* cartoons in the library where I used to live to realize that there might be more to the carving than I'd first thought. So I went over to the ruby and looked at it—*really* looked at it—using my sight magic to peer through the gem's many winking facets.

There was something behind the wall.

Some space, some room, some sort of open area. And that's where the magic was coming from—the entire stone carving was cool to the touch. Now, I just had to figure out how to get in there and see what Victor thought was important enough to hide—

"My office is just through here." Victor's voice sounded beyond the closed office doors.

I froze, realizing that I'd just jinxed myself. Curses rose in my throat, but I swallowed them down.

A key scraped in the lock. Victor was here, and he'd brought someone along with him.

CHAPTER THIRTEEN

Time to leave.

Since I couldn't get back out through the main entrance, I hurried over to the only other exit—a door set in the middle of the fourth and final office wall, one made entirely out of glass.

I unlocked the door, slipped through to the other side, and rushed over to the edge of the balcony, looking for a drainpipe or a trellis I could climb down. It was full dark now, and spotlights glimmered in the lawn, highlighting the guards patrolling the area, including one right below the balcony. My sneaker kicked a loose bit of stone, which *plink-plink-plinked* across the balcony. The guard's head snapped up, and I barely managed to lurch back out of his line of sight—

Creak.

My head snapped around, and I realized that I hadn't shut the patio door all the way behind me. It swung open a treacherous inch, then another one, but I didn't dare dart forward to try to close it. Not when I could see the office doors opening, and Victor striding inside.

So I scuttled over to the far side of the balcony, where the glass gave way to the stone of the mansion, and sandwiched myself in between the stone wall and a wooden trellis filled with red roses. Now, I just had to hope my hiding spot was good enough to keep me safe from Victor in his office and the guard patrolling the grounds below.

"Please," Victor's voice drifted outside to me. "Make yourselves comfortable."

I scooted forward just far enough so that I could peer in through the glass wall. Victor was in the office, along with Nikolai and Carl Volkov. I didn't see Katia, though. Maybe she was hanging out with Blake, while the adults talked. Poor girl, if that was the case.

Nikolai settled himself in a chair in front of Victor's desk. Carl sat down in another chair there, although he slouched to one side, obviously drunk. Carl was too out of it to look around the office, but Nikolai wasn't, and his dark eyes scanned everything, lingering on the dragon crest carved into the wall behind the desk. Eventually, his gaze turned toward the glass wall, and I was able to look into his eyes long enough for my soulsight to kick in—and let me feel his sharp, pinching jealousy.

Nikolai desperately wanted all the gold and other fine things that Victor had. Maybe that was why he'd agreed to an alliance with the Draconis. Maybe Victor was paying the Volkovs for whatever reason.

Instead of sitting down behind his desk, Victor moved off to a wet bar in one corner of the office and started pouring them all glasses of scotch.

"I hope you've been considering my proposal, Nikolai," Victor said. "I think that merging our Families into one unit would be most beneficial to us both."

Shock rippled through me. So that's what Victor was up to—or at least part of it.

Victor's back was to him, so he didn't see Nikolai smirk. Perhaps their alliance wasn't a done deal after all—or perhaps Nikolai was already thinking about how he could betray Victor. That would be a dangerous game to play.

"It is an interesting proposal," Nikolai replied in a neutral tone. "One that I have given a great deal of thought. But, as you know, there are serious obstacles to any such merger. The other Families would never allow it."

"Because our combined forces would be too big a threat to them," Victor finished. "I'm well aware of that. But think of it this way. If we were to combine, then none of the other Families would be able to stand against us, including Claudia Sinclair."

"True," Nikolai murmured. "Very true."

They didn't say anything else. Carl kept staring off into space, sliding down and then hoisting himself upright in his chair over and over again.

Victor had just poured the last glass of scotch when he stopped, frowned, and looked over at his desk. A breeze was gusting in through the open door and ruffling the papers there, something that his sharp, narrowed eyes had picked up. He would have to have a Talent for sight, or maybe one for hearing, to notice something like that, given that he was on the opposite side of the office.

Victor realized that the breeze was coming in from the balcony door, and his frown deepened as he headed in my direction.

I silently cursed and slid even farther back behind the white trellis in the corner of the balcony, trying not to rustle the roses any more than necessary. The thorns slid off my spidersilk coat, since they couldn't penetrate the smooth fabric, but several scratched my hands and neck and one particularly troublesome thorn tangled in my hair. I gritted my teeth, ripped free of the thorns, and pressed myself as flat as I could against the stone wall behind the trellis.

Victor pushed open the glass door and stepped out onto the balcony. I froze, staying absolutely, completely still, barely even daring to breathe and desperately pretending that I was just another part of the wall.

Because if Victor spotted me, then I was *dead.*

He'd yell for the guards, or worse, come after me himself. I held back a shudder. I'd seen what he'd done to my mom, how he'd carved her up like she was a slab of meat before he'd finally killed her. He hadn't cut her so many times just to murder her. He'd done it because he'd *wanted* to, which made him a special kind of cruel.

White stars flashed on and off in front of my face in warning, but I ruthlessly blinked them away. I couldn't afford to let my soulsight throw me back into the past to relive my mom's murder. Not now, when my own future was so very much in doubt.

"Something wrong?" Nikolai asked.

Victor waited several seconds before answering. "Seems I forgot to shut the door when I was admiring the view earlier."

He went back into the office and closed and locked the door behind him.

As much as I wanted to bolt from my hiding place and get out of here as fast as possible, I made myself stand absolutely still, in case he decided to look out the door again.

Sure enough, a second later, Victor stepped in front of the glass again, peering out into the night. He knew—or at least suspected—that someone had been in his office. All I could do now was hope that he thought it was Blake or some other Draconi.

After several long, tense seconds, Victor moved away from the glass, took the drinks he'd fixed over to Nikolai and Carl, and sat down behind his desk. They started talking, but the glass muffled their words, and I couldn't hear what they were saying. Besides, I'd been here long enough, and I'd pushed my luck as much as I dared to.

So I slipped out from behind the roses, waited until the guard below the balcony had moved away, climbed down the closest drainpipe, and vanished into the night.

* * *

I made it across the grounds and back over to the woods that ringed the castle. Victor's office had been on the opposite side from where I'd gone in, so I had to circle all the way around the compound. I had almost reached the trail that would take me back to the Sinclair mansion when I came across something else interesting—the Draconi Family cemetery.

It was just like the Sinclair cemetery, a clearing ringed with a wrought iron fence, with one notable difference—almost all the tombstones said *Draconi*. Apparently, the Draconis preferred to bury only their blood relatives here, instead of all those who had been loyal to their Family like the Sinclairs did. Exactly what I would expect from Victor.

I should have kept walking, since it was getting late and I needed to get back to the mansion, but I found myself stopping, opening the gate, and moving deeper into the cemetery. It took me several minutes, but I found a single white tombstone set off all by itself at one edge of the cemetery, like a lonely kid being left out of the rest of the cool crowd. Only a few simple words flowed across it: *Luke Silver.*

My father.

My heart squeezed tight as I stared at the marker, all sorts of emotions bubbling up inside me. This was the first time I'd ever seen where he was buried. This was the first time I'd ever seen any tangible proof that he'd ever truly existed, other than a few old photos my mom had shown me.

I'd never known my father, but my mom had told me all about him. Luke Silver had been the Draconi Family bruiser—before Victor had him killed. Victor hadn't liked Luke's relationship with my mom, especially after he'd proposed to her. Victor had thought that my dad was being disloyal to the Draconis by being with her, so he'd sent my dad out to deal with a copper crusher that had invaded one of the Family businesses.

It should have been a routine assignment, but Victor hadn't told my dad that there was a whole nest of copper crushers, and Luke had been ambushed, overwhelmed, and killed by the monsters. My mom had left Cloudburst Falls shortly after his death. He'd never even known that she was pregnant with me.

I turned my star-sapphire ring around and around on my finger—my mom's engagement ring—even as my heart twisted and twisted in my chest as though a copper crusher was coiled around it and squeezing the life out of me.

I'd once told Felix that Romeo-and-Juliet relationships between the Families never worked; because if Victor could so easily betray his bruiser, his right-hand man, his supposed friend, he wouldn't hesitate to arrange some sort of similar accident for Felix.

All the stupid, senseless Family plots and politics were another reason that I wanted to leave Cloudburst Falls as soon as possible—after I made sure that Felix, Devon, and the rest of the Sinclairs were safe.

This part of the cemetery wasn't as well tended as the rest, and bunches of wildflowers had grown up along the fence. I reached down, picked another blue forget-me-not, and laid it on my father's tombstone. I opened my mouth, but I didn't know what to say, so I clamped my lips shut and settled for turning my sapphire ring around on my finger one more time.

I sighed and rubbed my head, which was aching. There was nothing *to* say. Luke had loved my mom, and he'd been killed because Victor didn't approve of their relationship. Yet another love story with a tragic, bitter end.

There was nothing in this cemetery but ghosts, hurts,

and regrets. That was the way I felt about all of Cloudburst Falls sometimes—the Midway, the squares, even the sweeping views from the mountain. All of it reminded me of my mom and everything I'd lost.

And all of it made my heart keep right on aching from the deep, jagged wounds that would never, ever heal.

So I sighed again and turned around, ready to leave the cemetery and all the painful memories behind, and go back to the Sinclair mansion for the night. I looked up, my breath catching in my throat.

A woman stood at the cemetery gate.

CHAPTER FOURTEEN

I was so surprised that someone would be out here after dark that my brain ground to a complete halt, and I didn't even think of doing the smart thing, like vaulting over the fence and running away. Instead, all I could do was stare at the woman, my mouth gaping open.

Long, golden hair, dark blue eyes, pale skin that shimmered in the moonlight. She was one of the most beautiful women I'd ever seen, like a fairy-tale princess come to life, but something about her seemed strangely . . . familiar. Like I'd seen her somewhere before, although I didn't think I had.

For as beautiful as she was, her appearance was also a bit strange. A long, flowing white garment covered her slender body, looking more like a nightgown than an actual dress, and her feet were bare, despite the sticks, rocks, and other woodsy debris that littered the cemetery. One lock of her golden hair was braided down the right side of her face and tied off with a sapphire-blue ribbon, while a white wicker basket full of blood-red roses dangled from her hand.

The woman stared at me, obviously seeing me despite the mist and the darkness, which meant that she had some sort of sight magic. I expected her to open her mouth and yell for the guards, but to my surprise, a soft smile curved her lips. The warm, welcoming expression made her look even more beautiful, like an ethereal ghost come to frolic in the moonlit cemetery.

"Serena!" she said, tossing her basket aside and racing over to me. "You finally came back!"

I couldn't have been more shocked than if she'd started doing cartwheels. *Serena?* She thought I was my *mom*? Why? Why would she think that? Sure, I had my mom's black hair and blue eyes, and I was even wearing her sapphire-blue coat, but I obviously wasn't *her*.

But the woman didn't seem to realize that. Instead, she stopped in front of me, reached out, and drew me into a tight hug.

"Oh, Serena," she said in a choked voice. "It's been so long. So very, very long."

I stood there, my mouth still gaping open, my arms hanging by my sides, wondering who this woman was and why she thought I was my dead mom. After several seconds, the woman drew back, still smiling.

"Oh, Serena," she said in a light, lilting, almost singsong voice. "I have *so* much to tell you. About Deah and Lila and everything else that's been going on between the Families."

More shock jolted through me. She knew my name? But if she knew that I was Serena's daughter, then why did she think that I was my mom?

I looked into her eyes, and I realized that they were unnaturally bright, as though two glittering jewels had been set into her face. But the weird thing was that my soulsight didn't automatically kick in the way it usually did whenever I locked gazes with someone.

I waited . . . and waited . . . and waited . . . but I didn't feel any of her emotions, even though she was obviously very glad to see me. No warm happiness, no blazing conviction, nothing. Instead, this strange, almost floating sensation filled my mind as if my head were full of the light, airy mist that surrounded us, as if I were somehow drifting away from the rest of my body—

I blinked, and the sensation vanished, although the woman's eyes remained as bright as ever. I tried to step away from her, but she reached out and grabbed my hands, hard and tight enough to tell me that she had a strength Talent.

"We have to warn the girls about the wolf," the woman said in a low, urgent tone. "The wolf wants to devour them both, gobble them up until there's nothing left but bones and blades. . . . No blood, just bones and blades . . . bones and blades . . . bones and blades. . . ."

She shuddered and let go of my hands. She wrapped her arms around her body and hugged herself tight as though something terrible had happened.

"Are you okay?" I asked, having no idea what was going on or why.

The woman looked at me, her face dark and troubled. Then, in the next instant, she blinked, her lips stretching up in another sunny smile. "Just fine now that you're here, Serena."

And then she turned around, retrieved her basket of roses, and skipped past me. Seriously, she was *skipping* as though she didn't have a care in the world. The woman headed straight to my father's tombstone, then dropped to her knees, pulled the red roses out of her basket, and started arranging them on his grave, humming a soft tune all the while.

All I could do was just stand there with my eyes bulging and mouth gaping open even wider than before. I felt like Alice falling down the rabbit hole. Things just kept getting stranger and stranger.

"I thought that was you at the tournament today," the woman said. "But, of course, I was up in the box, so I couldn't be sure."

So she was the woman who'd been sitting in the Draconi box, the blonde wearing the white hat. That still didn't tell me who she might be in the Family, but that didn't matter. What did was getting out of here before someone else spotted me—

A branch *cracked* behind me, and a hand touched my shoulder.

Instinct took over. I grabbed the hand, turned my body into the one behind me, and flipped my attacker over my shoulder. The guy landed on his back with an audible *thump*, then let out a low groan of pain.

Felix blinked up at me. "Ouch. That hurt."

"Felix!" I hissed. "What are you doing here?"

"I'd say the better question is what are *you* doing here," another voice chimed in.

I whirled around to find Deah standing in the cemetery as well, her hand resting on the hilt of the sword strapped to her black leather belt. My hand curled around the hilt of my sword as well, and the two of us stood there, staring at each other, daring the other to make the first move.

"What are you doing here?" Deah demanded again. "You're trespassing."

I couldn't exactly tell her that I'd been sneaking around her house and spying on her dad, so I went with the first lie that popped into my head. "I was looking for Felix."

Deah crossed her arms over her chest and glared at him. Felix sighed, then held out a hand. I reached down and helped him to his feet.

"Is this another one of your girlfriends?" she snapped.

I rolled my eyes. "Don't be an idiot. I came over here

to make sure that no one spotted your Romeo—like, say, Blake or your dad."

"How did you even know I was coming over here?" Felix asked.

I snorted. "Please. You're crazy about her. As soon as she stomped off at the tournament today, I knew you'd probably sneak over here tonight and make some grand romantic gesture to win her back. Am I wrong?"

Felix winced, but he didn't deny my accusation.

"Don't be so cross, darling," another voice piped up. "It's always nice to have visitors."

The blond woman had finished arranging the roses on my father's grave. She got to her feet, skipped back over, and stopped next to me.

"What are you doing out here?" Deah asked, concern creasing her face. "You know you're not supposed to leave the house after dark. It's not safe."

The woman beamed at me. "Talking to Serena. What does it look like I'm doing, silly? And it's perfectly safe. Serena knows all about the monsters and the best ways to handle them."

Deah sighed. "Mom. . . ."

My eyebrows shot up in my face. "This is your *mom*?"

"Yes," she snapped. "This is my mom. Seleste Draconi. Do you have a problem with that?"

Her eyes glittered with anger, and her hand dropped to her sword again in a clear challenge.

"Now, don't be mad at Serena," Seleste said. "We were just catching up. It's been so terribly long since I've seen her. We're family, you see."

Seleste patted my shoulder, her touch light and soft. Us? Family? Why would she think *that*?

Deah frowned. "What's she talking about? Why does she keep calling you Serena? Did you do something to her?"

I held up my hands. "I didn't do anything to your mom. I was out here looking for Felix when she came skipping into the cemetery."

"What did she say to you?"

I shrugged. "Nothing really. Just some weird, random stuff."

Deah tensed, her jaw clenching. "She talked to you? Tell me what she said. Tell me the *exact words*."

"Why? It was all just gibberish about bones and blades and stuff."

She opened her mouth, probably to demand that I tell her what her mom had said, but another voice boomed through the night.

"Deah!" Blake shouted. "Where are you? Your crazy-ass mom got out of her room again!"

She sighed and closed her eyes for a moment. Then she turned and yelled back to him. "I'm over here, Blake! I found her! We'll be there in a minute!"

Blake didn't respond, although a door slammed somewhere in the distance as though he'd gone back inside the castle.

"You two need to leave," Deah hissed. "Now."

Felix held out his hand. "But—"

"No buts. Just go." Her face softened. "I'll text you later. Okay?"

He nodded. Deah stepped up, put her arm around her mom's shoulder, and gently steered her away from me. Still smiling, Seleste looked back over her shoulder and gave me a cheery wave.

"So nice to finally meet you, Lila. I'll be seeing you again soon," she called out in that eerie, singsong voice.

Deah tightened her grip on her mom, opened the cemetery gate, and hurried toward the castle. She never looked back.

I waited until they were out of earshot before I looked

at Felix. "What was that about? Why does Deah's mom act like that?"

He sighed and kicked at a tuft of overgrown grass. "Because she has a Talent for sight, specifically for seeing the future. She's always been like that, for as long as I can remember."

"Deah's mom can see the future?" I'd heard of folks having that power, but it was a rare Talent, and I'd never met anyone before with it.

He nodded. "Yeah. She's always saying strange stuff, calling people by other names, seeing monsters that aren't there, things like that. And she's always wandering off. Deah has to watch her all the time to make sure she doesn't get too far from the house and accidentally hurt herself or get eaten by a monster. Once, Seleste managed to get all the way down to the lochness bridge in town before Deah and the guards caught up with her."

I winced. That sounded like a rough life for Deah and her mom. "Is Seleste always so . . . out of it?"

Felix shrugged. "It comes and goes. Apparently, she's pretty clear during the day, but the sight or visions or whatever get worse at night." He looked at me. "What did she say to you? According to Deah, she's pretty accurate. The rumor is that's why Victor married her—for her visions."

We have to warn the girls about the wolf. . . . The wolf wants to devour them both, gobble them up until there's nothing left but bones and blades. . . . No blood, just bones and blades . . . bones and blades . . . bones and blades. . . .

Seleste's urgent, singsong voice whispered in my mind. This time, I was the one who shuddered. I didn't know if she could actually see the future or not, but those files and notes in Victor's office had me worried enough already, without thinking about bones and blades, or whatever her warning really meant.

"Nothing that made sense," I said, answering Felix's question. "Deah's right. We need to leave before one of the guards decides to patrol through here. Let's go."

Felix and I left the cemetery and headed through the woods toward the Sinclair mansion. Well, I walked and Felix trudged, banging into more trees and crashing through more bushes than he maneuvered around, since the white mist had now fully engulfed the forest.

"Slow down," he muttered, after bouncing off yet another tree. "Some of us don't have magical night vision, remember?"

"Well, then, it's a good thing you can use your healing Talent to stitch up all those cuts and scrapes you're getting."

"You are *so* not funny," he groused.

I grinned, even though he couldn't see me. "I'm a laugh riot and you know it."

Felix grumbled something under his breath that I was probably better off not hearing.

"Actually, I don't think that trespassing on Draconi property is really a laughing matter," a low voice drawled.

My hand dropped to the hilt of my sword, ready to pull it free, while Felix stepped up beside me. But instead of a Draconi guard, Devon stepped out of the trees right in front of us.

"Busted," Felix muttered.

Devon crossed his arms over his chest, his mouth fixed in a flat line. A black cloak covered his shoulders to help him better blend in with the shadows, and a sword was belted to his waist. Devon rarely carried a weapon, and the sword told me how worried he'd been about us. He was also holding a flashlight, the circular beam shooting off into the trees.

Devon raised his eyebrows. "Care to tell me what the

two of you are doing way out here where you shouldn't be?"

Felix opened his mouth, but for once, words escaped him. He clamped his lips shut and looked at me for help. I shrugged. I didn't have any lies ready either. There was really no good reason for either one of us to be out here, and all three of us knew it, especially Devon.

"Let me see if I can explain things," Devon said. "Felix went over to the Draconi compound to see Deah, apologize, and explain to her why Katia was flirting with him at the tournament."

"Dude!" Felix said. "How do you know about me and Deah?"

Devon gave him a look. "It's kind of obvious. I've known for a couple of weeks now, ever since that dinner for all the Families, when the two of you were staring at each other all night. Besides, every time we run into her on the Midway, you suddenly, mysteriously disappear for a while."

Devon was smart, able to pick up on subtle things like that, piece them together, and figure out what was really going on. That's how he'd realized who I really was and that I had transference magic. Just by watching and listening and putting together all the small, inadvertent clues that I hadn't even realized I'd let slip about my past and my power.

"I was hoping that you would come clean with me, but you didn't," Devon continued. "I went to your room, but you weren't there, so I figured you must have hiked over here. And when Lila wasn't in her room either, I decided to come look for you both."

Felix chewed on his lip. "And what do you think about me and Deah? Are you going to tell your mom?"

Claudia wouldn't like the idea of Felix dating Deah, especially not now, when the Draconis seemed poised to strike out at the other Families. She would order him to break things off with Deah, and he would have to do it. Claudia's word was law with the Sinclairs, and you either followed it, or you left the Family—for good.

Devon sighed and ran a hand through his hair, the mist turning his dark locks more black than brown. "I don't have a problem with Deah. She's always been nice enough to me, given that she's a Draconi. But she *is* a Draconi—and not just someone who works for the Family. She's Victor's daughter and Blake's sister. You couldn't have picked a worse person to sneak around with."

Felix's shoulders sagged. "I know that, all of that. But I love her, Dev. I have for a while now."

Devon looked at his best friend. "I know you do, and I think Deah cares about you too. That's why I'm not going to say anything to my mom . . . for now. But something's gotta give, man. You need to figure out if she's really worth all the trouble that being with her will bring down on both of you."

Felix momentarily brightened; then his face sobered. He wasn't just talking to his best friend right now, and he gave Devon a curt, respectful nod, realizing that the Family bruiser was giving him a chance to make things right—for everyone.

Devon turned to me, his gaze lingering on my long coat. "And you came over here to spy on Victor."

I smoothed down my coat, making drops of mist slide off the spidersilk. "And why would you think that? Maybe I saw Felix leave and was following him instead."

"Three reasons. You stayed behind in the library to talk to my mom earlier today, you only wear that coat when you're up to something sneaky, and we're still standing on Draconi property." Devon ticked the points off on his fingers. "Victor's up to something, isn't he?"

There was no use lying to him. "Yeah. Although I still have no idea what it is."

I told him and Felix everything I'd seen and overheard at the Draconi castle. When I finished, they were both frowning.

"What do you think those notes in the Draconi files mean?" Devon asked. "What sort of things was Victor going to give his people to increase their magic? Or whatever he's doing?"

"Not a clue. I took photos of the files, though. Maybe Claudia or Mo will be able to make sense out of them."

"And Victor has a file on Deah?" Felix asked. "You don't think he would actually . . . *hurt* her, do you?"

He chewed on his lip again and started pacing back and forth.

"Of course not," I said in a smooth voice. "His notes were all about how proud he was of her mimic magic. Nothing else."

Devon could tell I was lying, and he nodded his approval at me. There was no need for Felix to worry any more than he already was.

Felix opened his mouth to ask me another question, but Devon cut him off.

"We can talk more back at the mansion," he said. "I don't think that the Draconi guards patrol this far out, but I don't like waving this flashlight around where they might see it either. Let's go home."

Devon turned around, the flashlight swinging in a wide arc. I was just about to fall in step behind him when the beam swiped across something that was a bright, glossy red.

Blood.

"Wait," I said. "I see something. Shine your light back over here."

I pointed as I walked toward the spot where I'd seen the splash of crimson.

"Lila?" Devon asked, peering into the trees and mist around us. "What's wrong?"

I shook my head. I didn't know yet. But something *was* wrong because it was once again quiet in the forest—too quiet.

No owls hooted in the trees, no rockmunks scuttled through the underbrush, no monsters peered out at us from the bushes. I glanced around and realized that this was the same place where I had noticed the eerie silence before, on my way over to the Draconi estate.

I skirted around a couple of dead, fallen trees, with Devon and Felix trailing along behind me. I hopped over the last fallen tree and stopped, since the ground dropped away into a sharp, rocky ravine that was about ten feet wide.

My friends stood on either side of me, with Devon shining his flashlight back and forth, straight out in front of us, highlighting the dense thicket of trees on the far side of the ravine.

"I don't see anything," he murmured.

Me neither. So I looked around, searching for the blood I'd seen before. A second later, I spotted it, splattered on a tree to my right, with smears on the ground as well. A horrible thought occurred to me.

"Shine your light down," I whispered. "Into the ravine."

Devon did as I asked, the beam of his flashlight sinking lower . . . and lower . . . and lower. . . .

Until it hit the first body.

A tree troll was lying on the ground about ten feet down in the ravine, its furry gray arms and legs splayed out at awkward angles. Deep, vicious cuts crisscrossed the creature's chest and belly, and a few small pools of blood surrounded its body, although not nearly as much as I would have expected, given the horrible wounds.

And it wasn't the only one.

Devon moved the light back and forth, from one side of the ravine to the other, revealing more than a dozen dead trolls. All of them were in various states of decomposition, and many had been reduced to nothing but bones, although none of them had been killed as recently as the one closest to us.

"What do you think did this?" Felix whispered. "A bear? A copper crusher? Another monster?"

I shook my head. "I don't know. I doubt a bear would be this close to the Family compounds, not with all the people, lights, and noise. Of course, monsters are everywhere, but they usually like to stay hidden. But if it was a copper crusher or some other monster, why wouldn't it have eaten the tree trolls, bones and all? There are *so* many of them—"

"Too many for one monster to eat." Devon finished my horrible thought. "Way too many."

"But why kill a tree troll if you aren't going to eat it?" Felix asked. "It just doesn't make any sense."

I thought of the murdered troll we'd found behind the dumpster yesterday. Once again, that soft, evil laughter echoed in my mind, making me shiver.

"Maybe . . ." my voice trailed off. "Maybe it was just about the killing. Maybe whoever did this didn't care about eating the trolls at all."

Felix gave me a horrified look. "You think someone did this *for fun*? That they caught and killed a bunch of tree trolls? How would they even do that?"

"They'd have to have some sort of trap," Devon said.

He lifted the flashlight, shining it up into the trees around us and moving the beam back and forth.

I sucked in a breath when I spotted the cage.

It hung about ten feet up in a blood persimmon tree off to our right. A cage. Someone had actually put a cage out here so they could trap, torture, and murder monsters. Anger roared through my body, and I ran over, took hold of the trunk, and started scrambling up the tree.

"Lila," Devon said. "Be careful."

I nodded and kept climbing. A few seconds later, I was at eye level with the cage. It was a small, metal contraption, about the size of a pet carrier, with bars all around it. The door on the cage was open, and something flat and gold gleamed inside. I reached through the opening—careful not to trip the lever that would send the door shooting down—snagged the object, and dragged it out where I could see it.

A dark chocolate candy bar.

My stomach twisted, and bile rose in my throat. Someone had deliberately put the chocolate here to lure a new troll into the cage since they'd already killed the monster who'd been trapped earlier tonight—and all those other poor trolls before it.

"Lila?" Devon called out. "What is it?"

I tucked the chocolate bar into one of my coat pockets, then took hold of the metal cage.

"Use your compulsion magic and tell me to destroy something," I snarled. "Now."

Devon drew in a breath. When he spoke again, his voice held a cold crack of magic. "Lila, *destroy*."

Devon's voice wrapped around me like the mist cloaking the trees. The second I heard his command, invisible hands took hold of my arms, moving them this way and that. Devon's power soaked into my body and quickly melted into a familiar, icy wave of magic flowing through my veins, so cold that it was almost painful. Suddenly, I was stronger than before—and I used that strength to rip the metal cage apart with my bare hands.

Bit by bit, bar by bar, I tore the trap apart, the pieces *ping-ping-pinging* off the tree branches and disappearing into the darkness. I had just snapped off the final bar when the last of Devon's magic burned out of my body. I exhaled and took a moment to get my emotions under control before I threw away the remains of the cage and climbed down the tree.

"The trap?" Devon said, shining his flashlight at the broken pieces of metal that had fallen to the ground.

"Yeah."

"But who would do such a thing?" Felix asked. "And why? Who would deliberately be that cruel to a bunch of harmless monsters?"

I thought of Victor and Blake. Both of them were definitely that cruel. Both of them could easily kill monsters—and people too—just because they wanted to. Just because it amused them. Just because they thought it was *fun*. But I didn't understand why they would bother with tree trolls.

"This must be what's driving the trolls down the mountain and into the squares," Devon said. "They know that someone's hunting them."

The three of us moved back over to the ravine, with Devon shining his flashlight down the rocky slope again. We stared at the broken, murdered creatures, but there was nothing we could do for them. We didn't have any rope to climb down to get to them, and we didn't have any shovels or other tools to bury them.

Besides, all around us, blue, green, and red eyes appeared, glowing brighter and brighter as the other monsters crept closer and closer, drawn by the scent of fresh blood. Whoever had killed the troll was long gone, which meant that the danger had passed. But there were still other things lurking in the mist, hungry things that would be happy to snack on the dead troll—and us too, if we didn't leave soon.

"Let's go," Devon said. "There's nothing we can do for the trolls, and it's not safe for us to stay here any longer."

He moved away from the edge of the ravine. So did Felix. But I stayed behind, staring down at what was left of the dead tree trolls.

No blood, just bones and blades . . . bones and blades . . . bones and blades. . . .

For some reason, Seleste Draconi's warning whispered in my mind. I shivered, clutched my sword a little tighter, and hurried after my friends.

CHAPTER FIFTEEN

We made it back to the Sinclair mansion without running into any more problems—or finding any more dead monsters.

The three of us headed to the library, where Claudia was sitting behind her desk, shuffling through papers and pointedly ignoring Mo, who was lounging on a white velvet settee by the fireplace, sipping some delicious-smelling hot chocolate.

I went into the library first, and Mo straightened up.

"Where have you been, kid?" he asked. "I was getting worried."

"Oh, I picked up some company in the woods on the way back." I jerked my thumb over my shoulder.

Felix and Devon stepped inside the library, with Devon shutting the doors behind him.

"We need to talk," Devon said. "About exactly why you sent Lila to spy on Victor."

Claudia sighed, took off her silver reading glasses, and sat back in her chair. Mo looked at me, but I shrugged. I hadn't been here all that long, but I'd quickly learned that there was no stopping Devon when he wanted answers about something.

Devon marched over to Claudia's desk, crossed his arms over his chest, and glared at his mom. "Why didn't you tell me that you were sending Lila to spy on the Draconis? I'm the Family bruiser. I should know about these things."

"Because I knew that you'd try to go with her," Claudia said.

"And what would have been wrong with that?"

She arched her eyebrows at his harsh tone, but Devon didn't back down.

"Because Lila is a thief and a very good one at that," she said in a cool voice. "She's used to getting into and out of places she isn't supposed to be with no one seeing her."

"You'd better believe it," Mo chimed in, toasting me with his cup of hot chocolate and extolling my virtues, such as they were.

Claudia ignored him. "This job required the Family thief, not the Family bruiser. Besides, there was more risk of both of you getting caught if you went with her." She looked at Felix. "Although I see that you took Felix along with you . . . unless he had some other reason for going over to the Draconi compound?"

Felix gave her a tentative smile, but Claudia's gaze was hard and knowing. It looked like Devon wasn't the only one who'd noticed Felix and Deah making googly eyes at each other. Then again, it was Claudia's job to know everything that was going on with all the Sinclairs.

"Felix saw Lila leave, and we went after her," Devon lied. "But that doesn't change the fact that you should have told me what you asked Lila to do, especially given how dangerous it was. She's only been here a few weeks. You should have sent someone else, if you were that worried about Victor."

"I'm *always* that worried about Victor," Claudia snapped. "And with good reason. You know he's plotting something against the other Families, against *us*."

"And you sent Lila to try to find out what it was?" Devon shook his head. "You should have sent someone else. You should have sent *me*."

"And you need to set your feelings aside and trust Lila to do her job," she snapped again. "Just like you trust the guards to do theirs. Just like I trust you."

Devon opened his mouth to keep arguing with her, but I stepped up beside him.

"She didn't *send* me anywhere," I said. "The whole thing was my idea—hiking over to the Draconi property, sneaking into the castle, searching Victor's office. I *wanted* to do it."

He threw his hands up in the air. "Why would you want to do something like that? Something so dangerous? Do you know what the Draconis would have done if they'd caught you, Lila? Victor would have executed you on the spot."

Frustration blazed in his eyes, along with more than a little stomach-churning fear. He'd been worried about me. That was why he'd come looking for me. His obvious concern touched me, but it also annoyed me. Because Claudia was right—I was a good thief, a good fighter, and Devon needed to trust me to do the job I was here to do.

"It was a risk I was willing to take."

"Why?"

"You know *exactly* why—because Victor murdered my mom." I ground out the words, my hands clenching into fists, my whole body trembling with fury. "And I will do everything in my power to make sure that he pays for what he did to her. I don't care what I have to do or how dangerous it is. I would go right back over there this very *second* if I thought it would help us and hurt him."

Everyone stared at me. They could all hear the rage and need for vengeance in my voice.

"So what did you find out?" Claudia asked in a neutral tone, trying to diffuse the tension that blanketed the room.

"Lots of things. For starters, Victor, Blake, and Deah were having dinner with Nikolai Volkov. Carl and Katia were there too."

"What did they talk about?" she asked, leaning forward in her chair. "Tell me everything. I want to hear every single detail."

So I told her, Mo, Felix, and Devon everything that had happened while I'd been skulking around the Draconi castle, except for Felix and Deah hooking up in the greenlab.

"So Victor wants to combine the Draconis and Volkovs into one Family," Claudia murmured. "Interesting. That's a bold move."

"But Victor has to know the other Families would never allow that," Mo said. "It sounds to me like it's just a distraction. Victor gets everyone stirred up about a possible merger, while he's really planning something else."

Claudia picked up her glasses and *tap-tap-tapped* them on her desk. "For once, I agree with Mo. But if the merger isn't his main goal, then what is?"

"Maybe it has something to do with all those creepy files in his office," I said.

I filled them in on the files and e-mailed the photos I'd taken to everyone. Claudia, Mo, Felix, and Devon all pulled out their phones and scrolled through the pictures.

"All the files had these weird notes in them?" Claudia asked. "With all these *CC2* and other codes?"

"All the files have notes about the person's magic, but the Draconi files were the only ones that also had the codes. At least, from what I could tell."

Her green eyes glinted with interest. "How many Draconi files were there total? If you had to guess?"

I thought back, picturing the tall stack of files on Victor's desk. "Probably around twenty or thirty. However many people he has competing in the tournament. But that was just on his desk. He could have had more files in his office, maybe one on every single person in the Draconi Family. I didn't have time to search everywhere."

I thought of that secret space I'd discovered behind the stone dragon carving. Victor had *something* hidden back there, and I was going to find out what it was. But I didn't say anything to the others. Claudia might have risked my going over to the Draconi castle once, but I didn't know if she would approve a second trip. Then again, I didn't plan on telling her about it—until after I was back.

"Files on people, notes about their magic, talk of increasing their powers." Mo let out a low whistle. "It sounds like Victor is trying to build an army."

Claudia didn't say anything, but her mouth pinched with worry. This was not what she'd wanted to hear. But at least she knew that Victor was trying to ally with the Volkovs now, even if we had no clue what his files or notes were really about.

She looked at Mo. "This is more serious than we thought."

He nodded. "I'll reach out to my sources. See if anyone else knows that Victor is trying to merge with the Volkovs or why he has detailed records on everyone in the tournament, including his own people."

Mo pulled out his phone and started texting.

"There's one more thing," I said.

I told them about the dead tree trolls we'd found in the ravine close to the Draconi compound. I also pulled out the candy bar I'd taken from the trap and showed it to everyone, but it was just chocolate, the sort of thing you could buy at any store.

"That just sounds like Victor being Victor," Claudia said. "He's always been the sort to pull the wings off a butterfly just because he can. Trapping and killing tree trolls is right up his alley."

"Blake's too," Devon agreed. "Either one of them could have put that cage in the woods."

"But what about the troll we found next to that dumpster yesterday?" I asked. "That wasn't anywhere near the Draconi section of the Midway."

Devon shrugged. "Blake could have done that too. We ran into him and Deah a few minutes before we found the troll, remember?"

I nodded. He was probably right, but I still couldn't help but feel there was something more to the monsters' deaths. Sure, Victor and Blake delighted in their cruelty, but they also didn't waste their time on things that wouldn't help them. What could they possibly hope to gain from murdering a bunch of monsters?

I didn't know, but I had a bad, bad feeling that it was the key to Victor's plot against Claudia and all the other Families.

There was nothing else for us to report, so Devon, Felix, and I said our goodnights. Mo shooed us out of the library, claiming that we needed to get as much sleep as possible, since the Tournament of Blades would start bright and early again in the morning.

Yippee-skippee.

I went back to my bedroom, where Oscar was sitting on the front porch steps of his trailer. Tiny was on his back, snoozing in the corral, not looking like he had moved an inch in all the hours I'd been gone, although the tortoise's feet were twitching in time to the twangy country music drifting out of the pixie's trailer.

Oscar drained the rest of his honeybeer, then crumpled the miniature can in his hand and tossed it out onto the lawn, where it clattered against the ones already littering the grass. His violet gaze locked onto my coat. "I see you've been out."

I shrugged out of the sapphire-blue spidersilk and hung it up on one of the posters on the bed. "It's what I do."

"And where did you go skulking off to tonight?"

"Nowhere special," I said. "Just the Draconi compound."

"What!" Oscar's voice rose to a shriek that was loud enough to drown out the music.

Tiny grumbled and cracked one of his black eyes open, giving the pixie a reproachful look for disturbing his nap. Oscar ignored him and hopped to his feet, yanking his black cowboy hat off his head and whipping it back and forth in agitation.

"Why in the world would you go over *there*?" Oscar demanded, his voice climbing up another octave. "Don't you know how dangerous that is?"

I winced at his screech. "Of course I do. But it wasn't any more dangerous than living on the streets for four years. First Devon, now you. It seems like all anyone ever does around here is tell me what I shouldn't do."

"Well, maybe you should listen to us," Oscar sniped back. "Because we've been doing this a lot longer than you have, cupcake. Call me crazy, but I'm not in a hurry for you to get yourself killed, especially not over a piece of scum like Victor Draconi."

I winced, this time at my own stupid thoughtlessness. Oscar had lost a lot of friends to the Draconis over the years, so he was a bit sensitive about my putting myself in danger. In a way, the pixie and I were just alike. We didn't want to care too much about people because we knew how easily they could be taken away from us—and how much it hurt when your heart was broken over and over again.

"Oscar, I'm sorry. I didn't meant to worry you—"

"Forget it," he spat out. "I don't care to hear your lame-ass apology right now."

The pixie glared at me, then slapped his cowboy hat back onto his head, stormed into his trailer, and used one of his boots to kick the door shut behind him. The resulting *bang* was hard enough to rattle the trailer windows and make a few more loose shingles slip off the roof and drop down onto the lawn. A few seconds later, Oscar turned his music up as loud as it would go, assaulting my ears with the twangy tunes.

I sighed. So far tonight, I'd fought with Deah, Felix, and Devon, and now Oscar was upset too. Plus, I still had no idea what Victor was really up to, I'd gotten some creepy, cryptic warning from Seleste Draconi, who might or might not be able to see the future, and I'd stumbled upon a mass grave full of tortured, murdered monsters.

Perfect end to a perfectly miserable day.

I took a shower, but I was too restless and frustrated to go to bed, so I threw on a T-shirt, a pair of shorts, and some sneakers. Country music still blared from Oscar's trailer, so I went out onto the balcony and climbed up the drainpipe until I reached one of the mansion roofs that formed a wide terrace.

The terrace was open on three sides, and three lawn chairs were perched close to the iron railing to take advantage of the spectacular view of the Midway and all its flashing lights down in the valley below. But I wasn't here to admire the view. No, tonight I wanted to hit something—*repeatedly*.

So I headed over to a series of metal pipes that jutted out of the mansion wall, snaking up and down like an elaborate jungle gym. Several punching bags dangled from the posts. An open footlocker full of boxing gloves and other sporting gear sat close to the pipes, with a cooler full of ice and drinks over by the railing.

I didn't bother taping up my hands or grabbing a pair of gloves from the footlocker. Instead, I marched over to the closest bag, raised my fists, and just started hitting it. I slammed my fists into the heavy bag over and over again, all the while imagining that it was Victor's smug face I was pummeling. He'd gotten rid of my father and had murdered my mother, and now he was threatening to hurt everyone else I cared about. And I had no idea how to stop him.

Whack-whack-whack.

And the ironic thing was that Victor didn't even know I existed. Oh sure, he knew that Lila Merriweather was a new guard for the Sinclairs and was competing in the Tournament of Blades, but he didn't know that I was *really* Lila Sterling, the daughter of the woman he'd tortured and killed.

And he especially didn't know how much I hated him.

Whack-whack-whack.

Then again, it wasn't like I'd shouted my true identity from the rooftops. Just the opposite. I'd worked hard to keep who I really was on the down-low. Even among the Sinclairs, only a few folks knew the truth about who I was, what Victor had done to my mom, and why.

That had never bothered me before tonight, but going over to the Draconi mansion, seeing Victor so smug in his own home, so secure and confident in his own power, and reading through that file he had on me had flipped a switch inside me. Suddenly, I wanted him to know *exactly* who I was—and that I wasn't going to let him hurt another person I cared about. Not a single one.

Whack-whack-whack.

I whaled on the heavy bag until my knuckles bruised, my arms ached, and my legs trembled, but I kept right on hitting it. I drew back my fists for another strike when a voice sounded behind me.

"You keep that up and you won't have anything left for the tournament tomorrow."

I looked over my shoulder at Devon, who'd stepped through the door and out onto the terrace. "I don't care about the stupid tournament."

He let the door swing shut behind him. "You should. You could win it. Wouldn't that make you happy?"

I smashed my fist into the bag again. *Whack.* "Not as happy as hitting Victor would make me."

Devon didn't say anything, but sympathy softened his face. His dad had been murdered because of Grant Sanderson's schemes, and he'd felt the exact same rage and frustration that I was feeling right now. He stepped over and held out his hand. I looked at his outstretched fingers instead of into his eyes. I didn't want to see how sorry he felt for me.

But Devon was as stubborn as I was, and he wasn't going to take no for an answer. He stepped even closer, and I finally sighed, all the anger draining out of my body, and put my hand in his. Devon gave my fingers a soft, understanding squeeze, then led me over to the lawn chairs next to the railing.

We sat down, and I started to pull my hand out of his, but Devon wouldn't let go. Instead, he opened the cooler, reached down, and drew out a small bag of ice, which he gently placed on my bruised knuckles. I hissed at the cold sensation.

"You hit the heavy bag like you're trying to punch right

through it and you're wincing at a little ice? Crybaby," Devon teased.

I gave him a dark look, but that only made him grin wider.

He sat there, cradling my hand and keeping the ice in place before doing the same thing to my other hand. Even after the cold had eased the ache in my knuckles, Devon still held on, his touch firm but gentle.

"You want to talk about it?" he asked.

"No."

But he went on as though I hadn't spoken. "I know it must have been hard, being that close to Victor tonight and not being able to take a shot at him—especially after what he did to your mom."

I shrugged. "No harder than it's been all the other times I've seen him over the past four years."

Devon fell silent. He couldn't argue with that.

For several minutes, we both were quiet, staring out into the night. A faint breeze gusted down from the top of the mountain, clearing away some of the mist and letting us see the summer fireflies as they fluttered to and fro, their lights burning bright as they did their mating dance.

"You know," Devon said. "There might be a less dangerous way to get your revenge on Victor . . . and Blake too."

"How?"

He looked at me. "By winning the Tournament of Blades. Nothing makes Victor prouder than having a Draconi win, whether it's Deah or Blake or one of the guards. If you won, you would spoil the whole tournament for him. You would finally get to take away something he cares about."

"For a change," I muttered.

"Yeah. For a change."

Devon removed the ice from my knuckles and handed

me a cold bottle of water before grabbing one for himself. I mulled over his words. It would be satisfying to take something away from Victor, even if it was just winning the tournament. At the very least, it would prove that the Draconis didn't always get exactly what they wanted whenever they wanted it—at least for one day and in this one small way.

"All right," I said. "You've convinced me. I'll do my best in the tournament. Cross my heart and everything."

I drew an X over my heart, and Devon grinned again, the hot spark shimmering in his green eyes warming me from the inside out the way it always did. I dropped my gaze from his and took a long swig of my water, trying to cool off in more ways than one.

"So you'll do your best in the tournament, and Felix will do his best to juggle two girls at once," Devon snarked.

I laughed and almost spit out a mouthful of water. I gave Devon a mock glare. "You did that on purpose."

His grin widened. "Would I do something like that?"

"Absolutely."

He laughed. "Okay, okay. So I did do it on purpose. Just to cheer you up. But that doesn't mean it's not true about Felix, Deah, and Katia."

I snorted. "Oh, I doubt that Deah will let Felix juggle her. You should have seen how upset she was tonight when he came to the Draconi compound. Like it or not, she really does care about him."

"I know," Devon said. "I've seen the way she looks at him when she thinks no one's watching. But Katia likes him too. She was crazy about him last year."

"And what about you? Do you have a summer love who's come back to town for the tournament?" I teased, although my stomach felt strangely heavy as I said the words.

"Nope." He paused. "There was a girl once, though."

My heart squeezed tight in my chest, but I forced myself to ask the inevitable question. "And what was she like?"

He shifted in his lawn chair and stared out over the railing, his eyes locked on some spot far, far away in the Midway. "Well, we didn't actually get a chance to talk. All I really remember is that she had the most amazing blue eyes I'd ever seen." He looked at me. "And she still does."

Despite all the water I'd drunk, my throat felt as dry as a dirt road in the summertime. He was talking about the day we'd first met, when my mom had saved him from being kidnapped by the Draconis.

Every time I thought that I'd put some distance between us or done something that would piss him off for good, Devon came right back at me with something like that—something so sweet and so thoughtful and so damn *sincere* that it melted my defenses in a heartbeat. He didn't need his compulsion Talent to make me like him. He didn't need any magic at all.

He did it just by being himself.

But I was me, and I didn't do feelings. I didn't do attachments, and I especially didn't do relationships. Not since my mom had been murdered. I was a thief. I knew better than anyone else that it was much, much safer to keep my heart locked up tight, instead of putting it out there on display for everyone to see, where it could so easily be stolen—or broken again.

Devon kept staring at me, but I didn't let my eyes meet his. I didn't want my soulsight to kick in and show me everything he was feeling. Or how his emotions mirrored my own.

Instead, I chugged down the rest of my water and got to my feet. "Well, I should get some sleep. Tomorrow will be a busy day with the tournament. I need to rest up if I want to have any chance of winning."

"Yeah," Devon said, not bothering to hide the disappointment in his voice. "Busy."

He got to his feet as well. I gave him a small, nervous smile, still not looking into his eyes, then hurried around him, went over to the drainpipe, and climbed back down to the safe, lonely emptiness of my room.

CHAPTER SIXTEEN

"This is ridiculous," I grumbled. "Completely, utterly *ridiculous.*"

White feathers fell down in my face. I huffed out a breath, trying to blow them out of my eyes, but the feathers dropped right back down to where they'd been before. Annoyed, I reached up, yanked several of them out of the brim of my black cavalier hat, and stuck them in a nearby trash can. The motions made my black cloak billow out around my shoulders before dropping neatly back into place, while my black, knee-high boots *creaked* with every step I took. Tight black pants and a sleeveless white silk shirt completed my ridiculous ensemble.

"Tell me again why we have to dress up like extras from a *Three Musketeers* movie while we're fighting?"

"Because the tourists expect us to dress like this. It's all part of the show for them." Poppy grinned and tipped her purple hat at me. "Just be glad that your Family colors are black and white. I look like I'm wearing a bunch of grapes on my head."

I grinned. "Well, as long as the rubes are entertained."

She grinned again and rolled her eyes.

It was day two of the Tournament of Blades, and Poppy, Devon, and I were standing by the chain-link fence that ringed the stadium floor, waiting for the one-on-one matches to start. The other competitors milled around the area, all of them dressed like us in sleeveless white shirts and black pants, with cloaks and hats bearing their Family colors.

I looked up at the Sinclair box, where Claudia, Reginald, and Mo were sitting, with Oscar zipping around and around them just like he had yesterday. The pixie had started stuffing himself with junk food the second we'd gotten to the fairgrounds, and he was now on his third cinnamon-sugar pretzel. With his sugar rush, I half expected him to forget there was a sheet of glass in the front of the box and fly straight into it.

I scanned the rest of the crowd, my gaze finally locking onto the Draconi box. Victor was sitting up there, along with Seleste, who was gesturing with her hands and seemed to be talking a mile a minute. She was wearing a pretty white sundress with black polka dots, and her blond hair was sleeked back into a high bun, making her look far more normal and sane than she had last night.

Seleste noticed me staring and actually got to her feet, stepped up to the front of the glass, and waved at me, her whole face lighting up with happiness.

I wondered if she remembered me, Lila, from last night, or if she still thought that I was my dead mom. Hard to tell. Either way, I didn't wave back at her.

The officials, still dressed in their neutral white, stepped onto the stadium floor. The obstacle course was gone, but the cold spring and rock formations remained, since they were a natural part of the landscape. They would make the duels more exciting, providing obstacles for the fighters to maneuver around, duck behind for cover, or use as springboards to lash out at each other. A separate, foot-high ring of stones enclosed the larger rocks and the cold spring.

This was where the one-on-one matches would take place. Devon had told me that a smaller version of the rope ladder was usually included in the ring as well. Not this time. Maybe the officials had realized that yesterday hadn't been an accident and didn't want a repeat performance.

A low drumbeat rang out, and the crowd hushed, anticipating the start of today's action.

"And now, last year's returning champion, Deah Draconi!" a voice rang out through the sound system.

After yesterday's fiasco with the obstacle course, Deah had been seeded first as the reigning winner and had the privilege of having the first match of the day. She strode out into the center of the stadium, her red cloak rippling behind her like a wave of blood. Deah stopped outside the stone competition ring and bowed low to one side of the stadium, then the other. Cheers erupted, and a smile split her face. In that moment, she seemed genuinely happy.

Then she glanced up at the Draconi box. Seleste was on her feet again, cheering and clapping, but Victor stayed seated, his hands folded in his lap. Deah's smile slipped off her face, and her eyes dimmed, although she covered it up by whipping off her red hat and cloak and passing them over to one of the officials.

Deah's competition, a Volkov guard, was announced. He also removed his hat and cloak, and the two of them faced each other in the center of the stone ring. Devon had explained the tournament rules to me on the ride down here this morning. For today's rounds, everyone could use their weapons of choice, and the person to draw first blood won. Debilitating or killing blows were not allowed and would get you tossed out of the tournament immediately. Healers from each Family, including Felix and Angelo, were standing by the white tent with their magic and bottles of stitch-sting, ready to patch up the folks who got bloodied first.

The official in the ring with Deah and the Volkov guard

raised his hand, then dropped it and scurried out of the way, and the match began.

The Volkov guard went on the attack, raising his sword high, charging at Deah, and trying to overpower her with his opening blow. She gave him a cool look, then spun out of the way. The guard stumbled past her, but she was already whipping around and going on the offensive.

I'd never seen Deah fight before, but I could see why she was the tournament champion. She was quick and decisive, with no wasted movement or effort. The Volkov guard had a strength Talent, and she knew better than to engage him head on. Instead, she kept moving around him, always making him skirt the rock formations or hop over them to come after her, then sliding away. A minute into the fight, and the guard was already sweating and sucking wind, while Deah looked as calm and composed as ever.

"She's good," I said. "Much better than I'd thought she would be."

"Why do you say it like that?" Poppy asked. "Did you think she won by cheating or something?"

I shrugged. "She's a Draconi. The thought had occurred to me."

Devon shook his head. "There's no way for anyone to cheat. Not in the individual matches. The officials make sure of it. We can use our magic and weapons, but they make sure that's *all* we're using."

Just like he said, the five officials were stationed around the ring, watching the competitors' every move.

Deah hopped up onto a long, jagged, three-foot-high rock. The Volkov guard slammed his sword down onto the rock, hard enough to make chips fly out of it, but Deah had already skipped out of the way and jumped off the other end. I couldn't help but be impressed. With moves like that, she would make a good thief.

The guard let out a loud, frustrated bellow, knowing that she was just toying with him. So he screamed, raised his sword overhead, and charged at her, which was exactly what she wanted.

At the last second, Deah slid to the left and sliced her sword across his bare upper arm, opening up a long cut. The guard yelped, knowing he'd lost. And, as if that wasn't bad enough, he hadn't realized that Deah had positioned herself directly in front of the spring, and he stumbled past her and plunged headfirst into the cold water. He came up sputtering.

"First blood!" an official called out, stepping into the stone ring and raising Deah's sword hand, declaring her the winner.

Deah grinned, and cheers rang out. Up in the Draconi box, Victor clapped politely, but Seleste surged to her feet, put her fingers to her lips, and let out a loud, ear-splitting whistle that sounded through the whole stadium. Victor frowned as though displeased by his wife's antics, but Deah waved at her mom, happy at the show of affection.

My heart squeezed with jealousy. It was just like something my mom would have done, if she'd still been alive.

Poppy, Devon, and I were standing by the fence gate, and Deah had to walk past us to get out of the stadium.

"Nice fight," I said.

Poppy and Devon called out their congratulations as well.

"Thanks." Deah gave me a guarded look, nodded at Poppy and Devon, and then headed for the Draconi tent.

Poppy, Devon, and I hung out and watched the other matches, cheering for the Sinclairs and Itos and clapping for everyone who won, even the Draconis.

About halfway through the first round, it was Devon's turn to fight, and he strode out to the center of the ring to some of the loudest cheers of the entire day. Everyone knew, liked, and respected Devon, and I even spotted some of the Draconis cheering for him. Not Blake, of course, who openly jeered and *boo-boo-booed* like the jackass he was, but Deah politely clapped the way she had for all the competitors.

Devon was facing a woman from the Ito Family who was armed with two short swords. Devon loosened up his shoulders, then raised his own sword and faced her. The official stepped out of the way, and the fight was on.

The woman had a speed Talent, and she came at Devon almost too fast to follow, swinging her swords every which way. But he recognized the pattern and defended against it. Back and forth they fought, with the Ito guard moving faster and faster, trying to rattle Devon, but he kept his cool and matched her move for move. Not only that, but he started pushing the fight toward the left side of the ring where some of the smaller rock formations were.

Finally, when she was going as fast as possible, Devon kicked a baseball-size stone at her. The Ito guard lurched out of the way, but the unexpected motion threw her off balance long enough for Devon to step up, slice his sword across her arm, and win the match.

Poppy clapped, but I hooted and hollered, along with the rest of the Sinclairs and a good portion of the crowd. Poppy went over to speak to the Ito guard, while Devon jogged back over to me.

"You did great!" I said.

Devon grinned, his eyes bright and happy. He rushed forward, picked me up, and swung me around before setting me back down. Our gazes locked, and a hot spark sizzled in my chest, followed by a happy, dizzying rush of feeling that made my toes curl inside my boots. I suddenly felt too warm, and it wasn't from the sun blazing down overhead.

I cleared my throat, stepped out of his arms, and clapped Devon on the shoulder. "Good match."

"Thanks."

He held my gaze another second, making sure that I knew exactly what he was feeling, then turned and went over to the Ito guard to shake hands with her.

I let out a breath, but I went over and joined him, Poppy, and the guard. Despite all my fears and worries about Devon and this thing between us, there was no place I would rather be right now than celebrating with him.

The day wore on, and the matches continued.

Blake was up next, and he used his strength Talent to slice an Ito guard's sword in two. Even though the guard raised his hands, ceding the match, Blake still stepped forward and sliced his sword across the man's arm just because he could. Yeah, he was a complete and total jerk that way.

Vance won his match as well, using his strength and speed Talents to easily defeat a Salazar guard. Vance had kept his cloak and hat on while fighting, and when the match was finished, he pulled his hat off his head and swept into a low bow, as though he were an old-fashioned knight. Of course, the tourists loved it, cheering, taking photos, and chanting his name. I rolled my eyes. All the rubes were doing was inflating Vance's already enormous ego.

On his way out of the stadium, Vance stopped and smirked at me. "See? I told you that they'd be cheering for me. Try not to suck too much out there, okay, Lila?"

He swaggered past me and went over to Katia, who was standing by the fence a few feet away. Vance had been chatting up Katia all day long, although she kept ignoring him and looking over to where Felix was stationed with the healers. I even saw her wave to him a couple of times. Felix waved back, but his smile was strained.

Poppy was up next, and she used her speed Talent to run circles around a Volkov guard, easily winning the match.

Then it was Katia's turn. Agile, cunning, always on the move. She was a good fighter, one of the best I'd seen, right up there with Deah. But one thing seemed to be missing—her speed.

Katia didn't seem to be using any of her speed, her magic, today. Oh, she hopped up onto the rock formations and back off, leaped over the smaller stones, and skirted along the edges of the cold spring, but she didn't do any of those things any faster than a regular mortal would have. It was odd, especially given her blazing speed on the obstacle course yesterday. Maybe she just hadn't found her groove yet. But she still managed to slice her sword across the arm of her opponent when the Draconi guard tripped.

Katia smiled and waved, but a scowl spread over her face the second she turned away from the crowd. She stormed over to the fence and slammed her sword into the gate, shoving it open. When she realized that I was watching, she stopped, her cheeks red and her hazel eyes bright. I couldn't tell whether she was embarrassed or angry I'd seen her mini-meltdown.

"I should have done better," Katia growled, trying to explain her temper tantrum.

"You won. That's all that matters, right?"

She thought about it. "Yeah, you're right. Thanks, Lila."

She flashed me a smile, then moved over to her previous spot along the fence, accepting congratulations from the other Volkov guards.

Vance went over and started talking to her again. Instead of ignoring him the way she had before, Katia stared up at him, a thoughtful expression on her face. Then she sidled a little closer and started talking animatedly to Vance, who was hanging on her every word.

Katia's match had been right before mine, which was the last one of the opening round. To my surprise, a few nervous butterflies started flying around in my stomach. I handed my hat and cloak to Devon, who grinned.

"You'll do great," he said. "I know you will. Go out there and show everyone what you can do. Especially Victor Draconi."

I'd never been a fan of pep talks, but that was exactly what I needed to hear right now. I nodded and grinned back at him. Then I drew in a breath, pushed through the gate, and made my way to the stone ring in the center of the stadium.

From what I could remember of Felix's ramblings yesterday, my opponent was a Salazar guard around my age with a strength Talent who was holding a sword that looked more like a crowbar than a black blade. Even though it was twice as large as my sword, the guard moved the weapon from one hand to the other like it didn't weigh anything at all, making the muscles in his biceps ripple with the smooth motions.

The announcer called out the guard's name—Julio Salazar—and he waved to the crowd. Then it was my turn to step up and face the music, such as it was.

"And now making her tournament debut . . . Lila Merriweather!" the announcer yelled.

Cheers rang out, along with the usual *boo-boo-boos* from Blake, but I tuned those out and raised my sword high, soaking in all the happy noise. When the cheers, claps, and whistles had died down, I nodded at my opponent. Julio did the same, and we both raised our weapons and waited for the official to give the signal.

"For honor . . . for glory . . . for Family!"

The second the official stepped out of the way, Julio Salazar charged at me, lifting his sword high, wanting to smash my weapon out of my hand with one hard blow. I tightened my grip on my black blade and let him come at me, the same way Deah had with her opponent. She might have her mimic magic, but I had my transference power, and I was going to put it to good use.

Julio smashed his sword into mine, the blow strong enough to make me fall to one knee. The crowd gasped, thinking I was done for already, but it was all part of my plan. Julio grunted and bore down, trying to either make me let go of my sword or snap the blade outright, but I tightened my grip and waited—just waited.

Even as he pressed forward, my transference power kicked in, magic blossoming in my body like a frost-covered flower unfurling its icy petals one by one by one. I closed my eyes a moment, centering myself and directing the stolen strength flowing through my veins down into my legs. Then I shot to my feet, throwing Julio up and away from me.

The crowd gasped again, this time at my sudden surge of strength. I grinned. If only they knew. But I was perfectly happy letting everyone think I had a strength Talent. In a way, I did. People just didn't realize that their magic was what made me stronger.

Julio Salazar didn't realize it either. He frowned, whipped up his sword, and smashed it down on top of mine again, thinking that his magic, his power, was greater than mine. But all he did was make me as strong as he was—and then some.

That chill of magic grew and grew in my veins, until my whole body was ice cold and my breath frosted faintly in the air, although the sun was so bright and hot that I doubted anyone else could see it but me, not even Julio.

With the stolen strength, I threw Julio off a second time, and then I went on the offensive. Again and again, I smashed my sword into his, seemingly using the same brute strength he'd shown. Well, really, it *was* the same brute strength since it was his own power I was turning against him.

Julio blocked my attacks and tried to punch me in the face with his free hand, but I ducked the blow, spun away, and came right back up swinging at him. One, two, three moves later, I sliced my sword across his arm, drawing first blood.

"Winner!" the official called out, stepping into the ring, grabbing my arm, and raising it high.

The crowd cheered. Devon was clapping and yelling as loud as he could, and so were Felix and Angelo with the healers. Up in the Sinclair box, Claudia, Reginald, and Mo were all on their feet clapping and cheering, with Oscar flying dizzying circles around them.

I grinned and waved to all my friends, then turned and waved to the other side of the stadium. But the smile froze on my face. Because I'd forgotten that the Sinclairs and the tourists weren't the only ones watching me.

So was Victor Draconi.

Up in the Draconi box, Seleste cheered, clapped, and whistled as loudly for me as she had for Deah. I wondered why she would do that. Maybe she thought I was my mom again.

Either way, Victor wasn't happy about his wife's enthusiasm. He looked at her, then me. Even across this distance, his golden gaze locked with my blue one, and my soulsight kicked in, letting me feel all his cold curiosity about me.

My smile vanished, and the chill I felt now had nothing to do with the lingering magic running through my body. No, the icy sensation creeping up my spine had everything to do with Victor. I wondered what sort of notes he would add to his file on me. I shivered. Part of me didn't want to know.

I might have been invisible to Victor before, but I wasn't anymore. And I wasn't so sure that was a good thing.

CHAPTER SEVENTEEN

Another round of matches was held, with the two rounds whittling the field down from one hundred twenty-eight to sixty-four and then thirty-two. Tomorrow's rounds would determine the tournament winner. Devon, Poppy, and I all advanced, along with Deah, Katia, Blake, and Vance.

The competitors congratulated each other a final time, even those who had lost, and everyone was in a good mood as we headed to the Family tents to change clothes. I was grateful to strip off my white shirt, black pants, and black boots and replace them with a blue T-shirt, gray cargo shorts, and gray sneakers. I also belted my sword around my waist again. The person who had sabotaged the rope ladder was still out there, and I wasn't going to be taken by surprise again.

I grabbed my duffel bag, then streamed out of the fairgrounds with my friends. The matches had taken most of the day. It was after seven now, and the summer heat and humidity had finally eased. But instead of going back to the parking lots, getting into their cars, and driving home, everyone headed out of the fairgrounds and stepped onto some gray cobblestone paths that wound into the trees.

"Now what?" I asked. "Why aren't we going back to the mansion?"

Felix grinned. "And miss the after-party? Are you kidding? It's the best part of the tournament."

"After the first day of competition, everyone gets together for a little food, music, and fun," Devon explained. "It's tradition. Tomorrow night's party after the tournament ends will be even bigger and better."

I didn't particularly want to party, but Devon and Felix grabbed my hands and dragged me along. We walked about half a mile through the woods before the trees opened up onto a sandy beach. It was odd, seeing such gleaming, white sand in the middle of the West Virginia mountains, especially since we were hundreds of miles away from the ocean, but it was another thing that made Cloudburst Falls special. Every year, the town officials, with the Families' help, trucked in tons of sand to create and maintain a beach that wrapped around the lake.

Bloodiron Lake had always been one of my favorite places to visit. It looked like one of the vacation postcards you could buy from any cart on the Midway—the white, sandy shore, the glittering, deep blue surface of the water, the green pine trees surrounding everything. Even the sky was perfect, clear, bright, and dotted with puffy, marshmallow clouds.

Wooden picnic shelters ringed the perimeter of the lake, set back in the grass that surrounded the sandy shore. All of the shelters featured metal grills, along with heavy-duty, blue and green fiberglass picnic tables where folks could sit and enjoy their hamburgers and hot dogs.

The butlers and pixies from the Families must have come over here as soon as the tournament had ended because the grills were already going strong, with smoke wafting through the air. My stomach rumbled in anticipation. Was there any better summertime scent than grilled food?

A line had already formed in front of the grills, where

Reginald was overseeing Oscar and the rest of the Sinclair pixies. Devon, Felix, and I got in line, and soon I was loading up a plate with a cheeseburger, topped with plenty of bacon, along with macaroni salad, fresh summer veggies, and a mound of cheese fries sprinkled with, you guessed it, more bacon.

I grabbed a cup of lemonade, then followed Devon and Felix over to a picnic table where Poppy and Katia were sitting.

Katia flashed Felix a smile and scooted over to make room for him. He hesitated, but I bumped his shoulder with mine, nudging him forward. He shot me a dirty look, then smiled back at Katia and sat down beside her. I took the seat next to Poppy, with Devon sliding in on the bench next to Felix and across from me.

Everyone must have been as starved as I was, because we spent the next few minutes chowing down on our food. The cheeseburger was so good that I polished it off, then went over and got a second one, this time with even more bacon. The macaroni salad was rich and creamy, the veggies were cool and crunchy, and the fries were the perfect mix of crispy potatoes, ooey, gooey cheese, and smoky bacon. The ice-cold lemonade was tart and sweet and just the thing to hit the spot on a hot, humid day.

By the time we scarfed down our burgers and fries, Reginald and the pixies had set out several desserts, including a chilled strawberry pie topped with vanilla-bean ice cream that was so cold and sweet it made my teeth ache—but in a good way. I had three big pieces of pie, more than anyone else.

Katia smiled, amused by all the empty paper plates littering the table around me. "You must have been hungry, Lila."

Felix rolled his eyes. "She's *always* hungry. You should see how much bacon she eats for breakfast every day."

"And why is that a problem?" I said. "Besides, fighting and upholding the Family honor and stuff is hard work."

Felix rolled his eyes again. "Yeah. That's it."

Katia, Poppy, and Devon all laughed.

"Well, I'd say that Lila has earned all the bacon she can eat," Katia said. "I saw you fight. You have a strength Talent, right?"

"Right," I said in a neutral voice. "Just a minor one, though."

"That must come in handy, especially during the tournament."

"Sure," I said, staring at her so she wouldn't realize that I was lying.

Devon and Felix both frowned. They knew how important it was that no one realize the truth. Strength was a common Talent, but my transference power was not. It was the kind of rare magic that people would kill to possess, just like Devon's compulsion power.

But Katia didn't seem to notice our unease and turned her attention to Devon. "And you did well too. So did Poppy."

Devon and Poppy both murmured their thanks, and I decided that it would be better to talk about something else, anything else, than what magic we'd used to help us win our matches.

"You did good too, Katia," I said. "You moved really well out there."

She scowled and shook her head. "Not well enough. Not *fast* enough. I didn't think that guy would be as good as he was. I almost let him get the best of me. But it won't happen again. I'll make sure of that."

She looked at me, her hazel eyes locking with mine. A second later, her rock-hard determination flooded my body, along with hot, desperate need.

Sweat popped out on my forehead from the strength and burning heat of her emotions. I dropped my gaze from hers, but her fiery feelings kept simmering in my own body. Katia's desire to win the tournament was much more intense than I'd expected.

We talked about the tournament for a few more minutes, along with music, movies, and more. All around us, folks finished their food and got up from their tables. Some of them drifted back to the fairgrounds to play carnival games or get junk food, but most folks headed down to the water's edge to bake themselves on the beach, play volleyball and badminton in the sand, and swim out to the floating platforms in the middle of the lake and back again.

Katia got up, dumped her plate and cup in the trash, and came back over to our table. She gave Felix a sly smile.

"You want to get out of here?" she asked in a soft voice. "Go to our spot at the old boathouse and finally catch up?"

"Um, well, sure," Felix said. "That sounds . . . nice."

Katia frowned, hearing the reluctance in his voice. "Is something wrong? I thought that we'd hang out tonight, just like we did last year. I've been looking forward to it. Haven't you?"

"Sure," Felix repeated, trying to smile but not having much luck at it. "It'll be nice to talk with an old friend."

Her frown deepened. "Old friend?"

"Well, yeah," he said. "That's what we are now, right?"

She kept staring at him, as if she couldn't believe what he'd said—that he'd just put her squarely in the friend zone.

Devon got to his feet. "Lila, Poppy, why don't we go down to the lake and let Felix and Katia talk in private?"

Poppy and I shot to our feet, along with Felix. We didn't want to stay and see what was about to happen, but

Katia had other ideas. She didn't want to wait to talk to Felix alone. Instead, she took a step back, slapped her hands on her hips, and glared at him.

"Are you avoiding me?" she asked point-blank.

A guilty blush crept up Felix's neck. "Of course not. Why would you think that?"

"Oh, I don't know—maybe the fact that you haven't called me and that you've barely responded to any of my texts while I've been in town. Plus, every time I see you, you always run off somewhere else."

That guilty blush flooded his cheeks, turning his bronze skin as red as a tomato. Felix might be a great flirt, but he was a terrible liar, and he couldn't even look at her without wincing—a guilty expression if ever there was one.

"Come on, guys," Devon repeated. "Let's go down to the lake."

Katia snapped up her hand, stopping him. "Don't bother. This won't take long."

She kept staring at Felix. He looked back at her for a second, then dropped his gaze and started drawing a line in the grass with the toe of his sneaker.

Katia's eyes narrowed, and her face hardened with understanding. "There's someone else, isn't there? That's why you stopped calling and texting me a few months ago."

Felix winced again. "Yeah. I met someone earlier this year. I didn't plan on it. It just . . . happened."

"I understand." But the cold, clipped tone in Katia's voice said the opposite. "Who is she?"

"Does it really matter?"

Hurt shimmered in her hazel eyes. "No, I suppose it doesn't."

She kept looking at Felix, and he back at her, with Devon, Poppy, and I all shifting uncomfortably on our feet.

"Well, then, I guess there's nothing else to say," Katia said in a stiff voice. "I'll see you guys around."

"Katia, wait—" Felix called out, but she ignored him.

Katia hurried away from the picnic table. She started toward the trees, but Vance called out to her. Katia looked at Vance, then Felix. After a second, she squared her shoulders and went over to where Vance was sitting with his friends.

Vance got up, pulled off his hat, and swept his cloak out around him, just as smoothly as he had during the tournament. He was the only person on the beach who hadn't bothered to change out of his ren-faire hat, cloak, and boots. He grabbed Katia's hand and pressed a kiss to her knuckles, still playing the whole knight shtick. Then he straightened up, grinned, and started talking. Katia laughed at whatever he said, although the sound seemed brittle and hollow to me.

Devon, Poppy, and I all looked at Felix.

"Way to go, Romeo," I said. "Way to let her down easy."

Felix sighed. "I didn't mean to hurt her. Really, I didn't."

"I know," I said in a softer voice. "But you did anyway."

He looked at Katia, who had left Vance behind and was heading toward the trees by herself. "Maybe I should go after her. Try to explain."

Poppy shook her head. "Maybe later . . . a whole lot later. Right now, she probably wants to be alone. I would."

Felix stared at the trees where Katia had disappeared. "Yeah, you're probably right."

Devon put his hand on Felix's shoulder. "Let's go play volleyball or something. Give Katia some time to cool off. I'm sure she'll come around in a day or two. She might even find someone else that she likes before she leaves town. Vance certainly seems interested in her."

"Yeah. I guess you're right."

Felix stared at the trees a few seconds longer before he let Devon steer him away from the picnic table.

Despite the awkwardness with Katia, the four of us went down to the beach, grabbed a volleyball and an open net, and started a friendly game, with Devon and Felix facing off against Poppy and me.

I leaped up into the air to get the ball that Devon had tried to hit over me, then spiked it back over the net. Felix dove for the ball, but all he got for his trouble was a mouthful of sand.

"Ha!" I said, pumping my fist. "Match point! We win!"

Poppy and I grinned and high-fived each other. Okay, okay, so maybe the game wasn't *entirely* friendly. Or maybe I was just that competitive. Yeah, it was definitely that last one.

Felix got up and dusted the white sand off his khaki cargo shorts. "Did you have to spike the ball right in my face?"

"Nope," I replied. "That was just an added bonus."

He gave me a sour look, but we all laughed, including Felix.

By the time we finished our second match, which Poppy and I also won, it was after eight, and the sun had started to sink behind the mountains. Pixies zipped along the sand, building bonfires on the beach, and the orange-red flames flickered up into the twilight sky, chasing away the worst of the shadows.

When the pixies were done with the fires, they zipped along the beach a second time, passing out chocolate bars, along with marshmallows and graham crackers so we could all make s'mores. Devon grabbed a couple of metal skewers and threaded marshmallows onto them, while Felix stacked chocolate bars and graham crackers together.

"Not too brown," Poppy said. "I want to taste the marshmallow, not burned goo."

"Yes, ma'am," Devon said, saluting her with the skewer of marshmallows. "Some lightly toasted marshmallows, coming up."

He held the marshmallows over the fire for a few seconds, and then we all stuffed ourselves with s'mores. Crispy graham crackers, melting chocolate, sticky marshmallows. So good.

Poppy drifted off to talk to some other folks she knew, and Felix tagged along with her. That left Devon and me alone in front of the bonfire. Even though it had been in the eighties today, it was cool down here by the lake, now that the sun had fully set, and I found myself shivering.

"Here," Devon murmured. "Maybe this will help."

He reached into his duffel bag, pulled out his black cloak, and draped it over my shoulders. I wrapped the cloak around my body, while Devon sat down in the sand beside me.

We didn't talk for several minutes, just enjoying the *crackle-crackle* of the fire, the steady, soothing, *splash-splash-splash* of the lake against the shore, and the distant murmurs of music and conversation that floated up and down the beach.

Devon reached up and slid his arm around my shoulder. Startled, I looked at him.

"You're not the only one who's cold," he said, grinning.

"Oh. Right."

I lifted up the cloak, and he slid in next to me, the warmth of his body soaking into my own and driving away the chill. I breathed in, and his crisp, pine scent filled my nose, even stronger than the trees around us. We stayed like that for a while, my body tense and rigid, Devon's totally relaxed.

I don't know when exactly it happened, but I slowly started to relax too. Devon scooted a little closer to me. I turned to look at him and realized just how close he was. I tried to duck my head, but I was too slow, and my eyes locked with his. My soulsight kicked in, letting me see just how much he cared about me, letting me feel just how intense that spark was deep down inside his heart, the one that flared a little hotter and brighter every time he looked at me.

The care, the feeling, the spark—it all terrified me.

Because I felt the exact same way about him.

We'd had this connection, this warmth, these feelings between us ever since I'd come to work for the Family, and with each passing day, they got harder and harder to ignore, no matter how much I tried.

But I couldn't let myself fall for Devon. Not when I was supposed to be protecting him and the rest of the Sinclairs. Not when I was trying to get my revenge on Victor. And especially not when I was planning to leave Cloudburst Falls as soon as he and the others were safe.

"Lila," Devon whispered and leaned in even closer to me.

The hot spark in his green, green eyes, the husky sound of his voice, the warm kiss of his breath against my cheek. It was all so romantic—and far too much to bear.

Before I even really knew what I was doing, I shot to my feet, mumbled an excuse, and ran away, just like I had last night on the terrace when he'd held my hands and iced my bruised knuckles. His cloak flew off my shoulders and landed in the sand, but I was too busy stalking away as fast as I could to care.

"Lila—" Devon called out, but I ducked my head, wrapped my arms around my body, and kept moving, as though I hadn't heard him.

I couldn't afford to *let* myself hear him.

A few more folks called out to me, including Poppy and Felix, but I didn't feel like talking to anyone, so I left the beach behind and stepped into the trees. It was darker here, almost pitch black in some spots, but I could see as clearly as if it were noon, thanks to my sight. I stepped off the trail and kept going, moving parallel to the tree line and deeper and deeper into the underbrush at the same time. Finally, I stopped and peered back through the trees at the beach.

Devon stood by the bonfire, looking in this direction, but he couldn't see me through the trees and shadows that separated us. He took a few steps forward, as though he was going to come after me, but he stopped himself. He stared this way for another minute before turning and facing the fire again.

I let out a tense breath, not sure if I was relieved or disappointed he hadn't come after me—

"Looks like I'm not the only one with boy problems," a voice called out.

Branches rustled, twigs cracked, and Katia stepped out of the shadows and up beside me. She followed my gaze and looked through the trees at Devon.

"You should snatch him up while you can," she said. "He's one of the good guys."

I sighed. "I know."

"Then what's the problem?"

I sighed again. "I'm not one of the good girls."

She gave me a puzzled look, but I wasn't about to explain my complicated life, so I decided on a simple answer.

"I'm supposed to be Devon's bodyguard," I said. "Not that he really needs one, but that's my job in the Family, which means that anything else between us makes my job . . . complicated."

Katia snorted. "Complicated? Really? The only decision you should have to make about a guy like that is where you're going to go to make out with him."

I winced. "I'm sorry. I'm being stupid and insensitive. I shouldn't even be talking to you about this."

She snorted again. "Why? Because Felix dumped me? Don't feel bad about that. You didn't dump me, and you're obviously not the girl he's seeing. Besides, it's not like Felix and I made any promises or anything to each other last summer."

"Then what is it like?"

She shrugged. "I just . . . really liked him. And the closer the tournament got, the more I thought about him. The more I was looking forward to seeing him again."

Katia looked out over the beach where Felix was standing with Poppy and the Ito guards. Poppy was talking and nibbling on some toasted marshmallows. Felix was right next to her, but he wasn't paying any attention to Poppy. Instead, he was staring at someone at the next bonfire down the beach.

Deah.

She had a cup of lemonade in her hand and seemed to be listening to Blake talk to the other Draconis. But she was staring right back at Felix, ignoring the people around her, many of whom stopped and congratulated her on her victories in the opening rounds of the tournament. Deah finally had to look away from Felix when two of the Draconi guards stepped forward, scooped her up, and started carrying her around on their shoulders. Even from here, I could hear her shrieks of surprise and laughter, and so could Katia.

"I hate people like her." Katia spat out the words.

"What do you mean?"

"People who get everything they want all the time, without even trying. Without even working for it. Without doing *anything* for it." She threw her hand out. "Look at her. They're carrying her around like she's already won the tournament. She's rich, pretty, a great fighter, and her dad is the most powerful man in town. Her life is perfect."

I thought of Deah's mom, all the strange things Seleste said, and how Deah had to watch her all the time. "I'm sure that Deah has her own problems, just like everyone else."

Katia let out a bitter laugh. "I doubt that. At the very least, her father's not a drunk like mine."

I followed her dark, hazel gaze over to the picnic table where Carl Volkov was sitting. Well, *sitting* wasn't really the right word. He was slumped over the table, his head resting in the crook of his elbow. A silver flask was cupped in his free hand, and I was willing to bet it was empty of whatever liquor it had contained.

"I'm sorry. That must be tough."

Katia shrugged. "Not anymore. Not since I quit expecting him to care about anything besides drinking. Besides, I'll be eighteen in a few months. Then I can leave him in New York and move down here like I want to. Uncle Nikolai's already promised me a position. If I win the tournament, he might even name me the Volkov bruiser."

I stared at her, wondering why she was spilling her guts to me, since I was more or less a complete stranger. Then again, maybe it was easier to reveal your secrets to a stranger, someone who didn't know you and had no expectations about you and your feelings.

"Once I'm down here working for the Volkovs, I can take the prize money I'll get from winning the tournament and go to college at night," Katia continued. "And once I leave New York, I don't plan on seeing my father ever again."

"Don't you think that's a little harsh?"

She scoffed. "Are you kidding? With a dad who's drunk

all the time? Please. My mom died in a car accident when I was ten, and I've been taking care of myself ever since then. I'm tired of looking out for him too. Besides, *he's* the dad. He's the one who should be responsible, instead of crawling up in a bottle all day, every day."

Even though it was dark, I could still see the glimmer of tears in her eyes, but Katia ruthlessly blinked them back.

"I've spent the last two years busting my ass at tournaments during the summer, trying to save up for college. But all he does is drink away my prize money. Well, not anymore." She lifted her chin. "Once I win this tournament and get that money, I'll be set, and I'll never have to think about him again."

Katia gave me a tight smile, then headed out of the trees. She stopped at the picnic table long enough to give her dad a disgusted look, then walked down to the beach. Blake waved her over, and she joined the Draconis by their bonfire. In a minute, Katia was laughing, talking, and joking with Blake and the other guards, as though nothing was wrong.

I stayed where I was, thinking about all the hurt I'd seen in her eyes, as well as her words. Katia wanted to escape, and so did I. But she was running away from something bad, and I, well, I just didn't want to get my heart broken again. Before tonight, I'd never really thought about how sad and lonely that made me.

Or how much of a coward.

CHAPTER EIGHTEEN

I stayed in the trees a few more minutes and got my turbulent emotions under control before going back down to the beach.

It was getting late, and the pixies were carrying buckets of water up from the lake to douse the bonfires, while everyone else was packing up to go home. Devon was shoving the cloak he'd draped around my shoulders into his duffel bag when I reached him and Felix.

"Hey," I said.

"Hey," Devon replied in a cool voice, his face blank, deliberately not looking at me.

Maybe that was a good thing. I didn't want to stare into his eyes and see how much I'd hurt him—*again*. Maybe Katia was right. Maybe I was being stupid. Maybe I should just give in to my feelings and risk everything.

Because Devon really was one of the good guys. He cared about me, and I cared about him. Why shouldn't we be together? What was I so afraid of? Another broken heart? My heart had been broken plenty of times before, and it was still strong enough. It could take one more beating . . . couldn't it?

I stepped closer to Devon and opened my mouth, ready to tell him how sorry I was and that I wished I could do the entire night over—

"Can we leave already?" Felix groused, stomping around and kicking sand in every direction. "This party *blows*."

I looked past him to see Deah talking with Julio Salazar. She laughed at some joke he made, the sound floating across the beach to us. Felix glowered at them, then kicked up another patch of sand.

"Yeah," Devon said, still not looking at me. "I think it's past time we all went home."

He zipped up his duffel bag, slung it over his shoulder, and stalked away from the bonfire. Felix kicked up another section of beach, and I spotted something gleaming dully in the sand.

"Hey, what's that?" I said.

I dropped to my knees and started digging through the sand. It only took me a few seconds to uncover the object—a black blade.

Curious, I pulled the sword free. The weapon was still sheathed in a black leather scabbard, as though someone had taken it off and laid it by the bonfire. I frowned. Who would leave their weapon behind? And why?

I held the sword up to the light streaming out from the picnic shelters so I could see the scrollwork better. A single, bushy tree was carved into the center of the hilt, with smaller trees clustered around it.

Devon and Felix realized that I wasn't following them, and they stopped and stomped back over to me, both of them still angry.

"What is it now?" Felix snapped. "Did you find some pirate treasure buried in the sand?"

"Not exactly."

I showed them the weapon and pointed out the scrollwork. "Do you know who it belongs to?"

Devon frowned. "That's Vance's sword. What's it doing here? He hardly ever takes it off. And where is Vance?"

We looked around, but none of us spotted him walking up the beach and back over to the fairgrounds with the rest of the crowd.

"Maybe he's back at the cars already and just forgot his sword. Let me check." Felix texted his dad. His phone beeped back a few seconds later, and he shook his head. "Dad hasn't seen him in a couple of hours, and neither has anyone else."

"Do you think . . . something's happened to him?" I asked. "I mean, this is Vance we're talking about. He never met somebody he didn't want to annoy."

"He's probably just making out with some girl in the woods and lost track of time. That's what he usually does after the tournament." Devon sighed, but he reached down and pulled a flashlight out of his duffel bag. "But we'll go look for him."

"Because you never leave anyone behind, right? Not even guys like Vance," I said, teasing him and trying to lighten the mood and the tension between us.

"Right," Devon said, but the corner of his mouth lifted up into a small smile. "Not even guys like Vance."

Felix texted his dad again, telling Angelo what we were doing. Then Devon snapped on his flashlight, and we started our search.

We checked around the other bonfires first, but Vance wasn't at any of them, and no one could remember when they'd last seen him.

"What's the matter?" Blake sniped when we approached the Draconis. "Did you misplace one of your loser lackeys, Sinclair? Here's a tip. Why don't the three of you get lost, just like Vance did, and stay that way—permanently."

Blake laughed, and so did all the Draconi guards standing with him. Deah was the only one who didn't join in with their chuckles. I frowned, wondering at Blake's harsh words and whether he knew more about Vance than he was saying. Had he done something to Vance?

"Always a pleasure to talk to you too, Blake," Devon muttered.

Blake scoffed. "Whatever. We're outta here. Let's go, folks."

He pushed past Devon, strode up the beach, and started across the lawns. The other Draconis sneered at us a final time, then followed him.

Deah paused a moment. "I hope you find Vance," she said in a low voice, then headed after her brother.

We kept searching, but we came up empty and eventually wound up back at the Sinclair bonfire, which was nothing more than wet ash now. Devon handed Felix another flashlight from his duffel bag, and the two of them headed up to check the picnic shelters, thinking Vance might be talking to someone up there.

But I stayed by the bonfire, squatting down a few feet away from the wet remains and staring at all the prints in the sand. There were hundreds of them, circling around and around the bonfire before branching off in all directions. But I kept scanning the shore, searching for one very particular pattern. And, after about two minutes, I finally found it.

A boot print.

Vance had been the only person still wearing boots at the after-party, since everyone else had changed back into their regular clothes. So I stepped over to that first boot print and searched the sand for a second one. I spotted it and then several more beyond it, all heading toward the trees on the west side of the beach, the same trees I'd been hiding in earlier, when I'd run away from Devon.

"Hey, guys!" I called out. "Over here!"

Devon and Felix jogged back over to me, and I showed them the prints.

"See? I told you," Devon said. "Everyone goes into the woods to make out. There's an old boathouse a couple of miles down the shore that people sometimes use, if they can wait that long."

He looked at Felix, who blushed, and I remembered what Katia had said earlier about their special spot.

Felix cleared his throat. "Anyway, Vance is probably in the woods with someone right now. Let's go find him and drag him home."

Since I had the best vision, I took the lead, still following the boot prints, which led straight into the woods, just as Devon and Felix had guessed. We stopped at the edge of the trees, and Devon shined his light into the shadows.

"Vance! Come on, dude! Time to wrap it up and go home!" he called out.

No response.

Devon looked at Felix and me, shrugged, and stepped into the woods. We followed him.

I took the lead again, weaving in and out of the trees. Vance hadn't been trying to hide his tracks, so his trail wasn't hard to follow. A broken branch here, some loose rocks there, more boot prints stamped into the ground. But he'd gone much farther into the woods than I had, so far that all the lights and noise from the beach faded away, replaced by the eerie whisper of the wind in the trees.

"Vance!" Devon called out again, annoyance creeping into his voice. "C'mon, man! You can see her tomorrow!"

No response.

Felix flashed his light around. "Um, does anyone else feel like this is turning into a really bad horror movie? You know, three kids go into the woods late at night, none of them come back . . ."

"Well, you can stay here . . . by yourself," I said in a sweet voice. "Because nothing bad *ever* happens to the person who stays behind while the heroes go investigate the creepy woods."

He swallowed and looked around again. "I'm just trying to avoid becoming a really bad cliché."

"Don't be silly," I said. "This is much worse than a horror movie. We have real monsters around these parts, remember?"

"Way to reassure me," Felix sniped.

But I drew my sword, just in case he was right. So did Devon.

We kept going, deeper and deeper into the woods. We didn't speak, and the only sound was the *rustle-rustle* of our passage through the underbrush, along with the steady breeze.

The wind was probably the only reason I spotted it.

Something fluttered at the edge of my vision, something that wasn't a shadow, a pile of leaves, or a branch dancing in the breeze.

"Hold up a second," I called out.

Devon and Felix stopped, shining their lights in my direction. I went over, crouched down, and picked up something smooth and silky from the forest floor. Despite the darkness, I could tell exactly what it was—a white feather from a Sinclair cavalier hat.

So Vance had been back here after all. But the weird thing was that part of the feather was dark and wet as though it had been doused in something sticky. I frowned and stuck the feather out into the beam of Felix's flashlight.

Blood glistened on it.

Felix cursed and almost dropped his flashlight. Devon whirled around, shining his own light back and forth, his sword up and ready in case a monster came charging out of the trees toward us. We all held our breath, but nothing happened.

And I realized that I hadn't heard any natural sounds the whole time we'd been walking. No trolls chattering in the trees, no rockmunks scurrying through the bushes, not even some bullfrogs bellowing out a low, steady chorus.

The woods were quiet—too quiet.

My stomach twisted. I knew what we were going to find, and so did Devon and Felix, from the worried looks on their faces. I got to my feet, and they came over and shined their flashlights all around the area where I'd found the feather. About five feet away, I spotted another one, and then another one a few feet beyond that.

All of them were covered in blood.

I tightened my grip on my sword and followed the blood-and-feather trail. Fifty feet deeper into the woods, I rounded a tree and there he was.

Vance.

He was sitting up against the trunk of a blood persimmon tree, ripe fruit littering the ground around him, and a sweet, sticky scent filling the air. Vance's legs were splayed out in front of him as if he'd had too much to drink and was sleeping it off out here in the middle of nowhere.

"Vance!" Devon called out, hurrying over to his side. "There you are! We were worried about you—"

His flashlight beam fell on Vance, and the words died on his lips. Vance's blue eyes were wide open in pain and fear, and his hands were zip-tied together. His cavalier hat was clutched to his stomach, feathers and all, as if he'd used it to try and stop the blood loss from the deep, vicious cut visible through his white shirt.

And it wasn't the only one.

Almost a dozen cuts marred Vance's arms, chest, and legs, the red wounds looking almost like the black grease-paint a football player would swipe across his skin. A piece of duct tape had been slapped over his mouth to muffle his screams, and his eyes were already cold and glassy.

Dead—Vance was dead.

Murdered.

We all stared at Vance. It couldn't have been more than a minute, but it felt like forever. Finally, Devon let out a vicious curse, got to his feet, and ran his hand through his dark hair.

"Who . . . who would do this?" he demanded. "And why? Vance might not have been the nicest guy, but he didn't deserve *this*."

Felix shook his head and clutched his stomach. He looked like he was going to be sick. Yeah. Me too.

I let out a tense breath. "Let me try something. We can't help Vance now, but maybe we can at least figure out who did this to him."

"How?" Devon asked.

I told him and Felix about what I'd seen and felt when I'd looked into the eyes of the murdered tree troll that we'd found beside the dumpster off the Midway.

Devon frowned. "And you think that has something to do with this?"

I shrugged. "I don't know. But it's all I can do for Vance now."

He nodded. "Do it."

So I sank down on my knees in front of Vance. Devon and Felix moved their lights so that they were focused on Vance's chest instead of glaring straight into his face. I drew in another breath, let it out, and moved over so that my eyes were directly in front of Vance's.

My gaze locked with his, and his pain knifed straight through my heart.

Over and over again, a dagger lashed out, cutting Vance's arms and legs and chest. Every time he tried to move, to run, to get away, he would see the black gleam of the dagger out of the corner of his eye. Then the weapon would erupt out of the shadows and slice into him again—and again—and again.

He couldn't yell, not with that duct tape over his mouth, and he couldn't fight back, since his hands were tied together. But I could hear his silent screams in my head as he staggered through the woods. *No, no, no, no!*

And that wasn't the only thing I could hear.

Soft, heartless laughter accompanied every single swipe of the blade, and it didn't stop. Not even for a second. Instead, the laughter got louder and louder, the more pain Vance was in, the more cuts were inflicted on him, the more he *suffered*.

It was the most horrible sound I'd ever heard.

I gasped, trying to look away from Vance's sightless eyes, desperate to wrench my gaze from his, but I couldn't—I just *couldn't*.

A choked sob escaped my lips, and more and more pain spread through my entire body, tearing through my skin and muscles one at a time as though that dagger were slicing through me instead of Vance—

Suddenly, Devon was there, pulling my face into his chest and away from Vance's awful, awful gaze.

"It's okay," Devon said, rocking me back and forth the way he might a child. "It's okay. It happened to him, not you. You're safe, Lila. You're safe. I've got you."

I buried my face against his chest, not even trying to hold back my sobs anymore. Devon's hand slid through my hair, trying to soothe me. I shuddered and let him hold me.

But all the while, that terrible, terrible laughter echoed in my head.

The same cruel, evil laughter I'd heard when we'd found that murdered tree troll behind the dumpster on the Midway.

CHAPTER NINETEEN

Felix called his dad and told Angelo what was going on. We stayed with Vance until the rest of the Sinclairs showed up. Claudia, Angelo, Reginald, Mo, Oscar. They all came, along with several guards, and they all stared at Vance's body, as shocked and horrified as the three of us.

I told Claudia and the others what I'd seen when I'd used my soulsight on Vance, and she and Mo put their heads together, wondering who might have done this. But I hadn't seen the killer, only heard that sick, sick laughter. I hadn't liked Vance, and he hadn't liked me either, but Devon was right. Vance hadn't deserved *this*—this level of heartless cruelty. And now, I couldn't even tell Claudia who had murdered him.

I felt like a complete and utter failure.

I didn't dare look at Vance again, not even for a second, so Devon put his arm around my shoulder and led me out of the woods, with Felix on my other side and Oscar fluttering around us. We got into one of the Sinclair SUVs, and Reginald drove us home.

Devon made sure that I got to my room okay, then handed me off to Oscar, who ordered me to take a hot shower, put on some pajamas, and get into bed. I did as the pixie asked, even though I felt disconnected from my own body as though someone else were going through the motions for me.

Oscar fussed over me, pulling the sheets and comforter all the way up to my chin. Then he flew over to his trailer, rustled around inside, and came back out with a pixie sword. It was no bigger than a needle, but a dull stain on the end told me that it had been dipped in poison, probably copper crusher venom. Poison was often the only way pixies could survive against larger mortals, magicks, and monsters.

Oscar fluttered back over and landed on my nightstand. "Don't you worry about a thing, cupcake. I'm going to keep watch tonight. Ain't nobody getting to you the way they did to Vance. Tiny will stand watch too, won't you, Tiny?"

Over in his corral, the tortoise let out a low, huffing noise that sounded like a *yes*, his black eyes strangely bright in his green face.

Oscar saluted me with his sword, then started marching back and forth on my nightstand, moving from one side to the other with quick, precise movements, like a soldier standing guard.

The idea of him watching over me was comforting, and I fell asleep with the steady *clack-clack-clack* of his cowboy boots ringing in my ears.

I didn't think that I would rest at all, much less sleep, but I didn't wake up until Oscar nudged my shoulder the next morning.

"What's going on?" I mumbled, my voice thick with sleep. "What's wrong?"

The pixie looked at me, his violet eyes dark and serious. "Claudia wants everyone down in the dining hall ASAP." He jerked his thumb over his shoulder at the black duffel bag sitting on the coffee table. "I've already got your stuff packed up for the tournament."

That cleared the last dregs of sleep from my mind. I sat up in bed. "The tournament? Don't tell me they're still having it? What about Vance?"

Oscar shrugged. "Claudia told the other Families, but they think it's an accident—that Vance went too far into the woods and got clawed up by a monster."

"A monster that can use duct tape and zip ties? Yeah, sure." I snorted. "A monster killed him all right—but it was a human one."

"I know," Oscar said in a somber voice. "I've never seen anybody cut up like that before. It was . . . vicious. Even though there wasn't all that much blood."

No blood, just bones and blades . . . bones and blades . . . bones and blades. . . .

Seleste Draconi's singsong voice echoed in my mind. I shivered the way I always did whenever I thought about her creepy warning, but this time I forced myself to really think about her words.

No blood, just bones and blades. . . . No blood, just bones. . . . No blood. . . .

That's what all the horrible things that had happened over the past few days had in common—no blood. The murdered tree troll behind the dumpster off the Midway. The slaughtered troll that Devon, Felix, and I had found on the Draconi property. All the other troll bodies in the ravine. And now Vance.

None of them had been as bloody as they should have been, despite all the deep, vicious cuts on their bodies. Of course, Vance's blood had probably soaked into the ground. But something about *no blood* kept nagging at me—

"—but surely, that's not the first time you've seen something as horrible as Vance's body," Oscar said. Apparently, he'd been talking this whole time. "I mean, that library where you lived was in a bad part of town. There are plenty of monsters there, especially at night."

I nodded. "Yeah. And every once in a while, I'd see the remains of some smaller creature that the bigger monsters had snacked on. But Vance . . . all those cuts on his body . . . it was something else. Worse than anything I've seen before, except for finding my mom's body—and watching Grant and those two guards getting eaten by the lochness a few weeks ago."

"But you were just defending yourself and Devon," Oscar said. "Grant betrayed the whole Family, and he tried to rip out Devon's magic. Yours too. At least the lochness got a meal out of him before the end. Monsters have to eat too, you know. But poor Vance. He died out there in the woods all alone. And for what? Nothing."

I frowned. Something about Oscar's words tugged at a corner of my mind. Something about Grant and the horrible things he'd done to Devon and me. Something about ripping out a person's magic.

And just like that, part of the puzzle clicked together in my mind.

"No blood," I whispered. "*No blood.*"

Oscar frowned. "What are you talking about?"

"Vance," I said. "He was cut to pieces, but there wasn't a lot of blood on him or even around his body."

"So. . . ."

I drew in a breath. "So there wasn't any blood because somebody *ripped his magic out of him.* That's why they cut him so much. They wanted his blood, his power, his magic."

I thought back, picturing that dagger I'd seen cutting into Vance again and again. I hadn't been able to see any scrollwork on the hilt, but the blade itself had been dark—pulsing with a midnight-black glow. I could have smacked myself for not remembering it sooner.

"The person who killed Vance had a black blade," I said. "And they used it to soak up all his blood, all his magic."

"But why take Vance's magic?" Oscar asked, his wings twitching in thought. "I mean, yeah, he had Talents for speed and strength, but Vance wasn't the most powerful guy around. If you were going to take someone's magic, wouldn't you try to get the strongest person with the most power?"

"I don't know," I said, throwing back the covers and getting out of bed. "But I'm going to find out."

I took a shower, put on my ren-faire getup, and went to the dining hall. Practically everyone in the Family was crowded inside, but the room was quiet, and the mood was somber. Everyone knew what had happened to Vance, and it had shaken up all of us.

I wasn't particularly hungry, but I piled a plate full of food, heavy on the bacon strips, and headed over to the table where Devon, Felix, and Mo were sitting. All of them looked tired, and they'd barely touched their breakfasts.

"Hey, kid," Mo said, his voice flat and lifeless as he picked at the pancakes on his plate. "I hope you got more sleep than the rest of us did."

"I think I know why Vance was killed."

That got their attention, and their heads snapped up. I leaned forward and told them what I thought had happened to Vance.

When I finished, Devon frowned. "But why Vance? Oscar's right. If you were going to rip out someone's magic, wouldn't you do it to someone more powerful? Or someone who had a more unique Talent?"

"Like soulsight, compulsion, or transference magic?" I asked in a wry tone.

Devon winced, but he still nodded. "Yeah. Like those."

"I don't know. Maybe Vance was already out in the woods. Maybe he'd been making out with a girl, like you said. Maybe he was just in the wrong place at the wrong time."

"But you thought Vance was a bad guy," Felix said. "That he was the one who cut the rope ladder."

I shrugged. "Maybe he did. Maybe he didn't. I don't know anymore. And I don't know how Vance's murder fits in with what happened to all those tree trolls."

"I asked around about your murdered monsters," Mo said. "It's probably some idiot in town for the tournament, trying to prove what a tough guy he is by trapping and killing a bunch of monsters. Some folks like to show off like that. It happened last year."

"What happened last year?"

"A couple of tree trolls were found all cut up," Mo said. "I heard about it from one of the Volkov pixies when I was making my rounds at the tournament yesterday. Their guards found the trolls on the edge of the Volkov property around this time last year. It wasn't a pretty sight, and it sounds just like what you, Devon, and Felix saw the other night."

I frowned. "Did the Volkovs ever figure out who had killed the trolls? Or why?"

Mo shrugged. "Not that the pixie had heard."

I started to ask another question, but Claudia strode into the dining hall, a sword dangling from her hand. Everyone stopped eating and talking and turned to face her. She was wearing another black pantsuit and heels, with her silver cuff flashing on her right wrist. Her makeup was flawless, but tired lines grooved around her mouth and eyes. No doubt she'd been up all night, dealing with the Vance situation.

Claudia looked out over her Family, her gaze moving from one face to the next. "By now, you have all heard what happened to Vance," she said. "That his body was found cut up in the woods along the lake. With the tournament and all the tourists in town right now, the other Families have declared it a tragic accident. They're saying that Vance wandered too far into the woods and was attacked and killed by a monster. As a result of their declaration, the Tournament of Blades will proceed as scheduled today."

Mutters of shock and surprise rang out, with the loudest and angriest ones coming from the table where Vance's friends were sitting, including Henry, who'd made a full recovery from his broken leg.

"But we all know that it wasn't an accident," Claudia continued in a hard voice. "That Vance was an experienced guard, too experienced to be taken down by some mysterious monster without fighting back for everything he was worth."

Murmurs of agreement rippled through the dining hall.

Claudia waited until the noise died down before she spoke again. "There is nothing I can do about the other Families declaring Vance's death an accident. So we will go to the tournament today, and we will fight, and we will honor Vance the best way we can. Understood?"

This time, the murmurs were much louder, and every single person nodded his or her head in agreement, including me.

"But know this. Someone has killed one of our own, and I will do everything in my power to find this person and make sure that he or she is punished accordingly." Claudia's voice rang with steely authority. "I promise it to every person in the Family, just as I promised it to Vance last night."

Silence fell over the room. No one spoke, and no one moved.

"But until then, we will do our absolute best today, and

we will show everyone—*everyone*—what the Sinclairs are really made of." Claudia raised her sword high, mimicking the Family crest. "For Vance!"

We all shot to our feet, raised our own swords, and echoed her words. "For Vance!"

And we all meant it—every single Sinclair.

CHAPTER TWENTY

After breakfast, we packed up our gear and went to the fairgrounds.

We got there early, but the stone bleachers were already full, and practically every seat was taken, since this was the last and most popular day of the tournament. I filed into the stadium with the rest of the Sinclairs. Everyone stared at us, with whispers springing up in our wake. Everyone had heard what had happened to Vance, and the other Families were waiting to see how we would react.

Claudia led the way, waving and talking to folks she knew, and acting like nothing was wrong. But she didn't so much as crack a smile, and anger still burned in her eyes. We all followed her example.

Claudia, Reginald, Mo, and Oscar headed up to the Sinclair box, while Angelo went over to the healers' tent. Devon, Felix, and I headed toward the chain-link fence to wait for the first match of the day to start. Claudia had arranged for Henry to take Vance's spot in the tournament, so there were still thirty-two competitors left, and the field would be narrowed to sixteen, then eight, then four. After a break, the action would pick up again this afternoon, and the final four would face off. Once the final match was finished and the winner determined, the tournament would wrap up, and a barbecue dinner and after-party would be held at the lake, just like it had been last night.

Devon, Felix, and I walked past Katia, who was standing with the Volkov guards who were still in the tournament. Katia smiled at me, then deliberately sniffed and turned her back to Felix. Couldn't blame her for that. I'd seen how much she cared about him, so I knew how much he had hurt her, even though he hadn't meant to.

Felix winced, but there was nothing he could do or say to make things better with Katia.

Poppy was waiting for us at the fence, and she rushed over the second she saw us. "You guys! I'm so sorry about Vance!"

Devon accepted her condolences on behalf of the Sinclairs. Poppy looked like she wanted to say more, but she realized that we didn't want to talk about it. So she hugged us all, then went back over to the Ito guards.

Several folks from the other Families also came up and offered their sympathies. Devon nodded and spoke graciously to all of them. So did Felix. But I didn't talk to anyone. I was too busy staring into their eyes and using my soulsight, trying to figure out which one of them might have killed Vance. But everyone radiated genuine shock and sorrow, instead of secret satisfaction. Nobody that I looked at had anything to do with Vance's murder.

Blake and Deah were the last ones to come over to us, with Blake swaggering out front and Deah behind him.

Blake stopped in front of Devon. "I'm supposed to come over here and say how sorry I am about Vance and blah, blah, blah. So there you go."

Devon's hands curled into fists as though he wanted to punch Blake in the face. "Wow. Thanks for the sympathy."

Blake snorted. "Whatever. If you ask me, Vance was an idiot for going that far back in the woods. He got what he deserved."

I stared into his eyes. His brown gaze was cold as usual, but I didn't feel that certain smugness that would tell me Blake's words had some deadly, hidden meaning. He might be a grade A jerk, but Blake wasn't the person who had killed Vance.

But if he hadn't, who had?

Devon's hands clenched together even tighter, his knuckles cracking from the pressure, and he took a step forward as though he was going to give in to his urge to punch Blake. But Deah sidled in between them.

"We really are sorry about Vance," she said. "I didn't know him, but nobody deserves what he went through."

Sincerity and sympathy filled her face, and her genuine words were enough to get Devon to loosen his fists.

"Thanks, Deah," he said. "Good luck today."

She nodded. "You too. Let's go, Blake. We need to get ready for our matches."

Blake sneered at us again, but he let Deah lead him back over to the rest of the Draconis.

Devon waited until they were out of earshot before he turned to me. "Did you see anything when you looked at him?"

I sighed. "Unfortunately, no. I hate to say this, but I don't think Blake had anything to do with Vance's murder. Neither has anyone else who's come up to us today."

"Then who did it?" Felix asked.

I stared out over the competitors with their cavalier hats and colorful cloaks, the tourist rubes in the bleachers with their cameras and cotton candy, the Family officials high up in the glass boxes.

"I have no idea," I muttered.

The officials announced that the tournament would start in five minutes, so Felix wished us good luck, left

Devon and me at the fence, and headed over to the healers' tent to join Angelo.

Katia was in the first match of the day. She smiled and waved to the crowd, then stepped up to face her opponent. The official lowered his arm, and the match began.

The Salazar guard raised his weapon and went on the offensive, but Katia slid out of his way too fast to follow. Seriously. One second, she was standing right in front of the guy, and the next, she was behind him, raising her sword. The guard barely managed to whip back around in time to bring up his weapon.

The match went on, with Katia moving faster and faster with every second that passed. It looked like she'd finally gotten her groove back. Or perhaps her anger at Felix and having her heart broken was what was fueling her magic, her quickness, today. Hey, you used what worked.

And it definitely worked for Katia, who was able to draw first blood barely a minute into the match. She grinned and saluted the crowd with her sword, and everyone cheered. Katia skipped over to the Volkov guards, basking in their congratulations as well. She saw me watching her and waved. I smiled and waved back, glad that she was happy.

The day and the matches wore on. Henry lost his match, but everyone gave him a long, loud standing ovation, and there was a moment of silence for Vance. It wasn't nearly enough, though, and I vowed again to figure out who had killed Vance.

Devon and I both won our first matches, putting us in the field of sixteen, along with Katia. Deah easily won her match as well. Blake also made it through to the round of sixteen, where he faced a familiar foe—Poppy.

A couple of weeks ago, Blake had humiliated and practically assaulted Poppy in front of his friends. He sneered at her the whole time the official was reviewing the rules, hefting the sword in his hands like he wanted to bring it down and split her skull wide open. He probably did. Blake was a sick jerk that way. But Poppy just twirled her two short swords around and around in her hands, ignoring him.

The fight began, and Blake raised his sword and charged at Poppy, trying to overwhelm her right away with his strength Talent. But she stepped up to meet him, used her speed magic to sidestep and trip him as he went by, and neatly sliced both of her swords across his left arm, drawing first blood and knocking him out of the tournament.

Poppy smiled and waved to the crowd, and I clapped, yelled, and whistled as loud as I could. I was glad that she'd finally gotten a little bit of revenge on Blake for the horrible way he'd treated her.

For a moment, Blake just stood there in the center of the ring, a stunned look on his face, as if he couldn't believe what had happened. That Poppy had beaten him. That he had lost so quickly. Then he slowly turned and looked up at the Draconi box, as if he was dreading what he was going to see.

Victor was on his feet, his arms crossed over his chest, his eyes narrowed, his lips puckered in displeasure. He didn't like Blake losing.

I wondered if Victor would call Blake a loser like he had Deah, after she'd lost the obstacle-course round to Katia. Maybe it was mean of me, but I hoped that Victor was even harder on Blake than he had been on Deah.

And I couldn't help calling out to Blake when he stormed by.

"Aw, too bad you got knocked out of the tournament already, Blake. And by a *girl*. That must be particularly humiliating for *you*, seeing as how you're a high and mighty Draconi and all."

Blake glared at me, his hand tightening around the hilt of his sword as if he wanted to pull it out and skewer me with it. "Ito got lucky, that's all. The same way that you and Sinclair have gotten lucky so far. Deah will still win the tournament. Just wait and see."

He gave me another evil glare and stomped off, probably to go up to the Draconi box, now that he was out of the tournament. Good riddance.

Poppy got knocked out in the next round, but Devon, Katia, Deah, and I all won our matches, then the ones after that, making us the final four competitors in the tournament.

It was just after noon when the officials called for a break, saying that the final matches would start at two o'clock sharp. All the folks from the Family boxes came down from on high to mingle with their guards and offer their congratulations to the folks still in the tournament. Claudia, escorted by Reginald, made her way through the crowd, stopping to talk to the other competitors, but Mo made a beeline straight for me.

"Keep up the good work, kid," he said, clapping me on the shoulder. "I've been placing a lot of bets on you. Everyone thinks that Deah is going to win, but we know better, don't we?"

He winked, and I had to laugh.

"Don't count your money just yet, Mo," I said. "Deah's a good fighter. So are Devon and Katia. Any one of us could win."

He waved his hand, causing the diamond signet ring on one finger to flash in the sunlight. "Bah. This tournament is yours to lose, kid. Just like it was your mom's before you."

Startled, I looked at him. "What? Mom competed in the tournament too?"

Mo nodded. "When she was your age. She won it too.

A couple of years in a row, including the summer she left town."

Before all the bad stuff had gone down with my dad. Before Victor had sent Luke out to be killed by that nest of copper crushers. Before my mom and dad could leave the Families and Cloudburst Falls behind like they'd been planning. That's what Mo really meant.

My mom had never hidden her past from me. She'd told me about working for the Sinclairs, meeting and falling in love with my dad, even the problems she'd had with Victor and the other Families. But I'd never known that she'd won the Tournament of Blades—and not just once.

"I didn't know that," I said in a soft voice. "She never told me about competing in the tournament."

Mo stared out over the stadium, his eyes dark and distant with memories. "This is where Serena and Luke actually met. They had to fight each other in the last round. Serena had knocked Victor out of the tournament to get to the final round, and it was winner take all between her and your dad. It was one of the best matches I've ever seen, but your mom finally drew first blood. And Luke was a good sport about it too. He and your mom started talking, and, well, things happened from there between them."

"Why didn't she ever tell me any of this?"

He shrugged. "She didn't like dwelling on the past, especially when it came to your dad. You know that."

No, she hadn't. My mom hadn't hidden her past from me, but she hadn't been very chatty about it either. Even when we'd come back to Cloudburst Falls every summer, I'd had to beg and beg her to tell me stories of what the town had been like when she was a kid, of all the things she'd seen and done, of all the plans that she and my dad had had for the future.

Plans that had never happened, thanks to Victor.

Mo squeezed my shoulder, sensing how much this meant to me, but I couldn't help wondering what else my mom hadn't told me. Sure, her winning the Tournament of Blades wasn't exactly an important secret, but what other things might she have kept from me—

"There you are!" a voice called out. "Darling, you were *fabulous*!"

Mo and I looked over. Seleste Draconi had come down from the Family box and was racing toward Deah, her arms outstretched, ready to hug her the second Deah was in range. Seleste was wearing another one of her long, flowing dresses, this one in a sapphire blue that made her look more beautiful than ever. Her hair gleamed like polished gold in the sun, although her eyes were the same unnaturally bright blue that I remembered from the cemetery.

Almost like . . . monster eyes.

That's what Seleste's eyes reminded me of. All the bright, glowing, jewel-toned eyes of the monsters as they crept through the shadows at night.

Everyone stared at Seleste as she drew Deah close, kissed both her cheeks, and then hugged her tight. An embarrassed blush flamed in Deah's cheeks, but she was smiling wide, and she hugged Seleste right back.

Jealousy pinched my heart. My mom would have done the same thing, would have hugged me just like that, if she'd still been alive.

But she wasn't, and Victor and Blake were to blame for that.

Deah hugged her mom back for a few more seconds before stepping out of her arms. "Thanks, Mom." She shot a nervous look at Victor, who had walked over and joined them. "But shouldn't you be up in the Family box resting? You know how the sun and the heat can get to you."

Victor sighed. "Your mother insisted on coming down and congratulating you in person, even though I told her that she could have just texted you."

"Well, that was nice of her." Deah brightened for a moment, but the expression wilted under her father's stern glare. "Wasn't it?"

Victor didn't respond. Instead, he studied the other competitors, the same sort of sneer on his face that was always on Blake's. "Well," he said. "If this is your competition, there's absolutely no excuse for you to lose the tournament."

His voice dripped with disgust, telling everyone within earshot his low opinion of the remaining competitors. But even worse was the sharp, pointed look he gave Deah, and all the malice shimmering in his golden eyes. It was a clear warning that she would win the tournament or else something very unpleasant might happen—to her.

"Yes, sir," Deah said in a faint voice.

Victor must have sensed my staring at him because he turned and looked in my direction. My gaze locked with his, and my soulsight immediately flared to life, letting me feel the absolute ice of his emotions and all his hatred for everyone around him—including his own wife.

In that instant, I realized that Victor barely tolerated Seleste and all her odd behavior, and only kept her around because her visions of the future were useful. The second she stopped being useful . . . well, I was willing to bet that Seleste would end up just like my parents—dead.

I shivered. I could easily imagine Victor tearing Seleste's Talent for seeing the future out of her. Part of me was surprised he hadn't done it already. Or perhaps he only wanted the information from the visions and had no desire to actually experience them for himself. Not if it meant being like Seleste.

Seleste noticed Victor staring at me, and she brightened

and headed in my direction. Mo grabbed my shoulder again, his fingers digging into my skin in a clear warning.

"No matter what she says, act like you don't know what she's talking about," he muttered.

"Why?"

"Just do it, kid," Mo hissed.

Seleste marched over and grabbed my hands. "Darling! There you are! It's so good to see you again!" she beamed at me, squeezing my hands tight in hers.

With her strength Talent, it felt like she was on the verge of cracking my bones. I winced, and she loosened her hold.

"Oops. Sorry. I don't know my own strength sometimes." She winked at me. "Just making sure that you were real. Sometimes, I have to do that, you know. I'm sure you remember that about me."

"Um, okay."

It seemed that she had mistaken me for my mom again, so it wasn't hard to pretend to be confused. But why did she keep doing that? It wasn't as if Seleste had actually known my mom . . . had she?

I frowned, but I didn't have time to focus on the thought, not with Deah glaring daggers at me, and Victor and Blake striding over, scowls fixed on both of their faces.

Seleste kept staring at me, but Victor stopped and looked at Mo, his lips puckering in thought.

"Um, who are you?" I asked Seleste, keeping up the charade that I had never met her before.

Just like that, her sunny smile vanished, and utter misery filled her face. "You know exactly who I am. I'm Seleste, your best friend. Don't you remember me?"

I looked at Mo for help. This time, I wasn't faking it.

"Hello, Seleste," he said in a soft, gentle voice. "I think you're a little confused. I don't think you've ever met Lila before. Lila *Merriweather*."

He put a little extra emphasis on my fake last name. I didn't know why, but it worked, and I could almost see the proverbial light bulb snap on above Seleste's head.

She looked at him, then me, then back at him. "Oh. I guess you're right. My mistake."

She shrugged, then turned, looped her arms through Victor's and Blake's, and started skipping away with them. At least, she tried to. They weren't having any of the skipping, but they let her drag them off into the crowd. Then again, they didn't have much choice, with her strength magic pulling them along.

Deah stayed behind, though, and she turned her hot glare to me the second her father and brother were out of earshot. "Who does my mom keep confusing you with?"

Before I could think of some lie, Mo answered her. "Lila's mother," he said, still staring after Seleste. "Her name was Serena."

Startled, I glanced at Mo. Why would he tell Deah my mom's name? If she told Victor and he put two and two together, then he would know that I was Serena Sterling's daughter. He might also realize that I knew he'd murdered my mom, and my anonymity, my only protection from him, would be gone.

Deah looked back and forth between Mo and me. "Is that name supposed to mean something to me?"

Mo gave her a sad smile and shook his head. "Of course not. But Serena was an old friend of your mom's. I was Seleste's friend too—before she married your father."

He muttered the last few words, and Deah's face tightened with even more anger.

"Well, whoever your mom was, stay away from mine," Deah snapped.

"Don't worry about that," I snapped back. "That crazy lady is all yours."

Her hands clenched into fists, and her blue gaze slammed

into mine, letting me feel all of her white-hot rage and how protective she was of her mom.

"My mom is *awesome*," Deah snarled. "She just happens to see the world a little differently from everyone else. But that doesn't make her crazy, and it certainly doesn't give you or anyone else the right to make fun of her. So why don't you keep your snotty opinions to yourself."

I held up my hands. I wasn't going to argue with her anymore. There was no point in it. Besides, she was right. I didn't have the right to make fun of Seleste, and I was ashamed that I had. Mocking people was something that Blake always did, and I had zero desire to be anything like him.

Deah glared at me another second, then stormed away.

The second she was gone, I turned to Mo. "Why did you tell her Mom's name? Why would you do that?"

Mo tipped his white straw hat back on his head. "I know, I know, it was stupid. It's just that I hadn't seen Seleste in so long. Most of the time, Victor keeps her locked up in one of the towers in the Draconi castle. Besides, I wanted to give her and Deah some kind of explanation."

My eyes narrowed. "How do you know Seleste anyway?"

He stared after the Draconis instead of looking me in the eye. "We used to be friends. Way back when we were about your age."

"Who was friends?"

"Me, Claudia, Seleste, and your mom. Well, really, it was the girls who were tight. I was more friends with Serena than anyone else. And, of course, Claudia and I weren't friends at all after we stopped dating."

My mouth dropped open. "You and Claudia *dated*?"

"Yeah," Mo said in a distracted voice. "For a while. Before she met Lawrence, Devon's dad."

I'd always thought that Mo and Claudia had some past

connection, but I never thought it was something like *this*. Calm, serious Claudia with cheery, boisterous Mo? I just couldn't picture them together. But if they'd broken up way back when, it would explain the tension between them now.

Mo kept staring in the direction that Seleste and Deah had gone, his eyes dark with memories and feelings he wouldn't let me see. After several seconds, he shook his head, as if clearing the cobwebs of the past out of his mind, and plastered a smile on his face.

"But that's all over with now, kid. How about I buy you a funnel cake? With tons of powdered sugar, just the way you like it? You're going to need a sugar buzz before the final matches start."

I frowned. Mo loved money as much as I did, and he never, *ever* offered to buy me anything unless he was trying to distract me. I wondered what had happened between him, my mom, Claudia, and Seleste, and why there was still so much secrecy and tension about it even now. But he'd changed the subject, which meant that the conversation was closed. Besides, I was never one to turn down free food.

"Sure," I said. "A funnel cake sounds great."

CHAPTER TWENTY-ONE

Mo and I went out into the fairgrounds, where he bought me the biggest funnel cake we could find. He started talking to some folks he knew from the Ito Family, and I finished my cake, murmured my excuses, and drifted away from him.

I had some time before the final matches started, so I wandered through the fairgrounds, looking at all the cheesy carnival games, T-shirts, flags, and more. If it was cheap, tacky, and brighter than a flashing neon sign, you could buy it here. The vendors called out to me, hawking their wares and trying to get me to play their games, but I ignored them.

I ended up on the edge of the fairgrounds, staring out toward the lake and trying to make sense of everything that had happened over the past few days, from the murdered tree trolls to Seleste's strange behavior to all the secrets Mo wasn't telling me.

The deep blue of the water shimmered in the distance, but instead of concentrating on the pretty scene, I started walking along one of the cobblestone paths until I reached the tree line.

My thoughts turned to Vance, and the image of his cut-up body filled my mind. I wasn't anywhere close to where he had been murdered, but I still found myself peering through the branches, wondering who had killed him and why. Why had the killer taken Vance's Talents instead of someone else's, someone with much stronger magic? And how did all the murdered monsters fit into this? Or were they even connected to Vance at all?

My mind spun around and around, trying to figure things out. But there were no answers to be found in the dappled shade of the woods, so I turned to head back.

And that's when I heard the giggles.

Giggles? Out here in the woods?

I was still wearing my sword, and my hand dropped to the weapon's hilt, despite the seemingly innocent sounds. I crept a little closer to the trees, tilting my head to the side, listening and looking into the thin afternoon shadows. The *crack-crack-crack* of twigs crunching underfoot sounded, along with more giggles. Through the trees, I spotted two figures heading toward me.

A second later, Blake stepped out of the woods about ten feet away from my position. And he wasn't alone—Katia was with him.

From their rumpled clothes and Katia's messy hair, it was obvious what they'd been doing. They saw me at the same time I did them, and the three of us stopped and stared at each other.

"Sorry," I said. "I was just taking a walk before the tournament starts up again."

Blake snorted. "Sure you were. Or maybe you just like to watch, you freak."

He shoved past me, driving his shoulder into mine and nearly knocking me down, but I ground my teeth together and held my tongue. The tournament was supposed to resume in fifteen minutes, and I didn't need to get into a fight with Blake right now.

Katia pulled her dark red hair back into a ponytail and smoothed some of the wrinkles out of her white sleeveless shirt. Then she lifted her chin, marched over, and stopped in front of me.

"Go ahead," she said. "You look like you want to say something."

I shrugged. "It's not really my place to say anything."

Her hazel eyes glittered, and she crossed her arms over her chest. "Say it anyway."

I sighed. "I know you're upset about Felix, but messing around with Blake won't make you feel any better in the long run. Blake is *not* a nice guy."

She shrugged back at me. "Maybe I'm tired of nice guys. After all, Felix was a nice guy . . . until he wasn't. Besides, how do you know what would make me feel better? You're too chicken to even do anything with Devon."

I stiffened. "I don't know what you're talking about."

Katia's smile was full of sneering pity. "I've seen the way he looks at you, and you look the same way right back at him. But instead of actually doing something about it, you keep him at arm's length. It's stupid, if you ask me. Especially since he's such a *nice guy*, right?" she mocked me with my own words.

I ground my teeth together and didn't say anything. There was nothing I *could* say because she was exactly right about me being scared of how much I cared about Devon. When it came to risking something as fragile as my heart, I was as skittish as a rockmunk facing down a copper crusher.

Katia sighed, and some of the ugly tension drained out of her face. "Look, I appreciate you trying to warn me about Blake, but I know exactly what kind of guy he is, and I can take care of myself. Drunk dad, remember? Besides, Blake and I were just messing around. Nothing serious. It's not like I think he actually *cares* about me or anything." Her features hardened again. "I made that mistake with Felix. Trust me, I won't make it again."

I didn't respond.

"Anyway, I've got to get back to the tournament, and so do you."

"Yeah," I said. "See you over there."

Katia moved off, heading back toward the fairgrounds.

I stood there for a few seconds, thinking about her harsh words, which hit a little too close to home. But I couldn't do anything about them now, so I sighed, turned around, and followed her back to the fairgrounds to get ready for the final rounds of the Tournament of Blades.

I had barely set foot back in the fairgrounds when Oscar came zipping through the air, stopping right in front of me.

"There you are!" he practically shouted. "I've been looking everywhere for you! Come quick!"

Oscar buzzed around and around my shoulders, trying to herd me toward the stadium.

"What's wrong?" I asked. "What's happened? Has someone else been hurt?"

Oscar shook his head, and his wings twitched in agitation. Even his tiny black cloak seemed to bristle with anger. "They shook up the tournament, flipped the brackets around and everything. That's why you need to get over there right now."

I frowned. "What do you mean they flipped the brackets around?"

"You'll see," he said in a dark tone.

The pixie shooed me into the stadium. I thought that

most of the Family higher-ups would be back in their boxes by now, including the Sinclairs, but Claudia, Reginald, Angelo, and Mo were standing by the chain-link fence, talking to the officials. Devon and Felix stood a few feet away, watching them.

"What's going on?" I asked, walking over to them. "Oscar said they changed the tournament."

Felix snorted. "Oh, they changed it all right—which is what Claudia and the others are arguing about with those idiots."

He stabbed his finger at the officials. Claudia was right up in their faces, her hands on her hips, her green eyes blazing with anger. I couldn't hear exactly what she was saying, but her sharp tone let everyone know she wasn't happy.

Mo looked over at us and shook his head. Devon and Felix both sighed.

"Good luck," Felix said, clapping Devon on the shoulder, then turning and doing the same thing to me. "I know this will be tough. I'll be rooting for both of you at the same time. No matter what happens, there won't be a loser here today. You guys know that, right?"

Devon nodded, but I was still confused.

"How can you root for both of us at the same time—" Suddenly, I realized exactly what was going on.

I'd been scheduled to fight Deah in the next round of the tournament, with Katia facing off against Devon. But the tournament had changed, and the brackets had been flipped—which meant I had to fight someone else now, and since there were only four of us left, that meant only one thing.

"Oh," I whispered. "Oh *no*."

"Oh no is right," Oscar said, landing on one of the fence posts.

I looked at Devon, but judging from his tense expression, he wasn't any happier about this than I was. Because now, instead of fighting Deah next, I had to fight another Sinclair.

I had to fight a member of my own Family.

I had to fight Devon.

CHAPTER TWENTY-TWO

Claudia kept arguing with the officials, but it was obvious they'd already made up their minds, and this was happening.

I looked at Devon. "I don't want to fight you."

He shrugged. "I don't want to fight you either, but this is what we have to do."

"But how did this even happen?"

Felix stabbed his finger up at the Draconi box. "Apparently, his royal highness didn't want you to be Deah's next opponent, so he had a word with the officials and convinced them to shake up the brackets at the last minute. Claimed it would add more excitement to the tournament. We all know that Victor is just trying to make things easier for Deah. After all, she's beaten Katia before, and you and Devon have both looked scary good during the tournament."

I frowned. "So he wants to give Deah a better chance of winning by having one of us Sinclairs knock the other out."

"You got it, cupcake," Oscar said, glaring at the officials.

I looked at Devon again. "So what are we going to do?"

He straightened up to his full height, a determined look flaring in his eyes. "We're going to fight. We're going to show everyone that the Sinclair Family has two of the best fighters in Cloudburst Falls. And we're going to do it honestly. No compulsion, no transference, no magic or Talents of any kind. Just you and me going sword to sword. No hard feelings no matter who wins. And whoever does win will kick ass in the final round and win the tournament. What do you say to that, Lila?"

I grinned at him and stuck out my hand. "I'd say that you've got a deal, Sinclair. Winner take all."

"Winner take all, Merriweather."

Devon grinned back, and we shook on it.

Despite all of Claudia's arguments, the officials announced the change in the brackets to great applause from the crowd. Devon and I were up first, and we strode out to the middle of the stadium. It was just the two of us, standing in the center of the ring, facing each other down. It reminded me of the very first day I'd come to the Sinclair mansion, sparring with Devon as a test to see whether I was good enough to join the Family or not.

The official introduced us and reviewed the rules before moving in, raising his hand, and starting the fight. Devon and I circled each other. This wasn't the first time we'd fought, so we already knew all about each other's strengths, weaknesses, and tendencies. But this match was for a spot in the final round, and we both knew what was at stake. Not only representing the Sinclairs well, but also having fun. Because there was nothing we both loved more than a good fight.

Finally, Devon moved in, raised his sword, and began the battle in earnest. Back and forth, we danced across the stone ring, neither one of us able to touch each other with our weapons to draw first blood. All around us, cheers and yells exploded over and over again in a continuous roar that rattled from one side of the stadium to the other. The crowd wanted a fight? Well, they were getting a good one.

A minute ticked by, then another one, and another. And

still Devon and I fought, our blades clashing together over and over again, up high, down low, side to side to side, each one of us fighting as hard and fast as we could. The crowd noise faded away until it was a dull roar in the back of my mind, and the world reduced to Devon in front of me, his feet moving in elaborate patterns in the grass, his hand clenching the hilt of his sword, his green eyes narrowed in fierce concentration.

I didn't use any of my magic on him, not my transference power and not even my soulsight to try to anticipate his next move. I wanted to win fair and square, just me and him and our fighting skills, with no magic of any kind, just like we'd promised each other.

So we fought and fought and fought, with the *clash-clash* and *clang-clang-clang* of our swords ringing out through the stadium, even louder than the crowd. At least, that's how it seemed to me. My ponytail slapped against my shoulders, sweat streamed down my face, and my arms ached from swinging my sword over and over again, but I kept right on fighting, and so did Devon.

Finally, though, Devon made a mistake.

He got a little too close to the cold spring, and one of his feet slipped off the edge for a second before he managed to right himself. It was a small mistake, a tiny error, and could just as easily have happened to me, but it would give me the opening I needed three moves ahead, and I was going to take advantage of it.

One.

Sure enough, Devon was late in bringing up his sword to block my next blow.

Two.

Then he was late again stepping back out of the way when I sliced out with my blade. He was barely parrying my blows, and he whirled away, trying to buy himself some space to get his timing back on track.

Three.

Devon faced me and raised his sword to attack me again, but I stepped back out of his reach and pointed my sword at him. Devon glanced down at the blood dripping down his bare arm.

He bowed to me. "You win, Lila." He straightened up and grinned. "I knew that you would."

The crowd went wild—hooting, hollering, and cheering—knowing they'd just seen the match of the tournament. Everyone surged to their feet, giving us a standing ovation and cheering louder and longer than they had for anyone else in the entire tournament.

The official stepped into the stone ring and raised my hand high, declaring me the winner. Devon started to move back to give me the limelight, but I grinned, reached out, clasped his hand in mine, and pulled him up next to me.

He grinned back at me and tightened his grip. Together, we raised our clasped hands high to the massive roar of the crowd. Devon looked at me, all the warmth in his eyes and heart reflected back in my own.

Felix was right. Nobody had lost here today. As far as I was concerned, Devon and I had both won.

Still hand in hand, Devon and I left the stadium floor and stepped behind the chain-link fence. We were swarmed and spent the next five minutes accepting backslaps, handshakes, and congratulations from the other competitors. Poppy and Felix finally muscled their way over to us, congratulating us as well, while Oscar buzzed around and around our shoulders.

Finally, the stadium quieted again, and we turned to watch the match between Katia and Deah that would decide which of them I had to fight in the final round.

Deah nodded at Katia as they faced each other in the

stone ring, but Katia didn't return the gesture. Instead, she kept twirling and twirling her sword around and around in her hand, loosening up. Every once in a while, she would turn toward me enough that I could see the determined glint in her bright green eyes. The official called out the instructions again; then the fight began.

Katia immediately went on the offensive, moving quicker than I'd ever seen her move before, even during the obstacle course. Her movements were almost too fast to follow, and the only reason Deah was able to block her blows was because she'd long ago memorized the moves and countermoves, just as we all had.

And it wasn't just that Katia was fast, but she also seemed stronger today, hitting Deah's sword as hard as she could over and over again and showing no signs of stopping. I'd known that Katia was upset about losing to Deah in the tournament twice before, but she was fighting like it was a real battle and giving it everything she had. Katia had told me how much she wanted to win, and I'd felt her desire for myself, but she was really putting it all out there.

But despite all her speed, sharp blows, and determination, Katia still wasn't able to get the best of the other girl.

Deah realized that Katia was trying to overwhelm her, and she did just enough to keep herself in the match, waiting for Katia's initial fury to burn itself out. And it slowly did. The longer the fight continued, the slower and weaker Katia became, almost as if she'd used up all of her speed and strength with that opening round of attacks.

I didn't know exactly how Deah's mimic Talent worked, but I'd thought it must be similar to my own soulsight. It seemed I was right. Deah stared into Katia's eyes the whole time, as if she was peering into the other girl the way I could look into other people. The longer Deah stared at Katia, the more she started to move exactly like the other girl, flowing from one attack position to the next, until it seemed as though Katia were fighting herself. And not only that, but it almost seemed as if Deah grew stronger and stronger as the match went on, while Katia kept slowly weakening.

Katia knew the tide was turning, and she snarled and lashed out with a series of quick attacks, designed to end the fight. But Deah was too smart, too experienced, too good, for that, and it didn't work. Every time Deah blocked her latest blow, it only made Katia that much angrier. My eyes locked with Katia's for a second as she whirled around, her hazel-green gaze burning brighter than ever before.

Her red-hot anger, rock-hard determination, and aching desperation punched me in the gut one right after another. *Bam-bam-bam.* Katia wanted to win the tournament, but even more than that, she had this hot, desperate *need* to beat Deah, as though it was more important to her than anything else.

But she wasn't going to be able to do it.

Deah was clearly the better fighter. Oh, she wasn't quicker or stronger than Katia—I doubted that anyone was right now—but Deah could think ahead and plan out her moves in a way that Katia couldn't, just as I'd been able to think ahead in my fight with Devon. Katia didn't realize it, but Deah was slowly driving her toward the cold spring in the center of the ring. In seven more moves, Katia would go into the water and Deah would win the match.

The fight dragged on, the cheers getting louder and louder with every sharp, ringing blow the two girls exchanged. Katia raised her sword high, putting everything she had into a strike aimed squarely at Deah's head, as though she really wanted to cleave Deah's skull in two with her sword. Everyone in the stadium gasped, including me—because if that blow connected, then Deah was dead.

But Deah managed to bring her own weapon up in time to block Katia's sword, the muscles in her arms standing out and showing what an enormous effort it was. Deah stared into Katia's eyes, dug her feet into the ground, and threw off the other girl, who shrieked in anger. Deah snarled back at her, and the two of them started circling each other again, with Deah still driving Katia closer and closer to the cold spring the whole time.

Katia was in a rage now, and she whipped her sword back and forth, and back and forth, moving harder and faster than ever before. But Deah matched her move for move.

Finally, Katia made a mistake, the same one Devon had made. She got too close to the edge of the cold spring, and her foot slipped. Katia windmilled her free arm for balance and Deah took advantage, stepping up and slicing her blade across the back of Katia's sword hand. That small motion pushed Katia over the edge and sent her toppling backward, straight into the water.

Deah stepped back.

Katia came up sputtering. She shoved her wet hair off her face and stared in disbelief at the blood welling up out of the shallow cut on her hand. Her fingers tightened around her sword, making more blood ooze out of the wound, and she scrambled out of the water and surged forward as though she was going to keep on attacking Deah, even though the match was over.

One of the officials quickly stepped in front of Katia, cutting her off, even as another official reached for Deah's hand and held it up.

"Winner, Deah Draconi!" the official yelled.

The stadium erupted in cheers. Deah glanced up at the

Draconi box, giving Seleste and Victor a happy wave. Then she went over to Katia and held out her hand for the other girl to shake, but Katia gave her a disgusted look, whirled around, and stormed out of the stadium.

Deah kept smiling and waving to the crowd. Beside me, Devon, Felix, Poppy, and Oscar were talking about the match, but I only had eyes for Katia.

I slipped away from the others and followed Katia over to the Volkov tent, which was deserted, since everyone had been gathered around the fence, watching the match. Katia slung her sword as hard as she could, and the weapon zipped through the air and stuck in one of the wooden poles holding up the tent, wobbling back and forth.

"Dammit!" she screamed.

Katia went on a rampage—knocking weapons off tables, dashing cups and plates to the ground, and slamming her fists into every single thing she could. I'd heard of 'roid rage before, but Katia was beyond even that. I moved away from the tent entrance, not wanting to embarrass her with the realization that someone was watching her epic meltdown.

Finally, after a couple of minutes, the noise and cursing stopped, and Katia stepped back outside. She saw me standing near the tent. She hesitated a moment, then strode over to me, looking out into the stadium. Deah was still there, smiling, waving, and signing autographs for some of the tourist rubes, as well as members of the other Families. Katia scowled, white-hot rage flaring in her hazel eyes.

"You fought a good match," I said, trying to cheer her up. "The way you moved out there . . . it was incredible how fast you were."

She gave me a disgusted look as though I'd just said the stupidest thing ever. "Not fast enough. Not good enough.

I'm never fast enough, I'm never good enough. Not with *her* around."

She glared at Deah a final time, then stomped off into the fairgrounds. I let her go. Yeah, it sucked to lose, especially to the same person over and over again, but that was life sometimes. Katia seemed to specifically blame Deah because she'd lost, but Deah had clearly been the better fighter. I might not like Deah, but she'd won fair and square, just as I had against Devon.

And there was something else about Katia that was bothering me—some small, nagging detail that I couldn't quite put my finger on. But the more I tried to figure it out, the deeper it sank into my brain.

After a couple of minutes, I gave up and moved on to the next thing—the final round of the Tournament of Blades. I wondered who would win, Deah or me. I looked down at the star carved into the center of my black blade and my star-shaped, sapphire ring.

I thought of my mom then, and I was determined that it was going to be me.

CHAPTER TWENTY-THREE

I headed back over to the fence to hang out with Devon, Felix, Poppy, and Oscar before the final match. It took me much longer than it should have, since people stopped me every few feet to congratulate me and wish me luck in the final round. One tourist rube with a camera even asked if I would let her take my photo. I didn't really want to, but I decided to be nice and pose for a picture, even though my smile was more of a snarl.

I had just moved away from the tourist and was blinking away the blinding camera flash when a hand settled on my shoulder.

I spun around to find Seleste Draconi staring at me with her bright, intense eyes—eyes that seemed to look right through me.

"You can't win today, Serena," she said in a dreamy voice. "You're my sister, but you can't win today."

I couldn't have been more shocked than if she'd zapped me with a bolt of lightning.

Sister? Seleste and my mom were *sisters*?

"You need to let the girls win," Seleste continued. "It's the only way they're ever going to find each other. They're blood, and blood should stick together."

I shook off my shock. Seleste was just spouting nonsense again or somehow saying that she and my mom had been as close as sisters. Mom had never mentioned having an *actual* sister. Not even once. Surely, Mom would have told me that I had an aunt—

My stomach dropped. Or maybe not, since that aunt was married to Victor Draconi.

"I think you're confused." I didn't want to hurt Seleste, but my voice came out sharper than I intended. "I'm not Serena Sterling. I'm her daughter, Lila. Remember? We met the other night at the cemetery."

For a moment, Seleste's face cleared, but then her eyes clouded over again, burning even brighter than before. "Lila . . . she finally came to her father's grave, just the way I saw she would. . . ." Her voice trailed off, and she seemed lost in her own thoughts.

This conversation was going around and around in circles, and I didn't need Seleste and her visions messing with my head. Not before the final match. I turned to head back to my friends, but Seleste latched out and grabbed hold of my arm.

She looked at me again, this time actually seeming to see *me*, and not my mom or some ghost or misty vision of the future. "You have to let Deah win," she hissed. "Whatever you want, I'll pay it and more. Just let her win the tournament. You're the only one who can beat her. And you're the only one who can beat *him*."

I shook my head. "I have no idea what you're talking about."

She tightened her grip on my arm, still staring at me. "Victor will punish Deah if she doesn't win. You know he will. The same way he punishes me when one of my visions turns out to be wrong or not what he expected. But he doesn't realize that I'm telling him the wrong things. Never the right things. Never the important things. He slaps me and locks me away with no food, but I don't care. Not anymore."

Seleste cackled, as if she was happy she was lying to Victor despite all the pain and misery it brought down on her.

"I'm going to do my best in the tournament," I said, trying to bring her back to the here and now. "Maybe Deah will beat me, and maybe she won't. But I'm not going to just *let* her win."

Seleste tightened her grip, her fingers painful and bruising on my upper arm. "But you *have* to. It's the only way Victor will ever be defeated—if you and Deah work together."

I had no idea what she was talking about. Deah loved her father and desperately wanted his approval. Even if she knew what a monster Victor was, there was no way she would ever turn against him. Especially not to help *me*. Deah hated me because I knew about her and Felix. Because I kept pointing out how stupid it was for the two of them to keep sneaking around when so many people could get hurt as a result.

"I'm sorry," I repeated in a firmer voice. "But I can't help you."

Seleste's face took on a sly, cunning look. "Not even to get your revenge on Victor for murdering Serena?"

Her words were like a slap across the face. "How do you know about that?"

No one knew about that, except for Mo, Devon, Claudia, and a few other people. It wasn't like Victor had announced he'd murdered my mom to all the other Families. I doubted he'd given the horrible things he'd done to her more than a passing thought over the years.

Seleste gave me a pitying look. "I saw it, of course." She sighed. "I see everything."

Anger roared through me. "Well, if you saw it, then why didn't you *stop* it? Huh? Especially since you were her friend. At least, that's what Mo said."

"Not just her friend—her *sister*," Seleste snapped back. "She was my sister, and I still couldn't save her."

More questions crowded into my mind, including why she kept insisting they were sisters. Seleste didn't look anything like my mom, with her blond hair and dark blue eyes, and she didn't even have the same kind of magic—

Wait a second. Blue eyes. Mom had had dark blue eyes. So did I. And so did Deah.

My mom had had sight magic. Seleste could see the future. I could see into people with my soulsight, and it seemed as if Deah could do something similar with her mimic magic.

Jolt after jolt, shock after shock, zinged through me. Could . . . could Seleste be telling the truth? Could she and my mom really have been sisters? That would mean . . . that would make Deah my cousin. We would be related. Family.

Blood.

"You have to believe me," Seleste said, pleading with me. "I tried to save Serena. I try to save everyone, but it doesn't always work."

Her voice dropped to a ragged whisper, and her entire body trembled. I looked—*really* looked at her—peering past the glaze of magic that coated her eyes.

Her aching regret slammed into me, making my heart hurt, my stomach twist, and knives slice through every single part of my body. The emotion was so strong that I staggered back, clutched my chest, and gasped for air, trying to get away from it for just one second. But Seleste . . . she couldn't get away from it. She felt this all day, every day. How did she live with it?

Seleste dropped her gaze from mine. "I really did try to save Serena."

"I . . . I believe you," I croaked out, the awful emotions vanishing and my breathing slowly returning to normal.

"And you have to believe me about this too. You have to let Deah win the tournament. It's the only way to save you both . . . *bones and blades . . . bones and blades . . . bones and blades. . . .*"

She grabbed my hands and stared into my eyes, but her gaze was foggy and distant, and I could tell that she wasn't really seeing me. Instead, she kept mumbling those same words over and over again. I wondered what sort of prophecy or vision of the future it was. Whatever it was, she thought it was going to kill either Deah or me or both of us.

And I was starting to believe her.

People were beginning to stare at us and whisper, so I pried my hands out of Seleste's and took a step back. She reached for me again, still mumbling about *bones and blades*, but I took another step back, staying out of her reach, and kept my gaze averted from hers. I didn't want to know what she was feeling. Not right now.

Finally, she seemed to snap back to her senses, and she gave me another sorrowful look.

"I hope you believe me," Seleste whispered. "I hope you do the right thing—for all our sakes. Or Victor has already won."

Then she turned and walked away without another word.

I slipped into a pool of shadows next to the Sinclair tent and drew in deep breaths, trying to push all the questions and worries out of my mind and compose myself. Easier said than done.

When I felt calm enough, I went back over to the fence where my friends were still standing. Felix, Poppy, and Oscar all wished me good luck, then turned to talk to some other folks who had come up to them, but Devon stayed with me. He touched my shoulder and steered me a few feet away from the others.

"What's wrong?" he asked.

I shook my head. "I ran into Seleste in the fairgounds. She said some . . . strange things."

"Like what?"

I told him everything she'd said, except for Seleste claiming to be my aunt and wanting me to throw the tournament so Victor wouldn't punish Deah for losing.

The longer I talked, the more Devon's frown deepened. "Bones and blades—that's the same warning she gave you at the Draconi cemetery. What do you think it means?"

"I have no idea. And really, I don't think I want to know. I need to focus on the match. Not get distracted by Seleste and her prophecies."

Devon touched my shoulder again. "Then don't—don't think about it at all. For the next five minutes or ten minutes or however long the match lasts, just think about how you can win. I would wish you luck, but you don't need it. And no matter what happens out there, I want you to know how glad I am that you're a member of the Sinclair Family. That you are a part of my life."

My mouth dropped open in surprise. Devon smiled, but he took care to not look at me, as if he didn't want me to be distracted by his feelings. Yeah. Fat chance of that happening. He opened his mouth to say something else, but Felix asked him a question, and Devon turned away from me to answer him.

My fingers curled around the hilt of my mom's sword, and I drew it out of its scabbard and held it up before me, staring at the stars carved into the hilt and streaming down the blade. I wondered what my mom had thought at this moment, the minutes before she would either win or lose the tournament. What she'd been feeling. And what it had felt like when she had finally won. When she'd finally proven herself to be the best fighter around.

So I twirled my mom's sword around and around the way I had so many times before, and the way she had so many times before me. I moved the weapon from one hand to the other and back again, clearing my mind for the fight to come.

And when I was ready, I dropped my mom's sword to my side and let out a breath, finally ready to fight for everything that I wanted.

CHAPTER TWENTY-FOUR

The officials announced that it was time for the final match, and I drew in a breath and stepped out into the stadium. Directly across from me, Deah entered on the opposite side. The crowd yelled and cheered, although I could hear a few, loud *boo-boo-boos* mixed in as well, from Blake and his crew.

I kept my pace slow and steady and concentrated on the feel of my mom's sword in my hand, more determined to win than ever before. As Devon had said, this was my chance to take something from the Draconis for a change, especially from Victor, and I wasn't about to screw it up by not paying attention to what mattered most right now.

My opponent.

Deah reached the stone ring before I did, her sword down and out by her side, just like mine was. Sunlight glinted off her weapon, and I finally got a good look at the symbols carved into the sword.

Stars covered the black blade.

I blinked, wondering if I was imagining things, but I wasn't. Five-pointed stars covered the blade of her sword, clustered together in tight groups, just the way they were on mine, almost as if her weapon was a twin to my own.

Or a sword that a mother had passed down to her daughter.

Shock zipped through me. My heart clenched tight, and in that instant, I knew that everything Seleste said was true. She was my aunt, which made Deah my cousin, and Deah had a Sterling Family sword to prove it.

More and more questions crowded into my mind. Mo . . . he had to know about this. So did Claudia. After all, they'd been friends with my mom and Seleste. So why hadn't they ever told me about Seleste and Deah?

But I pushed all the questions and revelations aside. Just because we shared the same DNA didn't make us *family*. Not really. It didn't matter if I was related to Seleste and Deah. It didn't have any bearing on the tournament at all. Because Deah was my opponent, the person standing between me and what I wanted, and I wasn't about to go easy on her just because some secret had been dragged out into the light.

So I stepped forward and listened to the official go through the rules a final time, even though everyone had already heard them before. Deah looked up at the Draconi box, and so did I. Seleste was sitting there, front and center, and she gave a big, cheery wave to her daughter before her gaze moved to me. She hesitated, then waved at me as well, although not as enthusiastically.

Victor was also in the box, sitting and talking to Blake, the two of them totally ignoring Deah, even though this was her big moment. Or maybe they were so sure she was going to win that they didn't even have to watch the match.

I looked into Deah's eyes, feeling all of her tight, pinching hurt. She desperately wanted her father's love and approval, and she never felt she had it, no matter what she did or how much she accomplished. Not even now, when she was in the spotlight, poised to bring such glory to the Draconis and win the Tournament of Blades for the third straight year.

It made me feel sad for her.

My mom might be dead, but she'd never ignored me the way Victor and Blake were ignoring Deah. She might still have both her parents, but in her own way, she was as alone as I was. Katia had been wrong. Deah Draconi didn't win at everything, and she certainly didn't have everything.

She didn't have very much at all.

Seleste noticed that Victor and Blake were ignoring Deah, so she waved to her daughter again, a big, happy smile on her face. I sensed that some of the hurt eased in Deah's heart, and she waved back to her mom. Then she dropped her gaze from the box and focused on her sword, swinging it around and around in her hand, gearing up for the fight.

I stared up at Seleste, and she looked at me again. Our gazes locked, letting me feel her aching desperation for me to throw the match and let Deah win. I wondered why it was so important and why she thought it was the only way that Deah and I could save each other. Even if I did throw the match, it wasn't like Deah and I would automatically become besties. It wasn't like we would ever be friends. Not when she was a Draconi and I was a Sinclair.

Not when her father had murdered my mother.

So I turned away from Seleste and looked over at the Sinclair box. Devon, Felix, Claudia, Angelo, Reginald, and Mo were all up there, with Oscar *zip-zip-zipping* around faster than ever before. All of them were looking at me, grinning, clapping, and flashing me thumbs-ups, but I focused on Devon. Our gazes locked, and his warm pride filled me from head to toe. Win or lose, friends or something more, he'd always be there to support me.

That knowledge shattered the last part of the shell around my heart, letting all the feelings I had for Devon pour in. I just stood there, with all these emotions flooding my body. Warm happiness. Rock-hard certainty. And a hot, dizzying rush that made my heart soar. But for once, they weren't someone else's emotions—they were *mine.*

Once again, Devon had stormed past all of my defenses without even trying, just by being the good guy that he truly was. Word by word, smile by smile, thoughtful thing by thoughtful thing, Devon had chipped away at the cold, brittle shell that coated my heart, the one that had encased it ever since my mom had died. I wanted to tell him that—and so much more.

But now wasn't the time for Devon and me, so I dropped my gaze from his and focused on Deah again.

"Good luck," she said in a soft voice. "May the best fighter win."

"Yeah," I said, tightening my grip on my sword. "You too."

The official lifted his hand, then dropped it.

Deah and I both raised our weapons and charged at each other.

My sword met Deah's, the resulting *clang* so loud that you could hear it throughout the stadium. This wasn't just about two people fighting each other to win a contest; it was representative of our two Families fighting as well, and the epic clash that had been going on between the Sinclairs and Draconis for years.

Deah and I stood in the middle of the stone ring, our swords locked together, each one of us trying to throw the other off, neither one of us having any success. Neither of us had speed or strength Talents, so we were evenly matched. I'd have to fight her with my wits and skills, like I had Devon.

I didn't have a problem with that.

Finally, we both backed off, untangling our swords and circling around and around each other. Then we both charged at each other again, whipping our swords back and forth, and back and forth, and falling into the steps we'd both danced to a thousand times before.

All the while, the crowd was going crazy, cheering, yelling, clapping, and screaming with every move Deah and I made, with every *clang* of our swords and every smash of our feet in the trampled grass. This was the last match of the tournament, and they wanted it to be a good one. Well, I planned to give them their money's worth—before I beat Deah.

But the longer we fought, the brighter Deah's blue eyes glowed, and the more her movements became exactly like . . . *mine.* The way she held her sword, the way she moved, even the snarl of her lips—it was all like a mirror image of myself—and I realized that she was using her mimic power.

The cold chill of her magic radiated off her body, and my own transference power stirred weakly in response. But unless she actually used her power on me in some tangible way—hit me, tripped me, whatever—then I couldn't absorb her magic and use it against her. I couldn't use her magic to make myself stronger. This wasn't the first time something like this had happened, but I found it more frustrating than ever before because if I was just a little bit stronger, I could overpower her and win the match.

So the fight dragged on . . . and on . . . and *on.* . . .

Since I was more or less fighting myself at this point, I couldn't win, but neither could Deah. One minute passed, then two, then three, and we fought on, both of us starting to suck wind. With every blow we landed, the crowd gasped, thinking that this was going to be the moment when one of us cut the other and drew first blood. But I blocked her blows, and she thwarted mine, and the fight raged on.

But the longer we fought, the more I realized I had one small advantage over Deah. She might be able to use her

Talent to mimic my every move, but she didn't actually have *my* magic. She didn't have my transference power, and she especially didn't have my soulsight. However her magic worked, she could see the moves I was making, how I held my sword, how my feet shifted around and around, and she could copy all of that right down to the squint of my eyes and the tilt of my head.

But she couldn't *see* into *me* the way that I could into her.

She couldn't feel my emotions, and most important, she couldn't anticipate what I was going to do next. Not exactly, not precisely, not for sure every single time the way I could with her.

And I finally knew how I could win.

Deah had been staring at me the whole time, looking into my eyes the same way I was staring into hers. I wondered if that's how her magic worked, if her mimic Talent was a form of sight. Did she have to see a person in order to copy their fighting style and everything else about them? It made sense, especially since it seemed that all the other women in our family had some sort of sight Talent. If that was how her power worked, then all I had to do was not look at her, not let her peer into my eyes.

So that's what I did.

I dropped my gaze from Deah's, instead focusing on her sword and the way the sun glinted on the metal, the warm rays highlighting all the stars carved into the hilt of her black blade—her Sterling Family sword.

For a moment, guilt surged through me, but I shook it off and went on the attack, whipping my sword back and forth and pressing forward with renewed energy.

And slowly, I began to take control of the fight.

At first, it was small things: Deah not putting her foot down exactly how I did mine, holding her sword a fraction of an inch lower than mine, gripping the hilt just a little too high. But slowly, all those little things started to add up. Deah was still a great fighter—one of the best I'd ever seen—but I was just a smidge better, someone she couldn't overcome without her mimic magic.

And she knew it too.

Her blows became quicker and more desperate and reckless. I couldn't see the future like Seleste could, but I knew with crystal clarity how the rest of the fight would play out. Five more moves and she would overreach, and then I could slice my sword across her arm and win the Tournament of Blades, just as my mom had before me. The thought made me so happy that I smiled and stared directly into Deah's eyes.

Her hot, sweaty desperation slammed into my gut so hard that I blinked and stumbled back from the force of it. I stared into her eyes again, and I realized desperation wasn't all she was feeling.

Deah was afraid.

Fear churned and churned like acid in her stomach. She knew that I was the better fighter and that she was seconds away from losing the match and the tournament. And she was afraid of what her father would do to her and Seleste when she lost.

It was weird, but in that moment, I almost felt I could see into Deah. That was nothing new, but I wasn't just feeling her emotions—I was actually *seeing* all the memories she had of growing up. Training so hard all the time so she could be the best fighter possible. Running after Seleste, trying to keep her from wandering off and displeasing Victor and Blake. Doing everything she possibly could to win her father's love and approval and knowing that nothing she did was ever truly good enough for him. That Victor preferred Blake and always would.

One after another, the memories flooded my mind until it was all that I could do to keep swinging my sword.

How did Deah live like that? Training so hard, worrying about her mom, being hurt by Victor's cruel words time and time again? How did she function when she knew that her own father didn't even love her? Neither did Blake, who saw her as just another tool he could use to do their father's bidding.

In that moment, I felt sorrier for Deah Draconi than I ever had before.

I could win the match, but for the first time, I didn't want to because I knew what it would cost her. I didn't like Deah, but I didn't want her or Seleste to suffer because of me. I'd *never* wanted that, but if the fight kept going the way it was, that was exactly what was going to happen. Deah and her mom would suffer miserably at Victor's hands, and there would be nothing that I or anyone else could do about it, since it would happen behind closed doors at the Draconi estate. No one there would dare to interfere with Victor and Blake, and none of the other Families would care enough to get involved, except for Claudia. But even then, I didn't know what Claudia could do to help them, since the Sinclairs and the Draconis were on the verge of going to war anyway.

I sighed, knowing what I had to do. It was the exact same thing my mom would have done. She'd always tried to protect people who needed help, and she'd never once complained about it. I wasn't as good or noble as she had been, but I knew a hard truth. That sometimes, doing the right thing sucked out loud, and this was definitely going to be one of those times.

So I sighed again, lowered my sword just a fraction, and slowly lessened my pace, as though I was exhausted and finally fading. Deah pressed her advantage, and I made my blows weaker and weaker, letting her get a little closer to cutting me every single time. I could have recovered, I could have taken her out, but I decided not to.

Besides, maybe Seleste's prophecy was right and Deah and I needed each other to survive. Either way, I wasn't going to win this fight. Not now. I wasn't going to be the cause of someone else's misery—especially not someone who had as much hurt in her battered, broken heart as I did.

So I counted down the moves in my head, wondering if she would take the opening I was going to give her.

And she did.

I pretended to trip on the edge of the water and stumbled past Deah. An instant later, I felt her black blade slice into my arm, and the hot spatter of blood sliding down my skin.

Just like that, it was over.

I sighed, lowered my sword, and turned around. Deah stared at me, dumbstruck, as though she couldn't believe that she'd actually, finally won.

The official hurried over, grabbed her hand, and raised it high. "And the winner of the Tournament of Blades is Deah Draconi!"

The crowd erupted into loud, roaring cheers, each one like a sword slicing my heart to ribbons. They should have been cheering for *me*. They should have been yelling and clapping for *me*. They should have been chanting *my* name over and over again, not hers.

I dropped my head, trying to ignore all the jubilation, as though I was exhausted and disgusted with myself. Not too much of a stretch right now.

Yeah, sometimes, doing the right thing was the most painful feeling in the entire world.

CHAPTER TWENTY-FIVE

The members of the Draconi Family stampeded down the bleachers and stormed onto the field, shoving everyone aside, including me. Blake hoisted Deah up onto his shoulder. A Draconi guard stepped up on Deah's other side, and he and Blake carried her around and around. All of the Draconis were clapping, cheering, and yelling—except for Deah.

She kept glancing back over her shoulder at me, her eyes dark and troubled. She knew I'd let her win, but she didn't know why. Well, I wasn't about to tell her.

But I'd made my choice, and the fight was over. There was no taking it back, so I trudged over to the fence at the edge of the grass. Devon and Felix were already waiting for me, their faces filled with sympathy that I didn't want to see and especially didn't want to feel right now.

"Um, good match, Lila," Felix said, wincing, obviously torn between consoling me and being happy that Deah had won. "You'll get her next year."

"Yeah," I muttered. "Next year."

Devon frowned, suspicion flaring in his eyes. He realized that I'd thrown the fight, but he didn't ask me about it. Maybe he knew I didn't want to talk about it right now. That I never, *ever* wanted to talk about it. That I just wanted to go back to the mansion, hole up in my room, and not come out for the rest of the summer. Maybe by then all the talk about the stupid tournament would finally be over. Yeah, right. It would *never* be over. Blake and the rest of the Draconis would gleefully rub my defeat in my face for as long as I stayed in Cloudburst Falls.

The Sinclair guards climbed down from the bleachers and headed over to us. I plastered a smile on my face and gritted my teeth through everyone's congratulations and condolences. The guards quickly drifted away, and Claudia, Mo, Reginald, Angelo, and Oscar came down from the Family box and gathered around me. Reginald and Angelo wore sympathetic expressions, but Mo and especially Claudia seemed much more thoughtful. Oscar was absolutely crestfallen, barely twitching his wings enough to hover in the air beside me.

I turned to Mo. "Sorry I didn't win. I hope I didn't cost you too much money."

He grinned and slung his arm around my shoulder. "Don't worry about it, kid. Easy come, easy go." His black eyes narrowed. "Besides, you did your best, right? That's all anyone can ask of you."

"My best. Right."

Mo stared at me, and I realized that he knew I'd thrown the match as well. But apparently he decided not to call me on it in front of the others.

"Besides," he continued. "I might have . . . hedged a few of my bets, so to speak, just in case things didn't go the way I wanted them to. If you can't win, you might as well break even, right?"

I frowned. Something about his words bothered me, although I couldn't say exactly what it was. Something about hedging your bets and trying to stack the odds in your favor, although I supposed that everyone in the tournament had tried to do that as much as they could over the past few days—even if Devon had told me that there was no way to cheat in the one-on-one matches.

I frowned. Or was there a way to cheat? Maybe all you needed was—

"You did well, Lila," Claudia said, interrupting my train of thought. "I'm proud of you, regardless of the outcome of the match, and so is everyone else."

Sincerity flashed in her eyes, but her mouth was set in a hard line, telling me that she, too, realized I'd thrown the fight. I was sure she wanted to know why, although she was polite enough not to demand an answer in front of everyone.

But my friends' suspicions were nothing compared to having to watch Deah bask in the winner's glory.

She was still riding shoulders, still the center of everyone's attention. Finally, though, the officials stepped forward again and broke up the crowd as best as they could. A few seconds later, a low, rolling drumbeat sounded.

"Now what?" I muttered.

Devon gave me a sympathetic look. "Now, the officials will present the winner's trophy . . . and the one for the runner-up."

I groaned. "Please don't tell me that I have to go back out there."

He winced. "Sorry, Lila."

Sure enough, one of the officials came over, gesturing for me to go back out into the middle of the stadium, where a small stage had been erected inside the stone ring. By the time I reached the stage, Deah was already standing on it, and I had no choice but to go over, climb the steps, and stand right next to her.

The head official started talking about what an honor it was to oversee the tournament every year, how fiercely all the competitors had fought, and blah, blah, blah, blah. The only thing that mattered right now was the fact that I'd lost. But I plastered a tight smile on my face, raised my hand, and waved to the crowd when I was supposed to. Deah did the same thing, smiling just like I was, although she kept looking at me out of the corner of her eye.

"Why did you let me win?" she muttered during a particularly loud round of applause. "What possible reason could you have had for doing that?"

"What does it matter?" I muttered back. "You won. So shut up, and be happy about it."

She shook her head. "I didn't want to win like *that*. I wanted to *earn* it for myself. I don't need your charity or especially your damn *pity*."

I opened my mouth to snark back that with her ungrateful attitude, she didn't have to worry because she wouldn't be getting either one of those things ever again. But the official stepped forward and presented me with a small silver cup before I could get the words out.

I ground my teeth together, forced myself to smile again, and held the cup up over my head as though I were absolutely thrilled with second place. No bloody way.

After the polite applause had faded away, I lowered the cup and *tap-tap-tapped* my fingernail against the side of it. Solid sterling silver and worth a pretty penny. Well, at least I'd gotten something out of letting Deah win. Maybe I'd let Mo hock my trophy, such as it was, at the Razzle Dazzle. I certainly didn't want to keep it and be reminded of how I'd lost.

"And now, I am pleased to present this year's winner of the Tournament of Blades . . . Deah Draconi!" the official yelled.

Deah got a gold cup—real gold from the way it glimmered in the sun—and hoisted it up and over her head. The Draconi dragon crest had already been stamped into the cup, along with Deah's name and the date she'd won the tournament. Wow. The engravers around here worked fast. The thought further soured my mood.

The crowd cheered again, the sound rising to a deafening roar, and Deah smiled and waved, although I was the only one who noticed how thin and brittle her expression really was.

Maybe that was because it matched mine perfectly.

Finally, the stupid ceremony wrapped up, and I could leave the stage. I stomped down the stairs and back over to the fence where Devon and Felix were waiting for me, along with Oscar.

"Don't worry," Oscar said, fluttering over and landing on my shoulder. "You'll get her next year."

"Right," I muttered. "Next year."

If one more person said that to me, I was going to scream.

"Come on," Felix said. "Let's get you cleaned up and out of those clothes so we can go get some food. I know you must be starving."

"And how would you know that?"

He grinned. "Because Lila Merriweather is *always* starving. They've already set out the food down by the lake. And doesn't bacon make everything better?"

Felix waggled his eyebrows, trying to cheer me up by using my own line against me, and I actually found myself laughing, just a little. Sure, losing had sucked, but I wouldn't trade places with Deah for anything. She might have won the Tournament of Blades, but I had something way more important—my friends—friends who would never, ever desert me no matter what happened.

"Come on," Felix said, a wheedling note creeping into his voice. "I'll even let you have my allotment of bacon too."

I eyed him. "Promise?"

He made an *X* over his heart. "Promise."

I laughed again, the sound coming to me easier this time. "Good. Because you're right; bacon does make everything better. So point me to it."

We stopped at the Sinclair tent, where Felix used his healing magic to patch up the slice in my arm. I also took off my tournament clothes, exchanged them for my normal blue T-shirt, gray cargo shorts, and gray sneakers, and put my silver cup in my bag with the rest of my things. I strapped my sword back to my waist, then balled up my black pants and white shirt and stuffed them into the nearest trash can. I never wanted to wear them or be reminded of this day again.

When I was finished, I threaded one arm through Felix's and my other one through Devon's. Together, we left the stadium behind and headed out of the fairgrounds.

It was after seven now, and the party was already going strong by the time we reached the lake. People were milling around the picnic shelters, laughing, talking, and scarfing down food. Someone must have gotten hold of Oscar's playlist because twangy, old-school country music sounded. The smells of grilled meat filled the air, and my stomach rumbled.

"See?" Felix said, nudging me with his elbow. "I knew you wouldn't be down for long. Not when there's free food."

I laughed and we got in line in front of the stand that Reginald and the Sinclair pixies were manning, with Oscar fluttering over to help them out. Tonight's menu was barbecue, which meant meat and lots of it. Pulled pork, pulled beef, smoked brisket, and lots of grilled sausages slathered with this spicy barbecue sauce Reginald told me he'd gotten from a restaurant called the Pork Pit. I piled a plate high with meats, then another one with coleslaw, onion rings, baked beans full of bacon, and some delicious sourdough rolls to sop everything up with.

Devon, Felix, and I went over to a table and sat down. I wanted nothing more than to eat my food in peace, but to my surprise, folks from all the different Families came over and congratulated me on the tournament yet again. Nobody said that I would get Deah next year, though, so I didn't have to break out my best scream on anyone.

I smiled and made the appropriate noises, but the congratulations only made me feel even more like a stupid, stupid fool. Yeah, I might have done the right thing, but the aftermath was torture. Especially since Deah was in the middle of the lawn, surrounded by her adoring admirers, with that gold cup glimmering on the table beside her like a neon sign flashing HERE SHE IS! SHE'S A WINNER! ISN'T SHE GREAT!

I focused on the cup. Maybe I could go over and swipe it while everyone was paying attention to Deah. Too bad I didn't have my spidersilk coat with me. It would have been perfect for hiding that gold cup and smuggling it away from here.

Blake and the rest of the Draconis might be showering Deah with attention, but not everyone was happy about her win. Some of the other competitors were giving her sour looks, including Katia, whose eyes glittered an eerie green. I frowned. Something about her gaze bothered me—

Devon bumped his shoulder into mine. "What are you thinking about?"

The thought, whatever it was, vanished back into the bottom of my brain. I shook my head. "Nothing."

He stared at me, his eyes shining in his face. He leaned down and wet his lips, as though he was about to ask me something, and I was suddenly aware of just how hard my heart was hammering in my chest. Especially because this time, I was going to tell him yes.

Yes, I cared about him. Yes, I wanted to be with him. Just . . . *yes*. To everything there was between us.

"Well, well, well," a familiar, unwelcome voice sneered. "If it isn't the first loser, hiding out with the rest of her loser friends."

I looked up to find Blake standing beside our table. My hands curled into fists in my lap. More than ever before, I wanted to wipe that smug smirk off his face. Devon put a hand on my arm, warning me against doing anything.

"Did you really think you could hide over here?" Blake said, his voice booming out like thunder.

Folks stopped what they were doing to stare at us, and I realized that Blake wanted me to get mad. He wanted me to look like a sore loser. Well, it wasn't going to happen.

I shrugged, not rising to his taunting. "I wasn't trying to hide. Just wanted to get some food."

Deah had heard Blake, and she grabbed her gold cup off the table and walked over to stand by her brother. Of course she would. She might have Sterling blood, but she was Draconi through and through.

"Blake," she said. "Leave her alone. I won. That's the important thing, right?"

Blake gave her a cool look. "Of course you won. You were always going to win. You're the best fighter in town. And now that you have won, you need to show everyone else what their place is—below you. Below us. Below all the Draconis."

Deah bit her lip, looking back and forth between Blake and me. Her eyes cut to Felix for a second as well. She didn't want to go along with Blake, but I knew she would. She always had before, even if she knew her brother was a bully and hated the way he looked down on everyone else.

She sighed. "Blake, let's just go. Okay? There's no need to be mean about things."

He frowned. "You weren't saying that last year when you won. You spent the whole night telling the other contestants to suck it, and rightly so, especially Katia. So what's different this year? You won again, and we should celebrate. Why aren't you on board with that?"

Deah glanced at me, and my soulsight kicked in, letting me feel just how much she was struggling with this. She might have won the tournament, but she hadn't done it fairly, and it was eating at her. Her gaze fell to the gold cup in her hand, her fingers tightening around the handle.

"Come on, Sis," Blake said, that sneer creeping back into his voice again. "Everyone knows that you're the best. I just want to make sure these Sinclair losers realize it too."

"They're not losers," she said in a soft voice, her fingers tracing over the snarling dragon crest stamped into the cup.

"Sure they are," Blake said, his voice growing louder and louder. "Especially Morales. He didn't even get picked by his own Family to enter the tournament because they all know what a *loser* he is. He wouldn't have even made it through the first round. Scratch that. He wouldn't have made it through the first minute without getting bounced out of the tournament."

"Don't talk about Felix like that," Deah snapped. "He's never done anything to you."

Blake's brown eyes narrowed. "And yet, you're the one who's always defending him. Why is that?"

Deah's gaze flicked from Blake to Felix and back again, desperately trying to come up with some sort of answer.

I shot to my feet. "Maybe because she's tired of you

picking on him the way you do everyone else. I wouldn't want to have to listen to you either."

Blake stepped up so that he was staring straight down into my face. "Deah might have already beaten you in the tournament, but I can do it again. Right here, right now. Where it really *matters*. Where I can really make it *hurt*."

What he meant was where he could give me the beating he'd been itching to dish out for weeks now, ever since I'd humiliated him at the arcade by putting him in that wrist lock in front of his friends.

But I wasn't scared of Blake and his threats, and I laughed in his face.

"Please," I scoffed. "You couldn't beat me on your best day. And trust me. Today isn't that day."

Blake started toward me, but Deah stepped in between us.

"Hey," she said, putting her hand on his chest. "Just calm down, okay? Let's go back to our table and forget about them."

Blake looked down at her, his eyes glinting with a dangerous light. "Sure, we'll go back. After you show her who's really in charge around here. Go on, Deah. You beat her once. Do it again. And this time, really make it *hurt*."

Deah bit her lip again, but she didn't automatically say no. By this point, everyone was staring at us. The other Draconis had drifted over to the table, and they'd all gathered around, along with some of the kids from the other Families. Apparently, they didn't want the tournament to end yet, or perhaps they just wanted to see a little more blood sport, because all the other kids formed a circle around us and started chanting *Fight! Fight! Fight!* in louder and louder voices, with Blake, of course, leading them.

I looked at Devon and Felix, and they both stared back

at me, concern creasing their faces. But there were too many of the other kids around and not enough Sinclairs for them to do anything about Blake's suggestion of a new fight between me and Deah. So I stepped forward into an open space a few feet away from the table, my hand on the hilt of my sword. If Blake wanted a fight, he was going to get one.

Blake put his arm around Deah's shoulder and marched her forward. "Go on," he repeated. "Show her how Draconis fight. Show her how Draconis end things, especially Sinclairs."

He pushed Deah forward so that she was standing right in front of me. Panic and guilt flared in her eyes. She didn't want to do this. She didn't want to be here, but she was going along with her brother, just like always.

To my surprise, Deah shook her head and stepped away from me. "I'm not going to do it. I'm not going to fight her."

"Why not?" Blake said. "It's not like you're scared of her. You already beat her once. You can do it again."

Deah kept shaking her head, making her golden hair whip around her shoulders. She had the sick, panicked look of a wounded deer being hemmed in on all sides by a pack of hungry copper crushers and about to be dragged down and squeezed to death.

"No," she said. "I'm not going to do it. I'm not going to fight her. You don't understand."

Blake rolled his eyes. "Why not? Just do the same thing that you did in the tournament and teach this bitch a lesson. What is there to understand?"

"Lila let me win!" Deah screamed.

Her voice echoed through the evening air, seeming to bounce from one side of the lake and back again. Suddenly, everyone was quiet and still.

Deah looked around, breathing hard, her cheeks red,

realizing that she'd just shouted her secret to everyone. But she didn't try to take it back. Instead, her spine straightened, and she lifted her chin and faced Blake again.

"I didn't win the tournament," she said, all her heartache apparent in her choking voice. "Lila was the better fighter. She could have won, but she didn't. She let me cut her instead. Probably because she felt sorry for me. Isn't that right, Lila? Don't you feel sorry for me? The girl with the crazy mom, bully brother, and heartless dad?"

I didn't say anything, but my wince was answer enough for her and everyone else.

Deah let out a bitter laugh. "Yeah, that's what I thought. Here. Take this. You earned it. Not me."

She shoved the gold cup into my hands, broke through the ring of kids, and ran off into the woods.

CHAPTER TWENTY-SIX

I stood there holding the gold winner's cup, the metal strangely, sickeningly cold under my fingers. All around me, everyone was quiet, although I could feel their speculative gazes on me, wondering what had ever possessed me to let Deah win instead of taking the victory for myself. Yeah, I was asking myself that one too.

Blake gave me a disgusted glare, like he couldn't believe I'd actually let someone else win anything, then stomped off, heading back toward the fairgrounds. Obviously, he had no intention of going after Deah to make sure that she was okay. Some brother he was. I wondered if he was looking for Victor so he could tell dear old dad what she'd said. I wouldn't put it past Blake to be that kind of tattletale.

I wondered if Victor would punish Deah and Seleste anyway, even though Deah had technically won the tournament. I hoped not, but there was nothing I could do about it. I wasn't the one who'd let the monster out of the bag.

One by one, the other kids drifted away, going back to their own tables, although they all kept staring at me and whispering behind their hands.

I sighed. For the third day in a row, this was a miserable end to a perfectly miserable day. Yeah, bad things really did come in threes, and these last few days had been doozies all the way around.

Felix stared at me. "You really did let her win, didn't you?"

I shrugged.

He grimaced, then looked at the woods where she'd gone. "I should go after her. Talk to her."

I sighed. "No, let me. Besides, I still have to give this back to her." I held up the gold cup. "I don't want it. Not anymore."

I'd never be able to look at it without thinking about Deah's meltdown and the anguish shimmering in her eyes, anguish that I'd felt down to the bottom of my own soul.

Devon nodded. "Go talk to her. We'll wait for you here."

I nodded and headed off toward the woods.

We'd been sitting at a table near the front of the lawns, and I had to walk almost the entire length of the picnic area before I reached the woods. Everyone turned to watch my progress, although thankfully, the whispers died down the closer I got to the trees.

I clutched the gold cup to my chest, kept my head down, and hurried on. Even though it wasn't all that big, the winner's cup felt heavy and awkward in my hands, and I wanted to give it back to Deah as soon as possible. I wasn't even tempted by all that shiny gold, not anymore. And I didn't have the slightest desire to let Mo pawn it at the Razzle Dazzle.

I had thought that I was doing the right thing by letting Deah win, but now I wasn't so sure. Maybe I should have just finished the fight. Maybe I should have beaten her fair and square. Either way, Deah had been hurt, and now she and Seleste would probably suffer even more, once Blake told Victor about her confession.

I left the picnic area behind and stepped into the woods.

It wasn't quite eight o'clock yet, but shadows already filled in the spaces between the trees, giving everything a gloomy atmosphere. It matched my mood perfectly. Because not only had Deah been hurt, but now I would always be known as the girl who had *almost* won the Tournament of Blades, the runner-up and the first loser, just like Blake had said. Even if everyone remembered all about Deah's proclamation, her name was still the one on the gold cup—not mine. I kicked at a rock and sent it skittering off through the underbrush.

I didn't think Deah had been walking all that fast, but she'd already gone far deeper into the woods than I'd expected. For the first time, I realized just how isolated I was and how far away the noise from the picnic area was.

I wondered if Vance had noticed these same things before he'd been murdered out here.

The image of Vance's body and all the hideous cuts that had been inflicted on him filled my mind. I'd never been afraid of being alone before, not even in the bad parts of town where there were more monsters than shadows in the alleys, but a shiver went up my spine, and I found myself lowering my hand to the sword strapped to my waist.

And that's when I realized that the woods were quiet—too quiet.

It wasn't all that late, but here in the gloom, monsters should have already been stirring, waking up to hunt their dinner. But no brightly colored eyes flashed from the bushes or high up in the trees, and I didn't hear so much as a rockmunk rustling around in the underbrush, searching for nuts and berries. I shivered again. The silence was creepier than anything else—

A low moan sounded.

I froze, wondering if I had imagined the sound. But the moan came again, and then again. Someone was out here, and they were hurt, from the sound of things. Normally,

I would have rushed forward to help the injured person, but so many bad things had happened over the past few days that I decided to be extra cautious. So I drew my sword and slowly approached. Besides, just because those moans sounded human, didn't mean that they actually were. Many a monster had suckered in an unwary tourist or guard that way.

I crept deeper and deeper into the woods, searching for the source of the sound. Even though the shadows grew darker by the minute, I was still able to see everything around me clearly, thanks to my sight magic.

Including the body.

A crumpled form was sprawled in the middle of the trail up ahead, and the red shirt and golden ponytail told me exactly who it was—Deah.

I quickened my pace, scanning the woods around her, but I didn't see anything out of the ordinary. Just trees, trees, and more trees.

I reached her a few seconds later. Deah was lying on the ground, bleeding from an ugly gash in her forehead. Her sword was clutched in her hand, as though she'd tried to defend herself against whoever or whatever had attacked her. Worry shot through me. Deah was an excellent fighter, something she'd proved during the tournament. If something could get the drop on her, that meant it could do the same to me—or worse.

My head whipped left and right, but I still didn't see or hear anything moving in the trees around us. I'd have to take the chance that I could get her out of here before whatever—or whoever—had done this came back.

I dropped to my knees beside her, the gold cup tumbling from my hand and rolling away. "Deah! Deah! What happened? Are you okay? Who did this to you?"

She looked at me, her eyes hazy and unfocused, but she managed to croak out a single word. "Run. . . ."

She moaned, and her head lolled to the side.

"Deah! Deah!"

I shook her, but she was out cold. More worry filled me. I didn't have any strength magic, and she was too heavy for me to carry back to the picnic area. I'd have to call Devon and tell him what was happening. I reached for the phone in my pocket—

A branch *cracked* behind me.

"I did it to her," a familiar voice called out.

I froze, then got to my feet and slowly turned around.

Katia Volkov stood behind me, her arms crossed over her chest. A bit of sunlight streaming down through the trees highlighted the wolf stamped into the cuff on her wrist. Seleste's voice whispered in my mind.

We have to warn the girls about the wolf. . . . The wolf wants to devour them both, gobble them up until there's nothing left but bones and blades. . . . No blood, just bones and blades . . . bones and blades . . . bones and blades. . . .

I'd been so focused on *bones and blades* that I'd forgotten about the first part of Seleste's warning. Suddenly, I knew that the wolf was Katia, although I had no idea why she would want to hurt Deah or me.

Katia strolled toward me, and my hand tightened around the hilt of my sword. She wasn't going to take me by surprise like she had Deah.

But Katia walked right on past as if she didn't care about me at all, instead leaning down to pick up the gold winner's cup I'd dropped. Katia held up the cup in a fading patch of sunlight, admiring her reflection in it. Somehow, the glint of the gold made her green eyes seem even bigger and brighter than ever before.

I frowned. Wait a second. Why were her eyes green? They were hazel . . . weren't they?

I thought back to all the times I'd seen Katia over the past few days. Her eyes had been hazel the very first time

I'd met her in the Midway. I was sure of that. And they'd been hazel some of the other times I'd seen her around the tournament too. But they'd also been green at times, just like they were right now. Why would her eyes change color so often?

But even weirder than that, there was something so . . . *familiar* about the bright, emerald-green glaze to her eyes. I'd seen that exact same color somewhere before, sometime recently, and I knew it was desperately important for me to remember, just as I knew how important it was to keep myself between Katia and Deah.

Katia admired the gold cup a moment longer, then set it down on the forest floor and faced me again.

"What are you doing?" I asked. "Why did you hurt Deah?"

She shrugged. "Because I wanted to. I've been wanting to blindside her for *days* now. I tried to knock her out in the first round of the tournament when I cut the rope ladder, but she got on the platform before the ropes came loose. I was so disappointed. But when I saw her run into the woods, I knew it was too good an opportunity to pass up—that I could finally finish things with her."

I sucked in a breath at her casual confession. I'd been right when I thought that someone had been trying to knock people out of the tournament by cutting the ropes. But I'd blamed Vance, when Katia had been targeting Deah the whole time. I'd just been collateral damage that day—and I might be again tonight, if I didn't figure out a way to stop her.

Katia glared at Deah's still form, then looked at me again. "Did you know that she's the other girl Felix has been seeing?"

"How did you find that out?" I asked, trying to keep her talking, even as I slid my hand into my shorts pocket again, reaching for my phone.

She snorted. "I saw them making out behind the Draconi tent before one of the matches. They were so busy sucking face they didn't even notice me."

I'd always thought all that sneaking around was going to end badly, and it looked like I'd been proven right, just not in the way I'd expected.

Katia shook her head, making her dark red hair swish around her shoulders. "I can't imagine what Felix sees in *her*. Not that it matters. If he can't see how special I am, then he doesn't deserve me."

"Okay," I said, trying to speed-dial Devon. Kind of hard when I couldn't see the screen. "I know you're upset that you and Felix aren't together, but that's no reason to take it out on Deah."

Katia laughed. "You think I'm doing all this for a *boy*? Please. I thought you were smarter than that, Lila. I do things for *me*—nobody else."

I tapped my phone screen, hoping I was calling someone who would pick up, hear our conversation, and realize that something was wrong. "Okay. So what exactly *are* you doing then?"

She shrugged. "Deah beat me in the tournament. But it's the last time she'll ever beat me at anything."

"Why do you say that?"

She looked at me like I'd just asked the stupidest question ever. "Because I'm going to take her magic and make it my own the way I should have all along. I took Vance's power, thinking that would be enough to beat her, but obviously, I was wrong and he wasn't nearly as strong as he bragged he was."

I froze, my blood turning to ice in my veins. "You killed Vance? You took his magic?"

Too late, I remembered running into Katia the night Vance was murdered. I hadn't thought anything of her being in the woods at the time, just thinking she'd been hiding out there from Felix the same way I had been from Devon.

"Of course I took his magic," Katia said, her voice cold and hard. "Why else would I ask him out here last night? It certainly wasn't to make out with him like *he* wanted. He thought he was going to get lucky. Heh. You should have seen the look on his face when I zip-tied his hands and slapped that duct tape on his mouth and he finally realized what I was up to. It was *priceless*."

She laughed, but the sound made goose bumps crawl across my skin because it was the same sound I'd heard when I'd looked into Vance's dead eyes last night. And it was the same evil laugh that had echoed in my mind when I'd found that dead tree troll beside the dumpster.

"The tree troll. . . ." I said. "You killed Vance for his magic, but what about the tree troll in the Midway? Why did you murder it?"

"Yeah, that was one of mine too. I also whacked one of them up at the Draconi estate a couple of nights ago. I wanted to get more than one, but Blake and Victor had already killed all the others they'd trapped."

My mind whirled and whirled, trying to put everything together. "But why? I still don't understand *why*."

Katia gave me another of those you're-the-biggest-idiot-ever looks. "For its magic, of course." Her face turned sly. "You wanna know a secret?"

I didn't respond, but I didn't have to.

"I don't actually have all that much magic of my own," she said. "I have a very minor Talent for speed, but I found a way to increase it, to have all the magic I want, whenever I want it."

My stomach twisted. "By killing monsters and people and taking their power."

She shot her thumb and forefinger at me. "Bingo."

Suddenly, I realized why Katia's eyes kept going from

hazel to green and back again—because of all the stolen tree troll magic pumping through her veins. Devon had said there was no way to cheat in the tournament, but he'd been wrong.

So very, very wrong.

"The trolls' magic . . . Vance's magic . . . you wanted it for the tournament. You took their power and used it to try to help you win."

"Bingo again," Katia said. "Look at you, on a roll and everything. And now I'm going to do the same thing to Deah. Come to think of it, I should have done this last year, when I had the chance."

"You want her magic? You want her mimic power?"

"Of course I *want* it," Katia snarled. "With Deah's power, I can beat anybody and win any tournament I enter, and I can finally scrape together enough money to leave my father behind forever. And forget working for the Volkovs too. With Deah's magic, I can do things the way *I've* always wanted to."

She noticed my horrified expression. "Oh, don't look so shocked. You know what a loser my dad is. You see how he drinks."

"Yeah," I said. "And I know how much that must hurt. But that's no excuse for doing horrible things. Lots of kids have crappy parents, and they don't go around murdering monsters and people. Killing Deah isn't the answer to your problems."

"Sure it is," she replied. "And yours too. With her out of the way, they'll have to declare you the winner of the tournament like they should have all along. I saw your last fight with her, and I heard what she said to you at the picnic tables. You had her beat, so why did you let her win?"

"Because Deah's dad would have hurt her if she didn't win."

She snorted. "Please. Deah should protect herself from

Victor. She's strong enough to do it. She just doesn't have the spine for it." Katia paused. "At least, she would have been strong enough, but now, all that lovely, lovely magic is going to be *mine*."

I shook my head and stepped forward. "No way. I won't let you hurt her. It's sick and wrong and twisted, and you know it."

Katia laughed, the sound cold enough to chill my bones. "Sure, I know it. But *I don't care*. The only thing I *do* care about is myself and finally *winning*. You don't have any say in it. Don't try to stop me, Lila. You won't like what happens."

I raised my sword. "I'm not going to let you murder her."

She grinned. "You don't have a choice. And since you're taking her side, well, I guess I'll be getting two powers for the price of one today. More strength magic for me. Goody."

Katia drew out a dagger from the belt on her waist. I recognized it—it was the same dagger she'd used to kill Vance and the tree troll at the Midway.

I snapped my sword up into an attack position, but then she moved, almost too fast for me to follow. Of course, she was fast now. Her eyes were as bright and green as a troll's, which meant she had some monster magic running through her body.

I barely got my sword up in time to avoid her first blow and all the others she rained down on me. I'd fought people with speed Talents before, even during the tournament, but Katia was something else. She was just too quick for me, and it was all I could do to parry her lightning-fast attacks. A few more moves, and she would be able to disarm me. Still, I fought on, trying to figure some way out of this mess.

Clang!

Katia finally got the advantage and knocked my sword out of my hand. Desperate, I charged at her, but she easily sidestepped me. But that was okay because it gave me enough time to yank my phone out of my pocket. I hadn't managed to connect with my earlier swipes, but I hit the screen and speed-dialed Devon. I could hear the call going through.

"What do you think you're doing?" Katia hissed. "Who are you calling?"

She lashed out with her dagger, and I ducked out of the way. She made another move for my phone, but I threw it into the bushes before she could get her hands on it.

Katia rushed at me again, and I sucked in a breath to yell, hoping that Devon would hear the noise through my phone. But she was so quick that I didn't even get a chance to do that.

Even as I opened my mouth to scream, her fist zoomed toward my face. I tried to turn away, but she was faster than I was, and I couldn't avoid the hard, sharp blow.

Everything went black.

CHAPTER TWENTY-SEVEN

The pounding in my head woke me.

I groaned and realized that my neck was twisted at an awkward angle and that I was slumped up against a hard, wooden wall like a sack of potatoes. My eyes fluttered open, and a couple of overhead lights burned into my brain. I closed my eyes against the harsh glare and sat upright, even though it increased the pounding in my skull. For some reason, my arm was wrenched up above my head, making my shoulder ache as well. I tried to lower it, only to find that I couldn't.

Clank-clank-clank.

I peered up, squinting against the glare of the bare bulbs dangling from the ceiling. A thick shackle circled my right wrist, above my silver Sinclair cuff, with a chain leading from the shackle to a metal loop that had been driven deep into the wall. I sucked down a breath and yanked and yanked on the chain, but it was made out of hard, heavy metal, and all I could do was make the links *rattle-rattle* together like bones.

I forced down my panic and looked around, trying to figure out where I was and how I could get out of here. There was only one door, directly opposite from where I was shackled, and the entire structure was made out of old, weathered boards, including the wall I was chained to.

The wood might have been painted a cheery red at one time, but the color was now a dull, rusty brown. The wide open area and high A-frame ceiling reminded me of the picnic shelters by the lake. An old, dusty table and a couple of cobweb-coated chairs squatted off to one side of the room, along with two splintered oars and a wooden canoe with a gaping hole in its hull. The air smelled of fish, and I could hear the steady *rush-rush-rush* of the lake slapping against the shore.

The old boathouse. I was in the old boathouse that Katia had mentioned. Her special spot with Felix. I shuddered.

"You really should have stayed at the picnic tables," a voice muttered. "We both should have."

I looked to my left to see Deah sitting on the floor a few feet away. One of her arms was chained to the wall as well, and she'd been struggling against the shackle and chain for quite a while, judging by the red marks that circled her wrist.

"What's going on?" I asked, trying to focus despite the pounding in my brain. "Who did this to us?"

"You really don't remember?"

I shook my head and bit back another groan as that small motion made the ache intensify in my skull. I cradled my head in my free hand and took some deep breaths, trying to get the pounding pain under control.

Finally, I managed it and raised my head again. Deah sat slumped up against the wall, a miserable expression on her face. She kept glancing at the door across from us.

"She'll be back soon," Deah said in a flat voice. "I imagine that she'll get started then."

Suddenly, everything came rushing back to me. Finding Deah in the woods, hearing Katia brag about all the horrible things she'd done, fighting Katia, losing when she'd used her stolen speed magic to punch me out.

"How did we get here?" I asked.

Deah shrugged. "I was knocked out for most of it. All I remember is Katia throwing me over her shoulder and carrying me through the woods. She must have done the same thing to you, and now, here we are."

"We have to get out of here before she comes back."

Deah snorted. "Way to state the obvious, Lila. But it's not going to happen. Believe me, I've tried."

She cursed and rattled her chain again, but it didn't jerk free of the wall.

Thump-thump-thump.

Thump-thump-thump.

Thump-thump-thump.

Footsteps sounded outside, getting louder and louder as they headed in our direction. Deah scrambled to her feet, and I did the same, the links in our chains *clank-clank-clanking* together in a dark, ominous chorus.

The door to the boathouse slammed open, and Katia strolled inside. She gave me and Deah a thin smile, then went over and set down the gold winner's cup on top of the table. She also threw down two black leather scabbards next to it. Our swords. I tensed and so did Deah. If we could just get our hands on the weapons, we might have a chance.

Katia noticed us staring longingly at the swords and unsheathed first one, then the other, staring at the scrollwork carved into the hilts and black blades.

"Funny how they both have stars carved into them," she said. "Almost like you two were from the same family or something."

"That's because we are," I said. "We're cousins. Our moms, Seleste and Serena Sterling, were sisters."

Deah gasped, her eyes bulging in shock. She'd never expected me to say something like that. Even I wasn't quite sure why I'd revealed that particular secret right now.

Maybe because I was tired of people keeping things from me and didn't want to do the same thing to her.

Deah kept staring at me. I shrugged back at her.

"Seleste might get confused, but she doesn't get *that* confused," I said. "I do look quite a bit like my mom."

"Whatever. I didn't bring you two here to listen to your family drama." Katia held up my sword, admiring it. "But I have been wanting a new blade. Maybe I'll use yours, Lila. You won't be needing it anymore."

My hands curled into fists. "The only way you're getting my mom's sword is over my dead body."

She smirked at me. "Why do you think we're all here at the boathouse? So no one will hear the two of you scream when I take your magic."

Deah's hands also clenched into fists, and she surged forward, but the chain on her arm pulled her up short.

Katia grinned and clucked her tongue. "What's the matter, Deah? Feeling a little . . . tied up?" She laughed. "Or maybe you just don't know what to do now that you're not the center of attention. When there's no one around to make sure that I fight fair."

Deah didn't say anything, but if looks could kill, Katia would have been feeding the fishes by now.

"Now, you two just hang tight," Katia said. "I want to check my traps before we get started."

"What traps?" I asked.

She laid my sword down on the table. "Oh, the ones I stole from Uncle Nikolai last summer. He had several of them rusting away in a shed at the Volkov compound. I doubt he even noticed they were gone."

I remembered what Mo had told me about murdered monsters being found on the edge of the Volkov property last year. So Katia had been killing creatures last summer as well. I wondered how many monsters she'd tortured just to get their magic.

"This summer, I set some traps along the lake in hopes of catching more trolls than I did last year," Katia said. "There was a copper crusher in one of them when I looked earlier. I'm going to go take care of it right now."

I shuddered, thinking of the cage I'd found on the Draconi property—and how Katia would carve up the crusher to take its strength magic.

"Anyway, I'll be back in a few minutes, and then we'll see just how loud the two of you can scream."

Katia smirked at us again, then turned and left the boathouse, slamming the door shut behind her. Deah started pulling on her chain again, even harder than before.

I sighed. "Maybe we should talk about being cousins—"

"Shut it," Deah snapped, still pulling and pulling on her chain. "The only thing I'm concerned about right now is getting out of here. And you should be too."

She was right. Escape first, talk later. Still, her tone annoyed me.

"Well, that's not going to work, unless you have some strength magic that I don't know about," I said.

"Well, do you have a better idea?" she snapped.

"Maybe."

I held up my arm and looked at the shackle on my wrist. The shackle was old and thick, too thick for me to have any chance of breaking it, but Katia had snapped a tiny metal padlock through the loops to secure the two halves of the shackle together. A nice, new, shiny padlock that wasn't nearly as sturdy as it appeared to be. The sort of padlock that I'd picked open a hundred times before. I grinned. We were as good as out of here.

I reached up into my ponytail—but my chopstick lock picks were gone.

No picks meant no opening the padlock and no chance of escape. Panic welled up in me, but I forced it down and looked around the boathouse, hoping that the chopsticks had just fallen out of my hair and were somewhere in here.

A few seconds later, I spotted the two shiny black sticks lying on the floor—on the far side of Deah, well beyond my reach.

I cursed, and Deah stopped pulling on her chain to see what I was staring at.

"You want your hair sticks?" she sniped. "Really?"

"They're not just for my hair," I sniped back. "They're lock picks. You know, something that might actually help us get out of these." I held up my shackled arm. "Unless you have a better idea?"

She shook her head.

"I didn't think so. So can you grab them and hand them over to me . . . *please*?" I had to choke out the last word, but there was no way I could reach the chopsticks, so I decided to be nice.

"And why would I want to do that?" She crossed her arms over her chest at the snarky tone in my voice.

I rolled my eyes. "Oh, I don't know. So we can get out of here and away from the evil girl who wants to cut us up and take our magic."

Deah kept glaring at me. I sighed.

"Look, I don't like it any more than you do, us being related and everything that means, but working together is the only way we're getting out of here alive. Unless you want to be gutted like a fish and have your magic torn out of you just so Katia can win some tournaments?"

Deah sighed. "Fine. But that doesn't mean I have to like it. Or you. Or especially that secret you just dropped on me, *cousin*."

"I wouldn't dream that you ever would, *cousin*," I sniped back.

She glanced at the closed door, then slid to her left, moving slowly so as not to make her chain *clank-clank-clank* any more than necessary.

"Hurry up!" I hissed.

She gave me a withering look, but she increased her pace. Deah reached the end of her chain, then dropped to her knees and stretched her hand out as far as she could.

Short—she was three feet too short.

Deah stretched and stretched, but no matter how hard or far she clawed, she just couldn't reach the chopsticks. After about two minutes of heaving, she gave up, panting hard and trying to get her breath back.

"It's no use," she said. "I can't reach them. Now what?"

Instead of answering, I looked around the boathouse again, searching for anything that would let her bridge those final three feet and reach the chopsticks. But there was nothing. Our swords were out of reach on the table, and the only things Katia had left on us were our clothes and shoes. Even if they were closer to us, the splintered oars and busted boat were useless. The one thing that might have helped us was a fishing pole, but I didn't see any sort of fishing gear—

Wait a second. Fishing poles. I didn't have one of those, but maybe I didn't need one. Maybe I could just make my own.

I thought about things, working out the problem in my mind, then bent down, yanked off my sneakers, and stripped the laces out of them.

"What are you doing?" Deah asked. "How is taking off your shoes going to help anything?"

I tied the laces together, then threaded one of the ends through the eyelets on my right sneaker, tying it off into a tight knot. Now I had a sneaker with more than three feet of string dangling from it.

"Here," I said, passing the shoe over to her. "Think of it as a fishing pole."

Deah stared at the shoe, then me. "You are either the craziest person I've ever met or the smartest."

"Let's hope it's the smartest. Now, come on. Katia could come back any second."

Deah nodded and turned toward the chopsticks. She let out a breath, then threw out the shoe, careful to hold on to the lace on the end, so she wouldn't lose it.

Thump.

She hadn't thrown it hard enough, and it landed short of the chopsticks. We both froze at the loud noise it made, but five seconds passed, then ten, then fifteen, and no footsteps sounded. Katia either hadn't heard the noise or wasn't worried enough to leave her traps and come investigate it.

"Again," I said. "Again."

Deah yanked the sneaker back and tried again.

Thump.

This time, the sneaker bridged the distance but landed too far to the right of the chopsticks for Deah to snag them.

"Again!" I hissed. "Quick!"

"Be quiet!" she snapped back. "You're ruining my concentration!"

I really wanted to snap at her again, but I forced myself to grind my teeth together and keep quiet.

Eyes narrowed, Deah looked at the chopsticks lying on the floor—*really* looked at them, the same way I would have with my sight magic. She hefted the sneaker in her hand, judging its weight and the distance. Then she let it fly.

Thump.

The sneaker landed just beyond the chopsticks. Deah

and I both sucked in breaths, and she pulled the sneaker toward her, one slow, careful inch at a time. The shoe bounced across the floor and Deah stopped. She fiddled with the laces for a few seconds and managed to flip the sneaker right side up. Then, she slowly drew it toward her again.

The sneaker bumped up against the edge of the chopsticks—and sent them rolling straight toward Deah.

She snatched them up the second they were in range, turned, and handed them over to me. "Here. Work your magic, Merriweather."

I grinned. "All you had to do was ask."

She rolled her eyes, but she was grinning back at me.

I twisted open the chopsticks, revealing the lock picks hidden inside. I gestured at Deah, and she stepped forward and held out her wrist. I inserted the picks into the padlock.

"Come on, baby," I crooned. "Open sesame."

A few seconds later, the lock snapped open, and I slid it through the shackle and stuffed it into one of my pockets. Deah unhooked the shackle from around her wrist and carefully lowered it and the attached chain to the floor, making as little noise as possible.

The second she was free, she went over to the table, grabbed our swords, and hurried back with them. She strapped on her own weapon, and I did the same, both of us moving as quickly and quietly as we could.

"Now what?" Deah whispered. "Do we storm outside and try to take her by surprise?"

"First things first." I passed the picks over to Deah. "Here. Open my lock."

"What? Why can't you do it?" she asked.

I held up my shackled hand. "Because the angle's all wrong, and I can't pick it one-handed. So you're going to have to do it for me. Have you ever picked a lock before?"

She shook her head, making her blond ponytail slap back and forth.

"Then good thing for you and me, it's not that hard."

Deah took the lock picks from me, bent over my shackle, and got to work. I tried to talk her through it, but the picks kept slipping out of the padlock, and she just wasn't getting the hang of it.

"It's no use," she growled. "I can't do it."

"You have to, or we're both dead."

Deah sighed and went back to work with the lock picks, but she gave up a minute later, when the picks slipped out of the lock again. "I'm sorry. I can't do it. You stay here. I'll go get help."

"And I'll be dead by the time you get back with it."

"But I *can't* do it. I don't know how, and like you said, I don't have any strength magic that would let me break the shackle."

I tilted my head to the side, thinking about her words—and the magic that she *did* have. "What about your mimic power?"

She frowned. "What about it?"

"Well, you can do more than just fight with it, right? I mean, you can mimic the way someone moves, walks, talks, everything."

"Yeah, so what?" Deah asked.

"Then you could mimic me picking a lock, right?"

"I suppose so," she said in a doubtful voice. "I've never tried to do anything like that with my power before, though."

"Well, it's always good to learn new things," I snarked. "Now watch me and do exactly what I do."

I imagined that I was bending over an invisible padlock, holding the lock picks in my hands. Then I drew in a breath, slid my imaginary picks into my imaginary padlock, and went to work. I pretended as though I were moving the picks around and around, feeling for the tumblers, and trying to get them to slip into place so the padlock would pop open.

I felt stupider than I ever had in my entire life, but I kept right on working. Deah watched me the whole time, her dark blue eyes narrowed, her lips pressed tight in thought. After several seconds of concentration, she slid the picks into the real lock on my shackle again. It was awkward, with her standing right next to me, trying to work on my shackle while I was moving my hand around, but she managed it. Slowly, Deah began to mimic my movements, holding the lock picks just so and sliding them around and around inside the padlock in the patterns that I was showing her.

Seconds ticked by, then turned into a minute, then two. But we kept working together the whole time. The air was hot and stuffy. Sweat dripped down my face, hers too, given how hard the two of us were concentrating, and the only sounds were our ragged breaths mixing together in the absolute stillness of the boathouse—

Click.

And just like that, my padlock popped open.

Deah stared down at the lock, still holding the picks inside it, as though she couldn't believe what had just happened. "I did it. I actually did it!"

"And you can be very proud about that later. Now help me get it off," I said. "Hurry!"

She passed me the lock picks, which I closed and slid into one of my pockets, while she unhooked the padlock from my shackle. The second it was off my wrist, I grabbed the chain and lowered it to the floor.

"Come on," I whispered. "Let's get out of here before she comes back—"

The door to the boathouse slammed open again, and Katia strolled inside, this time holding a dagger in either hand.

"I'm back," Katia called out in a singsong voice.

She stopped short, realizing that we were free. For a second, the three of us looked at each other.

Then Katia laughed. She just laughed and laughed, as though our being halfway to escaping was the funniest thing *ever*.

Deah and I looked at each other. We both drew our swords and stepped together, forming a united front.

"Oh, how adorable," Katia sneered. "Two enemies teaming up together to try to save themselves from a fate worse than death. Too bad you're both still going to lose—everything."

"I doubt that," Deah snapped back at her. "I've beaten you before. I can do it again. And so can Lila."

"You'd better believe it," I chimed in.

Katia took a step forward. Deah and I both snapped up our swords, but Katia didn't attack us. Instead, she raised the two daggers in her hands—both of which were glowing a familiar, sickening, midnight black.

"Oh, I doubt that," she purred. "Considering that I have more magic in these two black blades than the two of you have in your entire bodies."

I eyed the gleaming weapons. "What kind of magic?"

"Strength from the copper crusher and speed, courtesy of another tree troll in one of my traps," Katia said, admiring first one blade, then the other. "I hate to use it all up killing the two of you, but easy come, easy go. That's the only problem with monster magic. It gives you a boost for a little while, but then it burns out of your system. It's not like human magic, like Vance's magic. His speed and strength are mine now forever. And soon, your powers will be too."

Katia grinned and twirled the daggers around in her hands. Deah and I both tensed, ready to throw ourselves out of the way should she decide to hurl the weapons at us, but that wasn't her plan at all.

Instead, Katia raised the daggers high, then stabbed herself in the heart with them.

CHAPTER TWENTY-EIGHT

I gasped in shock, and so did Deah.

Katia stabbed herself with both daggers. For a moment, a midnight pulse of blackness flashed, casting the entire boathouse in darkness, despite the bulbs burning overhead. Then the blackness faded and the light returned, but what it revealed was equally terrible.

Blood spurted out of the wounds, coating Katia's hands and the blades still stuck in her chest a dark, glossy crimson. But as soon as her blood touched the daggers, the blades soaked it right back up again, still glowing that eerie, midnight black.

Katia screamed in pain, and the midnight glow on the blades went out. In an instant, the weapons were their usual dull, ashy gray again. Katia gasped and gasped for breath, then doubled over.

Silence.

Then she started laughing again.

Katia laughed and laughed, the loud, wild, crazy sound bouncing around like a rockmunk trapped inside the boathouse.

Katia straightened up to her full height, and Deah and I both gasped again—because her eyes burned with magic.

The longer I stared at her, the brighter her eyes became, the color morphing from their normal hazel to a brilliant emerald green, with a spark of copper flashing every now and then. I supposed that it made sense that Katia's eyes would take on the tint of the monster whose magic she'd stolen—green for the troll and copper for the crusher. But the magic in her gaze kept flaring hotter and hotter, until her eyes were glowing much brighter than any monster's ever had.

Katia grunted, then pulled the daggers out of her chest. The black blades sealed up the wounds they had left behind, so it was as if she had never stabbed herself at all.

"A tree troll for speed," she purred, holding up one of the daggers. "And a copper crusher for strength." She held up the other dagger. "A perfect combo and more than enough magic to let me deal with the two of you."

Deah and I looked at each other. I nodded and she returned the gesture. We both knew that we'd have to work together in order to survive this.

Just like Seleste had told me.

Katia let out a loud scream and charged at us. Deah and I split apart, with me going right and her going left. But Katia was fast—so damn *fast*. And since she had two daggers, she was able to attack both of us at once. She lashed out at Deah with one blade, then pivoted back around to me, her movements almost too quick for me to follow. I barely managed to get out of the way of her black blade before she laid my guts open with it.

Deah stepped up behind Katia and swung her sword, but Katia lashed out with one of her daggers, catching Deah across the arm before she was able to get out of the way. Deah yelped and staggered away.

Katia turned back to me. She let out another loud yell and charged forward. I was standing by the table, and I kicked out, sending it skittering across the floor toward her. The gold winner's cup also flew off the top and clattered to the ground.

That incoming table made Katia stop short, but a cruel smile curved her lips.

"That's not going to save you," she hissed. "Nothing will. Not now that you've taken *her* side."

"I'd rather be on her side than yours," I said. "At least she doesn't go around murdering monsters just because it gives her some sort of sick thrill. No wonder you couldn't beat Deah. You were too worried about getting your next hit of magic to really focus on the tournament. Your dad might be a drunk, but you're nothing but a magic junkie *loser*."

I was deliberately taunting her, calling her the one word she hated most. And it worked. Katia screamed again and threw herself forward. This time, she slammed her fists into the table top, cracking it down the center and wading through the remains to get to me. Then she raised her daggers and slammed them into my sword as hard as she could.

I grinned because the second her weapons rammed into mine, my transference power kicked in, and that cold burn of magic filled my veins. Katia had stolen the tree troll's and copper crusher's magic. Well, I was going to take it away from her, blow by blow, bit by bit, piece by piece. This first attack was already enough to make me stronger.

But not strong enough.

Katia was in a rage now, and she slammed her weapons into mine over and over again, each blow harder and sharper than the last, until finally she knocked my sword away.

She raised her daggers to bring the blades down in my chest. I lurched back, trying to get out of the way, but my sock caught on a nail sticking up out of the floor, and I went down on one knee. I raised my right arm up, knowing that it was useless and that her daggers would lay my arm open to the bone—

Suddenly, Deah was there, slamming her sword into Katia's daggers and keeping her from killing me. I scrambled back up on my feet, grabbed my sword, and got back into the fight.

Katia kept whipping her daggers every which way, but as fast and strong as she was, it still took a lot of concentration to battle two enemies at once, especially two enemies who were as good at fighting as Deah and I were. We gave her all she could handle and then some.

But we were still going to lose.

With all that stolen monster magic pumping through her body, Katia was faster and stronger than the two of us. Despite her claims that monster magic didn't last all that long, she showed no signs of slowing down. Plus, she still had Vance's strength and speed Talents to fall back on. She was wearing us down, especially since Deah and I had fought so long and hard earlier in the tournament.

My blows were coming slower and slower, and it was all I could do to parry the hard, vicious slashes of Katia's daggers. Deah was slowing down as well. All Katia needed would be another minute, maybe two, and she would be able to disarm one of us. Then the other would fall and she could cut us up and take our magic at her leisure.

The magic chilling my body wasn't enough to help me defeat Katia. I needed more magic to stop her from killing us, which meant that I had to get closer to her. Had to get her to use her strength directly on me so I could absorb as much of her stolen magic as possible. Unfortunately, there was only one way to do that. I had to actually touch her.

I winced. This was going to hurt.

Deah managed to throw Katia back, and she lost her balance and stumbled over one of the chairs. I took the moment to creep closer to Deah.

"When I tell you, unload on her with everything you have!" I hissed.

"Lila! Lila, what are you doing?" Deah hissed back.

Katia got back up on her feet. I raised my sword and charged at her, screaming all the while. Katia smirked, realizing that it was a desperate tactic, but she let me come at her, just like I wanted. I lashed out with my sword, even though I knew that the blow wouldn't even come close to nicking her. Katia blocked my attack, but instead of stepping back, I dropped my sword and darted forward, wrapping my hands around her wrists.

The second my skin touched hers, cold magic surged from her body into mine. But Katia wasn't worried at all by my change in tactics.

"You stupid fool," she snarled. "You've just made it that much easier for me to do *this*."

She shook off my hold on her left wrist and slammed one of her daggers into my stomach. I screamed, even though the horrible wound sent even more magic spinning through my body, the power whirling around and around like an icy tornado inside me.

Katia yanked the dagger back out. She started to wrench herself away from me, but I lashed out and grabbed hold of her wrist again. We seesawed back and forth for a few seconds, with her trying to break my grip, and me digging my fingers and nails into her skin as hard and tight as I could. At the same time, I reached down and hooked my socked foot around one of her ankles, throwing her off balance and spinning her around so that her back was to Deah.

"Now!" I screamed.

Deah didn't hesitate, stepping forward even as my scream echoed through the boathouse.

Katia cursed, finally realizing what I was up to. Once again, she tried to break my hold, but it was no use. Even as she struggled against me, all she did was make me stronger and stronger, and I tightened my grip, my fingers pressing down, bruising the bones in her wrists.

A second later, Deah rammed her sword into Katia's back.

Katia let out an agonized scream at the mortal wound and arched back, as if trying to push Deah's sword out of her body. The daggers dropped from her hands, thumping to the wooden floorboards, and blood bubbled out of her lips.

Katia stared at me, her green gaze dimming by the second, the magic and color leaking out of her eyes as they resumed their normal hazel color. Her emotions slammed into me as well, even as the power and life drained out of her, and I felt every single agonizing moment of the red-hot wound in her back.

It matched the dagger wound in my own stomach.

Katia struggled and struggled, still trying to break my grip, but I tightened my hands around her wrists and held on. She let out one final, choked gasp, then slumped to the floor—dead.

CHAPTER TWENTY-NINE

Katia might be dead, but she was still going to take me down with her.

I was holding on to her so tightly that I fell on top of her, and it took me a few seconds to loosen my grip. I managed to roll off her, every motion making more and more pain shoot through my stomach. On the floor, I could see my blood mixing with Katia's, which was bubbling away like acid. I wondered if that's what stolen magic did to you—ate away at your insides like acid because it didn't truly belong to you. That would be some twisted poetic justice.

I pressed my hand over the wound in my side, but blood kept pouring out from between my fingers.

"Lila!" Deah rushed over to me. "How bad is it?"

"Bad," I rasped through the pain. "You need to get out of here . . . go get . . . some help—"

Thump-thump-thump.

Thump-thump-thump.

Thump-thump-thump.

Outside, footsteps pounded, coming closer and closer. Deah got to her feet, stepped in front of me, and whipped up her sword, ready to face whatever new danger this might be.

The door burst open, and Devon and Felix raced inside, both of them holding swords.

The three of them stared at each other for a second before Deah let out a tense breath and lowered her weapon. "You guys need to help Lila. She's hurt."

Devon dropped to a knee beside me, his eyes going wide with shock at all the blood on me. "Lila—" he said in a strangled voice.

"Here," Felix said, crouching down beside me as well. "Let me try to heal her, or at least stop the bleeding until Dad and the others get here."

Felix put his hands on top of my wound, making me gasp with more pain. But he ignored my choked sobs and let loose his power. His magic seeped into my body, trying to stop the bleeding, pull the ragged edges of the wound together, and undo all the damage that Katia had done.

And, for a moment, I almost thought it was going to work.

But Felix only had a minor Talent for healing, and my wound was definitely major all the way around. He was able to stop the bleeding for a few seconds, but then his magic burned out of my system, and blood started seeping out from between my fingers again. Felix had stitched up the wound as best he could, but it wasn't nearly enough.

Felix cursed. "It's no use. Her wound is too severe, and I don't have enough magic to heal her myself. If I had a bottle of stitch-sting. . . ." His voice trailed off because we all knew that he didn't and that there wasn't time to go get one from the fairgrounds before I bled out.

So Felix leaned forward and tried again, letting loose another burst of magic. I could feel his power inside me and my own transference wanting to kick in, even though it wouldn't do me any good. My transference power made me stronger, but right now, I needed magic to heal me, not give me enough muscle to swing a sword. If only Felix was as strong in his magic as Devon was, he could have easily healed my wound. But Devon's compulsion didn't have any sort of healing element to it, and he could only give people simple commands, like telling me to hold on when we'd been on the rope ladder or to run the night we'd been fighting Grant. Devon's magic had mixed with my own then, giving me the strength to run far enough to save us both from Grant and his goons.

I looked at Felix and Devon both huddled over me, and a crazy idea popped into my head. Felix might be the only one here with healing power, but he wasn't the only one with magic—and maybe raw magic was all I really needed.

I reached up and clutched Felix's hand in mine, then reached for Devon's hand, so that I was holding on to both of them at the same time.

"Felix," I rasped, blood bubbling up into my mouth. "Try to heal me again. Use . . . as much . . . magic as you can at once. Devon . . . at the same time . . . you tell me to *heal*. Put as much force behind it as you can."

Devon's eyes widened as he realized what I wanted, and he shook his head. "No. It's too dangerous. I've never used my magic like that before. I don't know how or even if it will work. It could kill you outright."

He didn't say anything, but I could see the wheels turning in his mind as he thought about it, trying to figure things out, the way he always did.

"If we don't try, I'm dead anyway," I rasped. "Do it . . . give me a chance . . . please. . . ."

My voice trailed off, and black and white stars began to flash in front of my eyes. I didn't have long, maybe another minute or two before I'd pass out. A couple minutes after that, I'd bleed out and die right here in the boathouse.

"We have to," Felix said. "I don't know if it will work either, but it's her only shot."

Devon nodded and stared back at his friend. "On three then. One . . . two . . . three!"

Felix tightened his grip on my hand and let loose another burst of magic, this one stronger than ever before, as though he was scraping up every bit of power he had left and funneling it into my body. Even as he blasted me with his healing magic, Devon leaned down so that he was staring straight into my eyes. He only said one word.

"*Heal.*"

The sharp crack of magic in his voice sounded as loud as a clap of thunder booming in my head. From one second to the next, his power took hold of me, and my insides started squeezing and squeezing together, trying to mash everything back where it was supposed to be. I screamed and arched back, my body growing colder and colder as Devon kept repeating his *heal* command to me over and over again, and Felix kept pouring more and more of his magic into me at the same time.

But then my own magic, my own transference power, kicked in, and all I felt was the cold burst of energy pulsing through my body, more intense than any I'd ever experienced before. Devon's command still tugged at my body, so I focused on obeying that order as much as I could, trying to add Felix's healing magic to the mix to get things done. It was weird, but I could almost picture my insides in my mind, all those torn muscles and severed blood vessels pulling themselves back together. And I realized that I could only feel the cold burn of magic in and around my stab wound—nowhere else in my body.

I wasn't sure if Devon's power and his command had

faded away, or if I just figured out how to use my transference magic in this new way, but I slowly started to get better.

I slowly started to heal.

I screamed and then screamed again as the blood loss slowed down and then trickled to a stop. My muscles pulled themselves back together, with my skin sealing itself shut over everything. It was worse than any stitchsting I'd ever used, worse than any pain I'd ever felt, even when Katia had stabbed me in the first place. Every second was utter, miserable, white-hot agony. But I screamed through it, and I focused on using the surge of magic to repair as much of the damage as fast as I could.

Slowly, my breathing grew easier, and the black and white stars faded from my vision. My screams died down to choked sobs and then even those dissolved into a silent stream of tears trickling down my face. It took me a minute to realize that I actually felt . . . okay. Like I wasn't dying anymore.

I blinked and realized that I was flat on my back on the floor, with Devon and Felix still holding my hands and looming over me, and Deah standing behind them, all three of them staring at me with tense, tight expressions.

"Did it work?" Devon asked in a shaky voice.

"I don't know," Felix said. "But she stopped screaming. That's usually a good sign."

"Well, pull her shirt up and look at the wound, you idiots," Deah said.

Devon and Felix kept gaping at me, so she dropped to her knees, shouldered Felix out of the way, and lifted up my T-shirt.

"Her skin—" Felix murmured, leaning forward and peering at my stomach. "It's whole again. There's not even a scar!"

"Well, then, I would say that it worked," Deah sniped.

But her hands were surprisingly gentle as she smoothed down my T-shirt again.

"Devon! Felix! Lila!"

Somewhere outside the boathouse, voices started shouting our names. Felix got to his feet and hurried over to the open door, waving his hands.

"Over here!" he called out. "We're over here!"

Felix stepped outside to get more help, while Devon and Deah helped me sit up and slump back against the wall.

Deah looked at him, then me, her eyebrows arching up. "That was quite a show, for a girl who supposedly only has sight and strength Talents and a guy who supposedly doesn't have any magic at all. If I didn't know better, I'd say that almost looked like transference power, along with compulsion."

Devon's face hardened. "And what if it was? You going to run and tell your dad? Because that's exactly what Blake would do."

Deah flinched at the mention of Victor and Blake, but anger sparked in her eyes. "No matter what you think about me, Sinclair, I'm not a monster."

"But you are a Draconi," he said in a cold voice. "And information like this would be very important to Victor."

"He'll try to kill us and take our magic," I said. "You know he will."

Deah stared at me. "Is it true? What you said to Katia. That your mom and mine were sisters? That we're cousins?"

Devon sucked in a breath at the revelation, but he didn't say anything. He knew this moment was between Deah and me.

"Look at my sword. Tell me what you think."

Deah went over, grabbed my sword, and sank back down beside me. She laid my sword out on the floor next to hers.

They were almost identical.

My sword had a large, single star carved into the hilt, whereas hers had three stars that were equal size. But the star patterns running down the blades were exactly the same, and it was obvious the swords were from the same family—the Sterling Family.

Deah stared at the swords for several seconds, all sorts of emotions flashing in her eyes, but I was too tired to use my soulsight to try to see what she was feeling. Finally, she got to her feet, grabbed her sword, and slid it back into her scabbard.

"What are you going to tell people?" Devon asked. "About Katia and everything else that happened?"

He was really asking again if she was going to blab to Victor about our magic.

"Nothing. Nothing at all." Deah's mouth twisted, but her voice was sad when she spoke again. "Don't worry. No one will ask me anything because no one will even realize that I was gone."

She looked at me a second longer, then turned and left the boathouse.

The rest of the night passed by in a blur. Claudia, Mo, Angelo, Reginald, and Oscar came to the boathouse, along with several Sinclair guards. I told Claudia and my friends the truth about what had happened, but Claudia decided to leave Deah out of things completely, since it would be easier for her and us if there was no mention of Deah being here tonight.

And just as Deah had said, I doubted that Blake and Victor would wonder where she had been. I just hoped that she didn't get in trouble for telling everyone that I'd let her win the tournament, but there was nothing I could do about that now.

Devon carried me out of the boathouse, and an hour

later, I was in the infirmary at the Sinclair mansion, with Angelo marveling over the fact that I'd used Devon's and Felix's magic to heal myself. He pronounced me fit enough to go back to my own room, where I took a long shower to wash off all the blood. Oscar fussed over me, zipping around and around my head and bringing up more food from the kitchen than I could ever possibly eat. But I did put a hurting on some BLTs. Yeah, bacon really did make everything better. Even a night as horrible as this one had been.

But there was one more thing I needed to do, so I finished my dinner, went out onto the balcony, took hold of the drainpipe, and started climbing.

Just as I'd hoped, Devon was on the terrace, sitting in one of the lawn chairs and looking down into the valley at the magnificent view. But I only had eyes for him tonight, so I scuffed my sneakers to let him know I was here. Devon got to his feet. He took a step toward me, then hesitated. But that was okay because I went over to him, both of us standing next to the railing.

Devon looked me up and down, his eyes lingering on my stomach, as if he was remembering the horrible wound and all the blood that had covered me just a short while ago. That made two of us. But tonight wasn't about that, not anymore, and I forced away the gruesome images and phantom pain.

"You must be feeling better, since you used the drainpipe to get up here," he teased.

I grinned. "Something like that."

His face turned serious. "How are you—really? I wanted to come see you, after everything that happened with Katia. But I thought you might want to be by yourself for a while."

I looked at him—*really* looked at him. The warm care and concern in his eyes took my breath away. Even now, after all the awkwardness between us and all the times I'd pushed him away over the past few days, his first instinct was still to make sure that I was okay. Katia had been wrong about a lot of things, but Devon wasn't one of them. He really was a good guy, and bad girl or not, I'd fallen for him.

And now, tonight, I was finally going to do something about it.

He frowned. "Lila, are you okay? You have this really weird look on your face—"

I stepped up, put my arms around his neck, and kissed him.

Kissed him the way I'd wanted to for weeks now. Kissed him the way I'd been dreaming about for so long. Kissed him with all the depth of these wonderful, dizzying, terrifying feelings I had for him.

And he kissed me right back.

We melted together, spinning around and around on the terrace, our lips, hands, and breaths mixing and mingling together. More and more of those feelings roared up inside me, until I felt as though every press of my lips against Devon's sent hot, electric sparks shooting out into the night air, the same way they were erupting in my heart over and over again. He pulled me closer, tighter, and I melted into him even more, breathing in his crisp pine scent. All I could see, hear, taste, touch, smell, *feel* was Devon.

And I loved it—I loved *him*.

The kiss was as perfect as perfect could be, everything I'd ever imagined and then some, and I never, *ever* wanted it to end.

But it slowly did, the way all good things eventually do.

Devon pulled back, his eyes slightly glazed and a goofy grin stretching across his face. "What was that for?"

"For just being you," I said. "For being there, for looking out for me the way you always do."

He smiled. "We save each other, remember?"

"Got it."

Devon stared at me, his eyes dimming just a bit. "So . . . what does this mean?"

I looped my arms around his neck again. "It means that you were right and I was wrong. I care about you just as much as you care about me. But I've been a stupid fool, worried about getting hurt again, about getting my heart broken again."

He frowned. "That could still happen. Not because I want it to, but because we both have a lot of enemies. And then there's Victor and whatever he's planning."

I let out a breath. "I know, but I don't care anymore. I almost died tonight, and we both almost died a few weeks ago at the lochness bridge when Grant came after us. If there's one thing any of that has taught me, it's that we should seize the moment, take a chance, because no one knows what's going to happen next. I was alone, on my own, for a long time. It's been hard for me to let go of that, to let you in, to trust you with my heart. I'm not a hundred percent there yet, and I don't know if I can ever get there."

His frown deepened. "Okay . . ."

"But I do know this. We could be—we *will* be—fantastic together. I've known it ever since our battle during the tournament, and I've been wanting to tell you for hours now. So if you'll still have me, I want to give us a shot, Sinclair."

Devon blinked and blinked, as if I'd surprised him so much that his brain just couldn't process my words right now. So I decided to put it in simple terms for him.

"You and I are totally going to make out now," I said.

"And then, maybe tomorrow night or sometime later this week, we'll go out on an actual date and see how things go from there."

Devon gave me a teasing, wicked grin, his green, green eyes shining even brighter and hotter than all the lights down on the Midway. "The first date of many, I hope."

"The first of many," I promised as I drew his lips back down to mine again.

CHAPTER THIRTY

The next night, Devon and I did go out on our first date.

Sort of.

If you counted me breaking into the Draconi mansion again an actual date.

But Devon was hiding in the woods, keeping an eye on the guards and texting me updates about their movements. Since I'd already been inside the mansion once, it was easy for me to slip inside again.

According to some chatter Mo had heard, Victor and Blake were having dinner at the Volkov compound tonight, which meant the mansion was mostly empty. So I didn't have any trouble going through the greenlab and picking open the doors to Victor's office.

Everything looked the same as I remembered, right down to the creepy files on his desk. They were still sitting in the same positions as before, one file for each person in the tournament, and five stacks, one for each of the major Families.

The only thing different was that my file was on top of the Sinclair stack now.

I opened it up, curious to see whether Victor had written any more notes about me, whether he'd realized that I had much more magic than I let on. But the file was the same as before. I guessed that Victor hadn't gotten around to updating it yet. But he would. I shivered and closed the file again.

Then I went over to what I was really here for tonight—finding a way into Victor's secret room.

The snarling dragon still glared from the wall, the same as before, with that ruby serving as the creature's eye. And once again, a cold chill of magic emanated from behind the stone. Something was back there, and I thought I knew exactly what it was, but I wanted to make sure before I told Claudia and the others.

So I ran my hands up and down and back and forth across the carving, searching for a loose bit of stone or some other mechanism that would open the wall so I could get to the room on the other side. But I didn't find anything. All the while, the ruby in the dragon's eye kept staring at me, smug that its secret was still safe.

I let out a soft laugh. Of course. How stupid of me. Always try the obvious first.

I reached up and pressed on the ruby. It sank into the stone with a whisper, and part of the wall slid back, revealing a large room.

I stepped inside, and a light clicked on above my head. Shelves lined all three of the walls from floor to ceiling. All of the shelves were filled with black blades, and all those blades pulsed with magic.

This was it—this was Victor's plan.

His dark heart of magic.

I walked along the first shelf, staring at the weapons—swords and daggers mostly, with an occasional mace or a hammer. Each weapon was on a peg by itself and carefully, neatly numbered with a tag. I recognized the letters and symbols as being written in Victor's hand, in the same code that had been on the files in his office: *TT29*, *CC2*, *RM55*, and the like. Now, thanks to Katia, I knew exactly what the initials meant.

At the boathouse, she had said that Victor and Blake had been catching trolls, which explained the trap I'd found on the Draconi property the first night I'd come over here. I wondered how Katia had found out what Victor and Blake were doing—if she'd discovered their cage in the woods last summer while she was planting her own traps out there. I didn't know the answer, and it didn't matter. But I had no doubt that Victor and Blake had trapped and killed the tree trolls for the same reason that Katia had.

They had stolen the monsters' magic.

"Tree troll number 29," I muttered, staring at a dagger that was the same size and shape as the ones that Katia had tried to kill Deah and me with. "Copper crusher number 2. Rockmunk number 55."

And the weapons and codes went on and on, all the way around the room. Even though it made me sick to my stomach, I pulled out my phone and snapped photos of everything to show Claudia and Mo later. It took me a while, since there were more than a hundred weapons inside the room, enough to outfit most of the Draconi guards.

Enough to win a war against the other Families.

Mo had been right when he'd said that Victor was building an army—and he planned to outfit each and every one of his soldiers with a black blade. All those extra boosts of magic would make the Draconis almost invincible; it could only be a matter of time before Victor decided to strike out at the other Families.

But we'd be ready for him when he did.

I'd made sure of that.

I stepped out of the secret room to find two people waiting for me in Victor's office—Deah and Seleste.

They both looked fine, and no cuts or bruises marred their faces. It didn't look as though Victor had punished them, despite Deah's confession that I had let her win the tournament. Making sure they were okay was another reason I'd come here tonight.

Deah had her sword out, but Seleste smiled when she saw me.

I smiled back at her. "Hello, Seleste. How are you?"

"Oh, fine, darling," she said, waving her hand at me. "Just fine."

"No more bones and blades?"

She shook her head. "No more bones and blades."

"Good."

Seleste smiled at me again, then started humming to herself and wandering around the room. Earlier today, I'd confronted Claudia and Mo about Seleste being my aunt and why they'd never told me about her and Deah. They'd said that my mom had wanted it that way, that she and Seleste had had a falling out when Seleste had announced her plans to marry Victor after he'd had my father killed. But I wanted to hear it from her.

Seleste went over to the bookshelf where Deah's trophies were sitting, picked them up, and started polishing them with the sleeve of her dress, still humming all the while.

Deah wasn't so accommodating, though. "What are you doing here?" she hissed, dropping her sword to her side. "Are you crazy?"

"No, just checking out a hunch. And I wanted to talk to your mom. I was hoping that she would come in here. You too."

I went over to Seleste. Now that I was looking for it, I could see how much she resembled my mom—same dark blue eyes, same straight nose, same mischievous curve to her lips. Seeing so much of my mom in her made my heart ache, but I kept my face and voice soft and gentle.

"Aunt Seleste," I asked. "What happened between you and my mom?"

Her hand curled around the trophy she was polishing, the gold cup from this year's Tournament of Blades. Someone—Felix, most likely—must have found it in the boathouse and returned it to Deah. Seleste stared at the trophy a moment, then carefully pushed it back into place on the shelf.

"I loved Victor. I thought he was different from what he really was. That he was a good man." She gave me a sad, crooked smile. "Mine is the only future I can't see, and I didn't realize what Victor was really like until it was too late. But Serena knew. She *always* knew. She tried to warn me, but I wouldn't listen."

Seleste drew in a ragged breath, then slowly let it out. "I didn't realize that Victor set Luke up to be killed by that nest of copper crushers. I thought it was just an accident. But Serena knew the truth. So did everyone else. But it was already too late for all of us. Claudia didn't want Serena seeing Luke, so they fought. Mo took Serena's side, so he and Claudia fought. Serena didn't want me seeing Victor, so we fought. Everybody fought, all the time, until there was nothing left of us."

Seleste stared at me, then Deah, who'd come up to stand beside me. "I don't want that for the two of you. You can't fight each other the way Serena and I did. You have to work together. Otherwise, Victor will win, and he'll destroy all the other Families."

Deah's eyes widened. "Mom, you don't mean that. Sure, Dad has his problems with the other Families, but he would never try to destroy everyone else."

Seleste stepped forward, reached up, and cradled Deah's face in her hands. "My darling girl, always wanting to believe the best of people, even when they don't deserve it.

You are the most wonderful thing that ever happened to me. Always remember that."

Seleste leaned forward and kissed Deah's forehead. Then her blue eyes glazed over, and she skipped away, humming and lost in her own world again. Deah watched her, a stricken expression on her pretty face.

I shook my head. "Open your eyes, Deah. Your dad has been plotting something against the other Families for a long time now. And I finally figured out what it is."

I pointed to the secret room, which was still open behind me. "Remember what Katia wanted to do to us? Well, your dad has already done the exact same thing to a whole bunch of monsters. He and Blake set out traps in the woods to catch monsters so they can rip their magic out of the creatures with black blades."

I stalked over to the desk and picked up one of the files there. "And he has files on all the Draconis, notes about how he can use those black blades to augment their magic, make them faster, stronger, better fighters. He even has a file on you, if you care to look."

Deah's face paled, and her mouth twisted as though she was going to be sick. "He wouldn't do that. Not to everyone in the Family, not to *me*. . . ." Her voice trailed off, and I could tell that she didn't even believe her own words.

"Go in there and look for yourself. Just be sure to close the door behind you when you leave."

I'd seen and heard everything I needed to, but instead of leaving the office like I should have, I stood still and kept staring at Deah.

"There's a war coming," I said. "Between the Sinclairs and the Draconis. And you're going to have to choose a side. I hope you choose ours, cousin."

Deah stared back at me, her blue eyes full of worry. All

the while, Seleste kept humming and skipping around and around us.

I nodded at Deah, then left Victor's office.

I met up with Devon in the woods, and we hiked back to the Sinclair mansion. We went straight to the library, where Claudia and Mo were waiting. I e-mailed the photos I'd taken to their phones and told them everything I'd seen in Victor's secret room, including all the black blades hidden there and what I thought he wanted to do with them.

Claudia put her phone down, took off her glasses, and rubbed her head as though it was aching again. "So Victor has enough black blades to give the majority of his guards more magic."

"Just a boost," I said. "Katia said that monster magic burns out of your veins quickly, that it's not permanent, like human magic is."

"How quickly?" Mo asked.

I shrugged. "She didn't say. But she'd set traps along the lake, and it sounded like she'd had to kill a lot of monsters just to advance through the tournament."

"It doesn't matter how long monster magic lasts," Devon said. "All Victor needs is an hour, maybe two, and he could wipe out an entire Family, including ours."

Silence descended over the library as we all took in that not-so-cheery thought. Claudia and Mo picked up their phones again, staring at the photos, but I wandered over to the bookshelf where that picture of my mom was. Now that I knew the blond woman with her was Seleste, I picked up the picture and looked at it again.

They both seemed so young in the photo, although they must have been about the same age as I was now. And they seemed so happy, smiling at each other, their arms slung around each other's shoulders. Whatever happened from here on out, I was going to take Seleste's advice—I wasn't going to fight with my friends, and I especially wasn't going to fight with Deah. She was my cousin, my family, my blood, and we would need all the help we could get to defeat Victor.

"So what do we do now that we know Victor's plan?" Devon asked, breaking the silence. "Do we tell the other Families and try to form some sort of alliance?"

"No," Claudia said. "That would just cause a panic. The fewer people who know about Victor's secret room and what's in it, the better."

"But we have to do *something*," Devon protested. "We just can't sit around and wait for Victor to decide to use those weapons against us."

I set the picture of my mom and Seleste back down on the shelf, making sure it was straight, then turned to face the others. "Don't worry about the black blades. I know exactly what to do about them."

Claudia arched her eyebrows. "And what is this brilliant plan of yours?"

"It's not a plan. It's what I do best."

I looked at Mo, and he grinned, picking up on my train of thought.

"Just like the Parker job?" he asked.

"Exactly."

Claudia frowned. "What's the Parker job? Or do I even want to know?"

"It's an assignment I sent Lila out on last year," Mo said. "This guy named Parker had bought a very nice diamond necklace for his wife, one that I had a buyer for. But Parker was mobbed up with the Draconis, so we couldn't steal the necklace without some serious consequences."

"So what did you do?" Devon asked.

Mo pointed at me, still grinning. "Lila had the bright

idea to, shall we say, replace Parker's necklace with one that I ordered from a jeweler in Cypress Mountain."

Claudia tilted her head to the side. "Lila stole the real necklace and replaced it with a fake."

Mo nodded. "And Parker and his wife still don't know the difference. She wears that necklace all the time to Family events. And I laugh to myself every single time I see all those fake diamonds flashing around her neck."

Claudia and Devon looked at me, questions in their eyes.

"We're going to do the same exact thing to Victor." I grinned. "We're going to steal all of those black blades and replace them with fakes. By the time he realizes the difference, it will be too late—for him."

Read on for a peek at *Bright Blaze of Magic,* coming in May 2016.

"You are the worst thief I have ever seen."

Felix Morales frowned, stopped walking, and dropped the large black duffel bag he was carrying on the ground. I winced at the *clank-clank* of the items inside the bag banging together.

"Why would you say that?" he asked.

"Oh, I don't know," I said. "Maybe the fact that you're tromping through the woods like you are trying to kill every single blade of grass under your feet. Not to mention hacking through the bushes with your sword like we're on a jungle safari. And then of course, there's the talking. There is *always* the talking. It's a wonder you don't pass out from lack of oxygen."

Felix's eyes narrowed. "And what is wrong with having a little light conversation while we hike through the woods?"

"Light conversation? You've been talking nonstop ever since we left the mansion."

"So?"

I threw my hands up in the air. "So you actually have to *stop talking* and *be quiet* to be a thief! That's why!"

Felix gave me a mulish look and started to cross his arms over his chest—until he realized that he was still holding on to his sword, the one he'd been swinging around like a machete for the past twenty minutes. He glared at me, but he finally slid the weapon into the scabbard belted to his waist. Well, that would cut down on some of the noise. Now, if I just had some duct tape for his mouth. . . .

Felix stabbed his finger at the guy standing with us, who was busy setting his own black duffel bag on the ground, although with far less noise than Felix had made. "And why aren't you lecturing *him* about being quiet?"

"Because Devon can actually walk through the woods without cracking every single branch he steps on."

Felix snorted. "You're just saying that because the two of you have been sneaking around the mansion sucking face for the last two weeks."

I tensed, still not used to having a relationship with a guy, much less talking about it with that guy's best friend. But Devon Sinclair stepped up and slung his arm around my waist, pulling me close.

"And it's been the best two weeks of my life," he said, grinning at me.

With his black hair, bronze skin, and dark, soulful eyes, Felix was undeniably cute, but Devon was the one who made my heart race like a tree troll hopping from one branch to another. The setting sun filtering in through the leaves brought out the rich honey highlights in Devon's dark, chocolate-brown hair, even as it cast his handsome face in shadows. But it was his eyes that always hypnotized me—eyes that were the same deep, dark evergreen as the forest around us.

I laid my head on his muscled shoulder and leaned in to him, letting the heat of his body soak into my own and his sharp, tangy pine scent seep deep down into my lungs. So far, being with Devon had been a wonderful dream, and sometimes I had to remind myself that we were really—finally—together.

Who would have thought it? Not me, Lila Merriweather, the girl who'd been living on the streets for four years before I'd gone to work for the Sinclair Family earlier this summer. And I'd never expected to fall for Devon Sinclair himself, the Family bruiser and the son of Claudia Sinclair, the head of the entire Family.

I might be a great thief, but I wasn't so great when it came to people, preferring to pick their pockets instead of making friends with them. But Devon had steadfastly ignored and overcome all my defenses, just by being the kind, caring, genuine, loyal guy he was. I hadn't done a single thing in my life to deserve him, but now that he was mine, I was going to care for and protect him as best I could. Technically, being Devon's bodyguard was one of my jobs within the Family, but he watched out for me just as much as I did for him.

Don't get me wrong. It wasn't like I'd gone *soft* or anything. I still picked plenty of pockets on the streets of Cloudburst Falls, West Virginia, and I wasn't above snatching phones, cameras, and other shiny things from people who could afford to lose them. After all, a girl had to keep in practice. But now I did most of my thieving for the greater good and with a little mob muscle behind me. Like my job tonight. One that Felix was endangering with his constant chattering and tromping around.

Felix rolled his eyes. "Enough with the lovey-dovey stuff already," he groused, grabbing his duffel bag and hoisting it onto his shoulder, making more *clank-clanks* ring out. "I thought we had places to break into and stuff to steal tonight."

Instead of letting me go, Devon wrapped both arms around me and pulled me even closer. "And you're just jealous that Deah's not here, or you would be doing the same thing with her."

Felix huffed. "Please. I would already be kissing my girl and telling her how beautiful she is—and that's *before* I took her for a moonlit stroll. Totally working my romantic A game from start to finish, which I intend to do the second we sneak into the compound and meet up with her. So, if you'll excuse me, my lady awaits."

He snapped up his hand in a cheeky salute, then whirled around and started stomping through the woods again, making almost as much noise as he had before. He might have put his sword away so that he wasn't hacking through the bushes anymore, but he started muttering instead. Felix wasn't completely happy unless his mouth was going a hundred words a minute, even if he was only talking to himself.

I sighed. "I don't know whether to strangle him or admire his confidence."

"Relax, Lila." Devon turned so that he was facing me, with his hands on my waist. "Felix will shut up once we actually get close to the mansion. He knows how important this is. We all do."

I nodded. "You always know just what to say to make me feel better."

He grinned. "That's part of being a good boyfriend, right?"

I looped my arms around his neck. "The *best* boyfriend."

Devon stared at me, his green eyes glimmering like dark emeralds. My gaze locked with his, and my soulsight—my magic—kicked in, letting me look into the depths of his heart and feel all of his warm happiness flooding my chest as if it was my own emotion. In a way, it was my own emotion, since I felt the exact same thing whenever I looked at Devon, whenever I heard his voice, whenever I made him laugh or smile or brightened his day in any way.

I stood on my tiptoes and pressed my lips to his. Devon's arms tightened around me, and he kissed me back, our lips crashing together time and time again, until I felt as though we were spinning around and around in dizzying circles, even though we were standing still.

"Any time you two lovebirds are ready!" Felix called out, his voice loud enough to make the rockmunks on the forest floor scurry into their stone dens.

Devon and I broke apart, both of us breathing hard and holding on to each other.

"Unfortunately, duty calls," he murmured in a husky voice. "To be continued later?"

I grinned. "Definitely."

Devon and I caught up with Felix, and the three of us headed deeper into the woods. The summer sun had set while Devon and I had been kissing, and darkness was quickly creeping over the land. We didn't dare use a flashlight, and Devon and Felix fell back, letting me take the lead, since I could still see everything around me as clearly as if it were noon. Not only could I use my rare soulsight magic to look into people and feel what they were feeling, but I also had the much more common and mundane sight Talent of being able to see everything around me with crystal clarity, no matter how dark it was.

And the place we were going was definitely dark—the Draconi Family compound, home of Victor Draconi, the most powerful person in Cloudburst Falls, the sworn enemy of the Sinclair Family.

And the monster who'd murdered my mom.

The longer we hiked, the darker it got, and the quieter the three of us became. Even Felix stopped talking and dropped his hand to his sword, his eyes scanning the trees around us, though he couldn't see through the thick fog that was slowly sliding down from the top of Cloudburst Mountain to invade the forests below. Every once in a while, I could hear the faint rush of water in the distance from one of the many waterfalls that tumbled down the mountain. The resulting clouds of mist from the falls always cloaked the top of the rugged peak, even during the brightest, hottest part of the day, but at night, after the sun had set, the fog grew thicker and thicker and sank lower and lower on the mountain.

But the white clouds did little to hide the eyes that stared at us.

Sapphire blue, ruby red, emerald green. The colors were the same as all the jewels I'd stolen over the years, but these were the bright, glowing orbs of the monsters that called the mountain home—tree trolls, rockmunks, copper crushers, and the like. Some were more dangerous than others, but lurking in the trees were plenty of monsters with enough teeth and claws to make meals out of all three of us.

Still, I didn't mind the cool clouds of mist, the watching monsters, or the soft sheen of dew that covered everything. It made for better cover for us.

Because if we were caught, we'd be executed on the spot.

Twenty minutes later, we reached the edge of the trees, crouched down, and peered at the structure before us. Technically it was a mansion, although the gleaming white stone and architecture made it look more like a castle. Tall, diamond-paned windows. White trellises with red roses curling through the slats. Towers topped with red flags bearing the Draconi Family crest of a snarling gold dragon. Everything about the castle made it seem as though it had been dropped on top of the mountain right out of a fairy tale. But there were no happy endings here—just danger, despair, and misery.

Devon, Felix, and I had been sneaking over here every night for the past two weeks on our thieves' errand, and we fell into our usual routine of watching the guards patrolling the grounds. It was almost full dark now, and

Devon and Felix were both wearing black cloaks to help them blend into the shadows. I sported my mom's long, sapphire-blue trench coat, made out of spidersilk, which also helped me melt into the growing darkness.

The Draconi guards were dressed in black boots, pants, and shirts, along with blood-red cloaks and matching cavalier hats, making them look like extras from a *Three Musketeers* movie. But they were far more dangerous than that. All of the guards had their hands on the swords belted to their hips, looking for intruders, as well as keeping an eye out for any monsters that might be creeping up on them. Many an inattentive guard had been snatched by a copper crusher and dragged into the forest, unlucky enough to be the oversize, venomous snake's dinner date.

"Are we good?" Felix asked, checking his phone. "It's almost time for us to meet Deah. You know how she worries if we're even one minute late."

With good reason. If she was caught helping the enemy, Deah would be executed right along with us, despite the fact that she was Victor's daughter.

Instead of answering him, I started counting the guards along the perimeter. One, two, three. . . . It didn't take me long to realize something was different tonight. My stomach knotted up.

"Wait," I whispered. "There are more guards patrolling tonight."

Devon frowned and squinted at the compound. "How can you tell?"

"I can see them. Trust me. There are more guards."

"Can we still take our usual route into the mansion?" he asked in a tense voice, his hand dropping to the large black duffel bag at his feet. "This is our last trip. If we can get in tonight, then we're done with this."

"Give me a second to work it out," I said.

Devon and Felix both fell silent, although they kept

looking from me to the guards and back again. I focused on the guards, staring at first one, then another. It took me less than a minute to realize that Victor had only doubled the number of guards, pairing them up in teams of two. He hadn't changed their routes, which meant that we could still get into the mansion the same way as before.

"We're good," I said. "Text Deah and tell her that we're on our way in."

Felix nodded, his thumbs flying over his phone. A second later, his phone lit up with a message. "Deah says that the coast is clear on her end."

"Good," I said. "Follow me."

Keeping low, I left the woods behind and hopscotched my way across the lawn, hiding behind various trees and bushes and only moving when the guards' backs were turned. Devon and Felix followed along behind me, both of them being as quiet as possible and clutching the duffel bags to their chests to muffle any telltale *clank-clanks*.

Less than two minutes later, we were at one of the side patio doors. I reached up and gently turned the knob. Unlocked. Part of me was disappointed. It was no fun breaking into a mansion when your inside woman left a door unlocked for you.

But I opened the door and ushered Devon and Felix inside. I slipped in after them and locked the door behind me, just in case one of the guards decided to check it. Then I took the lead again, creeping from one hallway and staircase to the next.

The outside of the Draconi mansion might resemble a castle, but the furnishings inside were the real riches. Just about everything gleamed with some sort of gold, from the chandeliers overhead to the gilt-edged mirrors on the walls to the trim on the tables and chairs. And Victor's snarling dragon crest was painted, carved, chiseled, embroidered, or stamped onto practically everything, from the crown molding that lined the ceilings to the stained glass windows set into the walls to the white flagstones underfoot.

All those dragons were creepy enough, but it seemed like every single one of the monsters turned its head, narrowed its eyes, and glared at Devon, Felix, and me as we crept past. I shivered. Sometimes, I would have been happy not to see so well with my sight magic.

We quickly made our way up several sets of stairs to the Draconi greenlab. Once again, the glass doors were unlocked, and the three of us slipped inside and moved through the area, which was part chemistry lab, part greenhouse, where a variety of magical and other plants were grown and harvested. The long, sharp needles on the stitch-sting bushes quivered as we hurried past them, but we didn't get close enough for the plants to lash out and try to scratch us for disturbing them.

We made it to the far side of the greenlab, and I sidled up to the glass doors there and peered out into the hallway beyond. The lights were turned down low in this part of the mansion, creating more shadows than not. Just the way I liked it.

Since the coast was clear, I stepped out of the glass doors and into the hallway—

A sword zipped out of the shadows, stopping an inch from my throat. I froze, my body tense, my hand curling around the hilt of my own sword, ready to draw the weapon and defend myself with it.

"You're late," a familiar voice growled.

Deah Draconi stepped out of the shadows, her sword still at my throat. I looked down at the weapon and the stars carved into the dull, ash-colored metal. A similar pattern adorned my own sword. Both of our weapons had been given to us by our respective mothers, and both were black blades.

Deah was quite beautiful with her golden hair and dark blue eyes, which were the same color as my own—another sign of our Sterling Family blood, along with our black blades. She was wearing white shorts and sandals with a red T-shirt, but my gaze dropped to the gold cuff stamped with the Draconi dragon crest that gleamed on her right wrist. Deah might be helping us now, but part of me still wondered whose side she would choose in the end, when Victor finally made his move to destroy all the other Families, starting with the Sinclairs.

"Hello, cousin," I drawled. "I didn't see you there. You're getting better at sneaking around. I approve. We might make a thief out of you yet."

Deah rolled her eyes at my calling her *cousin*, but she dropped her sword from my throat. Neither one of us had known about our connection until a couple of weeks ago, when it had come out during the Tournament of Blades, and we were both still getting used to the idea that we were family and trying to figure out what kind of relationship we wanted to have.

"How's Seleste?" I asked in a kinder voice, referring to her mother and my aunt.

"She went to bed early tonight." Deah hesitated a moment. "She's actually been doing a lot better these past two weeks. It's as if seeing you at the tournament and then us working together has quieted her mind and made her sharper, clearer, more focused."

I nodded. Seleste had sight magic too, but her Talent let her see the future, which led to her doing and saying all sorts of strange things. Most people thought Seleste was crazy or made fun of her, but I'd grown to like her odd ways. Besides, Seleste and Deah were the only blood family I had left now, and I was going to look out for them. That's what my mom would have wanted.

"Um, I hate to be whiny, but can we get on with things?" Felix asked, shifting on his feet. "These bags are heavy."

Deah looked at Felix, her eyes softening. "You know, I really like seeing you every night—even if it is because of my dad and what he's planning to do."

Felix's face lit up. "I like seeing you too."

Then he grinned, stepped forward, and slung his arm around her shoulders. "Have I told you how beautiful you look tonight—"

He started whispering to her as they walked down the hallway in front of us. Devon grinned and nudged me with his elbow. I rolled my eyes, but I was grinning too. I was glad that Felix and Deah had found happiness, despite how dangerous it was for them to be together.

The four of us made it to Victor's office, and Deah gestured at the double doors, which had two snarling gold dragons for knobs. The creatures looked like they might come to life and bite off the fingers of anyone who tried to open them.

"Locked," she said. "Sorry, but I haven't been able to get a key yet. I tried to open it earlier with those lock picks you gave me, but I'm still not as good with them as you are."

"No worries," I said, smiling. "Finally, something fun for me to do."

Deah shook her head. "You are seriously strange, Merriweather."

My smile widened. "You have no idea, Draconi."

While the others kept watch, I reached up and removed two thin chopsticks that were stuck through my ponytail. The sticks were the same black as my hair, but a twist of the wood revealed the lock picks hidden inside. The tools felt as familiar to me as my own fingers, and I started humming a soft, happy tune as I bent over the lock and inserted the picks.

Over the past two weeks, I'd had a lot of practice on this particular lock, and it *snicked* open less than thirty seconds later. Still, we all tensed, knowing that we were stepping into the dragon's den—and that he could come and catch us at any moment.

I stuck the chopstick lock picks back into my ponytail, then took hold of the knobs. "Here we go," I whispered and opened the doors.

The four of us crept inside, and I shut and locked the doors behind us. Victor's office was as richly furnished as the rest of the mansion, but I ignored the glimmers of gold and went over to the wall behind his desk. An enormous dragon was carved into the white stone there, with flames curled all around it, as though it were setting itself on fire.

I stopped for a moment, staring at the fist-size ruby that was the dragon's evil eye. I shivered again. No matter how many times I snuck in here, I never got used to looking at this particular dragon—or having it stare right back at me. Or perhaps it was what was behind the carving that worried me so much.

But I forced my unease aside, stepped forward, and pressed on the ruby, which sank into the stone. A second later, the wall slid back, revealing a large, secret room—one that was filled with weapons.

An overhead light clicked on in the room, revealing the black-blade swords, daggers, and more that lined the shelves covering the three walls. Each weapon was on a peg by itself and carefully labeled, with codes like *TT29*, *CC2*, and *RM55*—for all the tree trolls, copper crushers, and rockmunks that Victor had trapped and killed.

Black blades were made out of bloodiron, a special metal that grew blacker with every drop of blood that fell on it. Bloodiron could also absorb, store, and transfer magic from one person or monster to another. Victor had used these weapons to rip the monsters' magic right out of them so he could use their Talents for his own evil plan to destroy the other Families. I could feel the creatures' power pulsing through the blades, each one proof of Victor's cruelty and his delight in senseless slaughter. The cold burn of magic made me sick to my stomach.

"Let's move," I whispered. "I don't want to be in here one second longer than necessary."

Devon and Felix put their duffel bags on the floor and unzipped them, revealing the swords, daggers, and other weapons inside. They grabbed the weapons and handed them to me and Deah, and the two of us switched out the real black blades with the fakes.

We'd been coming here and doing this same thing every night for the last two weeks, slowly exchanging the magic-filled weapons for ordinary ones. We'd removed most of the black blades, but not all of them. I hated leaving a single sword here for Victor to use, but he had a lot of Talents, and I was betting that he could sense magic the same way I could. So we had to leave some of the real weapons here or he would realize what we'd done. Still, I made sure that we only left the blades that pulsed weakly with magic. I wasn't leaving Victor with any more power than I had to.

It only took us five minutes to switch out the last of the weapons, although it seemed much longer than that. By the time we were done, Devon and Felix were both sweating beneath their long, black cloaks. Deah was too, despite her T-shirt and shorts. I wasn't sweating, but my stomach churned and churned at the cold chill of all the magic in the air.

Devon and Felix zipped up the duffel bags with the real

black blades and slung them over their shoulders. I pressed the dragon's ruby eye again, and the wall slid back into place, hiding the secret room from sight.

"Well, I guess this is it," I said, trying to make my voice light. "No more late-night trips to raid Victor's secret weapons stash."

Nobody moved or spoke for a moment.

I looked at Deah. "Thank you again for helping us."

She nodded, but she stared at the floor instead of at me. Betraying her Family and her father was no easy thing, no matter how evil Victor might be.

I glanced at Devon and Felix, who both nodded. We'd discussed this for several days now, and it was finally time to ask Deah to do one more thing.

"Come with us," I said.

Deah's head snapped up, and she stared at me with wide eyes. "What?"

"You heard me. Come with us. Go pack a bag, get Seleste, and come with us. Right now."

She stared at me, and my soulsight kicked in, letting me feel all of her emotions. Electric shock. Sharp worry. Stomach-churning fear. For a moment, warm happiness mixed in with the other feelings, but it was quickly smothered by cold sorrow. I knew what her answer was going to be before she even opened her mouth.

She shook her head, her golden ponytail slapping against her shoulders. "I can't do that. You know I can't."

Felix stepped forward and grabbed her hand. "Please, Deah," he said. "You're not like the other Draconis. You don't belong here."

"But I *am* a Draconi." She looked at me for a second. "At least, part of me is. But that doesn't matter. I can't go with you. My dad would flip out if he realized that Mom and I were gone. And you all know what he would do if he found that we'd defected to the Sinclair Family."

We all grimaced. Victor would attack the Sinclairs with every guard he had in order to get back Deah and her mom. Deah's mimic magic and Seleste's visions were Talents that he didn't have and would never let slip through his fingers.

But Felix cared too much about Deah to give up so easily. "Please," he repeated. "Just come with us. We can figure the rest out later. Let's just get you and your mom out of here while we still have a chance."

Deah stared at him, and I saw and felt all the warm love she had for him. She bit her lip and shifted on her feet, as if she was actually considering changing her mind and coming with us—

One of the knobs creaked, and the doors rattled in their frames.

We all froze.

Someone was trying to get into the office.